PENGUIN BOOKS

The Obsidian Throne

J D Oswald is the author of the epic fantasy series The Ballad of Sir Benfro. *Dreamwalker*, *The Rose Cord*, *The Golden Cage* and *The Broken World* are available as Penguin paperbacks and ebooks. He is also the author of the Detective Inspector McLean series.

James runs a 350-acre farm in north-east Fife.

The Obsidian Throne

J D OSWALD

PENGUIN BOOKS

PENGUIN BOOKS

UK | USA | Canada | Ireland | Australia
India | New Zealand | South Africa

Penguin Books is part of the Penguin Random House group of companies
whose addresses can be found at global.penguinrandomhouse.com

First published 2016

001

Text copyright © James Oswald, 2016

The moral right of the author has been asserted

Set in 12.5/14.75 pt Garamond MT Std
Typeset by Jouve (UK), Milton Keynes
Printed in Great Britain by Clays Ltd, St Ives plc

A CIP catalogue record for this book is available from the British Library

ISBN: 978–1–405–93525–8

www.greenpenguin.co.uk

MIX
Paper from
responsible sources
FSC® C018179

Penguin Random House is committed to a
sustainable future for our business, our readers
and our planet. This book is made from Forest
Stewardship Council® certified paper.

For Alex
Now I can tell you how it ends . . .

GOLD COUNTRY
Mt Arnahi
RIM MTS
Cerdys
Gremmil
FOREST OF THE FFRYDD
Empty plains
CAENANT PLAIN
Cenobus
Ystumteun
Rhedeg Pass
Pwll
Emmass Fawr
Tochers
Betettown
Candlehall
KINGDOMS
HAFOD
River
Corris
Wright's Ferry
Beylinstown
Abervenn
Bay of Kerdigen
TWIN
Hafren River
Castell Glas
HENDRY
SOUTH
BOGLANDS

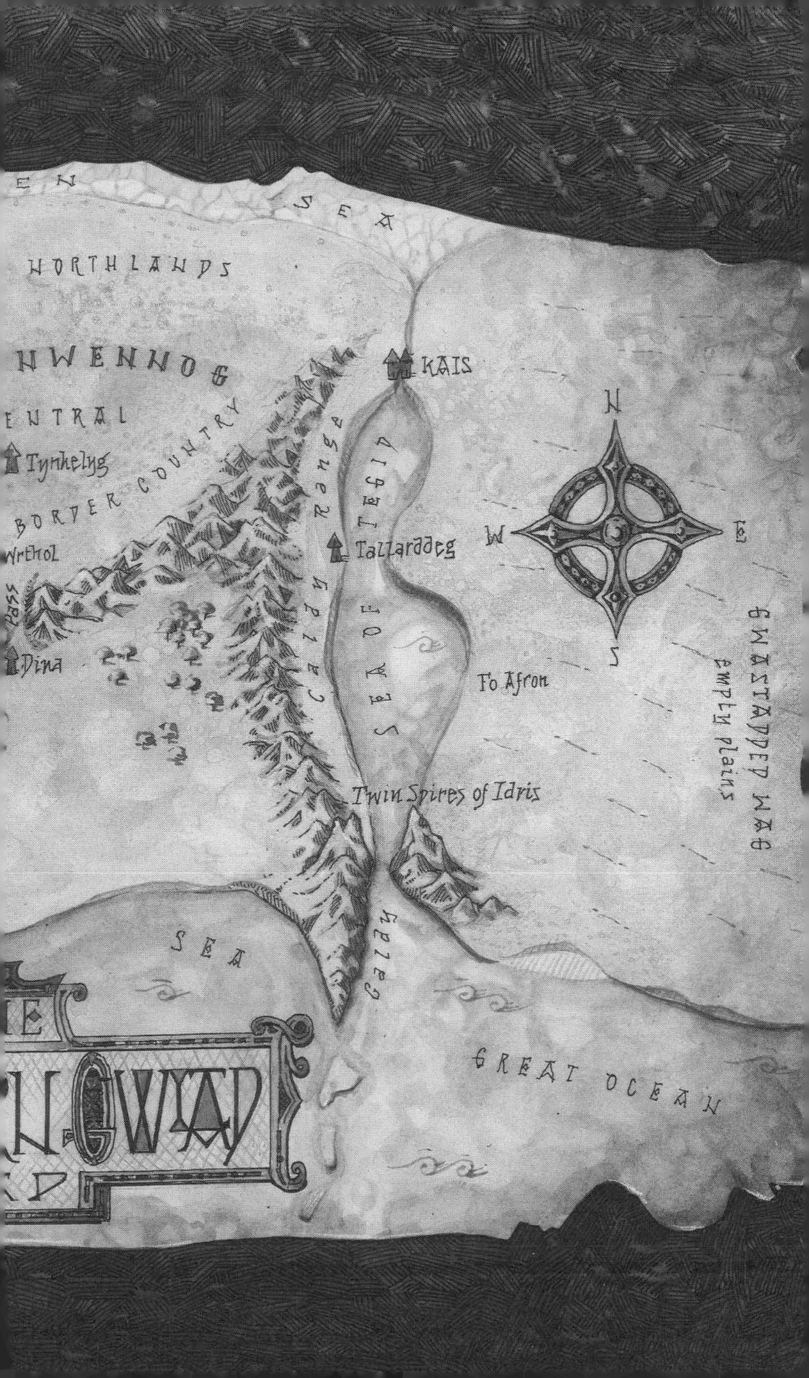

I

Lost another one today. A promising lad, he just disappeared from my study, leaving the fire to burn out and the plates uncleared. There is no sign of him in the castle, and the major domo knows nothing of him. A shame. I had high hopes.

I remain convinced that there is within men the capacity to know and manipulate the subtle arts. Many show an innate sensitivity to the Grym, which is the source of all life after all. If I can just find a way to increase their mental discipline and dampen down their innate curiosity, I am sure this experiment will succeed.

From the working journals of Gog,
Son of the Winter Moon

Cold wind whipped tears from his eyes as he tumbled tail over nose over tail. Benfro gripped tight on to his precious cargo, falling faster and faster from Gog's high tower. Still far away, the roofs of the smaller buildings that clustered about it like piglets round a sow were nonetheless hurtling towards him with terrible speed. And still all he could see was the image, the horrible echo from the past as Inquisitor Melyn's fiery blade crashed down. Cracked scale, ancient leathery skin, wiry flesh and arthritic bone no match for the concentrated power of the Grym. The conjured blade that had taken his mother's life now claiming another victim he was powerless to save.

He heard screaming, high-pitched and terrified, but it barely registered in his mind, still reeling from the shock. It was easy to tumble over and over, see the sky then the buildings, the dark storm clouds then the rain-slicked slates, shiny and ominous. Something small plucked and pecked at his arm and he glanced down almost casually. A lifetime ago Benfro recalled scooping the two people into his arms. The younger, the boy whose name he couldn't remember, was thrashing wildly, desperate to escape the dragon's scaly grip even though to do so would surely mean he would plunge to his death. The other one, the young woman, was calm. She fixed Benfro with her gaze, ignoring the way her hair blew around her like angry snakes, ignoring the iron grip he had around her even though it must have made breathing all but impossible, ignoring the rapidly approaching rooftops.

'You have to fly.'

The words were in his head, calm and serene as the Mother Tree. Or Lady Earith. She had eyes of deepest green, this young woman. Benfro could see them clearly, the flecks of gold that hung in the black pupils like stars in the deepest night. His missing eye showed him so much more.

'There is no time for that. Now you have to fly.'

This time the words came with greater force, pushing the fog from his mind. Or was it the vision of this woman in the aethereal, the aura that stretched and moulded around her a far bigger shape? Whatever it was, Benfro felt himself awaken, and realized then that he was falling fast. Acting on instinct, he snapped open his wings to their fullest extent, catching the air at the perfect moment to halt his tumbling and turn his plummet into a glide. The strain pulled at muscles still weak from his encounter with Fflint, pain rippling through his back and the older injury he had sustained in his escape from Mount Arnahi. For an instant he thought he was going to drop his precious cargo, held tight in arms that were beginning to feel the strain. He pulled them tighter, shutting off the screaming from the boy even as he suppressed the slow count that started at the back of his mind.

Try as he might, Benfro couldn't keep his wing tips feathered, the pain and the weakness bending them out of shape as cruelly as Fflint's mad temper. Looking down to the rooftops, far too close now, he tried to gauge his speed, pick out a route that would see them safely to the ground. It was all coming too quickly, and with a sickening sense of inevitability he realized he was going to crash.

'Hold tight,' he said, as if his companions had any choice in the matter. He held his wings wide for as long as he could, watching as the dull slate roofs rushed up to meet them. Then at the last possible moment he twisted in the air, wrapping his wings around the two terrified people, letting his back take the full force of impact.

Slate shattered in an explosion of noise, ancient rafters cracking like dead bones as his momentum took him through the roof. Benfro had the briefest of glimpses of an attic space, dusty and heavy with cobwebs, before his back jarred against a wooden floor, driving what little breath he had left out of him. Floorboards and joists shattered like dry tinder and he passed straight through.

The next floor was some kind of sleeping quarters, its ceiling far higher than the attic above it. Dazed by the twin impacts, Benfro could do nothing but scan the room as he tumbled, more slowly now, towards a floor covered in faded rugs. A platform raised in one corner formed a sleeping area much like the one he had used in Lady Earith's palace in Pallestre, only where that had been draped in finest white linen, this was heaped with the skins of great furred animals. A vast empty fireplace dominated one wall, but before he could take in much more than that and a large doorway, clearly built with dragons in mind, Benfro hit the floor.

This time it held, the rug cushioning a tiny fraction of the blow. Dust billowed up around him as the force drove the last remaining wind from his lungs. Something cracked in his back, pain spearing through the muscles like a hot knife. Benfro's head snapped back, bouncing off stone with a horrible crack that dulled his senses for merciful moments. He was dimly aware of something struggling in his arms. They were locked rigid and he could barely muster the energy to release them. His wings drooping by his sides, he could only lie there, stunned and confused. High above him, an ornately plastered ceiling had been ruined by his sudden arrival. Above the hole, he could see light, dull and grey and overcast, shining through the ruins of the roof.

And then a face blocked the view, straggly black hair hanging down until it almost touched his nose. Dark green eyes peered at him, an expression both quizzical and shocked.

'Benfro?'

This time the voice was in his ears, not his mind. She spoke much like Errol, only in a higher tone, a slightly different accent as if she'd spent more time speaking Draigiaith. Benfro tried to open his mouth in reply, found he couldn't even do that.

'Benfro? Come on. Wake up.' She leaned in closer, tapped at his nose with one finger a couple of times, then drew back her hand and slapped him hard across the snout. He tried to move, affronted by her actions more than anything else, but still he was paralysed, scarcely able to think.

'Damn you, dragon. You saved us from the fall. Don't die on us now.' This time the young woman slapped him harder, and with her touch he remembered her name. Martha. She was Errol's friend. The one they'd been looking for. He needed to find Errol, find Magog's jewel and take it to the place where the long-dead dragon mage's last mortal remains lay. Only then could he break free. But Gog was dead. Gog, who was the only one able to take him back. Without him, surely all hope was gone.

'Breathe, you great scaly beast.' This time the slap was more of a punch, and Benfro felt something even stronger behind it. He flinched instinctively as she drew back for another blow, took a deep breath for what felt like the first time in a thousand years. As his lungs filled, he felt his hearts hammering away in his chest, the burning sensation in muscles stretched too far. Something caught in his throat and he coughed, convulsing in agony and belching up a gout of pure white flame. Martha jumped clear just in time to avoid being scorched. The fire hung in the air like a living thing as Benfro coughed and hacked. He rolled over on to his front, seeing the boy Xando standing a short way off, face white, eyes wide and holding one arm like it might be broken. Without knowing how he did it, Benfro's missing eye showed him the swirling patterns of aura about the boy, confirmed the break. It would be easy enough to set, but it would take time to heal.

'Wh—' Benfro tried to speak, but his throat was tight from coughing. He levered himself up on to all fours, shook his head to shift the cobwebs clogging his thoughts. The motion set his wings swinging, and pain lanced up one, so sharp he almost blacked out. He fell forward, the shock jarring up his arms and setting off even more fire in his back and his damaged wing. Too soon after Lady Earith had healed him, he'd pushed himself further than was wise.

'Careful. You're badly injured. Best not to move too much.'

Benfro felt a touch on his shoulder, and with the words came a warmth that soothed away at least some of the pain. He looked up at Martha again, seeing that strange aura superimposed on her mundane self. A mystery he couldn't begin to unravel.

'Help the boy. His arm's broken.' His words came out in a hoarse whisper, as if he had been shouting at the top of his lungs for hours. Maybe he had. Martha cocked her head to one side, ever so slightly, then smiled. She took her hand from his shoulder and he instantly wished she hadn't. The pain came in waves, each breath jabbing

6

needles into the knot of muscles on his back at the roots of his wings. Slowly, tentatively, he reached out his senses, his missing eye seeing parts of him he could never have seen before and in ways he could only start to understand. As Martha tended to Xando's injuries, so he inspected his own.

Given the nature of the fall, he was mostly fine, just badly sprained muscles. His back was a mess of bruising beneath his scales that would ache for many days. His wings were largely undamaged, just sore from the beating they had taken from first the roof and then the attic floor. None of these injuries were causing him all the pain. That was a length of timber, a roof truss that his fall had broken off. Its sharp, jagged point had somehow wedged between two scales in his side and the impact with the stone floor of this sleeping chamber had driven it deep into his side. Thick black blood seeped around the edges of the wound, slicking his scales and dripping on to the dusty rug.

Errol remembered his brief time working with the old stable master at Emmass Fawr, before Father Andro had taken him under his wing and introduced him to the many wonders of the great library. He'd mucked out stables, carted shit and straw down the stone-arched corridors of the great monastery to the midden levels. He knew the stench of horse manure well. After a while it had faded. He would maybe catch a whiff of it under his fingernails where the scrubbing brush hadn't reached, or in his hair when he washed, but it was only an echo of the full-on stench. And even that had a certain charm to it.

Not so the filth he waded in now.

The air was full of it, making it hard to breathe. His head was light, thoughts hard to pin down, and no matter how long he was stuck in the great cave, no matter how many carts he loaded, pushed along their short rails and tipped into the deeper cavern, still the smell was as potent as ever. It clung to him like wet clothes. He was drowning in it, slowly losing all sense of self as the strange compulsion made him dig at the pile. For a moment, when the cry had gone up and more effluent had come crashing down, he had felt the faintest stirring of the Grym, but it hadn't lasted, and though he had waited for another flood with perhaps more enthusiasm than any of his wretched co-workers, no more had come.

Now the hem of his cloak was caked in a foul sheen of excrement, weighing him down more effectively than any chain. His feet were soaked in the caustic liquid that seeped out of the mess and into the cracks in the rock floor. His hair was matted, face smeared. He didn't want to think what condition his hands were in. Even if he could escape, find somewhere with fresh air and clean running water, it would take a lifetime of scrubbing to get the mess off. And even then he would still smell it. There could be no escape.

'You. Stop digging. Eat now.'

Errol was so wrapped up in his misery, so overwhelmed by the fetid air, that he didn't at first hear the words. And even when they did seep into his consciousness, he didn't really understand them, or think they were anything to do with him. The heavy slap to the back of the head was easier to understand. He cringed, leaning on his shovel, then turned slowly to see the supervisor standing behind him.

'Eat. Sleep. More digging tomorrow.' The supervisor took the shovel from Errol's weak hands, almost causing him to topple over into the mire. He pointed towards an opening in the cavern wall, flicked his hand dismissively. Too weak even to think, Errol could do nothing but comply.

His feet led him to a rough cave dimly lit by a fire that had almost gone out. A black cauldron was suspended over it from an iron tripod, something liquid and dark steaming inside. Errol looked around, but there seemed to be no one else having a break right now. He found a stack of rough wooden bowls on a ledge close to the fire, picked one up and ladled some of the food into it. At least he assumed it was food. He could smell nothing over the miasma wafting in from the great cavern. Despite the stench and the muck crusting his hands and fingers; despite the cloying sensation in his throat that made him gag whenever he opened his mouth, he was still hungry. Tilting the bowl to his lips, he took a sip of the lukewarm liquid, surprised that it didn't taste like everything else smelled. Thin and weak, it was still more nourishing than any meal he could recall eating. It took some of the foul taste away as it washed down his gullet, filled his stomach with residual warmth. He would have killed for some bread, but there was only the soup, so he ladled another bowlful, looking around guiltily as if expecting to be told he had taken too much.

Exhausted now that he had stopped working, his whole body cried out for rest. He bent down to examine a bundle of rags nearby, to see if there was something he could make into a bed, then recoiled in horror. The rags were clothes, wrapped around a man. Even in the minimal light spreading from the dying fire, Errol could see he was dead. He stood up too quickly, backing away from the corpse in horror. His foot caught on something and he stumbled to the floor amid a pile of rags that cracked like broken bones. Errol had seen death before, but something about this place amplified the terror. He scrambled towards the fire, convinced the dead were rising all around him, come to take him to their cold, empty world. There were people here he knew, their faces twisted in silent screams of agony. Alderman Clusster staggered towards him, leaning heavily on the tall form of Tom Tydfil the blacksmith. Godric Defaid was there, his eyes missing, hands little more than ragged stumps. Poul Gremmil sat weeping by the fire, and when he looked up, Errol could see the embers glowing through two holes where his eyes should have been. A hand fell on his shoulder, and he looked round to see Duke Dondal, his head tucked under one arm, his neck a bloody stump.

'Wha—?' Errol tried to speak, but the dead were all around him now, crowding in so close he couldn't breathe. The faint light from the fire darkened away to nothing, just the barest glow on the jagged rocks of the cave roof. And then as he fought for breath, the darkness engulfed him completely.

'We must reason with them. Find out what they want. Nothing can be gained from this fighting and destruction.'

Prince Dafydd glanced out of the palace window,

across the broken rooftops and away to the far plains below, where Queen Beulah's armies had massed for the siege. For a moment he thought the seneschal might mean to parlay with her, but even he knew that they had a better chance of reasoning with the dragons circling menacingly above the Neuadd than with the queen whose throne they had just stolen.

'Do you seriously think they'll talk to us, Padraig? I'm not even sure some of them can speak.'

Princess Iolwen sat on an ornate gilded throne placed on a raised dais at one end of the room. She looked uncomfortable, but that might have had as much to do with the situation as the chair. Usel the medic and Captain Venner of the palace guard made up the rest of the impromptu war council, with young Teryll the stable hand looking very much out of place as he sat beside the princess on a low stool. War council. Dafydd suppressed a hollow laugh at the thought. There was no war here, just annihilation. Either the dragons would destroy the city or Beulah would raze it to the ground, build afresh once she had put every man, woman and child within the walls to the sword. He had no doubt in his mind how merciful she would be.

'At least one of them spoke to you before. When they first arrived at the Neuadd.' Seneschal Padraig stood in front of the throne, hands clasped together in supplication, although to whom he was begging, Dafydd couldn't tell.

'Could you identify the beast, Usel?' Iolwen addressed the question to the medic, who was standing with his back to them all, staring out of the window. He said nothing at first, then slowly turned to face them.

'Beast is perhaps too strong a word. Sir Morwyr is intelligent, powerful in the Grym. I've felt his thoughts in my mind, as have you, Your Highness. He is not the leader of this party though.'

'If we could contact him would he act as a mediator?' the seneschal asked. 'We cannot hope to drive them off, nor can we flee the city. We must do something, surely?'

A silence fell on the room. Padraig was right. For the moment the dragons were mostly circling the Neuadd or prowling around the cloisters that surrounded the great hall, but it was only a matter of time before they set about the city again.

'I will go and speak to them.' Iolwen stood so suddenly Dafydd thought she might fall over. He rushed to her side.

'Iol . . . You can't . . . It's too dangerous.'

'I am the one claiming the throne, Dafydd. I am the one who would be queen to the terrified people down in the city. I cannot ask another to go in my stead.'

'Actually, Your Highness, you can.'

All eyes turned to Padraig, the changed tone of his voice cutting through the uncertainty that had dogged their meeting so far. He stood straighter, held his hands lightly together, no longer fretting.

'Padraig—'

'As seneschal of the Order of the Candle, it is my duty to represent the House of Balwen in all negotiations. I will present myself to these dragons, address this Sir Morwyr and press our case for peaceful coexistence.' He turned to the medic. 'I would appreciate your assistance, Usel.

My Draigiaith is perhaps a little rusty. It is a long time since last a dragon was presented at court.'

Without waiting for an answer, the seneschal bowed briefly to Iolwen, then turned and strode out of the room. Usel struggled to keep up, and Dafydd set off to follow them. Iolwen stepped down off the dais, Teryll just behind her.

'You should stay here, Iol. I'll take a couple of guards and make sure no one comes to any harm.'

For a moment he thought she was going to argue; it wouldn't have been the first time. But after a brief consideration, the princess just nodded. Dafydd took it as permission to leave, signalled the closest two guards to follow him and headed for the door.

By the time they caught up with Padraig and Usel, the pair were almost at the top of the stone steps leading down to the reception rooms at the front of the palace. The seneschal paused just long enough to allow a troop of guards to form up behind him, then he set off down the stairs. For an old man who had affected a doddering manner since they first met, he now seemed full of vigour. Dafydd tried to skim his thoughts, but Padraig's mental shields were tighter than any he had encountered since last he had sparred with old King Ballah. It was perhaps sensible, given how easily the dragon they had encountered before had pushed its way into his mind. Dafydd hung back in the shadows, drawing his own defences around him as he watched the seneschal step out into the daylight.

The parade ground in front of the palace had seemed vast when Dafydd first saw it just days earlier. Now it looked cluttered and small, littered with the carcasses of half-eaten animals and the occasional crumpled form of what might once have been a man. Two enormous dragons lay a few tens of paces from the entrance, basking in the afternoon sun. Another even larger beast was pacing slowly around the perimeter, peering at the stone walls, reaching out occasionally to touch something or leaning in to sniff. Three more dragons sprawled closer to the administrative buildings that formed the far perimeter of the grounds, and as the sun caught them they sparkled like jewels, a million different hues highlighting the patterns of their scales. Overhead, yet more dragons wheeled and cried in the sky, and as he looked up at them, Dafydd could hear the thunder of their voices battering against his mental defences. It was as well he'd prepared himself; unshielded he would surely have been knocked senseless by the noise.

'Sir Morwyr?' Seneschal Padraig now walked with his head bowed, taking slow steps towards the nearest of the dragons. Dafydd could not tell if it was the same one they had seen earlier, the one that had warned them to leave before its companions arrived. Something suggested to him that this creature was bigger, although it was the same deep black colour. It had been lying with its eyes closed, massive head resting on the flagstone path that speared arrow-straight from the palace doors to the far side of the parade ground. Now it opened one eye, bigger than Padraig's head, and sniffed the air as it focused.

'Sir Morwyr, I come on behalf of—' But on whose behalf he came, Padraig never said. With a swiftness that belied its great bulk, the dragon raised its head, opened its mouth and in one snap bit the seneschal in half. He didn't even have time to scream. Dafydd watched in horror as the dragon lifted its head higher, gulping down the morsel like a dog eating scraps. Padraig's legs and lower torso fell to the stone with a wet, bloody slap, and in an instant the dragon that had been lazing by the doors barged in and scooped it up.

In the space of a few heartbeats, Seneschal Padraig was gone, nothing left but a bloody smear.

A tense unease had settled across the camp, the army waiting, nervous. The common soldiers, drawn from the shires and hamlets, were a superstitious lot, and it had been in Beulah's interests to keep them that way. The brightest lads were taken at each year's choosing, trained to be Candles, Rams or warrior priests. The rest might learn a few letters, the rough calculations of the marketplace, maybe even a few words of Llanwennog if they were traders or seamen, but they weren't encouraged to deep learning. To them, dragons were creatures of myth, or at most fleetingly glimpsed timid creatures, not much bigger than a horse.

The two dozing on the plain looked like they could eat a horse in one bite.

Only the sight of the third, lying dead a few hundred yards further away, was keeping the panic from spreading. Anyone with a pair of eyes could look up towards the Neuadd, sitting proud on top of the great hill of Candlehall, and see the dozen and more huge beasts wheeling in the air around it. Where they had come from was anybody's guess, but that was unimportant. They were here, and they were more powerful than anything seen since King Balwen's time.

And Clun had bested their leader.

Beulah tried to project an aura of calm as she walked down the lines of tents, inspecting her troops. The land here was strong in the Grym, and with each passing day her ability to manipulate it grew, the dampening effects of her pregnancy leaching away. Even so, she struggled to find the right state of mind; the dragons tainted the air with their smell and the Grym with something even stronger, even more disconcerting. It was unnerving even the warrior priests, and that worried her more than anything.

'Is it true they fight on our side, Your Majesty?'

It wasn't the first time she'd been asked, nor would it be the last. The man who questioned her was a commoner, young and strong. A farm hand perhaps, judging by the colour of his skin and the set of his frame. He stood a little taller, a little straighter than the soldiers around him. And, of course, he had summoned up the courage to speak to his queen where all around trembled at her presence. She brushed his thoughts lightly, seeing only wonder and excitement there, a thrill at being part of this righteous war and pride at being in such exalted presence. He reminded her of Clun when first they had met.

'They fight for His Grace the Duke of Abervenn, and since he has pledged his allegiance to me, then yes, they fight for us.' Beulah put as much conviction into her words as she could manage, though in truth she had her doubts.

'Then we cannot lose, thank the Shepherd.' The young man bent his head and made the sign of the crook across his chest. It was a simple gesture, one Beulah had seen a thousand times and more, but something about it sent a shiver through her. Like a benediction for the condemned rather than a prayer of thanks.

'What is your name, soldier? Where are you from?'

'Siarl, Your Majesty. I come from the Hendry. Edge of the boglands south of Castell Glas.'

Beulah began to correct the lad about how she should be addressed, then realized just how silly the whole 'Majesty' and 'ma'am' thing was. 'You came with Duke Beylin? Helped retake Abervenn?'

'That I did. First ever fight I've been in and I never thought I'd be battling Hafod men.' The young man's face dropped, even as his eyes glanced briefly upwards to Candlehall and the Neuadd.

'Do not worry, Siarl. Some of my people may have turned their backs on me, given their hearts to the Wolf, but the Shepherd favours us. King Ballah is dead, Llanwennog taken. And now we have dragons on our side the siege of Candlehall will be short.' Beulah did not add that it would be bloody. She turned away from the young soldier, addressing one of the warrior priests who accompanied her wherever she went.

'Captain, this lad shows leadership potential. See to it that he is trained and given a commission. I need more men like him in my army.'

The young man dropped to his knees. 'Your Majesty. You do me great honour.'

'I do.' Beulah looked down at him, a shiver of premonition running down her back like cold water. 'See that you do not disappoint.'

2

Much has been written of the brothers Gog and Magog, who warred over the affections of Ammorgwm the Fair. It is said that when she died, the victim of one of their spells, so sickened were they that they split Gwlad in two. Rather destroy the world than have to share it with each other, they cared nothing for the incalculable damage their actions caused.

So much the legend has it, a warning to all about the follies of power and arrogance. But there is more to the tale than the bards tell, more truth to the story than even they suspect. Gog, Son of the Winter Moon, and his twin hatchling Magog, Son of the Summer Moon, warred with each other from their earliest days. They grew powerful in the subtle arts under the tutelage of the finest mages of their time, raised magnificent palaces and plotted such schemes as would bend the whole world to their will. Their rivalry urged them to ever greater deeds, each straining to outdo the other with their magic. Indeed it was such potent working that brought them to the attention of Ammorgwm in the first place.

The tale of their splitting Gwlad in two is often taken as a metaphor, a warning of the ultimate folly of those with too much power and too little responsibility. But like the rest of their tale it is in fact true. And not only did these two warring brothers somehow contrive to divide Gwlad into two separate realms, but each left in his brother's half a little gift that haunts us to this day. Magog sowed the seed that would grow into the malaise that afflicts our youngsters, a disaffection with learning and discipline, a reversion to old times when dragons were no better than beasts. And Gog left his brother's kin no better off, for he cursed them to wither even as he instilled in mankind, so long our friends and servants, a deep and irrational hatred of our kind.

From the journals of Myfanwy the Bold

The room at the top of the tower is always cold. The Old One doesn't appear to feel it, and neither do any of his followers. Dragons seem somehow immune to the weather, which he guesses makes sense. They can fly, after all. But there's more to it than that. Even on the coldest days, when he has to stoke the fire up high and dare not move away from it for long, the Old One still leaves the great glass doors open when he goes flying, sometimes even forgets to close them on his return. They are too heavy for the boy to shift. He knows; he has tried.

It is something to do with the lines and the Grym. He knows that too, is beginning to understand them. That was why the Old One chose him, plucked him from a life in the kitchens far below and invited him up to this high

19

tower. Because he could see something of the dragons' magic, their subtle arts.

'You have lit the fire. Well done, boy. You must have known I would be returning soon.'

That is another thing he doesn't quite understand – how the Old One can simply appear out of thin air, disappear too. True, the dragon mostly likes to leap from the top of his high tower and fly; who wouldn't? But there have been times in his short apprenticeship when the boy has been talking to his master, turned his back for just an instant and the dragon is gone. His return is often the same. Abrupt, unannounced. These are the magics the boy longs to learn.

'Where is it that you go to, master? When you disappear like that?' He pauses a moment, wondering whether he has the nerve to ask, then asks anyway. 'How is it that you disappear like that?'

The Old One observes him with eyes turned milky white with age, tilts his battered head ever so slightly. Some days a question will be ignored, some days it will earn the boy a swift rebuke, and some days – just occasionally – it will merit an answer. Today is one of the good days.

'Your first question is none of your business, clearly. My peregrinations are of concern only to myself. Had that been the depth of your curiosity I should have been most displeased.'

The boy hangs his head, more in disappointment than shame. It is an honour beyond honours even to be invited to the tower, let alone to have been picked to serve the Old One personally, to perhaps learn at his side. And yet for all the honour and all the promise, so far the boy's learning has been slow. He fears perhaps that the Old One has forgotten how humans live only short lifespans, fifty, sixty years. Perhaps a little more, but often much less. A dragon is barely adult in that time, and most of their kind in the palace number their years in the thousands. Or so they claim.

'But your second question. Yes, well that's the nub of it. That is a question that goes to the heart of all the subtle arts. I have been watching you, Melyn son of Arall. I didn't choose you at random to be my servant here. Quite the opposite. I have no great need of servants, but those of your kind who can sense the Grym all around them are few in number. Fewer still can reach out to the Llinellau and draw that power to them, use it for their own ends.'

The boy waits. He has learned these past months not to be impatient, or at least not to show his impatience. He has used his time alone in the tower, when the Old One is away on his journeys, to study what he can. There are scrolls and books so heavy he can scarcely lift them and written in dense scripts that swirl and change as he tries to read them, but he is nothing if not persistent. How else would he know his letters at all, a kitchen boy, son of an unimportant gatekeeper in a palace where the doors are never locked and all are welcome?

'The Llinellau Grym link every living thing in Gwlad. In some ways they are every living thing. When we are hatched – born in your case, I should say – we take some of the Grym into ourselves. And when we die – for all of us must die some day, even me – when we die we go back into the Llinellau to become one with all of Gwlad and for all of time. In that sense our lives are the aberration. Gwlad exists without us, the trees and the grass, the mindless sheep in the fields, the tiniest of insects and the largest leviathans roaming the wide ocean. These are all things of the Grym, but they do not know the Grym. That knowledge marks us out as different.'

The boy knows this, but only because he has read it in one of the Old One's books. This is the first time the ancient dragon has told him anything of the subtle arts. And yet it is not enough. It tantalizes him, knowing more already. What he longs for is to understand.

'You see the Llinellau, do you not?' The Old One moves closer to the fire, holds up his gnarled hands to the flames.

'They are everywhere, master. Sometimes it is hard not to see them.'

'Ah, you are rare among your kind, boy. To see with such ease what most men go their entire lives blissfully unaware of. There are even dragons who struggle to make that basic connection with the Grym. But tell me, what do you see of them here, in the flames?'

The boy is uncertain at first. He has never been asked something so directly before. But he is eager too, wants to show his mastery of this task so he might move on to more sophisticated magics. And so he jumps at the chance to excel, to impress his teacher.

The lines have always been easy for him to see, a constant companion on the edge of his vision. Now he summons them to the fore, thick and clear. The major lines delineate the room, arch into the roof overhead and criss-cross the floor. Focusing on the intersections he can see thinner lines, less structured, that nonetheless speak to how much life teems in even this seemingly barren place. And then he turns his attention to the fire.

A chaotic mess of Grym boils off the flames, lines arcing and snapping like the lightning storms he has sometimes seen through the great glass doors, so distant the thunder rumbles of their flashes take minutes to arrive. They jump and crack and flow out, mirroring the heat that he can feel on his face. He has never thought about it before, but he can sense the Grym leaping from the burning logs and into him just as much as the warmth from the flames. Perhaps more so. It is so easy just to reach out and bring a little more in, to push the deep chill from his bones.

And then it is too much. He stands fully ten paces from it and yet it feels as if he has put his hands deep into the fire. It is almost as if the Grym senses him, feels his call and answers joyfully. Now he doesn't know how to stop it. He pushes away, but that only makes things worse. He can feel the skin burning on his fingers, smell the stench of scorched flesh so horribly familiar from his earlier life in the kitchens.

'Enough.' The Old One's voice is all around him, enveloping him in a cocoon that separates the boy from the Grym entirely. It is almost as painful as the fire, but in a different way. Like hearing comforting voices all your life and then suddenly realizing they are gone. For an instant he is completely alone, and then the sound comes back, gently this time.

'You are too impetuous, Melyn son of Arall. Too hungry for the power. You will never control the Grym that way.'

'I am sorry, master. I will try harder next time.'

'Next time?' The ancient dragon tilts his head again as if the possibility is something he has not considered before. 'Perhaps. If you can learn to discipline yourself. You show great promise, but there is still a long way to go. Remember this lesson well, even after you have healed. The Grym is not your friend, neither your enemy. It is dispassionate, but it is more powerful than you can ever imagine. You must learn control. Learn discipline. Otherwise it will devour you. Now go and see the healer. You'll be needing a salve for those fingers.'

3

That ancient hall of the Neuadd has stood atop Candlehall's rocky hill since time immemorial. Some say King Balwen himself commanded it forth from the very living rock, but there are those who know it to be older even than he. Generations of his house raised the castle that surrounds the hall itself, extending and rebuilding into the great palace we see today.

There is no doubting the tactical advantages of the location of Candlehall and the Neuadd. Sat atop its steep-sided hill and overlooking the plains for leagues in all directions, it can be easily supplied by boats on the River Abheinn and so withstand even a protracted siege. In all its history there have been few direct attacks upon the city and never has it fallen, save through the treachery of Prince Lonk during the turmoil that was the Brumal Wars. And even then the true heir to the Obsidian Throne survived, escaped to gather his forces and retake his city.

How the prince could escape when the city was surrounded by an army a hundred thousand strong is one of the enduring myths that have grown around the House of Balwen and the magic that runs through its veins. The truth is both more prosaic and yet more wondrous, for it is said there exists beneath the solid rock of Candlehall hill a series of tunnels protected by ancient and powerful spells accessible only to those of royal blood. The magics needed to construct and maintain such powerful spells are beyond the comprehension of most, but it is no coincidence that the Inquisitor of the Order of the High Ffrydd, the most powerful mage in the Twin Kingdoms, spends as much time at Candlehall as at his order's mountain-top monastery, Emmass Fawr.

Barrod Sheepshead,
A History of the House of Balwen

'Hold still, won't you? I need to be very careful with this. Haven't ever had to heal a dragon before.'

Benfro lay on the sleeping platform, surrounded by animal skins that were more dust than fur. He couldn't have said when last this room had been occupied, but it was a long time ago. There was no trace of a scent of any previous visitor, just the background odour of cold stone, damp rugs and freshly broken timbers. It was cold, not helped by the large hole in the ceiling through which they had all fallen. Looking over at it, he could see tiny flakes of snow cascading down from outside. Since they had to get through the attic first, there must have been quite a snowstorm outside.

He gasped as an ice-cold knife of pain seared through his side. The young woman, Martha, bent to the task of removing the shaft of broken timber that had somehow slid past his scales and pierced his leathery skin. Benfro remembered all too well the agonies he had suffered at the hands of Fflint, but this was somehow worse. At least with his aethereal sight he could see the extent of the damage, guide his healer as she used all her strength to pull out the wood. As long as he could keep concentrating over the agony.

'Can I help?'

The young boy stood to one side, his arm splinted and hanging in a sling. Benfro had insisted Martha tend to him first, but even with her obvious skill both as a healer and at manipulating the Grym, he was going to take a while mending. They lacked the herbs and minerals needed to make the right poultices, and Benfro was too distracted by the pain to help. At least for now.

'See if you can find some kindling, Xando. Get a fire going.' Martha rocked back on her heels, rubbed her hands together for some heat. The Grym was all around them, she could easily have tapped it for warmth in the same way Benfro was already using it to heal his more minor injuries. He could see the wisdom behind her suggestion though. The boy was slowly coming out of his shock. He needed something to focus on, and he didn't seem to have any great skill in the subtle arts. A little bit of heat to help keep off the damp wouldn't have gone amiss either.

'Right then, dragon. Let's see if we can't get this out of your side.'

'Benfro.'

'I know. Sir Benfro. Your friend Ynys Môn told me many tales about you.'

For a moment Benfro was confused. 'Ynys Môn? How could you know him?' And then he remembered the jewels tumbling from his grasp as he flew over the palace gardens. But that had been him dreamwalking, not real. He had been sorting the jewels in Magog's repository, found his old friend among the ever-dwindling pile, fought against the control Magog had over him, and somehow found himself in this world.

'It makes no sense,' he said.

'Course it does. His jewels were reckoned. You did that. He was no more difficult to talk to than Sir Radnor. Much more chatty too.'

'But he was in Magog's world. I was there. And then I was here. That's not possible.'

'Silly dragon. You're here now. I'm here. There were always ways between the two worlds. You just needed to find them. Or for them to find you. It's them we pushed out the other side I'm worried about.'

'What do you mean?' Benfro asked.

Martha stood up for a moment. Facing him, Benfro couldn't help but see the blood soaking her forearms and smeared across her forehead where she had wiped her hair out of the way. His blood, and far too much of it for comfort.

'Has to be balance, see?' she said. 'Things slip back and forth all the time, but mostly they're simple-minded beasts and the like. When a dragon, or a person, stumbles across, well, something of equal power has to go the other way. You, me, Errol if he's in this world like he was trying. All that Grym has to be displaced back the other way. I imagine there's a fair few dragons find themselves in

Llanwennog or the Twin Kingdoms not really knowing how they got there. Or where they are.'

Something about her manner reminded Benfro of Corwen. Martha seemed incapable of understanding how he couldn't understand. And much like the old dragon mage, she seemed to find great amusement in his ignorance. Well, there were more important things to worry about. At least for now. He turned his attention back to the wound in his side, the broken rafter digging deep into his flesh.

'Hold still now. This may hurt a little.' Martha took firm hold of the short piece protruding from between two of his scales and pulled with all her might. The pain darkened Benfro's vision, even as it made his aethereal sight clearer. He could see the wood, his flesh and the organs deep inside his body. The point had missed anything vital, but only just. It lay far too close to one of his hearts for comfort. And there was something else about it.

'Stop!' The word burst from his mouth just as Martha began another heave. She let go instantly, falling back on to the heap of animal skins in a great billow of dust. When she stood up again her tangled black hair was streaked grey with it.

'What? I nearly had it.'

'There's a piece broken off inside.' Benfro closed his good eye and concentrated on what the missing one was showing him. 'When you pull the other bit, it's dragging it towards my heart.'

'I thought dragons had two hearts,' Martha said.

'We do. But they work together. I need both.' Benfro

moved as carefully as he could manage until he was in a more comfortable position, the wound well out of reach. He could feel the splinter working its way through him, little jabs of pain counting down the time until it would be too late. What would happen when that tiny piece of wood reached its target? Would he have any warning? It wasn't as if he could watch it all the time.

'This is beyond me. We're going to have to find a more skilled healer.' Martha stood up and shook her head, dust flying in all directions. She hopped down off the sleeping platform and approached the circle of broken timbers and plaster which was fast becoming covered in snow. Craning her neck, she looked up then backed away. 'But first we need to move. Won't be long 'til old Melyn comes looking for us.'

Melyn. The name sent a shiver through Benfro's whole body, from the tip of his nose to the end of his tail. How could he have forgotten Melyn? But in the chaos of the crash landing and his injury, the reason for their hurried escape had quite slipped his mind.

Gritting his teeth against the pain, he rolled back over on to his front. It took all his strength just to lever himself upright, get his feet underneath himself and stand. The room swayed back and forth, lightening and dimming in time to the throbbing in his side, but at least this way up the splinter of wood was pointing downwards. The tension between his scales held it in place and the blood appeared to have clotted around the wound.

'Where can we go?' he asked. Even the door seemed an impossibly long way away, the thought of walking with this impromptu spear in his side almost too much to bear.

He remembered the fiery red light in Melyn's eyes, the twin blades of fire, the terrible, familiar rage. 'You saw what he was like. He can go anywhere. He knows everything. Where can we possibly hope to hide?'

'Your Highness, we can't stay here. It's not safe.'

Prince Dafydd shuddered at the words, the memory of Seneschal Padraig's sudden violent end still fresh in his mind. He looked away from the balcony to where Usel the medic stood by the door. Usel's observation wasn't exactly news. The open windows let in the screams of the good people of Candlehall, the rushing of wings and crash of toppling masonry. Every so often a dark shadow would swoop past, but by and large the dragons were keeping their destruction to the lower part of the city, concentrating their efforts around the main gates. Dafydd had been watching the destruction with ever-deepening despondency. He had seen the armies of Queen Beulah form up on the plain, distracting the dragons after their first attack. Part of him had hoped that the creatures would turn to the easier target, but after a brief hiatus they had set about their terrible destruction of the city with renewed vigour. It was quite clear now that they were working on the side of the queen. He couldn't quite bring himself to describe it as fighting; that implied there were two sides to this conflict, where in fact all the Candlehall Guard could do was flee or die.

'Where can we go, Usel?' Dafydd turned back to the window, horrified by the carnage but determined to witness it. These people had welcomed him with open arms. They were his wife's rightful subjects, innocent men, women and children whose only fault was to wish for peace. They didn't deserve this fate but he was powerless to do anything about it.

'The cavern beneath the throne has more exits than one, sire.'

Dafydd turned to face the medic again. In all the rush since their arrival, the ceremony in the Neuadd, the appearance of the dragons and the subsequent carnage, he'd quite forgotten the cave and its endless rows of dragon jewels. Was that what had attracted these great beasts? Were they seeking revenge for their fallen brethren, killed over millennia?

'How do you mean? I thought you said there was only the one door into the place. Where are these others? Are they as well protected?'

'By the most ancient and potent of magics, or so I am told. I only know stories – I have never seen them myself – but consider this: the House of Balwen has not ruled over the Twin Kingdoms for so many centuries by allowing its children to be trapped in a walled city. There have always been ways to escape from Candlehall, even under the very eyes of besiegers.'

'And these secret passages. Could they let everyone out? The whole city?'

Princess Iolwen strode into the room, closely followed by Lady Anwen, Teryll the stable lad and the remainder of the palace guard who had accompanied them on this mad quest. She had changed into travelling clothes, and carried Prince Iolo in a sling around her shoulders like some common working woman.

'Your Majesty, I—' Usel began, but Iolwen cut him short.

'Enough "Majesty". I have no throne, no more right to call myself anything other than Iolwen. And if I leave these people to their fate I don't even have that right. Can we evacuate them all?'

'I don't know,' Usel said. 'I don't know how many people are left in the city, but it must number in the thousands. And the cavern, the jewels. That is a secret the House of Balwen has kept for millennia. I don't know how we could move so many people through it and not have them disrupt the delicate balance of the place. Just one jewel taken could cause chaos.'

'Look around you, Usel. Chaos is here already. It won't be long before the gates are down. Do you think my sister will show any more mercy to her people than her dragons have done?'

'If the seneschal were here—'

'Padraig is dead. And he didn't run this city on his own. There's an army of Candles in the palace. Set them to work. I will go and unlock the door.'

Usel paused for a moment as if weighing up his options. Dafydd could see the uncertainty in the medic's face, the conflict between saving as many lives as he could and endangering the secret he had spent a lifetime keeping. Eventually he made his decision, nodding once.

'I will have the word put out around the city. We will have to hurry though, and you will have to open the escape routes from the cavern. None but a direct descendant of Balwen himself can do that.'

'Hurry then, Usel. I will meet you at the door in half an hour.'

Dafydd watched the medic as he gave the briefest of

nods, then left the room. 'Is this wise, Iol? We can't save them all.'

'I can't abandon them either.' Iolwen hefted the sling into a more comfortable position, prompting a gurgling cry from the sleeping infant within. 'But Usel is right about the jewels. I don't care a jot about the secrets of the House of Balwen, but we can't risk them being taken. They're dangerous in unskilled hands.'

Dafydd recalled the vast cavern, the endless rows of stone pillars each with their hundreds of carved alcoves and individual piles of jewels. One such gem was a thing of great power and value. What lay beneath the Neuadd was a treasure beyond counting. Could they possibly protect it?

'Might I make a suggestion, ma'am?'

All eyes turned to Teryll, perhaps as much because he spoke Llanwennog rather than Saesneg. The young man had been taking lessons in the language of the Twin Kingdoms from the princess, indeed had reinvented himself as something of a servant to her alongside his duties of looking after their horses. He was still hesitant, over-whelmed by the situation he had put himself in.

'I am always open to suggestions, Teryll. Not so sure about being called "ma'am" any more than "Majesty".'

'Sorry.' The stable lad made a half-bow, half-nod. 'It's just sometimes when we've to move young fillies that spook at everything, we cover up the walkways so they don't get distracted. And sometimes, when they're too spooked even for that, there's some of the old trainers have a way with the Grym. There's an old saying – "In the brain, down the rein" – and it works just as well with people. Long as you're calm yourself, you can spread that feeling out.'

Iolwen let out a short laugh. 'Why is it that it takes a common man to show us the sensible way? You're right, of course, Teryll. We need to cover up as much of the distraction as possible, and then I can work to keep everyone calm. Like I did when the dragons first arrived.'

'Can you do that, Iol?' Dafydd didn't want to doubt his wife, but he was all too aware of the enormity of the task. 'It's not an easy thing to calm a few hundred. There'll be thousands of people and they'll all be frightened.'

Iolwen hefted the sling over her head, cradling her infant son close so she could kiss him gently on the forehead before handing him over to Lady Anwen. 'Not on my own, no. It's too much. I'll need your help, Dafydd. And I'll need the Obsidian Throne.'

'Is he dead? Think he's dead. Skinny wee runt of a thing. Dint reckon he'd last long. Dibs on his cloak, aye?'

'Saw 'im first, dint I? Is mine by right.'

Errol heard the voices in the darkness, their accents so thick as to be almost incomprehensible. He wasn't sure where he was at first, but then the smell hit him and brought the memories with it.

'Bin 'ere longer, int I? I gets first go.'

He opened his eyes slowly, feeling the crusty muck on his face. At first he thought he was blind. The darkness was almost complete, just a slight lessening in the shadows overhead, a subtle sense of movement. He was so cold, so tired, he just wanted to lie here and sleep. But the ground was hard under his back, the smell made breathing difficult, and the voices were getting louder, closer.

'Fight you for it. Good cloak like that don't come round often. Reckon it's worth a fight.'

With a low groan, Errol struggled upright. His hand touched rough cloth, cracked long-dead bones underneath. He remembered the dead man, all the dead bodies lying strewn about the floor like so much garbage. The fear was gone though. There were no ghosts here, just empty husks. Sitting up, he saw the fire still burning low, the pot of stew on its tripod hanging over the embers. Two figures stood to one side, frozen like schoolboys caught in some guilty act. Like everything else in this place, they were covered in a thick layer of dung, but he could see the whites of their eyes, wide with surprise.

'Wh . . . where am I? What is this place?' Errol's words came out thick and slurred, and only as they were gone did he realize he'd spoken in Saesneg. The two dark figures grasped each other, blinking. One let out a shout of alarm, then the other joined him, and finally they both ran from the cavern. Their screams echoed down the passageway for long moments before slowly dying away.

Bemused, Errol struggled to his feet. His head felt too light, as if it might pop off at any moment and float to the ceiling high overhead. He staggered across to the nearest wall, held out his hand to the cold stone for support. The touch sent a tiny jolt of energy up his arm, the merest hint of the Grym, which nevertheless felt like a draught of the freshest water he had ever tasted, a bite of the most delicious food. Instinctively he pressed his hand hard to the rock, seeking out the source of that power, but it was gone as fleetingly as it had come, leaving him a little more awake, a little stronger, but still without hope.

He slumped slowly to the ground, resting his back against the curve of the rock wall. The Grym had warmed him briefly, but now the cold began to seep back into his bones. Errol hugged his cloak around him, feeling something heavy drag at the hem as he did so. Intrigued, he pulled the cloth up close so that he could see in the near-total darkness, felt around the shit-caked material until he found the opening of a deep pocket sewn into the lining. A dim memory stirred as he pushed his hand in until he could feel what lay within. Scraps of cloth wrapped around something hard. He gripped one of them tight, began to pull it out, see what it was.

And then a heavy weight landed on his shoulder.

'Not dead. Can work.'

Errol looked up into the eyes of the supervisor leering down at him. How had the man got so close? He found himself lifted off his feet by the front of his cloak, and gripped the rag tight as he pulled his hand out of his pocket, trying to get hold of the supervisor's arms with the other one. The back of his head clattered off the rock wall, dazing him slightly, and he almost dropped his precious cargo. Then the supervisor had a hold of the slim silver chain looped around Errol's wrist. He muttered something under his breath and Errol found himself once more unable to resist as he was led out of the cave, back to the vast cavern and its enormous midden.

'Dig. Move.' The supervisor grabbed a shovel, pushed it hard into Errol's chest until he grasped it, palming the package he had found in his pocket. Before he had time to do anything else, the supervisor had shackled him to a cart. He gave Errol a heavy slap across the back as he departed with the ominous words: 'Ten carts. Drink. Ten more, then you eat.'

It was hard going. Harder than the first time. The manure was thicker and it stuck to his shovel so that each load was heavy and had to be bashed against the side of the cart to loosen it. The cloth in his hand made it difficult to grasp the handle properly too, but he didn't dare stop to look at it or even to shove it back in his pocket. He kept two fingers clasped around it, feeling a soft warmth emanating through the material that helped to soothe the pain in his arms and legs, ease the compulsion so that he could work at a pace that didn't leave him too exhausted to think.

When he had finished the first load, he stuck his shovel point down in the dirt like the other dishevelled workers before pushing the cart along its tracks to the tipping site. He had timed it so that no one else was there, which gave him a few fleeting seconds to catch his breath and finally unwrap the magical parcel he had found. The cloth was frayed at the edges, torn from some piece of clothing. Memories buzzed around the edge of his mind like flies, impossible to ignore but even harder to catch. He saw his own hands tearing that cloth, using it to protect his bare flesh as he reached out for a dark red flame.

The last piece unfolded to reveal a pebble-sized jewel of purest white crystal. It blazed amid the dirty fabric, beautiful beyond compare. A stark contrast to the muck and deprivation all around him. Entranced, Errol reached out a shit-caked finger, trembling like an old man, and gently touched the jewel.

A wave of purest relief flooded over him, so strong he

sank to his knees, letting out a gasp of surprise. The fog that had blanketed his thoughts was blown away as if by a tempest. And then a voice filled his head.

'Where is this place? What—?'

Flinching at the noise, Errol broke contact with the jewel. Immediately the warmth began to seep away, the fog edging back into his thoughts. He looked round, expecting to see the supervisor behind him, but there was no one to be seen. He looked back at his hands, shaking more severely now. The jewel still lay in its nest of torn fabric, and he slowly closed his fingers into a fist around it, letting his skin touch the cool surface.

'I cannot feel the Grym.' The voice spoke Draigiaith, but pure and perfect. Not like the heavily accented words of the men in the caverns.

'There are no lines here. I think we're deep underground.' Errol spoke the words aloud, then cringed at the thought he might be bringing attention to himself. How long before the supervisor came? Or just one of the other diggers? Why had he let them push him around like that? Why had he gone along with it?

'You have been placed under a compulsion. It's a very crude working, but I've seen similar before.' There was something about the voice that sparked a memory. It was far off, as if he had lived a lifetime since last he'd thought about it.

'Morgwm,' he said finally. 'Morgwm the Green. You're Benfro's—'

'Mother. Yes. Or a part of her. I cannot sense the rest of me. Not surrounded by all this rock. Where are we? Where is Benfro?'

'I lost him. Weeks ago. Possibly months. We were in Llanwennog, at Tynhelyg. Melyn was there. He captured me, was going to kill me. Benfro came back to save me. Then I . . .' Errol stopped, partly because the memories were confused and muddy, partly because he could hear voices in the tunnel. He couldn't let them catch him, couldn't let them take him back there. Worse, what if they found the jewel and took it from him? He looked around the ledge where his cart still stood waiting to be emptied. Light flickered from a line of greasy torches in iron sconces bolted into the rock face. It illuminated only a few feet either side, thickening the darkness of the pit into which all the excrement was poured. The tunnel mouth reflected more light, orange and dirty, moving closer as another cart was wheeled towards him. There had to be another way out, surely?

He took a couple of steps, then stopped as the thin chain around his wrist snagged. He tugged at it once, twice, hoping that it might break, but it held tight. A cart trundled from the tunnel on squeaky wheels, continuing its slow journey to the edge. Errol froze as the man pushing it reached for the lever that would release the load. Perhaps if he kept still he wouldn't be seen, wouldn't be missed yet.

And then the supervisor stepped out, flaming torch held high as he scanned the ledge from side to side.

4

One aspect of Gog's curse upon his brother's half of Gwlad that is not well understood concerns the long decline in fertility of the dragons of that realm. Our lives are long, and it takes our kind many years – perhaps centuries – to reach maturity. We are very selective of our mates and breed infrequently. Even so for two thousand years and more the dragons of Magog's realm dwindled in numbers, their kind becoming increasingly aged. What few young were hatched were only daughters – no sons of Magog would ever rise to take on his mantle.

And yet all curses can only run for a finite time, even if that time is measured in aeons. As the curse upon our realm lessened, and some of our young began to abandon the feral life and seek once more our learning, so in the other realm it was only a matter of time before a male kitling was hatched.

I have felt that moment, a tremor in the Grym as if Gwlad herself shivers with anticipation. So long divided, can it really be that our world shall soon be whole again?

From the journals of Myfanwy the Bold

His hands are healed now, the tips of his fingers shiny and smooth where once they had been rippled with prints. In time they will return to normal, that is what the old healer told him anyway. He doesn't mind; just feeling them is a reminder of the power that surged through him, boiling off the fire. He has spent the time since that incident trying to feel the Grym again, trying to control how it flows into him rather than just letting it burn him up. At first it took all his effort just to see the Llinellau around him, but now he can feel them without even needing to look, especially here at the top of the tower, where they are so abundant. And he can let the Grym warm him just enough to keep the morning chill from nipping at his ears and nose.

He still needs to build the fire though. Even though he has magic the boy can't even begin to imagine, the Old One likes to have his fire waiting for him when he returns from his travels. It's hard work, hefting logs as big as his legs from the stack beside the fireplace. He doesn't know how they get there, has never seen anyone haul them up the long spiral staircase from the palace far below. Indeed, he has never seen a tree save for in pictures. All his life has been bounded by stone walls and the view of the city roofs that greets him when he summons up the courage to venture out on to the wide ledge beyond the big glass doors. Roofs stretching to the hazy distance and then the mountains capped in white snow. On the clearest of days he has seen an indistinct green smudge in the far distance to the south and imagined that is the fabled forest of which he has read. Mostly he knows wood only as the logs that feed the fire, the floorboards and furniture, doors and servants' stairs, and the rafters high overhead in the deepening gloom.

'You are letting your mind wander again, my young apprentice.'

The boy spins, seeing the Old One standing in the open doorway. His wings hang half open, as if he has just landed on the wide ledge that surrounds the tower, but the boy cannot recall hearing his dragon master's landing or even the familiar sound of his approach. Was he really so lost in his thoughts, or is this the other magic? He studies the Llinellau around the Old One, looking for clues, but he doesn't know what is a clue and what is normal.

'How are your fingers? Not burned any more?' The Old One folds his wings tight and weaves a route through the collected apparatus and curios that fill this vast room. The boy has no idea what most of them are for – mainly it seems collecting dust that he then has to clean off.

'Much better. Thank you, master.' He bows his head in deference as the Old One approaches the fire, withered hands outstretched towards it. Whether the great dragon can see through his ancient eyes clouded white by the years, he cannot tell, but the boy has long since learned not to guess.

'Good. Good.' The Old One stares sightlessly into the flames, falling silent in that way of his the boy has become used to over the year since first he was summoned from the kitchens. Quite how the dragon had even known of his existence, he is unsure, but know of him he did. The Old One had known the boy's family history going back tens of generations, names he himself had never heard before, people long since forgotten even by their direct family. And yet the Old One had recited them as if reading from a book only he could see. It had seemed important to him, almost as if he were trying to justify something. To this day he refers to him as 'Son of Arall' even though that is not the name of the boy's father. He was just 'boy' until the Old One called him 'Melyn', the name of another man who died over a thousand years earlier.

'Your studies? You are progressing through the scrolls?'

'I have read all the ones you have given me, master. Some more than once.'

'More than once, eh? That's good. Knowledge does not come from a casual glance but a deeper consideration. You would do well to remember that. Still, I must look out some more for you. Come.'

He follows the ancient dragon across the room to where the writing desk stands. Beside it, shelves are crammed with rolls of parchment, scrolls and leather-bound books. The boy has looked through most of them when the Old One has been away, but most mean nothing to him.

'Here is a history of the first times, when men were little more than beasts roaming the dusty plains of Eirawen. There is much to be learned from it. And here . . .' The Old One reaches up high, pulls out a slim volume with a cover made of some strange green material that shimmers in the light falling on it from the candles nearby. 'This is my own copy of Aderyn's *Educational Notes for the Young*. I think you will find it, well, educational. And perhaps you might like to . . .'

The Old One falls silent. His white eyes never look

focused on anything, but now they take on that faraway stare the boy has come to recognize. Soon his master will leave, though whether through the glass doors and on the wing or by the subtle arts he cannot tell.

'I must go. Just briefly. Read these words, young Melyn son of Arall. Absorb them, their meaning. I will quiz you on them upon my return.'

He takes the scrolls and the book, light for a dragon but almost enough to drop him to his knees. Without any further word, the Old One steps around the writing desk and then is gone. At least that is what the boy's eyes tell him. His other sight, the view of the Llinellau he has been practising ever since he burned his fingers, tells him a different story. Without even a thought, the dragon has become the Grym, stepping into the Llinellau, and then . . . what? It is not hard to imagine the Old One using this magic to travel along the lines at the speed of thought. It happened so quickly, but the boy is certain he saw a flash of brighter Grym moving along one of the lines, dissipating so fast he might have missed it had he not already suspected. Had he not been looking for it.

But how was it done?

Holding tight to the scrolls and book, the boy seeks out the nearest major line of the Grym. He can sense it in a way that is not seeing nor hearing, but elements of both and all his other senses. There are voices calling him, glimpses of places he doesn't recognize, smells both exotic and revolting. For a moment there is heat on his skin, but not the burning of the fire. Then he is so cold it might be midwinter in the deep snow piled up around the main courtyard behind the kitchens. All these sensations and more flood him, tug at him, tempt him. Is it so easy as to just choose one and step? But which one? There are so many, so enticing, so exciting.

And then he sees it. A tree, vast, with leafy green branches spread wide. He can hear the swish of wind in its leaves, smell something like the scent that comes from the logs, only this is far more vital, more intoxicating. It is so real, so near he could just reach out and touch it.

So that is what he does.

5

Woe betide the novitiate who does not master self-discipline and self-knowledge before attempting to use the lines and the power of the Grym. It is a skill required of all who would serve the Order of the High Ffrydd, and only those who show an innate talent are chosen, but still the almshouses of the mindless swell their numbers each year. For the Grym sings a siren song to all who would connect with it, promising a world of infinite wonder should you just answer its call. Harden your heart to it, ignore the voices, the sights and smells. They are nought but illusion and to acknowledge them is to surrender to a fate far worse than death.

Quaister Timmins,
On the Workings of the Grym

'The walls cannot hold much longer, Your Majesty. Candlehall will be ours by tomorrow at the latest.'

Queen Beulah stifled a yawn as she received yet another report from yet another nameless general. None had anything new to say. The dragons had been alternately smashing rocks and occasionally themselves against the massive entrance gates or lying around on the plain in front of the city bickering with each other and sleeping.

They seemed to have an insatiable appetite for beef, preferably served still mooing, but at least they hadn't tried to kill any of her soldiers. Not yet.

'I'm sure I heard a very similar report yesterday, General. Come to me when you have something useful to tell me, or don't come at all.' She sat behind a large table in the command tent, strewn with maps and endless lists in Lord Beylin's distressingly tidy handwriting. The man himself sat to the left of her, the seat on her right empty where Clun should have been. His Grace the Duke of Abervenn had a knack for missing all but the important briefings. He was probably out riding that great horse of his, scaring the common soldiers even more than the dragons. On the other hand, he was the only one those same dragons would take orders from, so it was as well to keep him sweet. He had other uses too, the thought of which brought a slight flush to her speckled cheeks.

'Enough of this.' Beulah pushed herself up and out of her chair. 'We can plan and strategize and revisit the figures all we like, but the truth of the matter is we're stuck here until those wolf-cursed beasts break down that gate.'

'I rather think they would be quicker about it if we gave them less to eat.' Lord Beylin had risen from his seat at the same time as Beulah, as was only correct, but she could see by the way he hovered that he really wanted to sit back down and carry on counting his cows. Damn, but he was an irritating man. He had his uses too, not least of which was providing for her army. It was the slaughterhouses of the Hendry that fed this war, and Beylin would grow rich on it. She'd probably have to make him a duke too. Either that or cut off his head.

'Perhaps you would like to suggest that to them yourself?' Having him eaten by a dragon would solve her problems just as well.

Beylin nodded his head once in deference. 'I wouldn't dream of overruling His Grace the Duke of Abervenn, ma'am.'

'Good.' Beulah waved a dismissive hand at the papers on the table. 'You carry on with the admin, Petrus. I'm going to see if our captive has regained enough strength to be interrogated.'

Captain Celtin and a couple of warrior priests fell in behind her without being asked. Beulah considered dismissing them, but their presence was expected, and Clun would have their hides if he heard she'd been wandering the camp alone. She strode swiftly through the lines of tents. In truth she had almost forgotten about the man they had captured in Abervenn, the disciple of the so-called Guardians of the Throne. He'd been kept sedated for the journey up the River Abheinn and since they'd arrived. Her plan had been to wait until she had the power of the Obsidian Throne behind her, then peel away the layers of his mind one by one until she knew his every last secret. Weeks of being drugged should have battered down what few mental barriers he still had, even if it looked like she was going to have to wait a little longer before regaining her city and its magics. This close, she could use some of that power behind it anyway, and her skill was growing stronger by the day.

The soldiers had built a makeshift wooden hut to act as a prison, the drugged man its only inmate so far. Two warrior priests stood guard at the door and another two were stationed inside. All came to attention as their queen arrived; only the young man remained seated, leaning back against the rough wall of his cell. A quick skim of his thoughts showed his lethargy was feigned.

'When did you stop sedating the prisoner? I gave no order.' Beulah's anger had returned in the weeks following the birth of Princess Ellyn, and it too was stronger than before. She tried to keep it in check, all too aware that the prisoner was listening.

'Your Majesty, it was administered this morning. Same as every morning since you captured him.' Captain Celtin himself answered, his earnest tone going some way to ease her irritation.

'In his food? Has he eaten it?'

'He wouldn't eat anything, ma'am, so we've been force-feeding him with a tube. I personally supervised this morning's dose.'

'And yet he is awake and lucid, despite the act he hopes to fool you with. Restrain him.'

Beulah watched as three of the warrior priests entered the cell. The young man didn't put up a fight, but she could see the resentment in his eyes. Only when he was bound to his bunk with iron chains did she approach him.

'Do you feel stronger now you are close to your beloved throne? Not much of a guardian if you could let my sister take it so easily.'

'Princess Iolwen refused the throne. As did Prince Dafydd. Neither of them was ever a threat to our plans.' The man spoke slowly, his words slurring slightly as if he truly were drugged, and yet Beulah could see the clarity of his thoughts. He made no attempt to hide them.

'Our drugs still your body but don't affect your mind. Curious. I shall have to tell my men to up the dose.'

The man had been gazing at the floor, but now he raised his head slowly, weaving it from side to side like a drunkard as he tried to focus.

'You're too late, false queen. You'll never sit on your stolen throne again. His vanguard are here. I can feel them.'

'The dragons?' Beulah almost laughed. 'They are doing my work for me. They take orders from me. They serve me.'

'For now. Maybe. But they are only the first to come. He will follow, and he will not suffer our kind to be in his presence. Why else do you think your sister is betraying your family's oldest secret?'

Beulah paused before answering, once more skimming the man's thoughts but delicately, as she would when sparring with Inquisitor Melyn or Seneschal Padraig. She understood a little of what was happening now; the sedatives they had given this man might have dulled his body, but there was a walled-off part of his mind that was as sharp as a pin. Sharper, even. He was freed from the worries of bodily sensation. If he was an adept, then his aethereal self might well have been wandering far and wide while his body sat here guarded by her finest warriors. What might he have seen? Who might he have contacted?

'What do you mean, betraying our oldest secrets?'

As she had hoped, the answer to the question came swiftly to the front of his thoughts. Beulah saw the aethereal view of the Neuadd, first from outside, then inside with the massive bulk of the Obsidian Throne towering over everything. Then the view changed, sinking through the marble floor, the hard granite that formed the great mound upon which Candlehall was built, and then into the cavern deep below. The cavern that few were meant to know about and only those with the blood of Balwen in their veins could ever hope to enter.

'Balwen's seed is spread further than you think, false queen. We might even be cousins.' The young man managed to slump forward a little, but it was clear his body was not under his control. 'Kissing cousins.'

Beulah ignored the jibe. It had been intended to irritate her, but the news of her sister's betrayal had already done that. If it was true, of course. She couldn't take the chance though. Even if Iolwen shouldn't have known about the cavern, let alone the routes out of it and the ancient, powerful magics that protected them. She turned her back on the man, walked past the waiting warrior priests and out of the grim wooden prison.

'Kill him,' she said to Captain Celtin in passing. He clasped a fist to his breast by way of salute and nodded to one of the guards. Beulah felt the tug on the Grym as a blade of light was conjured, the last gasp at the edges of her mind as the young man lost his head. She was already many strides from the execution though. She needed to find Clun, and then she needed to talk to these dragons.

'Keep very still. As long as you don't move he cannot see you.'

The voice in Errol's head came with a compulsion far more powerful even than the silver chain that bound him to the cart. It didn't need to, he had frozen the instant he had seen the supervisor emerge from the tunnel. Senses dulled by whatever strange magics this place contained, he hadn't really considered the man before. He was cleaner than the diggers, but the light of his torch showed a face still smeared and grubby, scalp shaved no doubt to make washing himself at the end of the day easier. His face was fuller than the others, a pronounced gut suggesting that he had access to more food than the rancid cauldron of slops. He was well dressed too, a short cloak revealing stout leather boots and trews made of some oiled material that glistened in the darkness. But it was the small leather purse strung from his belt that caught Errol's attention; a brief glimpse as the supervisor turned this way and that, swirling his cloak as he tried to see where the missing digger had got to.

On the face of it, there was nothing all that unusual about having a purse, except that down here in the caverns there wasn't much need for coin. And this purse had an aura about it, something he had never encountered before. Almost as if it were a repository of the Grym. Was that how the supervisor controlled the diggers? Could that be the source of his power in this otherwise lifeless place?

Errol wondered what had become of his own money bag, gifted to him by Poul Gremmil what seemed like a lifetime ago. It was probably back in Tynhelyg or the village where Nellore had lived. Where they'd tried to sacrifice him to their gods, the dragons.

Nellore!

The memory hit him hard. Sitting in the cave, trekking the lines to steal food. His companion for the weeks they had spent walking towards the mountains and Gog's castle. How could he have forgotten her? Except that he had forgotten everything.

'Still yourself. Keep your thoughts quiet.' The voice of Morgwm the Green was little more than a whisper but the scolding in her tone was unmistakable.

'His purse. It's where his magic comes from. It's what binds us all to this place.' Errol thought the words, still trying to hold himself motionless as the supervisor walked towards him. For a moment he thought he had been spotted, but the man's gaze slid over him, over the cart and on to the next set of rails.

'You have a rare skill for one of your kind. Of course there must be a source of power here. Had I been whole, had I been alive . . .' Morgwm's voice faded to nothing.

'Can we take it from him?' Errol wasn't sure how. The supervisor wasn't the biggest of men, but he was large enough, and Errol was weak.

'We?' There was a hint of amusement in Morgwm's tone. 'I'm not sure how much help I can be. I am incomplete and I am dead, and here the Grym is almost non-existent.'

The supervisor was close now, still looking everywhere but at Errol and the cart. He stepped to the edge, held out his torch and peered down into the inky depths. Had he been just a little closer, Errol could easily have rushed him, shoved him over. But the purse would have gone with him, and somehow it was linked to the chain that tied him to the cart and muddied his senses. He needed to get the purse. Needed to find out what lay within it.

Errol tensed as the supervisor turned once more, scanning a slow circle. This close, he could see the confusion on the man's face. He bent down and inspected the rough iron tracks along which the cart was wheeled. Stood again and followed them to the edge, clearly unable to see the cart itself. He let out a howl of pain as he walked straight into it, his shin smacking against solid wood. He dropped the torch, hopping as he reached down to clasp his injured leg. Bent double, his cloak folded back on itself and Errol saw the purse close up, within reach.

There was no time to think, no time to plan. He launched himself at the supervisor, knocking him to the ground. Even so, he had misjudged the man's bulk, jarring his own neck and shoulders with the impact. One hand still clasped tight around Morgwm's jewel, he reached out for the purse, only to find a strong hand wrap itself around his wrist, pull him up hard.

'Thought something smelled wrong. Hiding was he? Trying to escape was he?'

The supervisor struggled to get his footing. Errol tried to break his grip, but it was tighter even than the chain. He kicked out, his soft boot connecting with hard shin, and the supervisor collapsed again. He let out a roar of pain and anger, then swung his free hand around in a fist. Errol saw it coming, ducked as best he could, but it still clipped the top of his head, stunning him. This time when the supervisor stood, Errol was too woozy to fight back, could only dangle as he was lifted by his wrist.

Then Errol saw it, just within reach of his other hand. The dropped torch still burned, sputtering slightly in the greasy mess smeared all over the cavern floor. It was a good weapon, but to use it he would have to let go of Morgwm's jewel.

'In the pit he goes. No place here for them as don't want to dig. That's what Mister Clingle always says.'

Errol felt himself being hefted higher and knew all too

well what was coming next. He had no choice. 'Sorry,' he said as he dropped the cloth-wrapped jewel as carefully as he could. As it left his hand, so the compulsion to obey, to dig, came back. His thoughts began to dull, but he fought with every last ounce of his willpower. Snatching up the torch, he swung it round in a wide arc. The flame grew brighter, flaring in the darkness, and then it smacked into the side of the supervisor's head with a jolt that ran down Errol's arm and rattled his teeth.

For a moment he thought it hadn't worked. The supervisor looked down at him with hate in his eyes. Then something glazed over them. He staggered sideways, closer to the edge, his grip still tight around Errol's wrist. One step, two, lurching like a drunkard. Errol tried to get his feet down, but they slipped in the mire. He dropped the torch, reached out for the purse still tied to the supervisor's belt. Its touch was like holding Morgwm's jewel, only different. The compulsion to dig vanished, his thoughts cleared.

The supervisor took one more fateful step, backwards over the ledge. Something of a realization dawned on his face as he overbalanced, swinging his free arm around as if that might somehow help. Errol tried again to get his feet down, to anchor himself, break free. But the supervisor's grip on his wrist was too strong. And with a terrible wail that might have been either of them, they both went over the edge.

The corridors were quiet, the air undisturbed in many a day. It was just as well, really. There was no way Benfro could move quietly, not with the needle constantly jabbing deep inside him. Walking crablike helped, but meant his half-spread wings scraped against the floor and banged off the occasional pieces of furniture they encountered. He'd already sent a couple of old tapestries tumbling, collapsing into billows of dust and broken fragments of fabric. Everything was old, untouched, abandoned.

'Where are we, Xando?' Martha asked as they paused at a point where the corridor opened out on to a large landing. Dim light filtered in through glass skylights covered in a thickening layer of snow. Outside the storm was building, charging the air so that the young woman's hair seemed to float about her head.

'Don't really know.' The boy peered around the corner, looking left and right, then up. Finally he stepped out on to the landing, crossed to where a banister rose from the floor. It was clearly built with dragons in mind, the gaps in the carved stonework large enough for a man to walk through let alone the slight figure with his broken arm. He steadied himself with his free hand before leaning out and down. 'Long way up, wherever it is.'

Benfro shuffled out on to the landing and leaned over the banister himself. The drop was enough to take his breath away, a repetition of landings plunging down in ever-smaller circles. The storm-darkened sky couldn't light up the lower levels, but torches flickered yellow light, reflecting off a polished marble floor at the very bottom.

'Are we going down there?' He looked sideways to where a wide staircase dropped from this top level down to the next. Walking on the flat had been painful enough; the thought of stairs made him feel sick.

'Unless you feel up to flying?' Martha joined the two of

them at the edge, leaning over without a care in the world, or so it seemed. Benfro had no great fear of heights despite his many falls – possibly because of them. He had wings and had felt the strength of them holding him up in the air. There would be no saving Martha and Xando if they fell. As if sensing his thoughts, the boy took a step back, but Martha just leaned out even further.

'There are people down there,' she said. 'And dragons. Look.'

Benfro looked down again, and sure enough he could see shadows scurrying around like ants. And then a small band of men ran across the hall on some urgent errand. A moment later a large grey dragon followed them, and then another, smaller this time and mottled green. For a moment he thought it was the fold from the Twmp come to the castle now Gog was dead. The small one might even have been Cerys, but the others weren't quite right.

He was squinting, trying to make out details in the poor light, when a third dragon strode across the hall, then stopped suddenly in the middle. So large he could only be male, and old at that, he glanced from side to side, turned through a complete circle as if trying to pinpoint something, and then looked straight up. Benfro rocked back on to his tail and pulled his head away from the banister, desperate not to be seen, but he couldn't help thinking he had made eye contact for a fraction of a heartbeat.

'Did he see us?' he asked as Martha and Xando both backed hurriedly away from the edge.

'I'm not sure.' Martha crept forward again, keeping low to the floor this time. She peered down for no time at all before scrambling back. 'Oh yes. We might want to hide right now.'

'Hide?' Benfro looked around the landing. There were a few doors, the corridor down which they had come, a couple of open alcoves that looked like they might have been intended to house statues, but nowhere a creature his size could hope to hide. 'Where?'

'The shadows. Quick.' Martha grasped Benfro's arm in both her hands and tugged him towards the darker of the two alcoves. He couldn't begin to think how it could possibly help if the large dragon had seen him already, but he followed her lead and in moments all three of them were huddled together in a space scarce big enough for him alone.

'Your wings. Cover us. Then hide.' Martha emphasized the last word as if somehow Benfro didn't know what it meant. He knew how to hide perfectly well; he'd spent most of his early years hiding from Frecknock after all. There were ways of using the shadows and light to make it hard to see you; he just didn't see how that could work here. He wrapped his wings around them both, pulling himself into the shadows even more, but he was still as obvious and visible as a deer highlighted by a ray of sun through the forest canopy.

The forest. The deer.

Benfro remembered then, the trick that Ynys Môn had taught him all those years ago. The first working of the subtle arts. The simplest of magics. He stilled himself, pulling his aura in tight around him even as he stilled his breathing down to almost nothing, and withdrew himself from the Grym. The cold seeped into his feet and nipped at the tips of his wings, but he kept himself motionless and waited.

It didn't take long. With a rushing of wind, the dragon he had seen at the bottom of the stairwell rose past the banister on half-furled wings. Benfro almost lost his concentration there and then. He had never seen flying like it, so controlled, so accurate. The dragon could scarce have fitted in the space between the banisters were he to stretch his wings wide, and yet he hovered like a tiny bird, scanning the landing with eyes of deepest black.

'I could have sworn . . .' His voice was deep, cultured. It reminded Benfro of Sir Frynwy when he was reciting one of the great tales after a feast. He flicked the tips of his wings and came to rest on the banister before stepping down on to the landing itself as a second, smaller dragon appeared behind him.

'There's nothing up here. It smells like no one has been up here in years.' The second dragon didn't land in quite such an elegant manner, clattering her tail off the banister and knocking a chip out of the stonework. Benfro almost lost his concentration a second time, revealing himself to the both of them, for he recognized her all too well.

'You are wrong. I can sense something, Cerys.' The larger dragon sniffed the air again, moving his head from side to side. Benfro was surprised he could smell anything but his own musk. It rose off him like the stench off a week-dead rotting carcass, so thick Benfro could almost see it. Still, he kept motionless as the great dragon swept past him and on into the corridor where they had just come from. He took a few steps along it, Cerys trotting behind him until they were out of sight. Benfro began to relax, then heard the smaller dragon talking again.

'Now's not the time for this. We have to get to the palace. Myfanwy is waiting for me. The Old One—'

'Is dead, Cerys. Dead. He was immortal. Ageless. And this usurper, this feral creature that calls itself a dragon killed him. He showed it kindness and it cut his head off. Ah, by the sun and the moon, how can this have happened?'

'We don't know what happened. Some say Sir Enedoc is dead too, and that it was a man who killed them both.'

'A man?' The older dragon strode out of the corridor, Cerys between him and Benfro's hiding place. His attention was on his companion though, not searching any more. 'No man could best the Old One, and Enedoc would have bitten his head off before he could even speak. A man wouldn't be able to reach the top of the tower, much less breathe the Fflam Gwir. That's old magic, feral magic. This is no dragon but a base beast. Worse even than the ones Myfanwy took you from. We must hunt it down and kill it.'

Without a backward glance, he leaped over the stone balustrade, spreading his wings just wide enough to slow his fall. In an instant he was gone, but the smaller Cerys stood for a while, no doubt watching his descent. She looked around briefly, and for a moment Benfro thought he had been spotted. Then she hopped up on to the balustrade like a bird, fluttering her wings gently to keep her balance. Shook her head just once in a manner Benfro had seen his mother do a thousand times before, and then she too opened her wings and stepped into the void.

6

Perhaps Gog's strangest and most persistent pre-occupation has been his attempts to fully understand the nature of men. Even before he fell out with his brother over that strange creature Ammorgwm, he spent as much time studying the servants, and particularly their youngsters, as he did any other aspect of the subtle arts. He remains convinced that they are as much creatures of the Grym as dragonkind, and fully as capable of mastering our magics as any dragon.

It is strange but not unsurprising that one quite so advanced in his knowledge can yet fail to see the simplest of facts. Most dragons do not even begin their training in the subtle arts until they have seen a hundred summers. It can take decades to learn even just to see the Llinellau Grym, let alone know how to manipulate them. To become even the most base of adepts requires centuries of painstaking and diligent study.

In all my long centuries of life I have yet to meet a man who has lived beyond the age of ninety. Aggressive and warlike, they are apt to kill themselves and each other long before then, and those who do not succumb to axe or blade die from the diseases that spread through their woefully unsanitary towns and cities. It is a marvel that they reach an age where they can successfully breed, except that they seem almost to be born ready to procreate. Indeed their mortality is a blessing in disguise, for were they to live out their full natural lives soon Gwlad would be carpeted with them.

From the journals of Myfanwy the Bold

He is everywhere.

All of Gwlad is laid out before him. Every living creature from the tiniest mote grubbing around in dirty soil to the massive, lonely beasts roaming the vast emptiness of the Southern Sea. Every man, woman, child. Every dragon, even the Old One. For an instant that is almost too brief to exist he knows them all, sees through their eyes, knows their thoughts. In that single moment he is Gwlad, he is a god.

And then the pull of the Grym shreds him. There are no words to describe the agony as his being is torn into uncountable fragments, rendered down and down like the wheat he has seen pounded into flour in the kitchens, the sides of beef cut and cut and cut until they are nothing but mince. His sense of self is pared away even as he loses all feeling in his body, all feeling of ever having had a body. There is everything, and there is nothing.

But there is him.

He knows he exists even if he cannot remember who he is, where he is, what he is doing. Flashes of memory explode around him like lightning in a storm. The image comes to him then, standing on the threshold of a huge doorway, watching as a storm rages outside, beyond glass so clear it is almost as if it isn't there. Where?

Another explosion and the view is different. A clear sky, blue so deep it is almost black. There are rooftops far below; is he flying? Falling perhaps, and with that comes the sensation of fear. If he fears, then he must be. He just has to find himself, extract himself from this impossible situation. All he needs to do is remember who he is. What he is. Easier said than done when your thoughts are flighty things, spinning away before they can fully form.

Not a name. That is too much to ask for. He knows . . . what? He is something, a single point in this seething cauldron of light and sound and smell and everything. If he can just focus, just find a tiny bit of peace and quiet, he can work out what is happening, how to stop it. How to get back to normal.

Except that he doesn't know what normal is. He has no frame of reference, and even the view is gone. There is just white, fizzing with possibilities, each new discovery taking a part of him away, diminishing him until there is nothing left. He fights against it, tries to hold himself together even though he doesn't truly know what he is, how he came to be here.

There was something. He was doing something. Trying to work out how someone else had done something. These things are important, he knows, even though the sense of them is always just out of reach, slipping through his grip. Grip? He remembers fingers, burning flesh turned red from within, the whorls and twists of his skin turned smooth. It is a half-formed image, but he clings to it with a desperation born of a sudden understanding that

64

he won't die in this place, but simply cease to exist. Have never existed. No one will miss him. No one will mourn him. No one will care.

But he cares, and he has fingers. Damaged by the Grym radiating from the fire. Healing now. He can feel them, flex them, give them his entire concentration. And as he does so, the noise all around him changes, the light fluctuating, modulating so that he is falling once more, plummeting through air that whips at his hair, tugs at his skin, his body, pulls tears from his eyes and blurs the view. He blinks them away, sees mountains capped with snow, dark rock faces, cliffs and waves of deep green that must surely be trees. He is tumbling downwards, tries to flap his wings to slow his fall, but he has no wings. He is not a dragon, but a man. Falling.

The impact with the ground drives the wind out of him. For a long while all he can do is lie there in the grass, struggling to breathe, struggling to make sense of where he is, who he is. He is cold, skin damp and naked. His body feels all wrong, his limbs awkward and unresponsive. And then he hears voices off in the distance, coming closer. They speak a language he doesn't understand, but their tone is unmistakable. They are alarmed, hurrying towards him and jabbering at each other. Two people at least.

Hands take hold of him, pull him upright, and the world tilts dangerously into view. He sits in a field of long grass, looking out across a wide chasm towards mountains strangely familiar yet not quite right. Looking around he sees occasional trees, some animals he doesn't recognize, buildings a way off, and beyond them what he took for another mountain but is something more. A vast slab of stone like a perfectly vertical cliff face, only pocked with uncountable hundreds of tiny windows. And beyond it towers reaching up into a cloudy sky.

'Who let one of the mindless out, eh? Some novitiate's going to get into trouble.'

'Nah. Look at him. He's too young. And they all have loincloths on. Shoes if they're being took outside.'

He turns to face the men, not understanding their words. The tongue is like his but different, and their accents are strange.

'Here. He ain't no mindless after all.' One of the men leans down towards him, concern written across his features. 'What's your name, lad? How'd you end up out here?'

He doesn't know what they are asking, although the fact it's a question is clear. Do they want to know where he came from? He would like to know that too. And how he got here, who he is. But he can't remember anything except a long list of names, and at the end of it one that seems to fit.

'Melyn.' He sees their astonishment at his voice, sees their fear and feels a thrill at it. 'Melyn son of Arall.'

7

All living things are connected by the power of the Grym, from the tiniest of gnats to the largest of leviathans swimming deep in the Southern Sea. The mighty oak trees of the Hafod and Hendry are joined with the scrubby ice plants that cling to the bare rock of the frozen north, and the mightiest of dragons shares that bond with the basest of creatures. All is one with the Grym.

So what happens in a place where there are no Llinellau, where life itself is absent? What happens deep within the lifeless rock of Gwlad? Few such places exist that it is possible to reach, and they are places best avoided. To be removed from the Grym for a short while is uncomfortable, but prolonged exposure to these lifeless zones, these anghofieddau, will leach away first your memories, then your strength of will and finally your life itself. And when you die you will not become one with the whole of Gwlad, but simply cease to be.

Corwen teul Maddau,
On the Application of the Subtle Arts

It was never going to be enough.

Dafydd watched the lines of tired and frightened people

as they piled into the palace complex. What few city guards were left had put word out as best they could, going from house to house while trying to remain unseen by the great beasts flying overhead. There were lulls in the attacks by the dragons, and most of their attention now seemed to be focused on the main city gates and the walls on either side, but there were still a couple of the smaller ones patrolling. They had sharp eyes too, diving at the first sign of movement and grabbing whatever they could, man, woman, child, dog or goat. Some they would kill and devour on the ground, others they carried into the air, higher even than the top-most spires of the Neuadd, before releasing them. Dafydd didn't think he'd ever be able to forget the screams and the horrible wet sound of body hitting stone at speed.

There was work to do. He couldn't spare the time to watch these poor people as they filed into the vast reception rooms of the palace. His earlier worry that they might be panicked or intractable had proven unfounded. They were mostly too shocked to do anything but go where they were told. Some had to be physically led. Everything they owned was destroyed, and all because they had sided against their queen. They had welcomed him in, offered Iolwen the throne, and this was all the thanks he had to give them.

'We have to go to the cavern, sire. The princess needs your help.'

Dafydd turned away from his vantage point, where he had been watching the kitchen staff passing out bowls of nourishing soup, attending to wounds and generally making themselves more useful than he had ever felt. Usel stood behind him, a worried look on his face that suggested he was not used to plans unravelling all around him.

'Lead on.' Dafydd pointed in the direction of the corridor and stairs, then followed the medic. All around, the once-ornate palace was rimed with the dust of broken stone and cracked plaster. Pictures of long-dead kings and queens, princes and princesses hung askew or had fallen from the walls completely. No one had bothered to pick them up. There was no time, and few had good thoughts for their former leaders in this new crisis.

They reached the door to find it already open. Usel hesitated on the threshold, then disappeared down the spiral steps. Dafydd followed, feeling the growing power of the Grym as he came closer to the greatest collection of dragon jewels ever amassed. At the bottom of the stairs he found a small party of workers, mostly the soldiers who had come with him from Tynhelyg, but a few of the city guard as well. It was easy to tell the difference between them even without the darker hue of the Llanwennog skin. The Candlehall natives all stared in awe at the sights they knew they had no right to see. Some even covered their eyes, perhaps fearing that when this was all over – if this was ever all over – they might be punished for their transgression. His Llanwennog troops, in contrast, seemed unmoved by the magic of the place and knew nothing of the prohibitions surrounding it. Teryll had begun covering some of the nearest stone shelves with curtains and sheets, trying to explain to the workers in halting Saesneg what to do. A young man in the black robes of a predicant of the order of the Candle was helping him.

'Usel, Dafydd. You're here.' Iolwen spotted them through the throng and pushed past the people to join them. She still wore the clothes of a commoner, which was perhaps why no one paid her much attention. 'Teryll's covering what he can, but I need to find the escape route so we can make a passageway.'

'There are many escape routes from this chamber, Your Highness. All are protected by the same magic that prevents any but your family from opening the door in the palace, but they are also hidden from view. Please, let us move away from the crowd a moment.' Usel held out his hands. Dafydd took one and Iolwen the other. Dafydd felt that strange sensation he had come to associate with the medic's hiding spell, only here it was stronger, the air shimmering around them as they walked unnoticed towards the edge of the cavern. Only once they were out of sight of the entrance did he let go.

'What do you know of these tunnels, Usel? I assume they are tunnels.' Iolwen looked around the cavern, and Dafydd followed her gaze, seeing only rough-hewn rock. The ground beneath his feet here was hard-packed dirt and smooth stone, with no obvious sign of any path.

'Only what I have been told by others who have never seen them. Some lead to the foothills north of the city, others to the woods to the west. In some of the more fanciful tales they tell of a passage that takes but a few moments to walk and yet brings you out in Abervenn. If such a thing is possible, then it is truly a marvel. We will need to exercise caution when entering them though.'

'But where are they?' Iolwen turned on her heels, arms held out wide to encompass the whole cavern. As far as the eye could see, there was just the one way in and the one way out.

'Please. Give me a moment.' Usel stood motionless, his

eyes closed. Dafydd thought he felt something, the lightest of breezes past his ear. He closed his eyes and slipped gently into the aethereal trance the way his grandfather had taught him. Down here it was easy, the power radiating from the collected jewels almost overwhelming.

'I did not know you were an adept, sire. Nor you, ma'am, although it is your birthright.'

Dafydd looked around to see both Usel and Iolwen in aethereal form. The medic looked much as he always did, but Iolwen glowed a bright gold as if she stood in a ray of perfect sun.

'It is not something I have had much practice at. Nor anything in the way of tuition. It feels natural here. Safe.' The princess took a step forward but stopped when Usel placed a hand on her arm.

'Stay close to your true self, ma'am. The aethereal is easier to reach here, but it is also easier to become distracted. Now you are here though, look closely at the walls around you. Is there anything unusual? Anything that isn't there in the mundane?'

Dafydd scanned the rock, seeing nothing odd. Iolwen walked a few short paces to a point that seemed no different from the rest, yet when she reached out and placed her hand on the surface, the golden glow spread from her to form a neatly carved arch. With an effort of will, Dafydd slid back into himself, the aethereal view disappearing slowly. For a moment he had the uncomfortable sight of Iolwen's golden form in front of him, while her real body stood motionless by his side. And then the light faded, Iolwen stumbling slightly as she let out a little gasp. Instinctively he put a hand out to support her, but she pushed it away, striding forward to the exact spot her aethereal form had stood. Where before there had been nothing but rock, now a wide tunnel opened up on to blackness.

Dafydd wanted to stop and investigate, but Usel bustled Iolwen on to a further point along the cavern wall, where another tunnel soon appeared. Three more followed, bringing them eventually back to the point where they had started, the bottom of the spiral steps. A group of soldiers and palace guards clustered close to the entrance as if they dared not venture further into the room. The young predicant who had been helping Teryll saw them approach and bowed deeply to the princess.

'Your Highness, we are as ready as we will ever be.' He pointed at the nearby pillars, draped to conceal the jewels. Iolwen approached the young man, but he kept his head down, unwilling to meet her eye, so all Dafydd could see was a head of cropped straw-blond hair.

'What is your name, lad?' the princess asked.

'Predicant Trell, ma'am.' The young man finally looked up, revealing a face pale and thin, unremarkable save for the crooked nose that had clearly been broken in his childhood and not set properly.

'No longer predicant, I think. Precious few Candles left, and none of them dared come down here.'

'This place is sacred. We cannot enter without the permission of the queen. I suspect my fellow Candles still do not believe that has been given.'

'Well they're welcome to stay in the palace if they wish. I want you to lead the first group through the tunnels. We'll be sending them down just as soon as we've made it back up the stairs.'

The young predicant's eyes widened. 'You're going back, ma'am? Surely—?'

'I won't leave until I know the people are safe. And besides, there's something I have to do. Something only I can do.' Iolwen reached out and patted the predicant on the arm. 'Look after my people, Trell.'

He nodded once, then hurried away towards the nearest tunnel, tugging at the drapes as he went to ensure they were well fixed. Iolwen looked around until she saw Lady Anwen, still carrying Prince Iolo in his sling. Dafydd was still watching the young predicant as he walked over to the first hidden tunnel but turned when he heard a voice address him.

'We must go to the Neuadd, sire. The people are calm now, but that cannot last once word gets out that there is an escape route from the city.' Usel hurried them to the bottom of the stairs, letting Lady Anwen and Teryll go first, then Princess Iolwen. The moment she set foot on the first step, a cry of alarm echoed in the great cavern. Everyone turned, trying to locate the source of the noise. Dafydd spotted it first – the young predicant lying on his back and clutching his hand tightly to his chest. And then Dafydd noticed something else. The exit tunnel had disappeared.

'What's happening?' Iolwen asked as they hurried towards the recumbent Trell. He was moaning, clearly in pain, and as Dafydd reached him, he could see why. The young man's hand was a bloody mess. It looked like someone had taken a hammer to it, or it had been trapped in a rocky fissure as it slammed closed.

'Calm yourself, lad.' Usel knelt by his side, pressed a hand to his forehead and murmured some low words.

73

Dafydd felt the strange sensation of someone tapping the Grym, all-powerful in this cavern full of dragon jewels, and the predicant's moaning eased. Gently, Usel helped him up into a sitting position, took hold of the mangled hand and began inspecting the damage.

'It can be saved. Thank the Shepherd it only caught your hand. I don't want to think what might have happened if you'd been standing in the tunnel mouth.'

'It . . . it was there. Then there was a whistling noise. I . . .'

'Calm yourself, Master Trell.' Usel once more put his hand to the predicant's forehead, soothing him with his magic words. Only once the young man's breathing had steadied did he turn to face the rest of the party.

'I'm sorry. I should have known. It's in the verses, mad though they are. "The blood of kings will clear the way." Ah, by Gog's hairy balls I hate that damned seer.'

'What are you talking about, man?' Dafydd had been as patient as he could, but Usel's cryptic words and the uneasy atmosphere of the cavern, the silent whispering of all those long-dead voices, all were conspiring to give him a headache worthy of an epic night on the town.

'The escape routes. They will only stay open as long as one of King Balwen's heirs remains in the cavern. Step through them or back up the exit stairs, and the magic that conceals them reasserts itself.' Usel worked as he spoke, taking a long strip of clean white cloth from the bag slung around his shoulders and using it to wrap Trell's hand. 'The princess will have to stay here until everyone has gone through,' he added.

'I cannot. I'm needed in the Neuadd. If I don't use the power of the throne, there'll be riots before a hundred people have made it to safety. Before you've even got them down the stairs.'

Dafydd reached out and took his wife by the hand. 'I can go alone. I know as much of this magic as any of us. I can use the throne, just for this.'

For a moment he thought she was going to agree, even though he had made the offer hoping she would protest. The unlikely figure of Usel came to his rescue.

'You offer is well meant, sire, but it would not work. The Obsidian Throne is protected by many ancient spells. I have no doubt that given the time you would be able to circumvent them, but time is a luxury we cannot afford. The princess is a direct descendant of King Balwen himself. The throne will welcome her. You it will fight, and that conflict will spread throughout the city.'

The silence that fell after the medic finished speaking was as deep as the cavern in which they all stood. The situation was impossible, and as Usel had so helpfully reminded them, time was running out. How soon before the dragons destroyed the gatehouse and the walls? How soon before Beulah's army marched through the streets, putting everyone to the sword?

'There is a way.'

He almost didn't hear the words, so quietly did Iolwen speak them.

'Iol? You can't leave. The tunnels will close as soon as you do. You saw what happened.'

'No, Dafydd. I can leave. You can leave too, but Iolo must stay. His blood is Balwen's blood.'

'My lady, he's but an infant.' Lady Anwen cradled the sling with the still-sleeping child in it.

'I would rather die than let him out of my sight, Anwen, but I have no choice. Take good care of him. Teryll, stay with her. Keep out of sight of the people coming through. If you can bear it, sit nearer the centre of the cavern. We will be just above your heads, no higher than the Fool's Tower in Abervenn. If all goes well, we shan't be gone long.'

Iolwen bent low to her child, cradled in another woman's arms, and kissed him gently on the forehead. He stirred, let out a quiet gurgle of contentment, then settled back to sleep.

'Wait for us as long as you dare, but if all hope is gone, then take the rest of the palace guard and flee. He is our future. He can end these generations of needless war.'

'Where is His Grace the Duke of Abervenn?'

Beulah strode down the wide track between the ranks of white canvas tents so quickly that Captain Celtin and his warrior priests had to run to catch up. She had accosted half a dozen hapless soldiers already, none of whom had any reason to know where her husband was, and now she was nearing the edge of the camp. Beyond her lay the plain, the city rising in the distance, and a few hundred paces off a half-dozen dragons dozing in the afternoon sun. A light breeze blew towards the camp, bringing with it a stench that both turned her stomach and set the hairs on the back of her neck prickling. She had smelled that musk before, in a tiny village on the edge of the forest many hundreds of miles north-west of here.

'Your Majesty, I have sent word for His Grace. Would it not be better to wait for him in the command tent?' Captain Celtin was smart enough not to stand too close to his queen when suggesting such a thing. Beulah wheeled angrily.

'No, Captain. It would not. Send a man to the tent to tell Clun where I am. The rest of you can come with me.' She turned back towards the distant dragons and began walking across the grass towards the nearest. She had seen enough of them to know that this one was the senior among them, the one who had bowed to Clun and who seemed to be able to keep the rest in line.

'Your—' Captain Celtin began to protest but wisely came to his senses. Beulah did not turn, but she could feel him hurry to keep up with her even as she could feel his trepidation. Her own she hid, though she could not deny it was there. The beasts looked large from a distance, but as she approached them they were bigger still, the smell boiling off them in waves. Rotting meat, spilt entrails and something deeper, earthier and far more sinister. She thought her approach quiet; she was so small compared to the creature she was like a mouse approaching a carthorse, but the dragon opened one eye to stare at her as she neared.

'A visitor? Or maybe another meal.' It spoke directly to her mind, directly to all of their minds if the reaction of Captain Celtin and his remaining warrior priests was anything to go by. Lucky the man who had been sent to wait for the Duke of Abervenn.

'You know who I am, Sir Sgarnog.' Beulah did her best to speak the Draigiaith, dredging her mind for memories of being taught the dry, dead language as a child in Emmass Fawr. Her mouth wasn't designed to form the words; no human mouth was.

The dragon lifted its head slowly, moving to get a closer

look of the queen, sniffing the air as if it were possible to smell anything over its own rank odour.

'My queen,' it said after a while, addressing her in flawless Saesneg. 'To what do I owe this great honour?'

'The walls still stand. The gates are not yet open.'

'What can I say? You construct your fortresses too well. One of us might simply fly over the wall and open the gates from the inside, but none of us is small enough to fit into the gatehouse. So we tear it down, but it is hard work.' The dragon reached out one taloned hand in Beulah's direction, but slowly so as not to appear threatening. The fine scales around his massive fingers – more like the claws of some vast raptor – were scratched, the talons chipped and blunted. He flexed them slowly, studying his hand for a while, then pulled it back and started to push himself upright. 'I will rouse the others and we'll have another go, if that is what you wish.'

Beulah couldn't read the creature at all. It seemed to be genuine in its deference to her, no hint of sarcasm in its speech. She had more chance of reading the mood of Clun's horse, Godric, than seeing into the mind of Sir Sgarnog and his fold.

'Actually, I have another task for you. One that will be less painful. The people trapped inside the citadel are attempting to flee through tunnels protected by powerful magics. I would have you guard the exits, make sure none escape.'

'None?' The dragon arched a scaly eyebrow.

'These people have betrayed me. They have betrayed the throne and the Twin Kingdoms. I do not intend to let them skulk off into the night. My darling sister and her so-called husband least of all.'

Sir Sgarnog shifted slightly, his wings rustling as he shook them. 'Your Majesty, if I may offer some advice?'

Beulah didn't know whether to be offended or astonished, but she was rapidly reassessing her approach to these animals. She recalled the few pathetic creatures that had been paraded at court during her father's reign – occasional tithes from the far corners of the Twin Kingdoms. They had been a nuisance, an affront to decency but hardly a threat. Benfro had changed all that, revealing the lie that dragons had been telling all those years. But Beulah was a realist. She had seen the devastation wrought by Caradoc, had read the reports from her army marching north to Tynhelyg, and finally she had seen the damage just a handful of the great beasts had done to Candlehall. It was only luck that had seen them side with her. Luck and the foolhardiness of Clun. Close up, she could sense their power, feel the deep magic running through them. Nothing she had learned about their kind as a child was true any more. If it ever had been.

'This place you call Candlehall is your home, is it not? The centre of your realm?' Sir Sgarnog continued as if taking Beulah's silence as permission. She nodded once, prepared to hear him out, at least for a while.

'Much of your army is from here too, I would expect. If not the city itself, then the surrounding countryside, the smaller towns and villages I have seen all around here. I would also hazard a guess that many of the people within these walls are close to those in your army. Cousins, sisters, parents. Maybe just friends.'

'And yet an example must be made, or my right to be their queen is baseless.'

'True.' Sir Sgarnog tilted his head slightly, and, fixated on his eyes, Beulah imagined the earth itself shifted under her feet. She fought off the feeling, tugging her mind away from the aura that surrounded the dragon. Had he been doing it on purpose, or was it just the nature of the creature to swamp both her physical senses and those more attuned to magic? Beulah shook her head, building up her defences once more.

'So you think I should not put them all to the sword. Or feed them to you and your fold.'

'There's scant eating on a man, and I for one have never been fond of food that can talk. Much less food that can wield the Grym with such deadly effect as Master Clun. No, I do not think you should put them all to the sword. Their leaders, of course. String them up or feed them to Gwynedd Bach. She's not so fussy what she eats. But the commoners? I would show them clemency, or you may find you have a mutiny to deal with as well. Put them to work rebuilding your city, perhaps.'

Beulah considered the dragon's words. They were not so far from her own thoughts on the matter, now that the initial shock of finding her capital taken from her had passed. She would still raze much of it to the ground by way of punishment, but a large part of the city was overcrowded, the buildings old and dangerous. Demolishing them and making way for something new would be an improvement. The work would keep her people occupied too.

'I will consider your advice, Sir Sgarnog. But I still do not wish my people to flee. The tunnels must be sealed lest the leaders escape.'

The huge beast raised himself slowly, as if the effort of

moving that vast bulk were too much. He lifted his head, turned it this way and that, sniffing the air with a distant, faraway look in his eyes. After perhaps a minute he peered down at Beulah.

'Five routes. Most interesting. I had thought any Heolydd Anweledig would long ago have lost their potency, yet these are still strong. Some exit nearby but one leads too far for me to see without deeper investigation. It has been crafted with a skill in the subtle arts I would have thought beyond any man. Intriguing. We will have to inspect each exit closely. This is not just a matter of bolting a door or collapsing a tunnel. We will return when it is done.'

Sir Sgarnog dipped his massive scaly head by way of a bow, then carefully turned away from the queen and lumbered off to the nearest sleeping dragon. He barked out orders in guttural Draigiaith, so rapid Beulah could only make out one word in ten. And then with a rumbling in the ground like an earthquake the entire fold took off like a flock of geese disturbed.

Wafts of gas fouler yet than those that filled the upper cavern stung Errol's eyes and prickled his skin. He could scarcely breathe, flailing around in the darkness as he fell headlong into the abyss. And then with a snap that almost wrenched his arm out of its socket, he stopped, held in place by the chain looped around his wrist and still tied to the cart above.

Dangling over the edge of the precipice, he looked down and watched as the tiny speck of flame that was the torch tumbled end over end towards the bottom of this impossible cavern. Somewhere in the black, falling alongside it, the supervisor continued to scream until his cries were abruptly cut short by a sound more like a stone dropped into a muddy bog than a body hitting rock. And then light, blue and white, billowed out from a single point. Flame rushed up to meet him with impossible speed. Instinctively Errol turned away, screwed his eyes shut tight.

The heat enveloped him, drying the muck that encrusted his skin and soaked the hem of his travelling cloak in an instant. It was impossible to breathe, his lungs squeezed as if a giant hand had grasped him tight. The strain on his arm lessened as Errol found himself being borne upwards by an invisible force. For a moment it was as if he floated in a sea of boiling water, and then his hand was snapped down again, his body pulled around in an arc. Before he could do more than tense, he crashed heavily into something hard and unyielding. The wind was driven out of him like a punch to the gut, and the brightness that had shone even through his tightly closed eyelids turned inky black, just a few dazed stars flickering about the edges of his vision.

Slowly the roar in his ears subsided, the pain in his chest lessening as he managed to suck in a few shallow, unsatisfying breaths. It might have been minutes or hours, he had no way of telling, but eventually Errol started to feel the pain in his neck, the twisting of his back and the awkward way his arm was wrenched up behind his head. He shifted his body, looking for a more comfortable position, and only then realized that he had something in his free hand, clenched into a fist. He held the supervisor's purse, torn from the man's belt as he fell away into the pit. Gases, no doubt thick and noxious and oozing from what must have been a deep lagoon of manure, had ignited when the torch had hit. The explosion had lifted him in the air, swept him in an arc, tethered to the cart by the silver chain. Somehow he had landed inside it, and that had probably saved his life.

Errol shuffled on his backside towards the point where his arm was being stretched by the chain. He had no idea which way was which, but the cart started to tilt alarmingly, so he shuffled quickly back until everything settled. He dimly remembered tipping the contents of the cart into the abyss, but had he re-latched it when he was done?

Keeping as still as he could, he tried to undo the purse strings with his free thumb. It took a long time, and the cart wobbled precariously with every slight movement. Errol was convinced that it was balanced right on the edge, ready to plummet at any moment. The purse was a source of warmth and strength though, and he was almost certain he knew what was inside it, how it would help him escape. But the leather thong was tied tight. Eventually he resorted to using his teeth, spitting at the foul taste on his fingers until finally the purse loosened and its precious contents tipped out on to his palm.

The gem was smaller than the one that had come from Morgwm the Green, but it was the same brilliant white colour. His eyes had become accustomed to the near-total darkness and he had to squint against the glare. Discarding the cloth purse, Errol rolled the tiny jewel around in his palm, trying to sense the dormant consciousness inside it. He could feel nothing though, just an intense jolt of Grym with no intelligence behind it whatsoever. Intrigued, he pinched it between two dung-encrusted fingers and gently reached over, touching it to the loop of chain around his other wrist. With the slightest of clicks, the links parted and the chain fell away, and with it the nagging feeling that he should have been obeying someone.

Inching his way to the end of the cart that he didn't think was teetering over the edge, Errol stood up on unsteady feet and peered out. The explosion deep below had blown out the torches that hung on the cavern walls, and the light from his tiny jewel struggled to penetrate the deep gloom. There was a tiny pinprick of light not far off though. It called to him in the silence with a deepening panic.

Getting out of the cart wasn't easy. It rocked alarmingly as he hoisted himself over the lip and lowered himself to the ground. Errol gripped the edge tight, felt with his feet until he was certain he was putting them down on something solid. Only then did he let go. The cart tipped, knocking him backwards as it upended over the edge. For a while there was just the whistling of something large falling through still air, and then a dull thud echoed in the darkness, followed by a sound disturbingly like a fat man belching.

He gasped in great lungfuls of air, his heart thudding away in his chest as he realized how close he had come to dying. And then a sense of fear and desperation cut through his shock. He shuffled over to the tiny ball of light, closed his hands around it.

'What happened? Where did you go?' The voice of Morgwm the Green filled his head, louder than before as if the dragon's spirit were shouting in alarm. Perhaps it was; she had been left incomplete, alone in the darkness in a cavern where no Grym flowed. It was hard to imagine a worse hell.

'I had to drop you. I had no choice. I'm sorry.'

'This place is so cold. There is no Grym here at all. No voices.'

As the words formed in his mind, Errol remembered the other diggers, away down the tunnel in the next great cavern. Why had none of them come to see what was happening? Surely they would have seen the explosion; they couldn't have failed to hear it. What if they were angry at him? What if they caught him and threw him over the ledge like the supervisor had threatened?

'We have to get away from here.' He scrabbled around on the cavern floor until he found the strip of cloth in which Morgwm's jewel had been wrapped. For a moment he thought about wrapping the two jewels together, but the one from the supervisor's purse felt too different. It had no spark of intelligence, just a compressed power like a spring trap waiting to be tripped. Something told him it would be best to keep them separate. He began to wrap it, then realized that it was his only source of light, feeble though it was. Unwrapping it, he carefully put the piece of cloth into the pocket of his robe, down beside the other wrapped jewel – Magog's jewel – and the strange glass orb. He had lost everything else, and yet somehow these two things had stuck with him through all his trials. A pity the same couldn't be said for his companions. First Benfro and then Nellore.

'Where will you go?' Morgwm's question echoed his own thoughts as he clasped her jewel tight in his fist, holding the other in front of his face.

'I don't know. I should see what has happened to the other diggers, I guess. Maybe the explosion hurt them.'

Feeling around, Errol's hand brushed an iron rail set into the ground. He followed it slowly, expecting to find clear air, but it brought him eventually to the tunnel mouth, black as death itself.

The explosion in the large chamber had clearly swept along the tunnel and into the area where the diggers had been working. The force of it had extinguished most of the torches, upended all of the carts and thrown bodies around as if they were no more than dolls discarded in a child's tantrum. To make matters worse, a flood of effluent had cascaded over the mess, smothering anyone who might have survived the initial blast. Errol cast out with his mind, trying to feel any thoughts while at the same time listening for signs of life. There was nothing, but then the Grym was so weak in this place, almost missing entirely, he could get no sense of anyone. The low moan of a distant wind and the dripping of water somewhere off in the dark drowned out any nearer sounds.

Errol left the party of diggers reluctantly. He would have liked to have checked them all, made sure that they were beyond helping before abandoning them to their fate. But he was weak with hunger, desperately tired, his head ached from the foul air and the beating it had taken. Even if any of the other men had still been alive, there was little he could have done for them. Helping himself to one of the remaining lit torches, he took one last look at the carnage, then stepped into the narrow tunnel, searching for the room where he had first woken.

It was only when he came to a fork in the tunnel that it occurred to him he didn't know where he was going. His memories were jumbled, distant, like a bad dream that he had woken to find was still true. Taking the left-hand passage sent him down to another fork, only this time with three options. He retraced his steps, turned right and ended up in the cave where he'd eaten. The pot still hung on its tripod over the fire, but the embers had long since died and the stew congealed into something no more appetizing than the muck in which the diggers had drowned. All around the cavern, the dead lay unlamented, huddled bones wrapped in shit-encrusted clothes. The sight of them, and the occasional loud crack as he put a foot down in the wrong place, had the hairs on the back of Errol's neck standing proud. Still he fought down the fear and made a full circuit of the cave in search of another entrance. Finding none, he returned to the fork and took the left-hand passage again.

It went on for hours, or so it seemed. Errol found what he thought was the cavern where he had first woken up, but again there was only one way in, one way out. The passages had been carved in the rock and were big enough for all but the most massive of dragons to pass through without too much difficulty. Nonetheless they pressed in on him with each passing step. At each new fork in the route he marked the tunnel down which he went, though often he had to backtrack. The only consistent direction was down. He was free though, and for the first time in as long as he could remember, Errol had hope. He had escaped. He had survived. Now all he had to do was find the way out. Find his friends.

8

Men worship an invisible being they call the Shepherd. At least men of the Twin Kingdoms do. Those hardier souls to the north, in the land called Llanwennog, have abandoned all pretence of such belief. It is a curious thing to venerate a being that cannot possibly exist, and yet it is a clever way to bind a people together. The rich mythology that has grown up around this god of theirs, woven in with exaggerated tales of heroes from centuries – sometimes millennia – ago works on the credulity of the uneducated. The message is as simple as the folk to whom it is directed: while the Shepherd's boon is a welcome thing, the attention of his great rival, the Wolf, is to be avoided at all costs.

But perhaps the most fascinating aspect of this system of belief is that it requires faith in a being who will only reward you once you are dead, and the nature of that reward is based upon how closely you have adhered to the rules laid down by the priests and kings. For only they can know the will of their god.

Disobeying these rules rarely brings any kind of intervention by the Shepherd himself. Rather it is the priests who dole out his earthly punishments and by so doing keep the masses in line. The priests – and by extension the king – hold the power and will do whatever is necessary to make sure that they keep it. As a means to control the masses, this religion is breathtaking in its simplicity, and yet any creature with but a scale of curiosity can see it for the lie it is.

Corwen teul Maddau,
A Study of Men and Their Ways

He is beginning to understand their language now. It has similarities to his own tongue, but noticeable differences too. It is coarser, less nuanced in particular when it comes to the subtle arts. And yet these men he finds himself surrounded by are far more openly magical than any he recalls.

It is becoming harder to remember his life before he appeared in the field outside the village. They had assumed him one of the mindless, the empty husks of men who have tried to become one with the Grym and failed. Or perhaps succeeded too well. At first they had brought him to the almshouses, put him in a room filled with drooling, unresponsive bodies sitting in rows, waiting not so much patiently as idiotically for their next feed or for their nappies to be changed. It had smelled bad, a mixture of human waste and rotting flesh that turned his stomach. Leaving had been the only sensible thing to do, even if it had caused alarm and consternation among the men who had found him. They had seemed reluctant to accept that he wasn't one of their charges, until an old man in white robes had visited. Then things had begun to change.

The man in the white robes was called Lembath, and he was addressed as Quaister. The boy had no idea what that meant, or what Lembath was saying, but he was cleaner than the men who had found him, and kinder too. They had gone from the almshouses, under the great arch and into the enormous fortress that the boy understood was called Emmass Fawr. Its name had echoes of his own language in it, but the meaning eluded him. Even so, he had seen as soon as he had walked in through the massive gates that it was built for dragons. In those first few days, deep inside the building, he had kept looking out for any of the great creatures. They had been a part of his life before . . . but then every time he tried to think about it, his memory failed him. He had nothing but a sense of dread about them, a deep-seated resentment bordering on anger. Dragons had done him a great wrong, after all. Even if he couldn't remember what that wrong had been.

Days have turned into weeks and then into months. He has helped out Quaister Lembath in the huge library, and he has slowly begun to learn something of this place, the religious order and the god they worship. The Shepherd's story is a powerful one, the favours he bestows on his most faithful servants something the boy covets. He wishes to join this order, which has taken him under its wing, but first he must persuade them that he is old enough and worthy of the honour.

And so he prays daily to the Shepherd, waits for the sign he knows must come. The chapel set aside for the librarians is an ancient space deep within the heart of the mountain upon which this fortress is built. It should be cut off from the Grym, but instead the power that binds all living things together seems unnaturally concentrated here. It reminds him of a place from before, even if he can't remember what before was. Where before was.

'That is because in coming to this place you were reborn, my faithful servant.'

The boy looks up from his prayers, scans the small chapel for any sign of who might have spoken, but there is no one. He is alone here.

'Never alone. I am with you always.'

He understands then that he is hearing a voice without sound, deep inside his head.

'Who are you?' The boy speaks the words out loud, the first time he has used the language of these people.

'You know who I am, Melyn son of Arall. Are you not praying to me, after all?'

'You . . . you are the Shepherd?'

He feels the presence now, a warmth in his veins lending him strength and easing away the ache in his muscles that is the result of a long day carrying scrolls and heavy books. He is kneeling now, but bends lower until his forehead is pressed to the cold stone floor, eyes squeezed tight just in case he catches a glimpse of God and finds himself blinded by the experience.

'That is better. I expect humility in my chosen, and I have chosen you for great things.'

9

The Old One is the father of us all. Or so it is taught to us as kitlings. It is true that all the dragons of Gwlad can trace their lineage back to him, and many a feud has grown from a simple argument about who is more closely related. As if such a thing were of any importance.

Few in Nantgrafanglach have ever seen the Old One, and fewer still remember a time when he flew with his fold. Those who know him will tell you of a solitary dragon of such great age as to appear immortal. Alone in his great tower, he pursues knowledge and a mastery of the Grym like none before. He has no companion in this task, though servants among the men speak of young boys enlisted to help him. Such tales can be discounted, for no man could possibly assist the works of a dragon. But there is one whom history appears to have forgotten, for where the Old One is the father of all dragonkind, so there must also be a mother.

Myfanwy the Bold, or sometimes Myfanwy Bach, is perhaps even more mysterious a figure than the Old One himself. Mother to all of the great houses of Nantgrafanglach, she shows favour to none, keeping herself to her own residence close by the walls. And should you make the journey

through the deserted halls to meet her, chances are
you will be disappointed. It is said that she pursues
her own studies as avidly as her sometime mate, but
that where he seeks to understand all there is to
know about the Grym, her study is into the healing
arts and the malaise that has stricken our kind in
recent centuries.

Sir Nanteos teul Palisander,
The Forgotten Halls of Nantgrafanglach

'It's not much, but I found us some food.'

Benfro was roused from troubled sleep by the words.
He looked up from his resting place on the sleeping platform amid the dusty furs to see Martha at the massive
door. He would have leaped up to help her, but it had
taken long enough to get comfortable and he really didn't
want to move again. The young boy, Xando, had been
tending to the fire, its heat barely registering in the large
room. With one arm strapped up in a sling there wasn't
much else he could do.

After their narrow escape from the grey dragon and
Cerys, they had hurried back down the corridor, looking
for an escape route that didn't involve going down the
stairs and into the hall below. In the excitement Benfro
had forgotten the wound in his side and the sliver of wood
working its way ever closer to his heart, but a sharp jab of
pain had soon reminded him. There had been no option
but to return as swiftly as possible to the room they had
first entered via the ceiling, where he had collapsed on to
the sleeping platform. Xando and Martha had scoured

the room for cushions, wedging them around him until he felt he could relax again. The effort had left him exhausted, and he'd fallen asleep as the two of them argued quietly about what they were going to do next.

'It's mostly fruit, a few raw vegetables. But I managed to steal this.' Martha dropped a handful of what looked like small pumpkins on to the table in the middle of the room, then pulled a makeshift sling over her shoulder and opened it up. Benfro's stomach growled as the aroma of cooked ham wafted across the room.

'Where'd you find that?' Xando hurried from his spot by the fire, eyes wide. It occurred to Benfro that none of them had eaten in a while. The last thing he had done before leaping from the top of Gog's tower was to breathe the Fflam Gwir and reckon the old dragon's jewels. That always left him empty, but the shock of his injury had dampened his hunger. Now his stomach growled like an angry dog.

'It's chaos down there. Honestly, if they weren't looking for Benfro we could probably walk out unnoticed.' Martha stuck her hands into pockets in her cloak, coming out with apples and cheese and a loaf of dark brown bread, a knife and finally a bottle. 'I think this is wine, which is probably the last thing we should be drinking. We can melt some of the snow for water though.'

Benfro slowly inched himself upright while the young woman arranged the food on what was a low table for him but was higher than comfortable for her and Xando. The pain in his side had subsided a little. He concentrated, seeing into his body with his missing eye. The flesh had hardened around the piece of wood, but he could tell by the colours swirling about it that infection would set in soon, if it hadn't already. He needed to clean the wound properly, prepare the salves and unguents that would draw the foulness out. More than anything he needed to rest and build up his strength. But here, in this cold, damp room, hiding from dragons who thought he had killed their most revered leader, he could scarcely relax. And the food which Martha had stolen needed to be rationed as well as shared.

'Come, Benfro. Eat. You look fair fit to pass out.' Martha held up the cloth-wrapped ham. It would probably provide a dozen men with a couple of meals or more, but for him it was barely a morsel. And yet seeing what else they had, he couldn't bring himself to eat it all.

'You have some first. Xando too. Perhaps when I'm a bit more rested you can describe for me where you found it all. Then I can try and reach out along the lines, bring some more here for us.'

Martha brushed long black hair out of her face, peering up at him with her dark green eyes. 'You have that skill? I can do it, but it takes so much concentration, so much time. A place like here it's easier just to go looking.'

Benfro thought back to his time in Magog's retreat at the top of Mount Arnahi. Alone and hungry he had reached out along the lines and found a turnip. Where it had come from he had no idea, and as he had learned more of the Grym and the subtle arts, so he understood quite how dangerous it had been for him to even try. He had often wondered where Magog had gone during that time, why the dead mage had abandoned him to wander unchecked around his most secret hideaway. Something had clearly dragged him away, demanded his full attention, so clearly he wasn't as all-seeing as he claimed. The thought that Magog might have a flaw brought the ghost of a smile to Benfro's face.

'Eat, dragon. You won't heal if you're starved.'

Benfro started. He'd let his mind wander and almost fallen asleep on his feet. Martha stood in front of him, the ham in one hand and a knife in the other. She had cut several slices off, one of which Xando was greedily stuffing into his mouth.

'Are you sure?' Benfro took the ham. His stomach growled again, angrier than before, but he didn't take a bite. Not yet.

'We have bread, we have cheese. There's even some fruit. We're not going to starve, but if you collapse from hunger then we'll have to leave you here.'

Benfro nodded his head once in acceptance, then took a bite of the first thing he had eaten since leaving the mother tree what felt like a lifetime ago. The flavours exploded in his mouth. He took another bite, forcing himself to chew the meat slowly, not wolf it down and regret it later. If he could get back to the palace gardens, the gatehouse through which he had entered, would it lead him back to the tree? Somehow he doubted it. He knew so little of her ways, but if anyone could heal him then it was her. Or Lady Earith, of course. Although after what she had done for him already, the thought of asking more seemed rude.

'We need to make a plan. We can't stay here for ever. Sooner or later someone's going to notice the hole in the roof.' Martha wrapped a slice of bread around a thick wedge of cheese, took a bite and chewed a while before continuing. 'Xando, do you know a way out of the city?'

The boy had been methodically feeding his face in exactly the way Benfro wanted to. He stopped at Martha's question, swallowing hastily before answering.

'I've never left the palace. Born and raised here, I was.' He looked around the room again. 'Not actually sure where here is, to be honest.'

'I am told this is the guest wing for the elder nobles. The houses of Nanteos, Caerfyrddin and Rhydol lodge here during the Old One's summer festival. Or at least they used to back when there was a summer festival. By all accounts there's not been one in many hundreds of years.'

Benfro stopped with the remains of the ham bone halfway between table and face. Xando turned a shade of white almost paler than the snow piled up in the middle of the room. Only Martha seemed unsurprised, turning slowly towards the door and the source of the words.

The dark green dragon from the Twmp. Cerys.

Errol lost all track of time in the darkness. It should have been cold, cut off from the Grym by miles of lifeless rock, but he drew warmth and a little strength from the tiny jewel in the pocket of his cloak. The torch weighed heavy in his hand, its flame growing steadily weaker, the bubble of light around him shrinking ever smaller. Morgwm's jewel had fallen silent almost as soon as he had left the first cavern. It was warm in his fist, a comfort but not a distraction as he trudged the endless passageways. With her presence at the back of his mind, he didn't feel completely alone, but with each new turning, each dead end and backtrack, each angry growl of his stomach and parched dry swallow, he longed for more helpful company.

'You know my name,' Errol said after what felt like the thousandth turn in the endless tunnels. His voice sounded strange, muted by the silence all around, thin and weak. 'How is it you know that?'

'Ah, Errol. I have known you as long as anyone. I was present at your birth. The same day my Benfro hatched, at the height of the confluence.'

'Confluence?' It was the smallest of the many questions Morgwm's words demanded but perhaps the easiest to ask.

'Our kind venerate the sun and the moon, Fair Arhelion and Great Rasalene, the mother and father of all dragons. Once every hundred years they come together in the sky, and day becomes night for a while. A dragon hatched at such a time is destined to great things, or terrible. A boy born then would surely be marked too. Thus it was with Benfro, and thus it was with you.'

'But I was born in Pwllpeiran, wasn't I? There were no dragons there. Well, apart from Sir Radnor, but he hardly counts.'

'There are some would say you weren't born at all, Errol. Your birth was unusual, to say the least. And it didn't happen in Pwllpeiran, but in the cottage I called home for five hundred years.'

'I don't understand.' Errol found he had stopped walking. The passageway here was no different to any other in the endless warren. He sank to the floor, leaning the torch up against the rock wall to stop it from going out. He had not realized how heavy it had become, how stiff were the muscles in his arm. He flexed his fingers, trying to squeeze some life back into one cramped hand, then gently opened the other, palm upwards. Morgwm's jewel was so white, so small, and yet it contained so much.

'Hennas Ramsbottom is not your true mother, though she raised you as if she were. She could do nothing less, since she truly believed you were her son and your father was a young Llanwennog man cruelly slain by a mob of ignorant Twin Kingdoms folk. That was the story she asked me to plant in her mind. She feared she would not be able to hide the fact that you were fostered if someone skilled in magic came asking questions. How right she was to insist.'

Errol tipped his head back slowly until it rested against the cold stone. Morgwm's words were more like images in his head now, memories of events seen long ago. And yet somehow he knew the truth of what the dead dragon told him. He saw Hennas, someone he would always think of as his mother no matter what anyone else might say of her. She was younger than he remembered, and the cottage where he had grown up looked different – tidier perhaps, newer. She was sitting out on the porch at dusk when a dragon Errol instantly knew to be Morgwm the Green appeared from the shadows. Smaller than Benfro and with tiny vestigial wings, Morgwm was nevertheless an imposing figure, towering over Hennas in the gathering dusk. She carried a wrapped bundle in her arms, and when she held it out, Hennas took it without question. Morgwm reached out a surprisingly slender hand, touched Hennas lightly on the side of her head, then turned and walked away, disappearing into the darkness whence she had come. The whole exchange took only moments.

And then the scene changed, evening becoming night becoming day, cycling forward with dizzying speed. He saw himself crawling across the porch, then tottering on unsteady feet, then running. He grew before his own eyes from an infant to a boy, his life hurtling forward to the inevitable day when the inquisitor and the queen-in-waiting would swoop down on the village and spirit him away. It passed in a flash, and he saw the cottage grow cold, dusty and abandoned. It made sense, even as it saddened him. Hennas had married Godric; of course she would have moved into his house in the village.

Except that as he thought it, so his view, his dream, shifted perspective. He seemed to fly, rising above the cottage and its rough shingle roof. He saw the trees that stretched away behind it, his childhood playground. They formed the very edge of the great forest of the Ffrydd, where it spilled through the Graith Fawr, that massive hole rent in the circle of the Rim mountains. But long before they reached that distant point there was a far more recent scar in the land. Broken branches, whole trees uprooted, the ground churned into mud and dug up as if a herd of giant pigs had been let loose upon the woodland. Everything was destruction. As he focused on it, so Errol saw the scattered white of bones flecked with bits of flesh, scraps of wool and hide where some great creature had devoured sheep and cattle whole. And there in the middle, something that should have been impossible to see, more impossible than this dream turned nightmare, the all-too-recognizable bones of human prey. Two skulls atop a pile of jumbled limbs and bloodstained vertebrae. Hennas and Godric Defaid.

Errol started from his dreaming with a cry that echoed in the tunnel. His heart pounded and a shiver ran through him that had nothing to do with the cold. The image had been so real, and yet even now it began to fade. What had brought it on? He looked down at the jewel in his grubby upturned hand, purest crystal against the crust of shit. He could feel the warmth and reassurance from it, but nothing as strong as the voice he had heard.

'Morgwm?' He spoke the name aloud, thinking about the jewel as he did so. No answer came, and then the torch, propped up against the wall beside him, guttered a couple of times and finally went out. He reached for it, foolishly thinking he might be able to save the flame, and that was when he noticed that he could still see his hands, still see the gravel floor of the tunnel and the rock wall. Smoke spiralled off the charred end of the torch, away in the direction he had been walking. The faintest of breezes tugged at his matted hair and chilled the skin on his face. Straining in the gloom, he imagined he could make out the silhouette of something not too far off. He hauled himself up, clasping Morgwm's jewel in his fist, but leaving the dead torch where it lay. Perhaps no more than a dozen paces on, the light grew into an opening, the sound of distant crashing water tickling his ears. The breeze blew stronger, air so fresh it made him more giddy than any wine thrust down his gullet by Inquisitor Melyn.

Errol stepped into a wide cave. The rock glistened with light refracted through the wall of water that cascaded in front of him, clean and pure and cold. He stepped up to the falling water, reached out his free hand, let the flow wash away the filth. Leaning forward, he inched his face into it, felt the water strip the muck from his skin. Further in, and it pounded at his head, tugging the knots and braids from his too-long hair. Through the crashing water he could see daylight beyond and knew that this was a waterfall hiding a cave mouth like the one in the clearing where Corwen's jewels had lain. What had become of the old dragon mage? Where had Melyn taken those jewels? One more task to add to the list. One more friend to save.

He pulled his head back, blinking as the fresh water ran from his face. Still filthy, yet he felt cleaner now than ever he had. Stronger too, as the Grym came rushing into him, bringing with it a renewed resolve. Clutching Morgwm's single white jewel tight in his fist, Errol took a deep breath and stepped out into the stream.

'Benfro! It's really you!'

The dark green dragon rushed into the room, the door clattering closed behind her. Benfro had thought her young before, running with the rough and ready dragons of the Twmp. Now she looked civilized, her scales clean and polished, and that made her seem younger still. She could not have been more than twenty years old. Not much more than him, really.

'What are you doing here, Cerys? How did you get here? Who was that other dragon you were flying with?'

'Sir Nanteos?' He is one of the elders of the Council of Nantgrafanglach. I don't know why, but they look up to Myfanwy as if she were their leader.' Cerys hurried over to where Benfro lay. As she stood beside him, he became acutely aware of her scent, less powerful than when he had known her at the Twmp but still enough to make his head spin, his hearts beat a little faster.

'Myfanwy? The healer?'

'That's what I thought. All my life she's just been this mad old dragon living in the dead tree houses and tending to the sick and injured of the fold. But she's more than that, see. When I told her what had happened to Fflint, and to you, she changed. Became very serious all of a sudden. She's been teaching me about the old ways for a while now, so when she came here she brought me with her. Said it was about time I grew up and learned how to be a proper dragon. It's all very strange. She has a house, you know. It's enormous. Almost as big as the whole Twmp. And she has servants – dragons and men. Everyone here looks up to her, and because of her they have been kind to me. I never thought I would end up in such a wondrous place.' Cerys looked around the room, her eyes wide. Then she finally seemed to notice Martha and Xando. 'But who are you? You don't look like servants.'

'They are my friends, Cerys,' Benfro said. 'They were up at the top of the tower when Gog was attacked.'

'The Old One! Is it true what they're saying? He really is dead?' Cerys rocked back on her long tail.

'He is. Enedoc too. We would be dead with them had I not leaped off the tower into the storm. Just a pity my wings weren't up to carrying all that weight.' Benfro glanced across at the pile of snow on the carpet. Martha and Xando had collected up all the broken joists and rafters for the fire. 'I'd have been fine if Fflint hadn't tried to pull them off.'

Cerys stood again, walked over to the snow and stuck a foot in it, then looked up through the lazily spiralling flakes to the hole and the sky above. 'Oh.' She carried on staring, as if a stormy grey sky was something she had never seen before.

'Are they really searching for us? Do they think we're responsible?' Benfro asked after a while. Cerys took longer still to drag her gaze from the ceiling.

'The whole of Nantgrafanglach is in turmoil, but the palace is madness. It's like when Caradoc went missing and Fflint and his cronies fought over who was going to be in charge. Only here there are many more dragons than in the Twmp fold, and they're not so much fighting each other as arguing and crying and tearing out their scales. A few are angry and looking for whoever murdered the Old One, but in truth most can't comprehend that he's truly dead.' Cerys shook her head. 'How did he die, Benfro? Who killed him? And why are you all hiding in here?'

'We're hiding because they think we killed him, but it was Melyn.'

'Melyn?' Cerys cocked her head to one side. 'What is that?'

'Not what. Who,' Martha said. 'Inquisitor Melyn is the head of the Order of the High Ffrydd and possibly the most powerful mage in Gwlad at the moment. He is also possessed by the spirit of Magog.'

Cerys let out an involuntary squeak at the mention of the name. 'The cursed? Don't say his name or the wrath of the Old One will be upon us.'

'The Old One is dead, Cerys. His wrath is all spent.' Benfro laid a hand on her shoulder and was surprised to find her shuddering. It wasn't that cold in the room, at least not for those touched by the Grym, so it must have been fear.

Martha approached the two of them, a strange look in her eyes. 'If you truly know nothing of Melyn, then we can take some solace in that. We've been hiding from him as much as from the other dragons here, but he must have fled once his foul deed was done. He will be back though.'

'He will?' Through his touch, Benfro felt the shivering grow stronger.

'He burns with a desire to see all dragons dead. I cannot fathom why, since your kind are the source of all his power, but then he is quite mad. And very dangerous.' Martha sat down on the edge of the sleeping platform, a frown on her face. 'We have to warn the others about him, and yet I fear they will not listen. Not if they think Benfro killed Gog and we helped him.'

'If Myfanwy were here, she would probably knock some sense into them. They listen to her, see? But she's gone missing, off on some errand of her own, and nobody knows where she is.'

Benfro sank down on to the mouldy furs in defeat. For a moment he had hoped they might be able to get help from the old healer, but if she was away then they would have to stay in this room, pray that no one found them.

'Why did you come looking for us, then?' Martha asked. 'You say you saw us hiding. How? And why not tell the others?'

Cerys pulled herself up as if affronted by the question. 'As to how, it wasn't hard. Sir Nanteos has a musk it's impossible to ignore, especially when he's agitated, but I grew up on the Twmp, learned to hunt as a kitling. I can scent another dragon easily enough, especially one I know. Benfro's scent was all over the landing, but I couldn't work out how he could be there. I thought he was dead, gone back to the Grym. But I could smell him, and two people with him. So I looked to the lines, like Myfanwy taught me. Then seeing through the concealment was simple. Smart thinking using a hunting trick, though. An old dragon like Sir Nanteos would never consider something so simple.'

'So you saw us yet said nothing. Why?' Benfro asked.

'Why would you ask that, Benfro? Of course I wouldn't say anything. We're friends, aren't we? And anyway I could see you were hurt.' Cerys pointed at Benfro's side, then to Xando. 'He is too, though less severely and his injuries have been tended to, at least partially. I have some skill in healing, as you know. I thought I could help.'

Benfro made to nod his head as a sign of thanks and acceptance, but when he did, the splinter in his side pricked him like a hot knife. His legs lost all their strength, and he found himself toppling forward.

'Benfro, have a care!' Cerys stepped swiftly up to his side, catching him before he could hit his head on the edge of the table. Close up, he could smell her scent more clearly now, over the smoke from the fire, the tang of the foods that Martha had stolen and the cold damp air of the room. It was a warm, earthy scent that reminded him of summer and the forest, a scent that had enveloped him in a dark cave and protected him while he healed. He held on to that, gripping her arm tight as another stab of pain dulled his vision, the splinter working its way ever closer to his heart.

Then something exploded in his chest, and the darkness took him.

IO

The Order of the High Ffrydd is the oldest of
the great religious orders. Formed by Balwen
himself, its sacred duty is to protect the Twin
Kingdoms from the godless and spread the word
of the Shepherd throughout Gwlad. As befits the
first and greatest order, only the finest candidates
are selected for the novitiate, and of those fewer
than half can expect to pass into the ranks of the
warrior priests.

To step through the gates of Emmass Fawr and
swear your allegiance to the order and the House of
Balwen is to renounce all family, all thought of
anything but a life of training and service. It is both
the highest honour and the heaviest burden.

Father Castlemilk,
An Introduction to the Order of the High Ffrydd

He couldn't quite remember how he had come to be here.
Or for that matter where here actually was. It was as if he
had been motionless for days, a statue of stone and cold
only now woken by . . . what?

How long had he been kneeling? Melyn tried to remember the passing of time, but there was only the fight, his
blade of fire passing easily through the old dragon's neck.

The others had proven harder to kill, had distracted him while Benfro made good his escape.

Benfro.

The name brought with it memories, a confusing mix of his childhood before joining the Order of the High Ffrydd overlaid with flashes of the fight. He had been injured, he remembered that now. The biggest of the dragons had fought hard before it had succumbed to his blade.

Cold shivered through him, and without thinking Melyn reached out for the Grym. It soothed the aches in his muscles, warmed him from the inside and gave him the strength to stand. Even so he was as weak as a new-born, his head light and his vision blurred. He had to reach out to the nearest upturned table, putting a hand on the rough wood to steady himself as he looked around at the devastation.

The great glass windows were gone, blown off their hinges. Outside, a blizzard darkened the sky, snow whirling and turning in a terrible storm, and yet he felt barely a breeze ruffling his hair. For a moment he was puzzled. Not that there might have been magics cast about the tower room to keep out the elements even if the windows were open, but that they should have persisted after the dragon who had cast them had died. Then he saw the web of the Grym pushing out against the stone walls to form a near-perfect dome of protection, focused not on the pile of ashes that was all that remained of the great Gog, Son of the Winter Moon, but on him.

'You did not know it, my faithful servant, but you were gravely injured in your fight with Enedoc the Black. It was necessary to protect you while you healed.'

The voice was all around him, inside him. It brought the familiar feeling of strength, the healing balm of his god. Except that Melyn knew now that the Shepherd was a lie, and as that understanding grew, so the wonder of the Shepherd's touch waned.

'Healed?' Melyn raised his hands, clenching them into weak fists. His arms were heavy and his whole body ached. Spasms rippled across his stomach, as empty as if he had not eaten for days. His throat felt like it was made of sandpaper, his mouth as dry as the arid plains of the Gwastadded Wag. 'How long have I been up here?'

'What matters time when you are immortal?'

'Days, I would guess.' Melyn stumbled slightly, his legs awkward as he staggered around the room until he found a silver goblet so large it was more of a bowl to him. He carried it to the edge of the room where thin wisps of snow had leaked through the invisible barrier from the storm outside. He scooped handfuls in, packing them down, then summoned the Grym to melt it. The surface steamed gently as he raised the goblet to his lips. No wine could have been as fine, the water soothing his throat and filling his twisted, empty stomach.

'You could have just asked.' A heavy scent of fine wine filled Melyn's nose as the water turned a deep shade of red. The Shepherd's voice had an odd, teasing inflection as he spoke, but then Melyn knew now that the Shepherd was no god.

'What is a god, then? Have you so little faith, Melyn son of Arall?'

'Difficult to have faith when you have met your god and found him full of lies. You are a dragon, not a shepherd.' Melyn's words were quiet, his throat still dry despite the soothing water. He would have drunk more had it not turned into wine.

'I am so much more than a dragon. I was the greatest mage who ever lived. I stepped beyond life when I spread my unreckoned jewels throughout Gwlad. And I am a shepherd. I have guided men since the time of Balwen and before, taught them the ways of the Grym and the secrets of my kind. Everything I have done has led to this moment. I have lived in hope of seeing my hated brother dead. Truly dead. And you, Melyn, have been the perfect instrument of my revenge.'

Melyn heard the words, felt the surge of healing power that once would have forced him to his knees. Now it was a welcome gift, but he felt no gratitude. Does a sword feel grateful for being swung in battle? That was all he was, after all, a weapon forged long ago. He pulled at the ring on his left hand, meaning to take it off and fling it out into the storm, but his fingers could not grasp it properly. He tried the right hand with the same result. Turning them over, Melyn saw his fingertips glinting gold in the insipid light fighting its way through the thickening storm outside. He squinted, held his hands closer and saw tiny scales where once had been flesh.

'My gift to you, Melyn. A glimpse of your true form. You need never fear being consumed by the Grym now.'

'My true form? Or yours?' Melyn clenched his fists tight, conjured a blade of fire from each. The surge of power was intoxicating, so easy to control. He stared into the red light for a while before absorbing the Grym back into himself. A novitiate, even a battle-seasoned warrior priest, would have been consumed by the fire, but Melyn felt only the gentlest heat. He studied the protective wards that kept the wind and most of the snow outside. Then, with a thought, he pushed through them into the storm. The noise was sudden and brutal, engulfing him as the wind buffeted his body, threatening to pick him up and throw him over the edge. Still Melyn felt no fear as he approached it, peered over and down through the swirling storm to the grey rooftops far below. Somewhere out there was Benfro.

'He holds the key, my faithful servant. You must track him down, capture him and deliver him to me. Then you will know rewards such as you cannot comprehend.'

Melyn smiled inwardly at the thought. He knew so much more now, his earliest memories falling into place. He knew this palace and the city that surrounded it; he'd been born here after all. And more, he knew so much of the secrets of Gog, who had cast him out, and Magog, who had taken him in. 'He is linked to you by your jewels,' he said. 'And so he is linked to me. I can find him any time. There is something else I must do first.'

This was how it had all begun. Up here on this tower. A small boy learning secrets never meant for his kind, taught by a creature who looked down at him as an oddity, saw him as some strange project. Like trying to teach a sheep to walk upright, to read and write and talk. Melyn remembered now how that sheep had done so much more. Found the lines, the Llinellau Grym, and reached out along them into nothing, into everything.

He took one step forward into the gathering storm and disappeared.

*

Benfro knew he wasn't dead. Death could never have been such torment. Everything hurt: every breath, every twitch of muscle, even the thumpity-thump of his hearts beating their irregular rhythm brought with it little jolts of fire.

He didn't know where he was, but it didn't really matter. There was no way he could move. Something held him in place more firmly even than Circus Master Loghtan's drugs, even as it left his mind free to wander.

The darkness worried him until he realized his eyes were closed. Thinking about them, he felt the press of fabrics against one side of his face. Trying to open the other eye didn't seem to work, the darkness not changing at all. He remembered Fflint's hands squeezing, his pointed talon reaching in, the noise it made as it pierced his eyeball. He panicked at the memory, struggling against the bonds that held him down.

'I think he's coming round, see. Hold still, Benfro. We're not done yet.'

The voice confused him. It wasn't his mother, nor Lady Earith. Not even the Mother Tree. Yet something in the tone soothed his fear away, eased his anxiety just enough to let him relax. Then another wave of pain spasmed through him. It felt like a wild animal was gouging out his flank, ripping apart his scales and tearing great chunks of flesh away with its teeth.

'Hold still. We're so close.' Another voice this time. Lighter, smaller somehow. Benfro felt a tiny hand touch the side of his nose, the spark as the Grym flowed from that small point and into him, easing away the worst of the agony. The wild animal was still gnawing away at his side, but the pain was somehow once removed, as if he were watching someone else endure it.

'Ah. There you are. Have a care, Martha. This is going to be rough.'

Martha. The name meant something to him, but before Benfro could think what, the animal at his side thrust its whole head into the wound, drove its fangs deep into one of his hearts. He let out a great bellow, distantly aware that along with his breath and the noise had come flame, palest blue and magical. Even though he was blind, he could see it sweep over him in a protective wave, the feral beast leaping from his side in surprise. Only it wasn't a feral beast, it was a dragon. Small, young, with scales of dark green, the fingers of one hand squeezed together to a point and slick with dark red blood. His blood.

'Got it, by the moon. Quickly, Martha. Fetch me the salve.'

The pain in his side lessened, although Benfro still felt a dull throb in time with his heartbeats. He was weaker than a kitling and could barely summon the strength to roll his head over, open his good eye. Figures moved around out of focus, and then a face appeared close to his, long black hair tumbling in tangled curls around it. He knew that face, and as he saw, so he recalled the name that had already been spoken twice since he had woken.

'Martha.' His voice came out as a thin, dry, reedy sound, like wind through rushes. He was so very tired and thirsty.

'You're awake. That's good.' Martha frowned, an expression Benfro had seen many times on Errol's face as he set to a difficult task. 'I think that's good.'

She disappeared from view again, except that Benfro's

missing eye saw the whole room now. It showed her stepping past him to where the dark green dragon stood close to his wounded flank. Cerys. How could he have forgotten her? Martha handed her what looked like a stone bowl, which she held with hands wrapped in heavy cloth. As he saw it, so Benfro noticed the smell and began to understand what was happening. The sharp, jabbing pain in his side was gone, which meant that Cerys had removed the splinter of wood. The dull throb was the infection that had inevitably set in. The bowl would be a salve to draw out the foul humours and promote healing. He could think of a few different recipes his mother might have prepared, mixing the herbs with rare soils and heating them all up in a cauldron until they steamed. Too late he realized what would have to be the next step.

'This will sting a little, Benfro. Please try not to belch fire again. It gave me quite a shock.'

Cerys worked as she spoke. She had the bowl in one hand, using the other and a thin iron bar to lever apart Benfro's scales. Before he could protest, she tipped the contents of the bowl into the opening. No delicate touch here.

Benfro had scorched the tip of his tail on more than one occasion, not paying attention while he was about his chores. Once, out hunting with Ynys Môn, he had foolishly tried to catch a glowing ember and chuck it back into their camp fire. Each of these times he had been burned, if not badly then enough to remind him for a month or so not to be so stupid. The salve burned like nothing he had ever felt before. It was as if that glowing ember had been rammed deep into his side. Was it his imagination or could he smell charring flesh? The stench of the deer slung across the cooking fire too early, before the flames had died to nothing. He bit down on another great bellow of pain, steam jetting out of his nostrils. Or was it just that the air in the room was cold?

'There. That should do it.' Cerys gently eased the iron bar out from between Benfro's scales, stepping back the better to see her handiwork. The heat still burned through his flank, and Benfro wanted nothing more than to sit up and tear at it until he had removed every last bit of the molten mess. But he was too weak even to move his head, could only see the room directly ahead of him and the disorienting aethereal view from his missing eye.

Slowly the pain eased, his body absorbing the heat of the salve in waves that slowed the hammering of his hearts. He was completely helpless, could do nothing but breathe heavily, gasping in the cold air as if he had flown a thousand miles against a storm. Cerys walked past him over to the fireplace, where a much bigger fire than Xando's earlier effort was burning merrily. She ladled something from a large cauldron into a smaller bowl, then brought it back across the room to him. He could smell the herbs in the water, identify some of them as pain relievers, medicines for the infection, and something else he hadn't encountered before. It didn't matter; he was so thirsty he would have drunk from a muddy puddle.

The dark green dragon stooped down to his level, lifted up his head with a hand still covered in his blood. 'The splinter is gone. At least I think it is. But you've a lot of healing to do, Benfro. Drink this. It will help.'

She lifted the bowl to his lips, and he drank greedily. Fully half of the liquid ended up on the dusty furs surrounding him, but the half that made it into his mouth soothed his throat. It was hot, though not so hot as to burn like the salve. Instead the heat spread through him like the warming power of the Grym. It eased the aches he hadn't known were there, relaxed the tension in his wings and legs. And finally it moved up to his head, sweeping him away on a wave of glorious relief.

It took far longer to climb the spiral stairs up to the anonymous corridor in the palace than it had to get down them. People were starting to file through the door at the top, still calm although Dafydd could feel the barely contained panic. He tried his best to spread an aura of tranquillity, but it wasn't easy having just left his infant son in the care of a woman he barely knew. Ahead of him, Iolwen was a rock, radiating quiet determination to get the job done. She had changed in the months since they had left Tynhelyg, become more assertive, more decisive. He couldn't help but love her all the more for it.

'We should disappear. It will make things easier.' Usel the medic had gone first, and now he stood in the corridor waiting for them, hand outstretched. Dafydd reached to take it instinctively, but Iolwen stopped him.

'Easier isn't always best, Usel. My people need to see me.'

The medic paused a moment, then gave a curt nod. 'You are right. But whichever way we go, we must hurry.'

They set off down the corridor towards the old palace and the cloisters where Jarius Pelod had died. It wasn't long before the people queued up and waiting began to notice the princess. Iolwen insisted on stopping, talking to them, reassuring them that she wasn't fleeing and that their best hope for escape was in the opposite direction. Still a few insisted on following, so that by the time they reached the lower chambers there was a small army behind them. Dafydd bade them stay below while he, Usel and Iolwen climbed quietly to the top of the stone steps, where they could look out on the cloisters and the Neuadd without being spotted from above.

He didn't need to be able to see the damaged grass and stone paths leading to the great hall to know that at least one dragon still remained there. The smell was enough, mixed in with the battlefield stench of rotting bodies and spilled entrails. He hadn't noticed it when they had met the great beast on the island, but these creatures had a musk about them that struck fear into the hearts of the bravest men. Between them and the main door, still hanging open since Iolwen's ill-fated declaration, the neatly mown grass was gouged and battered, the flagstones cracked. The bodies of men, women, horses lay bloated and broken. Some had clearly been half eaten, bones stripped of most of their flesh, unwanted pieces scattered hither and yon. And there in the midst of it, back turned to them and wings half-furled, one of the largest dragons Dafydd had ever seen was continuing its grisly feast with horrible sucking and crunching noises. Was this the creature that had killed Seneschal Padraig? He couldn't be sure.

'How are we supposed to get across there?' Dafydd whispered the question although the great beast seemed oblivious to their presence, consumed by the task at hand.

'There are more ways into the Neuadd than these doors, sire.' Usel placed a hand on Dafydd's shoulder, pulling him further back into the shadows where Iolwen still stood, paler than before.

'Then why are we here?'

'We need to know how many of them are in the cloisters. Hopefully there are none in the Neuadd itself. That would make things . . . difficult.'

Almost as if it had heard them, the dragon swished its tail, crunched down on some particularly hard bones, then tossed aside what appeared to be half a cow. It let out a loud belch and strode off towards the Neuadd. In moments it had disappeared through the open doors.

'Ah, by Gog's hairy balls. That's most unhelpful.' Usel leaned back against the stone wall of the cloister and put a hand to his face as if in thought.

'Can you hide us? Could we walk in past it?' Iolwen asked the question, although it had occurred to Dafydd too. He noticed the slight waver in her voice as she spoke, but was heartened by her courage to even think it.

'I do not know. The magic fools men, unless they are adepts and are looking for it. Dragons are inherently magical creatures though. They see the world very differently to us. We might be invisible to the people down there and yet plain as can be to that creature.'

Dafydd shuddered at the thought. Bad enough to walk past one of the monsters knowing it couldn't see you, it would be madness to attempt if there were any uncertainty. They still needed to get to the throne though, and it stood in the middle of hall, no way to approach it without being seen. That was the whole point, after all.

'Beggin' pardon, Your Majesties, but I couldn't help overhearing.'

Dafydd and Iolwen turned as one, seeing a stout man standing two or three steps below them. He wore simple clothes and had the look of a store keeper about him. His heavy cloth cap was folded in his hands and he twisted it nervously as he bobbed his head in a simple bow. Greying hair clung to his shiny scalp, but it was clearly giving up the battle with age.

'You have a suggestion? Or were you just eavesdropping?' Dafydd stepped down until he was directly in front of the man, a head higher than him even without the added advantage of the stairs.

'Where're me manners?' The man bowed again. 'Name's Derridge. Mercor Derridge. Used to be in the city guard 'fore I got a bit of an injury to me leg.' He reached down and rubbed at his right knee just in case they were unsure what he meant.

'I'm sure you served the city well, Master Derridge,' Iolwen said, 'but I'm not sure how that helps us.'

'Well I reckon you're wanting to get into the Neuadd there. Probably need to do something with the throne you weren't so keen on taking afore them dragons turned up.'

'If I'm to evacuate the city, then I need to use the power of the throne to keep everyone calm.'

'And you can't do that with yon big fella in there, using the place as a toilet or whatever it is he's doing, yes?'

Dafydd took a step to the side as his wife came to join him above this strange old man. 'Something like that, yes. You think you can persuade him to leave?'

Derridge nodded once, looked over his shoulder to the gang of people at the bottom of the stairs, then back up again. 'Reckon me 'n' the lads could set up a fair diversion. Run along the cloisters here making enough of a racket. Should draw him out.'

'It's too dangerous,' Dafydd said. 'A creature his size could just smash the place down. You'd all be killed.'

'Can think of worse ways to go than helping our folk escape. And it's not like you're taking the easy option either, sir.'

'You command these men?' Iolwen asked, looking past the man to the crowd below.

'They do what I tell 'em, yes. And we're all here to help, Your Highness.'

'Then I accept your kind and brave offer, Captain Derridge.' She turned to Usel. 'How long will it take us to get to the Neuadd by the back route?'

'Ten minutes, ma'am. If we don't dawdle.'

'Very well. Give us ten minutes, Captain, then start raising hell. And if we both survive this your bravery will not be forgotten.'

Freezing cold knocked the breath out of him like a punch to the gut. Errol was swept down in a torrent of water so powerful he didn't even have time to gasp. The fall was short, and then he was plunged into a pool of bubbles and froth that couldn't support his weight, pressed down by the force of the cascade above him.

Currents surged and spun him round, knocking his arms and legs against rocks. He couldn't tell which way was up, which way down. All around was a rage of motion, muffled sound still deafening in his ears, light exploding in all directions. His manure-caked travelling cloak twisted around him like a heavy net, squeezing his legs together so that he couldn't kick out, swim like he had done so many times in the river back home. Like he had done that time he and Martha had both fallen into the pool at Jagged Leap.

'Calm your mind, Errol. Try to relax.'

The voice was in his head again, and for a moment he thought he was back there, listening to Sir Radnor. But the tone was wrong, and the currents far more deadly than the ones that had almost killed Martha.

'Be still. Let the flow take you downstream.'

The advice was reasonable, except that Errol was convinced he was being dragged in circles, held down by the waterfall, and he was fast running out of breath. The explosions of light were less intense now, his vision fading even as his limbs began to feel heavy and useless. Only his left hand was tense, clasped in a tight fist around the tiny jewel. He could not let that go. Would never let that go. Otherwise what was the point of struggling?

His head bumped against something soft, and Errol felt himself tumbled over a couple of times. Fine sand billowed about him, muddying his sight and stinging his eyes. He could taste the silt, and only then realized his mouth was open. Too much effort to close it. Too much effort to untangle himself from the cloak. It was easier just to be carried by the current. To finally rest.

'Come on, Errol. Wake up.'

The voice was in his head, but it sounded different somehow. Higher-pitched, it was more muffled too, as if the water had finished flooding his ears and was now working its way into his brain. Errol ignored it. He just wanted to sleep.

The current wouldn't let him. It tugged at his shoulders, rolling him over in the silty water. It lifted him up and shook him, his face breaking through the surface.

'Don't you dare be dead.'

The words confused him. They were in his head, and yet not. They were spoken by the dragon whose jewel he still gripped tight, and yet they were spoken by someone much younger, much more human. Errol tried to focus, but his eyes were gritty. He tried to speak, but his mouth was full of water. And then he was choking, spasms forcing the water back out of his lungs. He dropped, the river once more folding him into her embrace. Then he was being pulled up again, dragged by something that wasn't the current. More like a person.

Tangled in his sopping-wet cloak, Errol was dropped to the ground still wheezing and spluttering and trying to take a breath. His lungs didn't want to work. His arms and legs didn't want to work. Even his head had stopped working. Then something hit him in the small of the back with the force of a felled tree. He coughed up a small lake of water, belching and retching like Tom Tydfil on his way back from the tavern late at night. He was just about to try to breathe in when another tree fell on him and he spewed up yet more water, coughed even more from his lungs.

'You breathing?'

This time Errol managed to suck in some air, groaned as he let it back out again. Panting was all he could manage for a while, and then slowly he rolled on to his side. For a while he had been warm, or at least things had been happening too fast for him to feel the cold, but now it seeped into his bones. Without thinking, he cast out for the Grym, found it in abundance all around him. Pulling it in had always been a struggle before, but now it flowed through him as if he were an empty pot thrust into a great vat. How long had he been deep underground, walled off from the life force by impenetrable rock? It was hard to gauge, though it felt like a lifetime since he had been in a much smaller cave, with a merry fire, seeking out along the lines for food so that he wouldn't starve. Him and Nellore.

The memories flooded in as if they were part of the Grym too. His eyes were still gritty, but Errol blinked as much away as he could before looking up to see the face he had expected to see as soon as he had recognized the bodiless voice. She was better dressed for the weather than him, heavy leggings and sturdy boots damp from wading into the river, a thick jacket made from the fur of an animal well suited to winter. She was cleaner too, but unmistakably the young girl from the village.

'Nellore?' Errol wasn't quite sure why he made it a question, except that he couldn't understand how she could have come to be here, now, when he most needed rescuing.

'Who'd you think it was?' She hunkered down a few paces away from him, tilted her head at a curious angle. 'You going to stay lying in that cold water all day? Only you're starting to steam.'

Errol struggled with the soaked material of his cloak. Even with the Grym lending him strength and warmth, it was an effort to make his muscles work. Bruises cramped his every movement, reminding him of the battering he'd taken from the waterfall. Slowly he managed to get first one hand free, then the next, using them to lever himself upright and look around. He was lying half in the water on a sandy beach at the edge of a river not much wider than the one that flowed through Corwen's clearing. The banks on the far side rose high, rock cliffs topped with tall pines, their branches drooped with snow still tumbling from a sky the colour of wet slate. The water reflected it, deep and fast-flowing, the surface smooth but undulating. The waterfall was a lot further off than Errol imagined it would be, a tall chute dropping a hundred spans or more into a wide bowl of froth and spume. Its roar was distant, muffled by the snow.

'How?' He turned slowly to where Nellore was still squatting, a curious smile on her lips. 'How did you know I'd be here?'

'Probably wouldn't believe me if I told you.' She stood up, came closer, reaching out a hand to help him up. 'Come on. Let's get out of here before this snow gets any heavier. Never saw snow before. Not sure I like it much.'

Errol reached up and took Nellore's hand. She wore no gloves, but her touch was warm. Another mystery his mind wasn't capable of processing. It was hard enough just struggling up on to his knees and then to his feet. Swaying dizzily from side to side, he took a moment to get his breath back, another to cough and hack up yet more of the river from his lungs. At least his soaking had washed the worst of the cavern filth from his face, hands and hair. Bits of it still clung to his cloak though, the smell a reminder that it hadn't all been some terrible dream. He took a step, then another, his legs uncertain, as if he was only just learning to walk. His mind was full of too much strangeness, but he was certain he was missing something. Lifting his hand up to rub the last of the silt from his eyes, he realized what it was.

His hand was open, palm still streaked with muck, and Morgwm's jewel was nowhere to be seen.

11

Greatest care must be taken when using the Llinellau to travel from one place to another. This most complex of the subtle arts requires not just that you move yourself to your destination, but that an equal balance of matter take the place you have vacated. This need be no more than a volume of air equal to your own bulk. The Grym is unforgiving though, and should you fail to make this adjustment, as is so often the case when novices first attempt this magic, then it will fill the vacated space with whatever it can. You may find yourself stepping into another mage's palace only for them to be whisked away to the place you have just left. Or worse, to some part of Gwlad known to neither of you.

Corwen teul Maddau,
On the Application of the Subtle Arts

Warm air brushed his face, bringing with it the smell of burning hair and the reek of the charnel house. Melyn stepped out of nothing and on to the dais beside King Ballah's throne. How long had it been since he had succumbed to the madness? How many days had passed since he had walked out of here and into Gog's realm? He had seen the truth and for a moment it had been too much for him. Now he could accept it, understand it, use it. So his whole life had been built on a lie. That didn't make the power behind the lie any less real.

The throne room was empty, the throne exactly as it had been when he had left it. Even the heart stone still sat on one arm, dull and lifeless and almost pulled in on itself. Melyn saw through the magics that swirled around it, hiding it from all but the most skilled of mages. For a moment he thought the jewel had been hiding itself, something it was more than capable of doing, but then his enhanced aethereal sight showed him the weave of much more recent workings. Familiar workings. Someone had concealed the heart of the Shepherd, not wishing to touch it, nor for anyone else to claim it.

The old anger stirred in his breast, that someone could interfere with this most important of all magical artefacts. But as he studied the workings that had concealed it, so Melyn began to understand who had sought to hide the jewel he had found and claimed for his own. Magog's first jewel, pulled from his living brain by the most subtle of arts. This was his strongest link to the Shepherd and the Grym; holding it opened him up to the long dead dragon's influence, but it also gave him access to Magog's knowledge. And what wondrous knowledge that was.

Before he could reach out and take what was his by right, Melyn was distracted by the crash of doors being thrown wide. A dozen warrior priests surged into the throne room, blades of light conjured and ready. At their head, Captain Osgal scanned the room with wild eyes.

His face was a mess of suppurating sores where the burns Benfro had given him still refused to heal, and he moved with an oddly rolling gait that suggested his injuries were not confined to his face. He was halfway to the throne before he saw the inquisitor, and came to such an abrupt halt two of his men stumbled into him.

'Your Grace?' Osgal walked forward more slowly now, coming to within a few paces before falling to one knee. 'By the Shepherd. We thought you were—'

'Dead, Osgal?' Melyn grinned, feeling the fear that boiled off these battle-hardened warrior priests. What a sight he must be to instil such awe. 'On the contrary, I have never been more alive.'

'But . . . but sire? Where did you go?'

Where did he go? There was a question indeed. To the end of Gwlad and back in the blink of an eye. Beyond it even, to the realm of the Wolf. To slay the Wolf. Except that the Wolf was no more real than the Shepherd.

'Where I went is of no importance. Not now, at least. There is much work to be done here before we can return to the Twin Kingdoms. Where is Frecknock?'

Osgal stood up slowly. 'The dragon? She is in the dungeons, locked up so she can't slope off.'

'Slope off? I would have thought she would have run as fast as her little legs could take her.' Melyn stepped down off the dais and headed towards the door. There were quicker ways to the dungeon for him now, but he didn't want to unnerve his men any more than they already were. Not yet, at least.

'She came to the doors here, flung them open and called for our help. That was ten days ago.' Osgal had fallen in beside the inquisitor and for a moment at least it felt like old times.

'She came to you?' Melyn asked. That he had been gone ten days surprised him, but not as much as the fact that Osgal hadn't slain the dragon in that time.

'She did. Claimed you had just disappeared, sire. I half thought she might have killed you, but—'

'You searched the rooms?'

'I supervised the search myself, but we found no trace of a fight, nothing to suggest foul play. I thought perhaps it might have been a trap laid by King Ballah, but even the most skilled adepts could find nothing.'

Melyn knew Osgal well. He had tutored the captain when he had been a novitiate. He was a good soldier, but not the strongest when it came to wielding the Grym. His blade of light was short, though effective, and he had never been able to slip into the trance that would let him see the aethereal. Melyn could read his thoughts as easily as if they were written in the air above his head. Captain Osgal hated the dragon and all she stood for, but he also knew she was useful and far too timid to be a real threat. And a tiny part of him admitted that Frecknock had saved Melyn's life too. Much though he hated to acknowledge the fact. The captain also hoped that the dragon might be able to heal his wounds, but he hadn't found the courage to ask. No, not courage. Osgal had not found the humility yet.

All of this played across the captain's mind, open to Melyn like it had never been before. And woven around it, so deftly as to be almost impossible to sense, was a foreign thread linking all the ways in which Frecknock alive would be more useful than Frecknock dead. How wily the creature was, and far more subtle than he had ever given her credit for.

Faces stared as the small group marched out of the throne room and through the palace in the direction of the entrance to the dungeons. Melyn recognized some of the merchants and lesser officials who had been presented to him in the days after they had captured the city. Warrior priests were dotted here and there, but by and large Llanwennog people were running things. How long they could be kept in line was the question, and one he didn't have a ready answer to. The sooner they could get more men to Tynhelyg, more of Padraig's accursed Candles, the better.

The dungeons were formed from a maze of tunnels carved into the rock beneath the oldest part of the palace. Long corridors with cells on either side met in larger rooms, some with skylights, others lit only by smoky torches hung from the walls. In one of them Melyn felt something strange, saw with his newly enhanced vision the way the Grym swirled and eddied as if it were still recovering from some great shock. The room itself was clearly a torture chamber, dominated by a heavy wooden frame to which a body could be strapped for numerous inventive purposes. Tools that would have looked more at home in a carpenter's shop hung from racks on the walls, but where any self-respecting woodworker would keep his blades clean and free from rust, these were crusted with blood, some with pieces of flesh still clinging to their cutting edges.

'He was here. The boy. Errol.' Melyn stopped in front

of the frame, picked up a heavy iron hammer that lay on a nearby table, hefted it. 'They used this on his ankles.'

'Your Grace. How can you possibly——?'

'You doubt me, Osgal?' Melyn fought the smile that tried to force itself on to his lips. Before, he would have been irritated with the captain, but now he felt no need.

'No, sire. Not at all. I just don't understand how.'

'The Shepherd moves in mysterious ways, Jerrim. Now where have you put my dragon?'

Osgal stiffened at the use of his first name in front of the ranks. Melyn found he didn't much care about that either. He had the aethereal trace of Frecknock now, something he couldn't quite describe as a scent, but a haunting familiarity anyway. He headed down the passage just before the captain could lead him that way, seeing the violence carried out in this subterranean hell written into the patterns and swirls of the Grym. When he found the right cell, it came as no surprise to him that he could sense the echo of Errol there too. This was where they had kept him, and now Frecknock lay in the mouldering straw.

He looked in through the iron-barred window at the top of the stout wooden door, seeing the shadows resolve themselves into her familiar form. Her scales were so dark as to be almost black, but they glinted in the torchlight from behind him, sparkling like tiny stars. She seemed to be shivering slightly, or perhaps weeping. Melyn couldn't be sure which, but neither filled him with the joy it should have done. Not now he understood.

'Unlock it,' he commanded Osgal. The captain looked momentarily panicked, turning back the way they had just come.

'The key, sire. It's on a rack in the torture room.'

Melyn let out a sigh, closed his eyes and looked at the door. His aethereal sight soon unpicked the secrets of the lock mechanism, and with little more than a thought he stretched his aura out, through the keyhole and twisted. The lock clicked and the door fell open.

The dragon stirred at the noise, rising slowly with her back to the door. By the slump of her shoulders, Melyn could tell she had been waiting for this moment, certain that she would not be freed until it was time to put her to death. When she finally turned, her head was down, eyes to the floor in supplication.

'Why so sad, Frecknock?' Melyn asked the question in Draigiaith, perfectly accented. The language had always felt awkward in his mouth, but now it was as if he had grown up speaking it. With a wry laugh, he remembered that he had.

'Your . . . Your Grace?' Frecknock's eyes grew wide as she recognized him and he took a curious delight in the mixture of confusion and relief that poured from her. 'You came back for me.'

Dafydd had been expecting the back route to the Neuadd to be through rough tunnels hidden behind secret panels in the oldest parts of the palace, but Usel led them to a wide corridor with a high ceiling, its shiny marble floor reflecting the sun from carefully constructed light wells. There were torches in sconces at regular intervals too, though none had been lit recently. Such a lapse in palace maintenance was perhaps understandable given the circumstances. All along the route, alcoves held sculptures of past kings and queens. At least Dafydd assumed they were kings and queens; certainly they bore some similarities in their faces to Iolwen. The high set of the cheekbones, the thin nose and narrow, piercing eyes seemed to be something of a Balwen trait.

'This passageway leads to an antechamber at the rear of the building.' Usel spoke in a low whisper, slowing his pace as he approached a set of heavy wooden doors. He produced a key from the folds of his cloak, slipped it into the lock and turned it slowly. There was a heavy *clunk*, and he eased it open. It screeched like a cat whose tail has been trodden on, the sound echoing down the stone corridor for what felt like hours. 'I think we should maybe try the hiding spell now.'

Dafydd took Usel's proffered hand, felt Iolwen grasp his other one. The air shimmered around them as they withdrew themselves from the Grym. Much stronger here than anywhere outside of his grandfather's throne room or the cavern somewhere deep beneath their feet where hopefully the good people of Abervenn were even now fleeing the city, he felt its absence as a chill on his soul.

'We should try to be as quiet as possible. Maybe the beast didn't hear us.' Usel didn't sound like a man convinced, but he stepped forward anyway and Dafydd had no option but to follow.

Steep marble steps led them to a small room, dark save for scant light coming in under a door on the opposite side. Heavy wooden wardrobes lined the walls, no doubt storage for ceremonial robes or some such. They approached the door nervously, ears straining for any sound of the dragon they had seen enter earlier. Dafydd could hear nothing, not even the sounds of a diversion from the newly appointed Captain Derridge and his band of misfits. He wanted to call them fools, but they were brave men truly.

'Let us hope this is a little quieter than the one below.' Usel cracked the door open just enough to be able to peer through the gap, stood there for a long while with his head held close. Finally he stood back, opening the door wide.

'We may be in luck.'

They stepped into the great hall of the Neuadd and Dafydd almost gagged on the smell. He had thought the dragon musk unpleasant when they were outside, but trapped by the massive vaulted roof high overhead, the stench was unbearable. Thick and meaty, it reminded him unpleasantly of the sewers that ran beneath his grandfather's palace. There were undertones of dog mess in there too, only somehow worse.

'By the Wolf. What is that?' He coughed, burying his face in his sleeve without letting go of either Iolwen or Usel's hands.

'I think they might be using this place as a privy,' Usel said.

'But I thought they said this was a dragon-made hall? Isn't that what the one who spoke to us said? Sir Morwyr?'

'Which suggests to me it was possibly made by the wrong dragon. Either that or they feel it has been too long despoiled by our kind.'

The dais on which the Obsidian Throne stood was fully fifty paces away, the polished stone floor strewn with rubbish, broken glass and lead. They huddled together, not daring to break contact even though there was no sign of the great black dragon who had entered the hall earlier. A light breeze blew through the holes where the stained-glass windows had been, but it wasn't strong enough to disperse the reek. By the time they reached the first step up to the back of the throne, Dafydd felt like no amount of fresh air would ever get the smell out of his nose.

'Hold.' Usel stopped, pulling Dafydd close. Iolwen pressed up beside him, and peering around the massive base of the throne he could see why. It had been hidden before, but now they could see the black dragon, hunkered down not far from the main doors, over on the far side of the hall. It appeared to be preoccupied and hadn't noticed them. There was no way it could have smelled them over the stench, the fall of the light meant they were in shadow beside the throne, and the whole place was so awash with the Grym it would be all but impossible for any magical sense to spot them. That was what Dafydd hoped anyway.

And then a roar went up from outside. For a moment he thought it was another dragon, come to challenge this one or maybe just join it. Then Dafydd began to hear words, the sound of metal banging off metal. The dragon looked up, stretching its long neck to peer out through the doorway. It grunted something that might have been speech and then shook itself, flapping its wings half-heartedly before stomping out of the hall with all the grace of a duck on a frozen pond.

'Waste no time. Princess Iolwen, you must take the throne.' Usel let go of Dafydd's hand, and the magic shimmered around them as the concealing spell ended.

Walking round to the front of the great chair, Dafydd could see the full extent of the damage the dragons had done to the Neuadd. It was clear they were using it as a dumping ground and toilet, clear too that these creatures were not in any way civilized. Half-eaten bodies were strewn across the floor, piles of ordure in every corner. If most of the windows hadn't been smashed, the air inside would have been unbreathable. As it was, it was hard to concentrate for the stench. At least the throne itself seemed to have been left unsullied, and as he processed the scene, so Dafydd could see that the mess ended in a rough circle perhaps twenty or so paces from it.

'They're scared of it,' he said in a low voice. 'Or at least wary.'

'Scared of what?' Usel asked, then obviously noticed the exclusion zone himself. 'Oh. How curious.'

'Curious or not, we've a job to do.' Iolwen set her foot on the first of the small steps that led up to the throne, paused for a moment, then continued. She was still holding Dafydd's hand and pulled him with her.

'Iol. I can't. This is your throne, not mine.'

'No time for that, Dafydd. I need your help. I can't do this on my own.' Two more steps and she was there, Dafydd reluctantly following. He called back to the medic, still staring at the mess and the ominously open doors.

'Usel, keep watch. If that beast comes back we'll need to run.'

Despite its great size, there wasn't a lot of room to sit on the Obsidian Throne. Close up, Dafydd could see quite clearly how the much larger seat had been filled in to create a chair a king might sit in. Skilled masons had carved stone to bulk up the seat, widen the arms and fill the open back, but they had not managed to match perfectly the stone, nor the quality of craftsmanship that had gone into the original. As he touched its cold, unyielding surface, Dafydd almost cried out in surprise. If the Grym had been strong in the Neuadd and in the cavern deep below, here it was almost unbearable. He had barely brushed the throne and yet he felt like he was connected to the whole city. No wonder so many of the House of Balwen had gone mad, seduced by the power that eddied all around them.

'Sit. Please.' Iolwen had shuffled up close to one arm of the throne, leaving enough space for Dafydd to settle in beside her. She still clasped his hand, more tightly now than ever, and her voice was higher, slightly strained. He did as he was bid and understood why.

Candlehall was in a state of terror. Thousands of innocent people were trapped within its walls, threatened by the dragons overhead and Beulah's army on the plain beyond. Their only glimmer of hope was the rumour of an escape route under the palace, but even though many had descended into the cavern, there were still doubts.

'We must try to keep them calm, reassure them that they can escape, but it will take time. If there are any still out in the city, I will encourage them towards the palace.'

Dafydd concentrated, remembering the many hours he had spent being tutored in the magical arts by his grandfather. King Ballah's skill at manipulating the Grym was legendary, but he was more interested in defeating his foes with it than influencing his subjects towards peaceful ends. Still, the principle was the same, surely.

He relaxed a little into the seat, feeling the power radiating from the stone. The voices were everywhere, hard to distinguish, like standing in the middle of a large room full of people. Concentrating harder, Dafydd tried to fix on just one voice, one anxiety. It was close by, already in the palace. He couldn't speak directly to whoever's mind it was he heard; they were not adepts and his thoughts were framed by the Llanwennog language he had grown up with. Instead he tried to think of his most calming memory from recent times and settled on the few days they had spent on the island in the Southern Sea, halfway to Eirawen. The soothing sound of the waves on the beach, the warm sun and gentle evening breeze, all of these things Dafydd sent to the anxious voice. Once he was confident he was doing the right thing, he spread the influence further. Alongside him, he could feel Iolwen doing the same, spreading calm through the city along with the message that anyone who wanted to escape should make their way to the palace.

Aided by the power of the throne, it should have been an easy task, but Dafydd felt the pull of the Grym in ways he had never encountered before. He had to keep his focus or risk drifting away. At one point he recalled a lesson with his grandfather, and before he knew it he was seeking that familiar mind, reaching far out along the lines. Further than he had ever been before.

'Focus, Dafydd.' He could not be sure if Iolwen had spoken the words or just thought them at him, but the squeeze of her hand in his was enough to anchor him.

And so it went on, for what felt like hours. He was dimly aware of the sky darkening, the day passing into evening. Somewhere in the back of his mind he registered too that the clanging of swords on shields as Captain Derridge and his irregular army distracted the great dragon had faded away to nothing. Had he heard screams? The agony of dying men? He couldn't be sure. There were too many voices, too much to contain.

Then another feeling swept across him, and Dafydd felt the hairs on his neck stand up. It wasn't a voice, but it had the same keen intelligence, a sense of curiosity and hunger and irritation that was both utterly familiar and completely alien. Too late he understood what manner of creature could think such thoughts. Too late he felt the anxious shaking at his shoulder, opened his eyes to see Usel standing right in front of him, white as a sheet.

Behind him, framed in the open doorway, not one but two massive dragons stared straight at them.

There was something wrong with his hearing. Noises intruded into his darkness, muffled but annoying. He couldn't have said when he had first noticed them any more than he could have said where he was. For a moment he couldn't even have said who he was, but the thought sparked memories and the memories brought with them sensation, understanding.

'Hush now. I think he's waking.'

The noises coalesced into words, a voice he didn't recognize speaking Draigiaith. Not the pinched, slightly uncomfortable accent even the people of Gog's world spoke, but the pure pronunciation that could only come from a dragon's mouth. Slowly Errol opened his eyes, feeling grit in the corners that drew tears as he blinked.

He was in a large room, lying in a comfortable bed and staring at a ceiling high enough for it to be in the most grand of palaces. What little light there was flickered slightly, a flame in a lantern of some kind off to one side, but he didn't have the energy to turn his head and look. He didn't have the energy to move at all. It was enough to just lie there, warm, comfortable, enveloped in blankets that smelled of lavender and other soothing herbs.

'You awake then, Errol? Only you've been sleeping ages now.'

That voice he did recognize. It brought back memories of falling into the waterfall, being rescued, of the cold. He remembered leaning heavily on Nellore, staggering up the snow-covered riverbank towards the trees, distraught at the loss of Morgwm's jewel but too tired, too weak to do anything about it. And then his memories stopped.

'How did I get here?' Errol struggled to sit up, but the heavy bedclothes pinned him down.

'Lie back, Errol Ramsbottom. Rest. You've come closer to death than is wise, and there is much still for you to do.'

He collapsed back into pillows as soft as freshly plucked goose down. His tears had cleaned out the worst of the gunk from his eyes now, and he gazed at the ceiling high above, decorated with fine plasterwork. Intricate patterns wove themselves in shadow and light, depicting scenes from a story he couldn't help thinking he had heard before. It was yet another puzzle for his mind, another distraction from what he was supposed to be doing, but it was so hard to concentrate. Someone had just spoken to him, he really should have been more interested in find-ing out who, what they wanted from him, how he had come to be here. So many questions. He tilted his head to one side, towards the source of light, and saw what he had known would be there. It still came as a shock.

'Dragon?' His own voice was as weak as everything else about him, and his throat ached as if he had worn it out through shouting.

'Perhaps I should introduce myself.' The dragon bowed her head slightly in his direction, and Errol knew that she was a she though he couldn't have said how.

'I am Myfanwy the . . .' The dragon paused a while, then shook her head. 'No, just Myfanwy. None of that naming nonsense here. And you? You're Errol Ramsbottom. Heard a lot about you, so I have.'

'You have?' Errol felt the strain in his neck from holding his head at an angle and looked back up at the ceiling. 'From whom?'

'From your friend Nellore, mostly. I had an interesting conversation with a dragon named Sir Radnor too.'

'Sir Radnor? But he's—'

'Dead?'

'I was going to say he's back in Magog's world.' Errol frowned at the ceiling, too weary to do much else.

'Indeed he is, and I was not at all pleased to find myself there. The magics that Gog and his mad brother wove were supposed to have been impenetrable, but time has a habit of unravelling such things.'

'Gog. You know him?'

Myfanwy let out a deep rumbling laugh. 'Know him? He is the father of my daughter and my three sons. Yes, if anyone can say they know him, then I can. Or knew him, I should say, for we have long since parted ways. But something is wrong. I fear he is dead. The Grym is in turmoil around his great tower, and the entrance is barred to all who would enter.'

This time Errol managed to heave himself upright, wincing at the pain that shot through his head. 'Dead? But how?'

'That much I have yet to discover, but only something momentous could have displaced me into his brother's world. And I wouldn't have been able to find my way back so easily either, had he still been alive. That cursed spell of theirs is failing fast.'

Errol only half heard the dragon's words, his mind still reeling at the turn of events. 'Where is Nellore?' he asked.

'Right here, int I.'

He turned his head too swiftly, the pain starring his vision. As it cleared, so Errol saw her, sitting on a chair at the other side of the bed. He had scarce noticed it at the river, but now he could see a change in her. She was well dressed, for one thing, her face fuller as if she had eaten well for several weeks. And her hair had grown long, down past her shoulders rather than the boyish crop he remembered. That didn't make sense, surely? It was only a few days since they had been attacked in the cave.

'Far longer than that, Errol Ramsbottom,' the dragon Myfanwy said in her deep, slow voice. 'And yes, I can see your thoughts all too easily. You are open to the Grym like no man I have ever met before, and that makes you easy to read. Nellore is unusual too. I suspect that might have something to do with what you taught her of the Llinellau. It was through her that I was able to find my way back home, and for that I am most grateful.'

'I don't understand. Longer? How?'

Myfanwy paused a while before answering, as if considering how best to explain something very complicated to a child. 'There is a place deep beneath this palace where the Grym does not flow. A different magic works there, more ancient even than Gwlad herself. We call it the Anghofied, and it is where those things we wish to forget about are sent. It is also a punishment for those palace staff who commit the worst of crimes. I cannot begin to understand why you were sent there.'

Anghofied. Errol considered the word with his limited understanding of Draigiaith. It seemed to mean forgotten place or something like that, which was appropriate at least.

'I still don't understand how I escaped from there. How Nellore found me.'

'As to how you escaped, I have no idea. No man has ever done so before. Nellore found you because I guided her, rode her senses as I tried to find my way home. There was a power about you, something I had not felt in two thousand years or more. It confused me because it was not of this world. Had I realized you had brought it across with you, I might have been able to return sooner. Perhaps even saved the old fool from his untimely end. And perhaps if I had known Magog was dead too.'

'Magog.' The word sparked a memory and with it a surge of panic. Errol felt his chest, noticed for the first time that he had been dressed in a soft linen bedshirt, his old muck-encrusted clothing nowhere to be seen. Bad enough to have lost Morgwm's reckoned jewel, but had he lost the evil red one too? He pushed himself fully upright, ignoring the pain in his head as he shuffled to the edge of the bed. 'I had his jewel. Where is it?'

Nellore jumped down off her chair and went to a wooden chest at the end of the bed. She opened it and immediately a rank smell filled the air. Myfanwy wrinkled her nose, then waddled over to the window and threw it open as Nellore produced a tattered velvet bag and a rolled wad of fabric. 'The washerwomen wanted to throw it all on the fire and be done with it, but I managed to get these out of the pockets first. They didn't smell that bad then.' She shrugged, went to hand Errol the bundles, but Myfanwy stopped her.

'Give them to me, Nellore.'

'Be careful,' Errol said. 'The jewel wrapped in that cloth is a dangerous thing.'

'More so even than when he was alive.' Myfanwy placed the package on an upturned palm, then unwrapped it with careful talons. The jewel lay inert, darkest red like congealed blood. She peered at it for long moments before wrapping it up again and placing it back in the chest. 'Why are you carrying this, Errol Ramsbottom?'

'We were searching for a way back to the place where Magog died so that we could find a piece of his body. Then it can be reckoned and the hold he has on Benfro broken.'

'Benfro?' Myfanwy weighed the other bundle in her hand. 'Do you know where he is?'

Errol shook his head. 'We were separated. Back in Magog's world. Just before I walked the lines – the Llinellau – to the village near the Twmp. Where Nellore came from.'

Myfanwy stared first at the young girl, then back at

him, her eyes seeming to penetrate deep into their souls. Errol felt like he was being read the way Melyn had read him, but unlike the inquisitor, whose touch had been brutal and careless, Myfanwy skimmed his thoughts with the lightest of touches. He hardly noticed that she was no longer in his mind when she opened the soiled velvet bag and pulled out the orb. In her hand it looked like a child's marble, swirled with patterns of grey and white frozen deep within the glass where before it had been clear.

'You saw Benfro in this once before. Could you find him with it again?'

Errol took the orb from her, feeling the weight of it. He had no idea how he had managed not to lose it since fleeing Tynhelyg, but it sat in his hand inert. 'I don't know how it worked before,' he said. 'I just picked it up and there he was.'

Myfanwy took the orb back, held it up to the light for a moment, then slipped it once more into its bag as she shook her head. 'Its magic is unravelling, like so much else here. I had hoped I was wrong, that the storm gathering around the great tower was his defence, not the result of his demise. I can see that was just wishful thinking. Gog truly is dead.'

'But how? He can't be.'

'We must go to the tower. I have been detained too long. If the entrance is blocked, then I must take you another way.' Myfanwy held out both hands and, without knowing why, Errol reached for one as Nellore took the other. The room darkened, he felt a lurching, spinning sensation as if he had drunk too much of Inquisitor Melyn's strong red wine, and then they were somewhere else.

12

Empty bodies will burn
The wingless beasts will fly
Servant on master turn
And fire fill the sky.

The Prophecies of Mad Goronwy

'How much longer must we stay in this place? It's so cold.'

'There's nothing keeping you here, Xando. You know that as well as I do.'

'Nothing? They all know I was a favourite of the Old One. They'll read my mind. They can do that, you know. See right into your thoughts like they're just written out on your face. They'll know I was there. Know I did nothing to save him. It'll be the Anghofied for me. I know it.'

Benfro lay on his good side, surrounded by cushions and the dusty animal skins that covered the sleeping platform as he listened to yet another argument between the young boy Xando and Martha. He was still weak and drowsy from the potions Cerys had made, but they were beginning to work on his fever. How long he had slept, he could not tell, and whether it was this place, Martha's intervention or just that he was busy elsewhere, Benfro had not felt the tug of Magog's presence at all since they had fled from the top of the tower. Too much to hope that the dead mage had given up on him; his missing eye showed Benfro quite clearly the looping strand of rose Grym that faded into the rest of the Llinellau criss-crossing the room. He reached out for it with his aura, checking the knot was still tight, then raised himself from his slumbers as best he could.

'What is this Anghofied you keep talking about, Xando?'

His voice clearly startled the boy. He had been sitting as close to the fire as he could get, unable or unwilling to tap the Grym for warmth. Now he stood up as if he'd been caught doing something wrong.

'You're awake, Benfro. Good.' Martha sat on the other side of the fireplace, a bit further away from the flames. She stood slowly, reaching for a bowl keeping warm beside the fire. 'There's some stew here for you.'

The young woman carried the bowl across the room to him, but even before it arrived Benfro could smell the food within. His stomach rumbled in anticipation, and he struggled up into a sitting position, feeling the wound in his side as a tightness rather than the stabbing pain it had been before.

'Thank you.' He accepted the bowl of stew, large in Martha's hands but disappointingly small in his. It smelled good and tasted better but was soon gone.

'Your appetite is as healthy as ever.' Martha took back the bowl and returned to the fire. A whole cauldron of the stew sat close to the flames.

'Tell me about this Anghofied, Xando,' Benfro said to pass the time. 'It must be a terrible place for you to fear it so.'

'We are warned about it as children. It's where they send anyone caught stealing, or worse. People who go there never come back.'

'It sounds terrible. Where is it?' Martha asked the question before Benfro could, and paused as she leaned over the fireplace, ladling more stew into the bowl.

'Deep down in the bowels of the earth. Far beneath the palace. Or so they say.' Xando had not moved from his seat by the fire, but he leaned towards Benfro as he spoke, eyes lit up with the telling as if the flames were inside him.

'I've heard it's where all the sewage and waste from the whole of Nantgrafanglach goes, and the condemned have to clear it all up. There's no magic down there, not dragon magic anyway. And time moves differently there too. What feels like a day there can be weeks up here.'

'Sounds like a tale told to keep youngsters in line.' Martha returned with the bowl, brim-filled this time, and Benfro took it gratefully. Had he been feeling stronger he might well have stood up, crossed to the fireplace and helped himself to the whole cauldron. But that would have meant there would be nothing left for his two companions.

'The Anghofied is real. I've heard Sir Nanteos and the others speak of men sent there for the worst misdemeanours.'

All eyes turned to the door, and Benfro barely remembered his full bowl in time, only slopping a small amount of stew out on to the sleeping platform. Cerys stood in the doorway, glanced nervously over her shoulder before she stepped fully into the room and pulled the door closed behind her.

'It is good to see you awake, Benfro. And looking better. I fear you cannot stay here much longer without being discovered though.' Cerys strode over to the sleeping platform and put a hand to Benfro's forehead, both feeling his temperature and forcing him to sit back down even as he began to rise.

'Stay. You do not want to open up that wound before it can heal properly.' Cerys bent to Benfro's side, inspecting the poultice and running her hand over his scales in a manner that felt at the same time deeply awkward and most pleasant. Unbidden, a memory came to him of another time this young dragon had been close to him, wrapping her wings around him and warming him as he healed. And then again, in the darkness of the cave, clambering in beside him to sleep.

'You should be able to walk now, at least slowly. I would caution against trying to fly any time soon though. Stretching those muscles will just tear you open again.' Cerys' words startled him out of his musing and he realized she was standing very close to him. She smelled different now, her musk less obvious than before, but still there and still enough to make his head spin.

'I am forever in your debt, Cerys. If you hadn't seen us, I'd probably be dead by now.' Benfro glanced down at his stew just briefly as he spoke, and the green dragon smiled.

'Eat. You will be ravenous after the healing. It takes as much out of the patient as it does the healer. More, really. It's your body that does all the work, after all.'

Benfro wasn't sure why, but he felt the tips of his ears burn at her words. He turned his attention to the bowl, eating more slowly than before.

'How are we going to get out of the palace?' Martha asked. 'Where will we go?'

'Where were you going before?' Cerys asked.

'Away, as far as we could get from Inquisitor Melyn. Or whatever it is he has become.'

'This Melyn. You've spoken of him before. You said he was the one who cut off your hand.' Cerys pointed at Benfro's arm and he reflexively turned it, almost spilling his stew in the process. 'He is a man, and yet he has knowledge of the subtle arts?'

'You make it sound as if that is unthinkable,' Martha said. Cerys looked at her with an expression that Benfro found hard to read but suggested she thought very little of men and women or their abilities.

'That is because it is. Unthinkable, that is. I have heard stories of the Old One, how he was convinced your kind could be taught simple tricks of magic. But he failed every time.' She turned to face Xando. 'I believe he was beginning to teach you, was he not? Only your minds are too small. You cannot— Oh.'

If Benfro hadn't been watching the whole thing from a distance he would probably have missed it himself. Martha dissolved from view, reappearing almost instantly beside Xando. Benfro's missing eye showed him in the aethereal how she had moved along the Llinellau quite effortlessly. Before the green dragon could say any more, she had raised one hand, palm up, and conjured a small ball of fire in it.

'Cannot do this?' Martha asked.

Cerys sat back on her tail perhaps a little more heavily than she had intended. 'That is . . . astonishing. Sir Nanteos says—'

'I imagine your Sir Nanteos says a great many things that aren't true. Some day you'll be old enough to understand that.' Martha extinguished the flame then sat down beside the fire. 'Where I come from dragons are small, timid creatures who barely use magic at all. It is men, and in particular men like Inquisitor Melyn, who wield the power of the Grym. What they lack in subtlety, they make up for in brute force. Their weapon of choice is a blade forged from pure Grym, sucking the life from anything close by to feed it. Such a weapon is what killed Gog, and Enedoc too. We only escaped because of Benfro.'

At the mention of his name, Cerys looked over to where he was sitting, a strange gleam in her eye. For a moment Benfro thought she was going to get up and walk over to him, but she stayed where she was, uncomfortable though it looked.

'So it really is true. The Old One was not killed by a dragon turned feral, not by a monster, but a man.'

'A man and monster both. He killed my mother the same way he killed Gog. He hates all of our kind, has dedicated his life to hunting us down. And now he is more powerful than ever. He walked the Llinellau like Martha just now, but from much further away. He could appear at any moment and strike us all down.'

Benfro wasn't quite sure why he said the words, why he felt he needed to frighten Cerys. Perhaps because they had all been hiding from the fear, gathering their strength and their will to go on. None of them wanted to admit just how powerful and mad Melyn had become because none of them knew how to cope with that knowledge. The room fell silent, just the crackling of logs on the fire and the sigh of wind outside. No one spoke for a long time as they each considered what he had said. It was Cerys who finally broke the spell.

'I must try harder to find Myfanwy. I cannot speak to the council, but they will listen to her, and she will listen to you.'

'Where is she? Have you not spoken to her since you . . .' Benfro waved his arm in the direction of his healing wound.

'I do not know where she is. She left me here with Sir Nanteos and the others weeks ago, and nobody has seen her since. I am surprised she didn't come back the moment the Old One was slain. Even I felt that disturbance in the Grym, and I have little skill at the subtle arts yet.'

'Has she gone back to the Twmp, do you suppose?' As he asked the question, Benfro recalled Martha's earlier words. 'What if somehow she has been displaced to Magog's world and can't find her way back?'

'Is that possible?' Cerys asked, her alarm even greater than Benfro's.

'If what you say of this Myfanwy is true, then it would take a creature of great power crossing over to displace one such as her.' Martha paused for a moment before adding, 'Magog himself came across the divide, of course. It was he who guided Melyn's hand when he slew Gog. Such a powerful combination would surely have displaced hundreds of feral dragons. Or one of great power.'

'Then there is no hope, surely. If Myfanwy is in Magog's world, how can we persuade the elders of Nantgrafanglach of this new danger?'

'Don't give up so easily.' Martha stood up, waving her arms around the room. 'Gog is dead, Magog has been dead for thousands of years. The subtle arts they wove are unravelling fast. The barrier between the two worlds is fading. Can you not feel it?'

Benfro looked about, then saw it in the aethereal with his missing eye. The Llinellau shivered, there was no other way to describe it. As if they were the strings of some vast instrument, pulled tight and then plucked by an unseen musician. Only where their hum had always been tuneful, now it was discordant and angry.

'If the barrier is fading, then Myfanwy will surely find her way back soon.' He struggled to rise, ignoring the pain of the wound in his side. 'But if she can find the way, then so too can Melyn. And this time he will bring his warrior priests. Whether they will listen to us or not, we must warn the elder dragons. Before he comes back to finish what he started.'

'What he started?' Cerys asked.

'The annihilation of all dragonkind.'

Days had passed since his return to Tynhelyg and still Melyn felt unfocused. The shock at his discovery of the true nature of the Shepherd had worn off, the violent rage dulled now to his more customary simmering anger. The warrior priests were keeping their distance as best they could, used to his temper, but the palace servants had taken a while to learn. There was no getting away from dealing with King Ballah's administrators. The Llanwennog equivalent of Seneschal Padraig's Candles were grey-faced men with no discernible sense of humour. At least they were pragmatic; no sooner had news of the death of Prince Geraint and the rout of his army reached the city than they had accepted their new ruler and set back to their dull work. There had been a few who had harboured resentment, nursed grudges or secretly plotted some kind of revenge, but their minds had been easy enough to read and their heads now adorned the main city gates. In a way they had done him a favour, since Melyn had always intended executing a few of the more senior officials to ensure the loyalty of those lower down the ranks.

It hadn't taken long though, and it hadn't eased his discomfort. Physically he was as strong as he had ever been, but mentally he was like a river in spate. The calm, bored exterior hid a whirl of thoughts, a crashing cascade of images and memories only some of which were his own. It was as if holding the heart of the Shepherd – or Magog's first jewel if he were giving it the correct name – had opened up his mind to secrets and knowledge gleaned over millennia. Too much for him to process, this had sent him over the edge, plunged him into the madness that still haunted his dreams. Melyn had managed to recover a degree of control now, not least by removing both Brynceri and Ballah's rings, giving them and the heart to Frecknock for safe keeping. She lay on the floor beside the throne like a monstrous dog, scarcely stirring as the morning parade of merchants, minor nobles and peasants paraded in front of him, seeking favours or justice.

'I never wanted to be a king,' Melyn said as the last supplicant was escorted from the room by a pair of warrior priests. He felt the words echoing through his mind, bringing back images of other men who had said similar things in the past. Hastily he drew up his mental shields, recognizing the trigger for another crushing wave of someone else's memories.

'Your Grace?' Frecknock's voice was an anchor, and he reached out to touch her shoulder as she stood. She no longer repulsed him in quite the way she and her kind once had. He knew now the lie that had been behind his loathing, even if it was yet another part of his confusion.

'All this I have done in the name of the Shepherd.' Melyn waved his free hand at the empty throne room. 'The war between the Twin Kingdoms and Llanwennog has always been about their rejection of the teachings of our god. Strange to think that Ballah had the right of it all along.'

'Surely there's more to it than that, sire. Did not King Ballah send assassins to kill Queen Beulah? On many occasions?'

Melyn should have been surprised at the dragon's knowledge, but his own mind was so full of the experiences of others that it hardly seemed all that unusual. And she had a point. Talking of the queen reminded him that he had not checked on her lately. He would have slipped into the aethereal, sought out Clun or even Beulah herself if her magic was returned sufficiently, but to do that was to open himself up to the madness and he was too weary to contemplate fighting that now.

'Do you have news of the queen?' He opted for asking Frecknock instead, waited with uncharacteristic patience as she went very still. A part of him sensed her leaving her mundane body and heading out across Gwlad. He longed to go with her but knew better than to give in to that call. So much had happened since last he had communicated with Beulah and Clun he had some difficulty recalling where they were, what they had been doing. They'd been at Tochers when Beulah's child was born, ready to march through the pass and relieve the siege of Tynhelyg. But the siege had never come; Magog's dragons had put an end to that. Where were they now? Melyn wondered.

'Queen Beulah and His Grace the Duke of Abervenn are at Candlehall, sire. They have not recaptured the city yet, but it is only a matter of time. There are dragons helping them break down the gates, and the escape tunnels have been blocked. Prince Dafydd and Princess Iolwen have no way of fleeing.'

Frecknock spoke as if in a trance, her voice flat and monotone. Melyn sank back into the throne as he took in her words.

'Dragons? Are they the same ones who destroyed Geraint's army?'

There was a long pause before Frecknock answered, time enough for him to consider his next move. With Ballah and Geraint dead, Prince Dafydd was the only one with a claim to Ballah's throne, the only one who might gather some sort of rebellion around him. Destroy the boy and the whole of Gwlad was theirs. At least all of it that mattered. No point worrying about distant Eirawen; only savages lived there. Was it really that easy? Melyn shook his head even though no one could see. Nothing was ever easy when dragons were involved.

'I do not think so, sire. I cannot see them, but from what Master Clun tells me these dragons have some learning, some skill in the subtle arts. The creatures who attacked Prince Geraint's army were scarcely sentient.'

Melyn clasped his hands together, rubbing at his fingers where the rings had so recently been. He had an inkling now of where these dragons were coming from, but the idea of it sent a chill through him no amount of Grym could warm.

'Come back to me, Frecknock,' he said, then waited for the flutter in the air that only his long-trained senses could detect, the return of her thoughts.

'Sire.' The dragon slumped slightly as if the effort of communicating halfway across Gwlad had tired her.

'The rings and the heart stone. Give them to me.'

Without a hint of a pause, Frecknock opened the leather bag she carried with her at all times, slung over her neck and one shoulder. She withdrew a small box and a velvet bag, and handed them both to Melyn. Her eyes were full of questions, but she did not ask them. He couldn't help but like her for that.

Opening the box revealed the two rings, so alike and yet so different. Melyn sensed the presence of the Shepherd in them, of Magog, but they were merely conduits to a far greater power and knowledge. Snapping closed the box, he slipped it into the pocket of his cloak before untying the velvet bag and drawing out the heart stone, holding it up to the light.

Were it not for Magog's gift of fine golden scales, the heat that blazed in the heart of the Shepherd might have stripped the flesh from his fingers and palm. Melyn instinctively raised his mental shields as the constant background chattering of his thoughts became a cacophony. It was an intoxicating feeling, more heady than the finest wine, more intimate than any moment he had shared since Queen Ellyn had died. The memory of her, of them, surprised him. The guilt that had suppressed his past indiscretions no longer had any meaning for him. What cared he for the warrior priest's oath of celibacy when the god to whom it had been sworn was a lie?

'Your Grace. Are you sure this is wise? The jewel will consume you utterly.' Frecknock's voice sounded distant, as if she were shouting to him from the far side of the parade ground out beyond the palace walls. Melyn focused on the jewel, surprised just how deep he had sunk into its intoxicating lure. With a wrench, he dropped it back into the velvet bag, the voices still loud in his head, the knowledge still just out of reach.

'A man could spend a lifetime studying this jewel and barely scratch its surface.' He hefted the bag, feeling much more than its physical weight. It promised so much, but at what price?

'Or he could lose himself to it entirely,' Frecknock said, and Melyn was surprised to hear the worry in her voice, the real concern for his wellbeing. He paused a moment, taking in the whole of the throne room, the palace, the city. All his to command – was that not enough?

'Stay here. I know you don't like it where I am going.' He stood up, muscles aching from having sat on the uncomfortable throne all morning. He shoved the velvet bag into his cloak pocket alongside the box and its rings, stepped down from the dais and walked slowly to the screen behind it.

'Guard the entrance. I won't be long.' He took one last look at the throne room before heading down into the great cavern, adding with a hollow laugh, 'I go to speak with my god.'

*

157

'Little things. Little things. They smell of power. I wonder what they taste like?'

Dafydd stood, frozen to the spot by fear. The two dragons in the doorway looked almost identical, as if they were twins. They were thin for their kind, their necks long and sinuous.

'What are they doing in here? This is our place now.'

The two dragons moved as one, then found they could not both fit through the doorway together. For a moment they fought each other and the sheer comedy of their actions lessened Dafydd's terror. It was only for a moment though, and then one of the great wooden doors crashed off its hinges. The noise as it hit the marble floor echoed through the vast hall. Behind him, Dafydd sensed Iolwen's focus waver as the calm she had radiated began to dissipate. He reached up, grabbed her hand, not really wanting to turn his back on the dragons to face her.

'You must stop, Iol. The people don't need to feel your fear.'

She opened her eyes, glancing up and past him. He followed her gaze and saw the beasts had covered half of the distance between doorway and throne now. Their progress was slow, hampered by the mess and destruction around them, but they moved in a perfect synchrony, one with the other, that was oddly mesmerizing.

'We have to go. Now.' Usel had edged to the corner of the throne and Dafydd felt rather than saw the medic slipping into his invisible form. And then he let out a tiny shriek, his image solidifying.

'Mustn't try to hide. That's kitling magic that is.'

Dafydd heard the words deep in his head and knew

that one of the dragons had spoken directly to their minds. Given the words, it might have been both of them, so closely were they linked. They acted as one creature split in two, weaving from side to side sinuously.

'Who are you?' Dafydd spoke the words in a whisper, too quiet even for Iolwen and Usel to hear, but the two dragons stopped, lifting their heads towards him like curious animals.

'It speaks an ugly language, does it not?'

'It wants to know our name. Should we tell it?'

'Names are power. Let us not.'

'Names are only power to those who know how to use them. What can this little thing do?'

'Caution, brother. Is that not what Angharad said? These creatures are small, but one of their kind killed Sir Chwilog.'

Dafydd heard the conversation in his head, even though he could see no movement from either dragon as they bickered. He had hoped to distract them and it seemed to be working. Then he remembered the line circling the dais and throne, beyond which none of the dragons seemed yet to have ventured. Perhaps it was that rather than his question that was keeping them at bay.

'We are Ynys Faelog.'

'And we are Ynys Feurig.'

'And we would know what manner of creature you are. Like a man, but with the power of the Grym to command.'

Dafydd's head began to ache. It wasn't that the voices were loud or harsh, but they stabbed deep into his mind.

'I am Dafydd, son of Geraint. I mean you no harm, nor disrespect. You are twins, are you not?'

'Hatched from the same egg we are.'

Looking at the pair of them, Dafydd didn't doubt it. They were one creature really, split in two. They moved as one, spoke as one. He wondered what would happen to the other if one of them was injured. Would they both feel the pain? What if one died?

'Come away from the black chair, Dafydd son of Geraint. It is too dangerous to approach.'

Dafydd took two steps from the throne before he realized what he was doing. Iolwen's cry of alarm and Usel's firm grip on his arm stopped him in his tracks. He shook his head from side to side, trying to dislodge the compulsion in the dragons' words.

'The Obsidian Throne is no danger to me,' he said.

'Truly?' The twins stopped their pacing around the circumference, turning to face each other. Dafydd imagined he could hear some exchange between them, but the thoughts were so swift and so utterly alien he could tell nothing of what they meant. And then they turned as one, stepped over the invisible line.

'Run!' Usel's words were backed up with a sharp tug to Dafydd's arm. The medic didn't wait to see if he was being followed, just darted around the back of the throne and set off for the distant door through which they had entered. Dafydd couldn't take his eyes off the twin dragons as they moved ever closer. Their eyes were dark globes flecked with tiny sparkling points, like stars in a clear night sky. There was something hypnotic about the way their heads moved from side to side, like a snake bearing down on a mouse. Transfixed by that stare, Dafydd inched slowly backwards until cold stone blocked his path. He was trapped against the throne and would surely die here.

'Dafydd, up here.' Iolwen's voice broke through the fog in his mind created by the dragon twins. He felt her hand on his shoulder, dared to turn for long enough to find the neat steps that climbed up to the throne itself. He scrambled up on to the seat, embracing his wife as if he hadn't seen her in months, not the scant minutes that had passed since the dragons had first entered the Neuadd. The twins had reached the dais now and climbed on to it without so much as a backward glance.

'I'm sorry, Iol. I never meant for this to happen.'

'Hush now. She is coming. She won't let us down.'

'Who's coming? Iol? What are you talking ab—?'

Dafydd's question was cut short by a screech from the open door. The light dimmed as another dragon filled the entrance, the great black beast that had been chasing the captain and his men around the cloisters. It screamed something in their harsh, guttural language and Dafydd felt the twins withdraw from his mind. Only with them gone could he sense how much they had inveigled their way into his thoughts. Their sudden absence made him feel sick.

As a pair, the twins turned to face the other dragon, their response to his call a rapid shouting like the argument of magpies. They retraced their steps past the invisible boundary, movements less coordinated as they picked a path back to the door.

'Quick, Iol. We won't get another chance.' Dafydd grabbed Iolwen's hand and pulled her out of the seat.

'But she's coming. She'll take us away from here.' She resisted, a look of confusion spreading across her face.

'Who's coming? Iol, we can't wait. We have to get to the cavern. Our son's still down there.'

Mention of their child, and maybe Dafydd's touch, jolted Iolwen out of whatever dream had a hold of her. She looked first at Dafydd, then at the dragons bickering in the doorway. Then without a further word she leaped from the throne, landing gracefully on the marble floor. Dafydd followed her, and in moments they were running for the anteroom. Neither of them turned when they heard the roars of frustration and alarm from the dragons at the far end of the Neuadd, nor when the sound of wings beating at the air drowned out even that. Iolwen had a head start and was a faster runner than him, but Dafydd didn't relax as he saw her disappear through the open doorway. He could feel the hot breath of the beasts behind him, the tendrils of the twins' thoughts probing for any gaps in his mental shields. The ground shook beneath him as something vast crashed into it, the black dragon landing after its short flight across the hall. He imagined it rearing its head, mouth wide open, fangs still dripping with the blood of its last victim as it prepared to strike him down. With the last of his strength, he leaped for the door, crashing on to the floor in the small room even as the great beast let out another frustrated roar.

Dafydd scrambled away as the great black dragon pressed its snout to the doorway. Its head was too big to fit through, so it reached in with hands as big as a man, grabbed the door posts and pulled the whole wall away.

'I will eat you, little man.' It spoke directly to his mind, less subtle than the twins, the words battering down his defences. He couldn't get his footing, kicking away dust and rubble as he tried to reach the steps and escape. But the distance was too great, and all he could do was watch in terror as a scaly, taloned hand reached out to grab him.

The cavern reeked of power. Melyn had felt it before, but now his senses were so much more finely tuned to the Grym, he couldn't help but be intoxicated by it. He knew that the Shepherd – Magog – was not really down here, but the place was such a potent nexus it was that much easier to seek him out.

'Ah, Melyn son of Arall, I wondered when you would return.'

The voice filled him with wonder, lent him energy and eased away the aches and pains from sitting so long in Ballah's uncomfortable throne. It was the same thrill he had always felt when in the presence of his god, but now it was tinged with a certain sadness. And anger too that he had been so fooled.

'How long have you been planning this? How long—'

'Since I died?' The voice in Melyn's head suggested faint amusement. 'I did not die, my faithful servant. I am not dead. I merely left this plane of existence, as the holy books tell.'

'The holy books are a lie. The Shepherd is a lie. Your power—'

'You cannot begin to understand my power, little man. How far it reaches. What it can do. I have healed your body, kept it young past its time. I can just as easily age it until there is little left of you but a husk.'

Melyn felt pain grow in his joints as if someone had sliced them open with a razor-sharp knife and poured acid into the cuts. His fingers bent, the knuckles swelling and seizing them into claws. His back creaked and folded until he was stooped, squeezing his lungs and making it hard to breathe.

'Imagine that. The great Inquisitor Melyn grown old and decrepit. Easy prey for any upstart warrior priest who might want to take his place. Perhaps your Captain Osgal or maybe Clun Defaid. He shows promise, and he has no doubts as to my divinity.'

Melyn struggled against the weight crushing down on him, dragging at his thoughts and making him slow. He pictured the mindless, sitting in the almshouses outside Emmass Fawr, drooling on to their naked chests, shitting themselves, needing to be fed and cleaned until their bodies finally gave up. He would not go that way. Neither would he die at the hands of some upstart novitiate who had caught the queen's eye. He clenched his fists, using the pain that shot through his hands and up his arms, riding it as he pushed back against the presence that he had so long considered his god.

'Still some fight in you, eh? Good.' The voice of the Shepherd, the voice of Magog, had a sneer in its tone that was quite unmistakable, but as he spoke, so the pain lessened, the relief flooding through Melyn like a healing balm.

'Hard to be in awe of your god when you've killed his brother. When you know him for the false god he truly is.'

'Ah, Melyn son of Arall. What is a god if not someone who watches over his people, guides them, intervenes here and there to keep destiny on track?'

'You commanded we hunt down dragons, slay them. And yet you are a dragon yourself.'

'You have seen this place, Melyn. And you have seen its larger twin beneath the great hall of the Neuadd. There are others around Gwlad, in places of power. They are the points around which the Grym turns, the source of our power, my brother and I. But he betrayed that power. He gave it up for the love of that fickle creature.'

Melyn wasn't sure what the voice was talking about, but he could see it was important. This cavern with its vast collection of jewels was not the work of men, and neither was the great cavern beneath the Neuadd. True, he had overseen the placing of dragon jewels within its alcoves all the years he had been inquisitor, as had every head of his order before him. That had been one of their sacred duties, handed down to Balwen by the Shepherd himself. But the hoards pre-dated them, perhaps by millennia.

'How is it you persuaded the Llanwennogs to collect your precious jewels for you? They rejected the teachings of the Shepherd centuries ago.'

'You think too small, Melyn. My reach spreads further than the Shepherd and the Wolf. They form only part of the story. The House of Ballah has not increased the size of this hoard for many years. And there were few dragons in this part of Gwlad to begin with. Rejecting my teachings was all part of my plan. What better way to ensure enmity between the two houses, the two nations?'

'Divide and conquer. But why would you need us fighting? What could we do together that might possibly threaten your great master plan?'

'Threaten?' Again the voice in Melyn's head laughed and sneered. 'Nothing could possibly threaten me in this realm. I am everywhere, know everything. But the wars and the constant scheming have kept you occupied. Kept you distracted while I waited for the time to be right.'

'The time for what?' Melyn asked, even though he suspected he knew. The ecstasy of being in the presence of his god was hard to ignore, even knowing his god was false.

'The time to be reborn. For the Shepherd to return. So that the damage my brother did to Gwlad might finally be repaired.'

'For Benfro.' Melyn's words echoed in the empty cavern. Ever since uncovering the truth about the Shepherd he had found it hard to kindle the old anger that had fed his ambition through the years, but just thinking about the young dragon stoked it anew. Not the explosive rage at his very existence, this was a more narrow fury. One he could control and direct.

'He is the key. His hatching at the confluence was not a coincidence. Neither is his lineage, directly back to me through the male line. My brother worked hard to stop that from happening, cursed the dragons of this realm to have only female kitlings and cursed them doubly to become the shrunken, timid creatures you have hunted. They are not true dragons. It is only fit that their jewels add to my power, sustain me even as my mortal remains turn to dust.'

Melyn reached into the pocket of his robe and took out the heart of the Shepherd. Knowing now what it was, he could see its imperfections, the roughness of it. Not just unreckoned but unfinished, it was unlike most of the jewels he had handled in his long life with the Order of the High Ffrydd. It buzzed with power, uncomfortable to hold though not in any physical way. He rolled it around the palm of his hand just once, then placed it in the nearest empty stone alcove. From his other pocket he pulled out the box that had once contained Balwen's ring on Brynceri's dessicated finger. Where had the finger gone? He couldn't recall. It was no longer important. The ring nestled beside its twin, given to some ancestor of King Ballah so many years before. Looking at them together, he could see the differences in the jewels, and the similarities. Their colour was identical to that of the heart from which they had been expertly chipped. Magically chipped. He plucked them swiftly from the box and placed them in their own alcoves, all three jewels apart. Then he let the box tumble to the stone floor.

'I am still with you, Melyn son of Arall. I will always be with you.' The voice of the Shepherd was no weaker in his mind, the ecstasy still potent enough to drop a man to his knees. At least a lesser man.

'I know. But I also know I don't need these jewels for what I have to do. They are safer here.'

He turned from the alcoves and headed for the steps carved into the central pillar, felt the Shepherd's presence fade the way it always had before. That casual dismissal that had once left him bereft now left him relieved. Mind closed as tight as he had ever closed it, yet still Melyn wondered if his god knew that he was lying.

13

In ancient times the dragons of Gwlad were huge beasts, fire-breathing and ferocious. Unlike the timid creatures we see today, they ruled the skies, flying with ease on wings bigger than the sails of the great merchant ships that ply the Southern Sea today. The few tribes of men were spread across the lands now known as Llanwennog and the Twin Kingdoms of the Hafod and Hendry, living in caves and constantly in fear of violent death from above.

It is said that the dragons were the Shepherd's first creation and favoured by him above all, but they turned to the Wolf and spurned the teachings of their creator. In his wrath he raised up his second creation, the men who until then had lived in fear. Taking on their form, he came down from the safe pastures and walked among us. One he favoured above others, taught him the ways of magic and the Grym, gave him the wisdom needed to unite the warring tribes. His name was Balwen and his sacred task was to hunt down the creatures of the Wolf, slay them in the name of the Shepherd.

Father Charmoise,
Dragons' Tales

It happened so swiftly, Dafydd couldn't really understand what was going on. One moment he was screaming, stuck on his back and unable to get away as the great black dragon reached for him with a hand that would crush and rend him at the same time, the next he was staring at an empty space where the doorway and wall had been. There was an instant of perfect silence, and then it felt like the whole world had collapsed. The ground shook, dust clouded the air and a noise like the toppling of mountains bludgeoned his ears. Part of the wall collapsed, bringing down some ceiling with it in great lumps that Dafydd watched stupidly until something in his brain finally kicked in. Scrambling back as the last few blocks smashed into the space he had been occupying, he saw the black dragon through a gap in the wall. It was lying on its side, wings twisted around its huge body as if it had rolled up against one of the shattered windows of the Neuadd. The top of its head lay against the floor, neck and underbelly exposed like a dog sleeping in front of a log fire. It wasn't moving, although he could see the slow rise and fall of its breathing.

'What the . . .?' Dafydd struggled to his feet, his ears still ringing and his heart thudding in his chest. He slowly approached the broken wall, searching everywhere for the dragon twins, Ynys Faelog and Ynys Feurig, but they were nowhere to be seen. He looked back to the top of the stairs, down which he hoped Iolwen had already fled along with Usel the medic. The stairwell was jammed shut with fallen rubble, a beam thicker than his torso wedged across it. He hurried over, tried to move it even though he knew it was pointless. Straining to hear anything over the hissing that filled his head, he clambered up the pile of debris and shouted.

'Iolwen? Usel? Are you in there?'

He pressed one ear against the stones, listening for any sound from beyond. Was that a scratching noise? A voice? Dafydd tried to reach out with his mind, but he had never been as skilled in that magic as his grandfather. Now he was too anxious, too pumped up with fear to concentrate.

'If you can hear me, go. Escape with Iolo. I will find you. I promise.'

He waited for an answer, but there was nothing. Had the tunnel collapsed on them? Were they even now trapped in darkness or crushed beneath the broken floor of the Neuadd?

'Calm yourself, Dafydd son of Geraint. You wife still lives, her companion too.'

Dafydd spun round, fear choking his breath in his throat as he saw a dragon leering at him through the broken wall and ceiling. For a moment he thought it was the black monster, recovered from whatever calamity had befallen it and coming back for the kill. But then he saw that the beast looking down at him was smaller, its face iridescent in the light filtering through the broken windows. He had not seen many dragons in his life, just those that the circus brought to the King's Fair each year and now these brute creatures who had appeared out of nowhere to destroy Candlehall and devour its population. And one other, Merriel, daughter of Earith.

'I said before that if you ever needed my help all you had to do was ask. I heard the princess calling even though

I was on the other side of Gwlad and could not understand how her voice could be so loud and so clear. Now I think I know.'

Unlike the twins and the dragon who had forced his way into the Neuadd the day Iolwen had refused to take the throne, Merriel spoke aloud and in only slightly accented Llanwennog. She glanced over in the direction of the prone black dragon, then back at Dafydd.

'He will wake soon. Probably best we are not here when that happens.'

Dafydd climbed down off the pile of stones and plaster, picked his way to a hole in the wall that had once been a door and looked out across the Neuadd.

'Where are the twins?'

'Twins?' Merriel paused a moment, her head cocked slightly in thought. 'Ah yes. I thought there was something odd about them. They fled, will most probably be seeking help. We must hurry.'

She set off towards the main doors, paying no heed to the throne. Dafydd didn't follow, looking first to the stairwell blocked by rubble, then to the black dragon, who showed signs of stirring, and finally to Merriel. She had stopped just beside the dais and was staring back in his direction.

'We will find them later. Do not worry yourself, Dafydd son of Geraint. They are as safe as any can be in this place. We, on the other hand, are very much exposed. I had the element of surprise on my side when I bested that brute. I don't want to give him a second chance.'

Dafydd hurried across the hall to where she stood. 'How did you beat him? He's twice your size.'

'He is feral, a throwback to when our kind were base and mindless beasts. I've no doubt he can speak, but he has no skill at the subtle arts whatsoever.' Merriel raised her head and wrinkled her nostrils. 'They are using this place as a midden, I expect because they are confused by it. A place of great power, it calls out to us all, even those who don't understand the nature of that call. And yet when they arrived they felt only fear of the throne. You can see how none dared approach it. The Grym is strong here, as if there were a hoard nearby. But I cannot feel any individual thoughts from it. Were we not in such imminent danger, I would investigate further.'

'A hoard? Of jewels?' Dafydd looked at his feet, imagining the floor was no longer beneath them. 'There is a cavern directly below us, and it is full of jewels. Rows and rows of them.'

'Rows?' Merriel had been moving towards the open doors, but she stopped, turning to face Dafydd. 'Not a great heap?'

'That's not what I saw, no. There were countless stone columns carved with hundreds of alcoves and filled with jewels. They glowed red all the time, and I could hear whispering voices even though I couldn't tell what they were saying.'

Merriel stood as motionless as a statue for a while, all worry about the black dragon forgotten. Then she turned back to the throne as if studying it more closely.

'By the moon. He couldn't have. Surely not even Gog would do such a thing.'

'Do what? And who is Gog?' Dafydd wasn't sure where he had heard the name before. And then it came to him – Usel's unusual expletive.

'No time, no time. We must flee this place before it corrupts us entirely.' Merriel turned again, her tail whipping around with her and almost knocking Dafydd over. She hurried to the door, past piles of foul-smelling dung and half-devoured carcasses. Dafydd had to run to keep up, but he wasn't about to stay in the Neuadd alone. From the far corner by the smashed wall into the anteroom a low moan grew in volume, turning into an angry roar as the black dragon awoke. It was echoed by another, louder roar, but he was running too fast to tell where that came from.

Until he leaped over the fallen door and burst out into the daylight.

A dozen or more of the creatures, ranging in size from big to vast beyond comprehension, were lined up in the courtyard between the Neuadd and the cloisters. Dafydd had thought the black beast the largest of the creatures, but it seemed a pup in comparison to the one that sat across the flagstone path. It ignored him, looking straight at Merriel as it screeched at her in its strange language. The sounds hurt his ears, but that was the least of his worries. Most of the dragons were just sitting, watching and waiting, but the twins he had seen earlier paced around in their oddly joined manner, weaving in and out between the larger beasts, eyes fixed on him. There was something mesmerizing about their stare and their voices ringing in his head, so loud he almost forgot about the black dragon lumbering through the Neuadd behind him.

'Take my hand, Dafydd son of Geraint.'

The words startled him almost as much as the hand thrust in his direction. He had never really studied dragons, never really had occasion or desire to do so. Surrounded by them, dwarfed by them, Dafydd was learning quickly. For one thing, they were huge, far bigger than the poor downtrodden creatures he remembered from the circus and the King's Fair. Even Merriel, who was one of the slighter dragons in the courtyard, was the size of a small house. Her hand wasn't something he could easily take. A finger, on the other hand, he could just about manage.

'What am I—?' he began to ask as the world dissolved in front of his eyes. He felt the Grym surging through him with more power than he had ever experienced. Nothing to which his grandfather had ever subjected him could compare. It filled him to bursting, and then he was flying outwards in all directions, losing himself in a swirl of colour, flashing lights and heat.

'Keep a hold of yourself. Keep a hold of me. We are almost there.' The voice of Merriel filled his head, and as he heard it, so Dafydd remembered that he had a head, a body to go with it. He felt the fine-scaled texture of her finger in his hand and an ache in his arm as if he had been clinging fast for his life.

The light faded like the after-image of staring at the midday sun, and as his vision returned Dafydd saw a swaying green backdrop. He stumbled as if he had been moving forward at great speed and had only just now touched earth. Except that it wasn't earth beneath, nor the heavy stone slabs of the entrance to the Neuadd at his feet. He fell to his knees in sand, soft and white. The air was warmer than Candlehall's slight autumn chill too, and heady with a scent it took him a while to recognize.

'I am sorry I had to bring you here. There are few places I could think of that would be safe. Fewer still with enough shared memory for us both to reach.'

'I . . .' Dafydd struggled to his feet. He recognized the stone pier and derelict buildings, the sea as clear blue as Iolwen's eyes. He knew this place, just couldn't get his head around not being outside the Neuadd any more. 'How did I get here?'

'You travelled the Llinellau Grym. Not something your kind can do.' Merriel raised her head and sniffed the air, turning slowly through a full circle. 'No men have been here since you last left. There is food here, and fresh water. I must leave you now.'

Still reeling from the magic that had transported him halfway across Gwlad in the blink of an eye, Dafydd took a while to understand what the dragon was telling him. 'Leave me here?'

'I must return to the great hall. Even now I can hear Iolwen's plea for help. I made an oath, and a dragon's word is not something given lightly.' Merriel took two steps towards the sea and then seemed to dissolve into the air. Dafydd couldn't be sure, but he thought he saw the lines of the Grym pulse brightly, flashing into his vision unbidden before fading back to nothing. He stared at the spot where the dragon had been, his mind catching up with events, eyes slowly focusing out on to the still sea and the distant small islands of the archipelago. A seabird shrieked overhead, emphasizing the terrible stillness and quiet of the island. He was safe, it was true.

But he was utterly alone.

*

'Cerys has been gone too long. Something is wrong.'

Benfro paced the room, more anxious even than he had been while trapped in the circus. The green dragon's skill as a healer was evident in how little discomfort he felt from the wound in his side, although every so often it would send a little twinge of pain through his muscles, too close to one of his hearts for comfort.

'She will return when she has found Myfanwy, Benfro. Just be patient. Rest. Build your strength.' Martha sat at the table closest to the fireplace, although unlike Xando she clearly had no need of its warmth. Benfro's missing eye showed him how easily she tapped the Grym. It surged around her like a second skin, colouring her aura and constantly changing.

'I don't like it. We're trapped here if someone comes looking for us.' His pacing brought him to the nearest window and he stopped for a moment, creaked open the shutter and peered outside. Snow crusted the glass and the frame, sliding down into an ever thicker pile at the bottom. Through a gap towards the top he could see the storm still raging outside. Was that natural? He couldn't remember it ever having been so bad when he was in Magog's retreat at the top of Mount Arnahi.

'They're not looking for us any more, Benfro. They're trying to figure out where to go from here. Gog was ancient before his kin began to lose interest in the subtle arts. No one remembers a time without him. It's hardly surprising that they are in mourning. Myfanwy will be part of that too, even if Cerys doesn't understand. There will be ceremonies, meetings to decide what to do next, arguments. Dragons live a long time; I'd be very surprised if things didn't take years to settle down, not days.'

'Years?' Benfro turned away from the window too quickly and a stab of pain shot through him. He tried to hide it, but Martha saw. She hurried to his side.

'Rest, Benfro. I know it's hard, but there's nothing you can do right now that's more important than healing. We're as safe here as anywhere. Nobody's going to be out flying over the city while that storm's still raging, so they won't see the hole in the roof. I've a feeling it's not going to let up any time soon either.'

Benfro limped across to the sleeping platform and slumped down on to the bedding. He was tired, he had to admit. Despite all the sleeping he had done since they'd arrived here, he never seemed to wake up refreshed.

'Do you think it's natural, this storm?' he asked as he settled down on his good side. Martha dragged a chair across to the platform and sat down. Without needing to be asked, she extended her aura and tied it in a knot around the rose cord of Magog-tainted Grym that still joined Benfro to the jewel, wherever it was. While he was awake he could keep it distant, but asleep it would invade his dreams without someone to guard him. Martha had taken that task upon herself without any prompting.

'It's very likely. Gog's death has unravelled the last of the great spell he and his brother weaved. This storm is but one symptom of that. I've tried to go back to the tower using the Llinellau, but they are too confusing to travel safely that way. Two worlds merging back together. I don't imagine that's going to happen easily.'

'What do you mean?' Benfro's good eye drooped closed

even as the missing one opened to the Grym and the aethereal more clearly. It was true what Martha had said: the Llinellau were not the solid, reassuring presence he had grown used to. They shimmered like a heat haze and seemed to shift about unless he focused directly on them.

'Think about it.' Martha perched on the edge of her chair, leaning close to Benfro. 'Our world, Magog's world, is one where dragons are timid and small. They hide their magic, even if they are skilled at it. And it's a world where warrior priests wield the Grym like a weapon. You saw what Melyn did to Gog and Enedoc. He is not the only one capable of such terrible, violent acts. I have seen the dragons of Gog's world too, the ones who have turned their backs on the subtle arts. They hunt people for sport. Think of our great cities, Tynhelyg and Candlehall, Tallarddeg and Abervenn. How will they cope if a score or more beasts bigger than you descend upon them? There will be war between dragons and men such as we cannot imagine. Unless we can get between them, explain what has happened.'

'Between them?' Benfro was suddenly wide awake again. 'Between Melyn and . . .'

Martha looked straight at him, shook her head gently. 'I know. I keep thinking about it and I can see no way of reasoning with him. He is Magog's creature now, perhaps always was. Somehow we must find a way to stop him, I just don't know how.'

'Well maybe Myfanwy will have an answer. She's old and wise.' Benfro caught movement in the corner of his eye, then realized that it was his missing eye seeing beyond the room. He pulled himself upright, casting off the bedding so swiftly that Martha was caught by surprise. She dropped her grip on the rose cord and for the briefest of moments he felt something cold and angry and mad a long, long way away. Instinct kicked in and he snapped his own aura around the Grym, knotting it tight as he stumbled towards the door.

It flew open with a crash before he could reach it. The grey dragon, Sir Nanteos, stood in the doorway for a moment, scanning the room. 'Seize him,' he shouted, and a half-dozen more dragons flooded past him. With his missing eye, Benfro saw Martha shrink back into her chair, Xando flatten himself against the stone in the fireplace. He could do nothing to save them, nothing to save himself. Strong hands grabbed him, twisted his arms and forced him down on to his knees. Pain lanced up his side, the wound opening again at the rough treatment. It all happened so quickly he barely had time to breathe.

'Don't struggle, you'll only make it worse.'

For a moment, Benfro thought it was Sir Nanteos speaking, but then he understood the words were in his head, had come not from a dragon but from Martha. Her advice was timely – he would have fought and undone all the healing of the past days – but it also drew attention to herself. The grey dragon looked around the room almost like a dog sniffing out a scent until his eyes alighted on the chair. With a nod of the head he directed one of the younger dragons to fetch her, a third in the direction of the fireplace.

'Bring them too. They have clearly been helping the murderer. They can share in his fate.'

*

'Princess Iolwen, we have to go.'

She had always known the risks, understood that something like this might happen – probably would happen – but still Iolwen could not quite believe it. She stood at the bottom of the stone stairs, looking up at the wall of rubble and fallen masonry completely blocking any passage into the Neuadd. Somewhere up there Dafydd was alone with the dragon. He might be dead already, or trapped under a fallen beam, helpless as the great beast came after him. As if to emphasize her fears, something crashed down above her, shuddering the ground and sending little tendrils of dust down through cracks in the ceiling.

'It's not safe here. We have to go.'

She turned away from the stairs to where Usel the medic stood. He didn't look any more happy about the situation than she did, but he had ever been a pragmatist. She remembered that about him from her long journey to Tynhelyg as a child, so many years earlier. The rest of the party had been sombre, addressing her in Saesneg, but he had made a game of the trip and at the same time taught her rudimentary Llanwennog. She could still remember the little rhymes he had made up, nonsense mostly but funny enough to be easily recited, over and over again. How different might her life at King Ballah's court have been if she had not even been able to speak to the old man. What would he have thought of her then? What would Dafydd have thought?

'I can't leave him, Usel. He's my husband. The father of my son.'

'You cannot help him here, Princess. We must return to the cavern, do what we can from there. Prince Dafydd is very resourceful. I am sure if he can he will survive this and return to you.'

Even Usel seemed to struggle with that lie. Iolwen had always dreamed of returning to Candlehall, of being welcomed home by the people who had sent her to live with their sworn enemy as a hostage to peace. Now that dream was turned nightmare.

Another crashing noise from above and dust billowed from a larger crack, extinguishing all the nearby torches. Iolwen took one last look towards the stairs, dark now, then hurried down the corridor towards the palace.

They found Captain Derridge and his band of misfits in the corridor where they had first parted. Iolwen might have suspected them of having just stayed there and not distracted the dragons at all, were they not to a man bloodied and bruised. The captain himself had one eye swollen shut, his hair slicked red and he held his arm awkwardly by his side. Even so, he pulled himself as upright as he could manage when he saw the princess approach, his other eye searching past her for the rest of the party.

'The prince?' he asked. Iolwen said nothing, but she could see Usel shake his head.

'Ah, by the Wolf!' Derridge winced as he spoke. 'I'm sorry, Your Highness. We did our best to draw him off, that big black bastard. But there's more of them up there every time I look.'

'You did all you could, Captain. I never asked more of you than that.' Iolwen slumped her shoulders, the adrenaline that had brought her so far now leaving her. She would have sat down; they were safe enough this far inside the old stone buildings and there were benches along the wall, but that was not what a queen did in front of her subjects. She took a deep breath and was drawing herself up ready to command, even if she wasn't sure what that command would be, when the noise of running footsteps distracted her. She turned, her heart leaping at the thought that somehow Dafydd had escaped and was hurrying to join them, but the face that greeted her was not her husband. Instead a young lad, perhaps no more than twelve, appeared around the corner that opened on to the steps up to the cloisters.

'Cap'n, sir. Cap'n, sir. Oh.' He stopped in his tracks when he saw the princess, then made to kneel and bow at the same time, almost falling over.

'What's up, Beyn? Thought you were meant to be keeping a quiet eye on them beasts. Not running around shouting and drawing attention to yourself.' Derridge limped forward, catching the lad before he tumbled to the floor. He held him by the arm and turned him so they both faced Iolwen. 'My grandson, Your Highness. All the excitement's gone to his head, I fear.'

The boy looked terrified, but somehow Iolwen knew it was because of her, not the dragons destroying the city and killing anything they could catch. He stared at her, then realized he was staring and dropped his gaze to his feet.

'Begging pardon, ma'am.'

'There's nothing to pardon, Master Beyn. You were about to report to your . . . the captain. Go ahead.'

The boy had looked up again at her words, his eyes widening even more when she said his name. Iolwen smiled, even though she didn't really feel like it, and tried to send soothing thoughts to him. It wasn't as easy without the power of the throne to help her, but it seemed to do the trick.

'I was watching the big doors, like you said, Grandda—sir. After the big black one went inside, there was all kinds of crashing and banging. I thought the Neuadd itself was going to come tumbling down. Only then they starts swooping in. All the other dragons. And they're all landed in the courtyard, all facing the entrance. One of them doors has fallen off. I think the big dragon couldn't fit through. Anyway, I was watching and another dragon comes out. Only it's not the big black one. He's nowhere to be seen. This one's different. It seems, I don't know, cleaner? And it shrieks at them in that weird way they have of talking. And the big red one shrieks back. And, and, and then I saw him. I did. Tiny he was beside the dragon, but he was there.'

'Who was there, lad? You're not making sense.'

'The prince, sir. He was there, and then this new dragon, it looks down at him. He reaches out to it, and then they both just disappear.'

'Disappear?' Iolwen had lost her smile, but something of an idea, a hope, was forming in her mind. 'This other dragon, what did she look like?'

'She, ma'am? Couldn't have said if it was a she or a he. They all look the same to me. Big and mean and ugly.'

Iolwen skimmed the edge of the boy's thoughts, looking for an image of what he had seen. She wasn't as adept at the magic as her sister, not in the same league as King Ballah or Usel, but the blood of Balwen ran through her veins and with it the skill to influence others. And sometimes to read them also. It helped that the boy was all excitement and fear, the images boiling off him like steam. She couldn't see a clear picture, just snippets, details, the curve of a tail, the tuft of an ear. But she did see Dafydd in his mind, and that brought a surge of relief. That he was surrounded by dragons was less encouraging.

'How did they disappear?' She asked the question more to bring the image to the front of the boy's mind than in hope of an answer.

'It was like they just dissolved into the air. But fast, like.' True to her hopes, the scene played out on the edge of his thoughts, and as it did so, Iolwen saw more of what happened than perhaps the boy had been able to comprehend. Dafydd did indeed reach towards the dragon's outstretched hand, and the two of them faded away to nothing. It would have been impossible to believe, had she not seen it happen once before.

'Usel, is it possible that one might use the Llinellau Grym to travel to a distant place?'

The medic took a while to answer, which confirmed her theory to her before he even spoke. 'In the ancient stories that dragons tell to their kitlings some of their heroes can do this. Flow into the Grym and reappear somewhere else instantly. I had thought it just that, a story. But of course all dragon tales are teachings as much as entertainment so there may well be some truth in it.'

'And what about a man? Or a boy not yet grown to adulthood?'

'I have never heard of such a thing, ma'am. The alms-houses at Emmass Fawr are packed with the mindless remnants of men and boys who have lost themselves to the Grym. Their bodies stay behind, only their minds disappearing into the Llinellau. I do not believe it is possible for our kind.'

'And yet I watched a young man disappear from the executioner's block in Tynhelyg. Dissolve in front of my eyes and flow into the Grym. There was no dragon there to help him; he did it by himself.'

'Errol?' Usel frowned. 'But how?'

'I don't know, but it gives me hope that Dafydd lives still. The dragon we met on the island, Merriel. I think she may have come back to save us. I was calling to her when we were trapped near the throne.' Iolwen's answer was cut short by a roar from the courtyard, followed by a crash that shook the whole building. Stone blocks the size of a man's head tumbled down the stairwell and into the corridor as something battered against the cloisters above. 'But now is not the time for speculation. Now we must flee before these creatures destroy us all.'

14

The Order of the Candle is the youngest of the great religious orders of the House of Balwen. Founded in the time of King Divitie III, it initially consisted of six warrior priests of the High Ffrydd and six medics of the Ram, charged by the king with travelling the length and breadth of the Twin Kingdoms to carry out a census of his lands and peoples. A task that at first seemed simple in the end took more than twenty years, and was not in fact completed until the reign of Divitie IV was in its second year.

Such was the success of the census that the new king decided to make it an ongoing process, with each village and town being visited at least once every five years. The original warrior priests and medics had already been joined by a small army of clerks and predicants, and it was only a matter of time before the order became as much an administrative body as one charged solely with collecting information.

Through generations of service, the order has strengthened its hold on the administration of the Twin Kingdoms, and perfected its methods of record-keeping and information-gathering. It is perhaps the least glamorous of the orders, at least to

those not privy to its secrets. But whereas the Order
of the High Ffrydd is the king's sword, the Order of
the Candle is his eyes and ears. With clerks of the
Candle in every town and city throughout the
realm, it is said that no man can sneeze at dusk and
the seneschal not know it by dawn.

Father Romney,
The Order of the Candle – a Brief Introduction

'Have those Candles arrived yet? They should be here
by now.'

Inquisitor Melyn paced around the dais upon which
King Ballah's throne stood empty. He knew he could sit
in it and no one would complain. He had earned the right
by combat, after all, and taken it up not long afterwards.
Only now he viewed the throne with a mixture of unease
and disdain. It was a focus for the power of the Grym, the
subtle arts so beloved of dragons, but he didn't need it. He
didn't need the help of the vast collection of jewels deep
beneath the throne room either. The power was his to
wield wherever he was and whenever he felt like it. He
understood so much more.

'The first wave from Tochers arrived this morning,
sire, along with a good number of Queen Beulah's troops.'
Captain Osgal stood guard, for all that the inquisitor
needed a guard. He looked awful, the burns on his face
and hands still not healed. Melyn knew that he could fix
the captain the same way the Shepherd – Magog – had
healed his own injuries over a lifetime of service. A lifetime of lies. He wouldn't though, at least not yet. An

injured and irritable Osgal was far better at keeping the troops in line than one distracted by the spoils of conquest.

'Who is in charge? General Otheng or that oaf Cachog?'

'Otheng, sire. He was to be stationed at Tynewydd, but with Geraint's army routed and Tordu's men scattered, he thought it best to head straight here. He's waiting outside.'

'Excellent. Send him in then.'

Melyn waited while Osgal retraced his steps to the main doors, flung them open and barked a command to the guards waiting outside. The inquisitor should have been irritated, impatient that everything took so long, but now he felt only calm. The Shepherd – Magog – had lived for thousands of years, his spirit still powerful for thousands more after his untimely death. The passage of minutes, hours, days meant nothing when you could imagine millennia. There was still much to do, however, and at the speed of men rather than dragons.

'Inquisitor Melyn. It is good to see you well.' General Otheng bowed only slightly as he approached the dais, never taking his eyes off Melyn's. As the second son of the Duke of Dina, he should have shown greater courtesy to one his senior in rank, but he was perhaps the most seasoned soldier not in the Order of the High Ffrydd, and as such Melyn was prepared to allow him some leeway. Chances were that he would soon be Duke of Tynhelyg anyway.

'You have made good time. Tell me, is there any news of Tordu? Prince Geraint and his army are no more, but I don't want the people rallying to his uncle.'

'You need not worry yourself about him, Your Grace.' Otheng reached for the clasp on a leather bag slung around his neck. Fumbling it open one-handed, he pulled out a silver amulet set with a polished red jewel. 'Found him in the woods not far from Tynewydd. What was left of him, that is. He'd fought off some of those great beasts, killed one by the looks of the carcass lying close by him.'

'Tordu? Really? Was he alone?'

'A way off from the main fighting, for sure. I think he must have been trying to escape, for all the good it did him. Lost his guts in more ways than one.'

Melyn felt his side, the scar of golden scales where Benfro had almost done the same to him. Normally he might have enjoyed Otheng's joke, but now it fell flat.

'You found no curses on this?' He nodded at the amulet.

'I wasn't born yesterday, Melyn. I had one of your warrior priests with me; got him to check it over. No way I'd be holding it now if he hadn't. There were some nasty things lurking in it for the unwary, but it's fine now.'

Melyn regarded the amulet with wary eyes, remembering the fate of the poor soul who had foolishly picked up Prince Geraint's golden version of the same thing. 'Frecknock? What do you make of this?'

General Otheng's face paled as the dragon emerged from her resting place beside King Ballah's throne.

'Your Grace. I . . . You have a . . .'

'Dragon?' Melyn couldn't help but chuckle at the man's fear. 'Do not concern yourself. Frecknock serves me, and she is as skilled in the ways of the Grym as any man. Hand her the amulet. She won't bite unless I tell her to.'

Otheng held out the amulet on its chain, the shaking of

189

his hand making it jerk up and down like a man freshly hanged. Frecknock took it in one outstretched hand, tugging slightly until the general released his grip.

'This is very much like the other one, but silver where that of Prince Geraint was gold. The gem in the centre is not dissimilar to those in King Ballah's ring, smaller chips from the heart stone. I suspect that they might have been used for communication, among other things.'

'Other things?' Melyn asked.

'Like the ring it is a focus for the Grym. It gives the wearer greater control over the subtle arts. Both Tordu and Geraint were adepts, I am sure, and with these amulets they would have been able to read the minds of the weak-willed. Influence them. Perhaps even make them do things they would not ordinarily have done.' Frecknock approached the inquisitor, offering the amulet to him. He took it, feeling the force of the Shepherd in it, the force of Magog. It called to him, as did the other stones hidden away in the cavern beneath his feet, a siren song of power that was so sweet and seductive. But it spoke of something else too. A vast stone palace surrounded by familiar mountains. A tower so tall it pierced the clouds. Unfinished business.

'You had best take this, Otheng.' Melyn passed the amulet back to the general. 'It will help you maintain communication with the rest of the Twin Kingdoms while you establish our rule over this land.'

General Otheng was absent-mindedly wrapping the silver chain around his hand when the import of Melyn's words hit him. 'Establish rule? Me?'

'I cannot think of a man more qualified, and I'm sure

Her Majesty the queen will agree. Llanwennog is now a province of the Twin Kingdoms. It will need a duke to rule it. Have the clerks of the Candle begin a census. They'll need to work with those local administrators we have already vetted. King Ballah wasn't a fool; he ran his kingdom efficiently enough. I see no point in starting from scratch. You will be in charge, General. Make sure our soldiers treat the people of Llanwennog well. We're not here to pillage and then run. Do a good job and I've no doubt you will be well rewarded.'

Otheng stared for a moment. Melyn could read his thoughts clearly enough, but they were written across his face as well. The titles and land at Dina would always be his brother's to inherit, but a dukedom that covered the entirety of Llanwennog was a prize indeed.

'I will not disappoint, Your Grace.' He slapped a fist to his chest in salute. 'But will you not be staying? Your warrior priests—'

'Are needed elsewhere. You may keep the few who came with you, but my troops must take leave of the city. It is yours to rule now. I suggest you begin immediately.'

Only a few stragglers remained in the corridor when Iolwen, Usel and their newly formed guard of honour returned. Some black-robed predicants in a huddle were arguing with a few clerks of the Candle as to whether they should descend or not, and two of the Llanwennog palace guard were exchanging nervous glances. When they saw the princess they snapped to attention, but she could see their eyes roving over the group in search of the man they naturally deferred to.

'Prince Dafydd was separated from us. He has escaped, and so must we before my sister arrives.'

The two guards hesitated for a moment, and in the silence one of the clerks approached.

'Your Highness. This is most irregular. The secrets of the House of Balwen have been kept, well, secret for thousands of years.'

Iolwen drew herself up to her full height, still too short to face down the man as much as she would have liked. Still, he quailed. He was thin, as many Candles were, and his skin had the pallor of one who rarely ventured outside.

'Your name?'

'I am Ioan, ma'am, chief actuary to the victuallers' sub-committee. My remit is—'

'You are the most senior Candle here?' Iolwen didn't give the man the opportunity to bore her to death with a long description of his duties. She had left this palace as a six-year-old girl, but even at that age she had learned not to let a Candle speak for any longer than was necessary.

'I . . . That is to say, yes.' Ioan dipped his head in a bow.

'How many Candles are there still in the city?'

'Our numbers were not great to begin with, ma'am. Seneschal Padraig has spread us around the Twin King-doms, and many have been tied up with the administration of Qu— your sister's war against Llanwennog. Before your arrival our numbers were not more than three hundred, I believe.'

'And how many remain? How many have refused to enter the cavern?' Iolwen nodded at the open doorway.

'Perhaps half that number, ma'am. I am disappointed to say that most of the predicants have chosen to save their skins rather than serve the crown to which they have sworn fealty. Their names are recorded and they will not be added to the rolls when the time comes for graduation.'

'You do not feel my invitation is sufficient to allow entry?'

'Only the reigning monarch may grant that boon, ma'am.'

'So you will be staying here then?'

'I have no choice. My sacred oath forbids any other course of action.'

Iolwen studied the man's face. He wasn't old, maybe only in his thirties where men of his calling might well expect to see their eighth decade. He had about him that same dry, dense quality as the ledgers he no doubt spent all his time creating, studying and amending. If he kept away from the dragons, it was likely Beulah's army would simply set him back to his business; he was not senior enough to have been part of Padraig's conspiracy. The predicants behind him were a different matter. Young, scared and with only basic training, they were expendable. Iolwen could see them being strung up as a warning to others not to betray the queen. She addressed the nearest of them, a lad who looked like he'd only just stopped wearing short trousers.

'What is your name, Predicant?'

The youngster's eyes widened in surprise and fear. No doubt he was from a little village in the middle of nowhere, overwhelmed by the honour of being chosen. 'M-me, Your Highness?'

'Yes, you.'

'Umm, Bendle, ma'am.'

'Well, Master Bendle. Do you wish to stay here and take your chances with the dragons and my sister? Or would you rather flee the city and go home to your family? There is no shame in that, not in these circumstances.'

Bendle's eyes widened even further, until Iolwen feared his eyeballs might pop out. 'It is forbidden, ma'am.'

'Your seneschal was eaten by one of those dragons, you know. My sister appears to command them. Do you think she will treat you well or just feed you to the beasts?'

The predicant swallowed hard. His face had shown little colour to start with, but now it was paler than Candle Ioan's pasty complexion. Iolwen decided she could spare no more time trying to persuade them. No one could say she hadn't tried.

'Suit yourself.' She shook her head once, then turned back to her guard. 'Seize them, will you? If they're forced down the stairs then no one can say they broke their precious vows.'

Without another word, a dozen of the irregular soldiers leaped upon the predicants, put them into armlocks and marched them off down the stairs. Captain Derridge himself went for the clerk, but Iolwen put a hand on his arm.

'Not him. He can stay. My sister will have need of his skills. And besides, he doesn't really want to leave his beloved books.'

Ioan bowed his head in acceptance of her appraisal. His whole demeanour was so dry it made Iolwen's skin itch. He looked over to the doorway where the last of the barely protesting predicants was disappearing out of sight, then back to the princess with the ghost of a smile. 'I do not think your sister would have been so considerate. I will pray for your safe journey, Your Highness.' And with that he turned and walked off slowly down the corridor.

'He's a bit of an odd fish,' Captain Derridge said as the clerk of the Candle disappeared into the dusty gloom.

'His kind often are. It's their books. They dry out their brains from staring at them too long.' Iolwen tried a smile, then remembered who was missing from the party. For a moment she had been distracted enough to forget Dafydd's uncertain plight. She had to find the dragon Merriel, had to track her husband down. Bad enough that their triumph had turned so quickly to despair; she didn't think she could live without seeing his face again.

The first thing Errol noticed was the cold whistling around his bare feet and ankles. Flurries of snow whipped on the wind, carried in through the vast windows, which opened out on to a raging blizzard. The storm should have knocked him off his feet, such was its ferocity outside, but something held it back from the threshold, damping its force although doing nothing to alleviate the chill. His head was surprisingly cold too, and when he reached up to feel it he realized his hair had been shaved off. Without a thought he reached out for the Grym, tapping it for warmth, then yelped as it rushed into him with unexpected force. Concentrating harder, he calmed the unruly flow, seeing the lines more clearly now. They shimmered and writhed like disturbed snakes, twisted by some terrible cataclysm that centred around the spot where he had seen the great carved writing desk. As he looked, so he could see how they formed an invisible curtain over the great windows too. Once it would have been completely impermeable, but now it was failing, buckling under the onslaught of the weather outside.

Errol was certain this was the place he had seen before, but it was changed utterly. In his dreams the tower room had been cluttered, but there had been a certain order to it. The long workbenches had been the right way up, the strange apparatus arranged on their tops whole and unbroken. Now glass fragments glittered on a floor strewn with broken vessels and twisted metal. Chairs lay smashed against the walls and the great fireplace was empty, no flames leaping from the damp charred logs. The golden cage in which Martha had been confined lay on the floor close to the writing desk. Both appeared unharmed, but all around was a scene of chaos. Scrolls lay in haphazard piles on the floor, pages ripped from books fluttering in the oddly muted wind that whistled between the two arched openings where the glass windows had been. A few scraps of frame hung from one hinge, but the rest was long gone.

'So it's true. He really did meet his end here. But what manner of beast could slay one so powerful? And here in his lair?' Myfanwy picked her way around the room, moving broken furniture out of her way as she approached the fireplace and the writing desk. Errol came at it from the other side, but was distracted by Nellore.

'Freezing in here. How can you stand there in your bedclothes?'

She was better dressed for the weather than him, but only just. Her skirt was a thick dark wool, and fell to just above the ground, mostly covering a pair of shiny leather boots. She wore a jacket of the same material, embroidered around the lapels with fine silver thread. It was probably quite warm, but the blouse underneath it was thin cotton. Errol was about to tell her to use the Grym for warmth, then reminded himself that not everyone knew that magic. The people of this world seemed particularly ill-attuned to it. He looked around for something that would do as a cloak, which was when he noticed the body lying over by the entrance to the stairwell.

How he could have missed it, he couldn't be sure. It was a dragon twice the size of Myfanwy, and even though it lay on its back, wings twisted and broken, head lolling, its belly still rose higher off the ground than Errol standing. Perhaps it was the shadows, or maybe the complete lack of any spark of life. More likely that he had been too busy looking the other way to notice. Now he had seen it, however, he couldn't take in anything else.

Treading as carefully as he could, Errol moved across the room until he was right beside the dead creature. He didn't recognize it, but it was clearly not one of the feral beasts from the Twmp. It was too clean, its scales polished and shiny except for a half-dozen places where something appeared to have burned through them leaving perfectly round holes. There was no blood around the wounds, and when he leaned closer to inspect the nearest one, Errol could smell something that wasn't quite burning but gave the impression of fire. Like the tang of two rocks cracked together.

'I know what has done this,' he said, sensing Myfanwy beside him even though he hadn't heard her cross the room.

'Ah, Enedoc, you were meant for greater things than this.' She crouched down beside the dead dragon, reached out and gently touched his face.

'You knew him?' Errol asked.

'I raised him from an egg. Enedoc son of Gog was my eldest. He must be given the respect due all our kind in death.' Myfanwy set about arranging the dragon's body, carefully folding in his wings and arms. 'I will take him to the place of his hatching. He can wait there a while, but not too long. Oh, these old bones.' She reached out and took the dead dragon's head in both hands before fixing Errol with a look as weary as he felt. 'I won't be long,' she said, then disappeared, the corpse of Enedoc going with her into the Grym.

'Did she just leave us here?' Nellore had wandered across the room to see what was happening, arriving just in time for Myfanwy's disappearance. Now she stared at the dragon-shaped empty space on the floor with her mouth open, her arms hugged to her sides for warmth.

'Looks like it. Let's hope she's not gone long. Not sure how easy it will be to get back. Not sure where back is, if I'm honest.' Errol hugged his arms around himself, shivering as the cold wind whipped at his bedclothes and the bare skin of his feet. His shaved scalp leaked heat, chilling his head and making it hard to concentrate on tapping the unruly Grym for warmth.

'What is this place? What happened here?'

'This? This is the top of Gog's tower. This is where I saw Martha, trapped in that cage over there.' Errol stepped carefully through the rubbish towards it. Nellore hurried ahead, booted feet unconcerned by the shards of broken glass everywhere, so that by the time Errol reached it she was already inside. The bars of the cage had been woven through with stiff material, pieces of wood and discarded parchment so that it resembled nothing so much as the nest of some giant carrion bird. Nellore emerged from the darkness bearing a heavy woollen blanket and a silver bowl with a wooden spoon sticking out of it.

'Looks like someone's been living in here.' She sniffed the bowl, wrinkled her nose at something unpleasant. 'Not for a while mind.'

Errol took the blanket from her, lifting it to his nose. He didn't know whether he was expecting to smell anything; he wasn't sure he'd have recognized Martha's scent anyway after their long parting. But there was something in the rough fabric, an aroma of autumn leaves and dark loam that sparked a memory. He took another breath and could almost see himself back in the woods close to his mother's cottage. That long summer before Inquisitor Melyn and Princess Beulah had arrived in the village to destroy everyone's lives.

'Here, what's this? Looks like someone's been having a bonfire.'

Errol snatched himself out of the dream as he saw Nellore walk over to a spot behind the writing desk. The floor there was clear except for a pile of fine white ash roughly the shape of a dragon. The breeze picked at it, whittling down the heap so that in parts the flagstones of the floor showed through. He remembered a very similar pile of ashes in the long grass on the empty plains of north Llanwennog. The last remains of a man called Tibbits, devoured by dragon-breathed flame.

'Careful. It might be dangerous.'

'Nonsense. It's just ash.' Nellore scuffed at the edges of the pile with her boot. 'Oh, but there's something in here.'

Errol opened his mouth to tell her not to pick up what he knew must be there, but he trod on a shard of glass and let out a squawk of pain instead. It was enough to distract her for a moment, but she was already crouched down, hand reaching into the pile as the wind brushed the last of the ash from the top of Gog's reckoned jewels.

'Don't touch them!' He gasped out the words over the agony in his foot. Too late, Nellore's fingers connected with the jewels and they lit up like the sun. Her eyes turned bright as all the Grym rushed from the room into her, through her.

15

The conjuring of the Fflam Gwir for the reckoning of a dead dragon's jewels is the most important responsibility of a mage. While most dragons possess a varying degree of skill in the subtle arts, few have the depth of knowledge required to perform this key act. Instead, they must resort to using a potent mixture of rare oils and minerals to bring forth the flame, setting firm the memories and learning of the deceased.

Second in importance only to the reckoning, the mage is charged with taking the reckoned jewels and placing them with those of dragons already passed. For death is only a stage in our existence, and transitory at that. Collections of dragons' jewels, sometimes called hoards by those who do not understand them, are places of great power in the Grym. Laid to rest, the collected jewels feed off this power, the experience and wisdom of generations mingling as one. Such places are protected from accidental discovery by wards the mage will maintain daily, linked to their own life force. And when they die, for death must come to us all, those wards will be tied to the dead mage's own reckoned jewels, strengthening the protection already provided by mages long since passed.

It is for this reason that the reckoned jewels of dead mages are not laid to rest alongside those of their fellow dragons. Instead, they are hidden away in solitude, there to watch over us for all eternity.

Corwen teul Maddau,
The Way of the Mage

Unlike the corridors and palace above, the cavern deep beneath the Neuadd was packed with people. Only a small fraction of the number who must have passed through already, but it was still enough to make the air taste stale. A line of Llanwennog palace guards and nervous predicants of the Order of the Candle had so far managed to keep the crowd away from the stone columns and their priceless contents, but a couple of the curtains Teryll had draped over them had slipped, and the glow of the jewels bathed everything in a hellish red light. They seemed to burn brighter, or so Iolwen thought. Almost as if they were feeding off the Grym emanating from so many people collected in one place.

She directed Captain Derridge and his ragtag band of soldiers towards one of the exit tunnels, then set about finding Lady Anwen and Prince Iolo. They were close to the centre of the cavern, directly beneath the Obsidian Throne itself, and Iolwen found Teryll and Captain Venner there too. The people were subdued, but even a whisper can be loud when a thousand people are making it. Iolwen thought that the susurrus would die down as she moved away from the crowd. Instead it grew louder, and as she focused on the words, she realized that the voices weren't human, but the near-silent moans and wails of the jewels themselves.

She had barely taken her sleeping infant from Anwen's arms, scarcely had time to cuddle her child and shed a silent, hopeless tear at how much he resembled his missing father, before a cry of alarm went up close to one of the tunnel entrances. Clasping Prince Iolo tight to her, she hurried over to see what was happening. In the confined space it was hard to tell how many people there were, but it seemed to be more than before. The red light cast awkward shadows too, making it almost impossible to see the tunnel itself. Then she saw the young Predicant Trell, his hand still wrapped in blood-soaked bandages, gesticulating wildly as he tried to control a crowd of agitated people.

'All will be well. Do not panic.' Iolwen suppressed her own anxiety as best she could, projecting an aura of peace over the crowd. It calmed them a little, but she could feel the fear bubbling underneath the surface, the panic just waiting to erupt. She could ill-afford a riot in this confined space; no need for dragons if the people trampled each other.

'Master Trell, what is happening?' She hurried across to where he stood. His face was pale, his exhaustion clear in the way his shoulders slumped and he swayed ever so slightly. As he saw her, he straightened.

'I do not know, Your Highness. The line was moving slowly, but we'd got most of the people out. I turned my back for a second and when I looked again the tunnel was gone.'

Iolwen could see now. The shape she had taken for the

tunnel mouth was just a shadow on the rock. 'Make way,' she said, putting enough compulsion behind the words for the anxious mob to comply. When she reached the wall, there was no sign of an entrance. Only the tracks worn in the dusty floor by a thousand pairs of feet showed that anything had been here at all.

'How can this be?' She put a hand out, felt the rough stone. No magic coursed through it, and when she tried to summon the lines to her vision there was nothing to see.

'Take the prince, please, Anwen.' Iolwen passed back her sleeping infant with great reluctance, but this was not something she could do while carrying him. She steadied herself, blanking out the growing fear all around her, and let herself slip briefly into the aethereal. That was how she had located the tunnels before, but now the silver arch was gone. No trace in the stone that there had ever been a way out.

'What of the other tunnels?' Iolwen stumbled out of the trance and set off towards the next entrance. Before she was even close she could see that it was gone, and the next as well. The fourth exit sealed up as she approached it, the people who had been about to enter tumbling to the floor as if pushed away by an invisible hand. Beyond it the fifth entrance remained open, and the crowd surged towards it, their panic growing.

'Be calm, but be swift.' She placed her hand on the wall close to the tunnel entrance, feeling the surge in the Grym here as her presence reinforced whatever magic controlled this escape route. Tapping it for strength, Iolwen pushed the compulsion out across the room, backing up her words. The rush slowed, feet falling into a steady rhythm as they began to move like a well trained army on parade.

Soon the people were marching through the opening three and four abreast. Iolwen tried not to dwell too much on what might have caused the other tunnels to disappear. No doubt it was her sister's doing. That this one was still open left too many uncomfortable questions, but then the existence of the tunnels was just as troubling. Where they might lead, doubly so. What had happened to the thousands who had already left? Were they trapped in the rock, crushed like poor Predicant Trell's fingers? Or had they fallen into the waiting hands of Beulah's tame dragons?

Iolwen was aware of an increase in the noise echoing in the huge cavern, a general unease threatening to erupt into chaos. She tried hard to quell her own fears, knowing how easy it was to send them to everyone, amplified by the powerful Grym in the place. But the doubts were not easy to ignore, and the more she tried, the more she could feel control slipping away. Then a hand rested on her shoulder and she felt the familiar presence of the medic Usel.

'Take my strength if you need it. Calm yourself. There are not many left to go.'

Iolwen took a deep breath and focused on the central pillar that rose to the cavern ceiling. Above it stood the Obsidian Throne and seeped into that was the combined knowledge and skill of generations of the House of Balwen. Her father had sat upon that throne, and her grandfather before him. Back and back until the time of great Balwen himself. And now she could see that it had been there even before then, a centre of such potency she could not even begin to understand it. But she didn't need to understand, just needed to know that it had accepted her as it had accepted her sister. If they shared nothing else, then the blood of Balwen ran through both of their veins. She could save her people, ease their fear, help them escape.

'You can relax now, Majesty. We are all but done.'

The voice startled her out of what had almost been an aethereal trance. Sweat prickled Iolwen's face and her legs felt as weary as if she had marched a dozen leagues. She had not felt time passing, but hours must have gone by. There was no way that so many people could have entered the dark tunnel ahead of her in mere minutes.

'How long . . .?'

'Enough. That is all that matters.' Usel stood beside her, his hand still on her shoulder, but as he spoke so he lifted it off. Judging by the way he tensed at the movement he was as exhausted as Iolwen, the both of them strained almost to the limit by the effort of channelling such potent Grym. She looked around the cavern once more, noticing that the jewels had darkened again, the whispers become less intrusive. It was still an uncomfortable place to be, as was evident by the way the last few remaining people clustered around the tunnel entrance. Captain Venner and a half-dozen palace guards were still there, as was Teryll and Predicant Trell. Iolwen was pleased to see Mercor Derridge and his motley band had waited for her too.

'You must all go now. It can only be a matter of time before this tunnel disappears too. I will take the prince.'

The infant beamed a happy smile as Iolwen stumbled over to take him from Lady Anwen.

'Everyone else must leave before the two of us. I don't want a repeat of the last time.'

Trell nodded his understanding, then turned and stepped into the tunnel. Its mouth was black, no light shining from within and precious little of the dark red glow from the jewels penetrating beyond the entrance. Attuned to the Grym, Iolwen thought she felt a surge in the force as he disappeared and concentrated a little harder on the lines as the others walked through one by one. It was similar to what the young lad had seen when Dafydd disappeared, a feeling of displacement that was hard to understand. Could this tunnel be dragon magic? The thought was at once exciting and disturbing.

'I will see you at the other end, Your Majesty.' Usel was the last to go, giving her a solemn bow before he too was swallowed up by the tunnel. Iolwen paused a moment, looking once more around the now-empty cavern. In her arms, young Prince Iolo wriggled and then let out a tiny wail of impatience. The poor thing must have been starving, but it was not the time nor the place to feed him.

'O Dafydd, I hope you are safe, wherever you are.' Iolwen faced the black mouth of the tunnel, took a deep breath and stepped inside.

It was hardly the triumphal return Beulah had been expecting when she had left her capital all those months ago. Then her plan had been to tour the Twin Kingdoms, meet her people and drum up support for her war with Llanwennog, distracting King Ballah while Melyn found his way into the northlands. She had imagined returning to a city full of joy and welcome, its people happy that their queen had once and for all put an end to the menace of their godless neighbours. What greeted her was rather different.

The main city gates had been destroyed by the efforts of Sir Sgarnog and his friends. Stout walls that had stood for generations had been reduced to so much rubble in just a few days. The streets were empty save for the occasional stray dog searching for food. Here and there the half-eaten carcasses of larger animals rotted in the heat, and there were human remains aplenty too. When she had first heard of the treachery of Candlehall she had wanted nothing more than to raze the place to the ground, kill every living being within its walls. Now faced with her wish almost fulfilled, Beulah began to see the wisdom in restraint.

'This will take a long time to rebuild,' she said under her breath. Her horse pricked its ears as it heard her words, and beside her, looming on his massive stallion, Clun leaned forward.

'My lady?'

'I had not imagined there would be so much damage. It will take months, years to rebuild.'

'An opportunity to make it better, stronger. If more of these dragons appear, we will need to rethink the design of our cities.'

'More of them? I thought you said they considered you their leader. Will they not do as you say?'

'These ones, my lady, for now. But what if one of them challenges me for the leadership? What if all of them do? And dragons live long lives. Far longer than you and I. Who will control them once we are gone? It pains me to say it, but the warrior priests of the Order of the High Ffrydd are no match for these beasts.'

Beulah said nothing in reply. His thoughts mirrored her own. For generations the threat from dragons had been an abstract thing, the creatures themselves too small, timid and few in number to pose any kind of danger. All that had changed with the appearance of Caradoc. No, even before that, with Benfro. Where had they come from, these dragons so horribly reminiscent of the beasts of legend?

They took the route Beulah had ridden in a carriage on the way to her coronation, not the quickest way to the palace and the Neuadd, but the widest street. The steep, narrow way was blocked in at least two places by fallen buildings, impassable except on foot and even then dangerous. Slowly their small party picked its way past the rubble of destroyed lives, trying to ignore the stench that hung over the city like a curse.

Things were slightly better as they approached the palace itself. The parade ground to the front of the huge complex of buildings was mostly clear, even though the main gates had been knocked in and the heavy wooden doors hung broken. A smear of dried brown blood and ichor marked the marble steps in front of the entrance, where something, someone, had met a decidedly sticky end. Beulah felt a disturbance in the Grym here, but she was too much on edge to focus on it.

'We should sweep the palace before you enter, my lady.' Clun dismounted, letting his horse stand where it would. The great stallion didn't move a muscle until he patted it on the neck, then it lowered its head to sniff the stain on the steps once before walking purposefully over to the ornamental fountain for a drink.

'I'm not a helpless princess.' Beulah swung off her own horse, letting her senses expand around her. The warrior priests who made up her guard were tight behind their mental shields, and she knew them all well enough after months on the road. Sensing others within the building would not be difficult, especially given how few of them were left. She brushed past Clun, who looked like he was trying to decide whether to argue with her or not, and climbed swiftly up the steps to enter the palace. Her palace.

The first thing she noticed was the floor. Normally the rooms were kept scrupulously clean by an invisible army of servants. Now grit crunched underfoot, and looking up at the ceiling she could see cracks in the plaster, whole chunks of cornice missing entirely. Paintings hung askew on the walls, some fallen completely, as if the existence of dragons had twisted and buckled the world, picked up the whole hill and shaken it vigorously. In the outer reception rooms parts of the ceiling had fallen in completely, blocking the main stairs to the residential floors, so Beulah set off for the kitchen wing, Clun close at her heels.

They met no one, and the kitchens themselves were deserted. Beulah cast her thoughts out wide, touching the alien minds of the dragons wheeling in the sky overhead, but she could sense no one in the entire palace beyond their immediate group.

'Come with me,' she ordered, setting off up the servants' stairs at speed.

'Your Majesty, should we not proceed with caution?' Captain Celtin asked. He had already ordered two men to sprint up the steps ahead of them.

'The palace is deserted, Captain. We are in no danger from my sister's supporters.'

'I was more worried about a ceiling collapsing, ma'am. I never thought to see such destruction. Do these beasts not understand people live here?'

'Oh, I think they know that well enough.' Beulah reached the top of the stairs and headed swiftly down the corridor towards the door she knew would be standing ajar even though it was supposed to be the best-protected secret in the palace, if not the entire Twin Kingdoms. The dragons might not have much appreciation for the labours of men, but what Iolwen had done was a far greater act of vandalism. The closer they came, the more obvious it was that a great number of people had come this way. The dust was trodden by countless feet, the tapestries on the walls hanging at odd angles or ripped. A couple of benches close to the doorway had been knocked over in the rush, or so it appeared.

'Clun, you come with me. The rest of you stand guard. No one is to enter this doorway without my express permission.' Beulah didn't wait for acknowledgement, but set off down the steps, soon finding herself in the great cavern deep beneath the Neuadd.

'My lady, what have they done?' Clun stopped by her side, following her gaze. Curtains Beulah recognized from the public reception rooms had been draped about the stone columns that housed the royal collection of dragon jewels, no doubt to dissuade casual pilfering and dampen the magic that flooded the room. The deep red glow was muted too, making it harder to see in the perpetual gloom.

'Ignore it, my love. There are more pressing concerns.' Beulah set off around the perimeter of the cavern, studying the rocks for the places Inquisitor Melyn had shown her so many years before. What would she have given to have him by her side now? She shook her head to dismiss the thought. The inquisitor had his own business to attend to. He would return as soon as he was able, of that she was certain.

'It should be here.' Beulah placed her hand on the rock, felt the warmth of it like a living thing. The Grym was concentrated around this cavern in a manner she couldn't understand. Normally deep rock interfered with the life force, blocking it completely in places like the lower levels of Emmass Fawr and the dungeons of Castell Glas where they had interrogated Father Tolley. Perhaps it was the concentration of jewels, so inherently full of Grym, but for whatever reason, the magic was not working.

'Is something wrong, my lady?' Clun asked.

'Each tunnel is concealed by magic. Only one whose veins carry the blood of King Balwen can reveal it. This one has opened for me before. And yet now it remains closed.'

'It must be the dragons' doing. They said they would seal the exits.'

'I did not expect them to seal the entrances too. And too late, by the look of things. Everyone has left already. My traitorous people have fled.'

'Are they all sealed? Angharad the Red has not yet returned, so maybe that exit is still working?'

Beulah ran her hand over the stone once more, then set off for the next point, and the next. She could see the prints of many feet in the dirt floor that skirted the edge of the chamber. How many hundreds had passed through here? This place was meant to be a secret! How could her sister have betrayed the family so? But then the family had betrayed Iolwen, hadn't they? Sent her off to live with the enemy when she was only six years old. It was hardly surprising this was the way she saw fit to repay that kindness.

Four exits remained stubbornly hidden to her touch, and Beulah was almost back to the stone steps leading up to the palace now. Slow to follow, Clun caught up with her as she reached for the spot where Melyn had shown her the fifth tunnel. She took his hand for luck, then brushed the rock with delicate fingers. The Grym surged around her and the cavern wall dissolved into blackness as the tunnel was revealed. A faint wind ruffled her hair, warm and carrying a scent that she couldn't immediately identify. Distant sounds echoed from the stone, rhythmic and soft like waves on a beach. Beulah took a step forward, intrigued by the mystery, but a hand on her shoulder stopped her.

'My lady, it is not safe. Angharad the Red might close this off at any time. What would happen to us if we were inside it then?'

Beulah shrugged off Clun's concern, but she stepped back nonetheless. The tunnel remained open, and she stared at it for a while, wondering where it led. But there were more urgent matters than this to attend to. She took one more look around the cavern, then strode to the exit. At the top of the stairs, Captain Celtin and the warrior priests were waiting, spread out in an arc around the doorway as if they expected to be rushed at any moment. It would have been funny had the silence of the normally bustling palace not been so disconcerting.

'Captain, send word to the army to reoccupy the city. We'll need teams to begin clearing up the mess these dragons have caused.'

Celtin slapped a fist to his chest in salute. 'I will suggest to His Honour Lord Beylin that he might like to oversee that, ma'am. It is the sort of task he would relish.'

Beulah smiled at the joke. It was no secret Beylin was ill-suited to warfare. She was less happy about how much richer the reconstruction of Candlehall would make him, and how much more indebted to him she would be, but no one else would be up to the task.

'Good idea, Captain. Make it so.' She turned once more to Clun, took a deep breath and steadied herself, aware that this was the final task and the one she had been dreading. 'Now it is time we went and reclaimed my throne.'

Errol thought he was going to faint. The jewels sucked all the life out of the room, and from farther afield too, heedless of anything but their own desperate need. He dropped heavily to his knees, could scarcely muster the energy to put a hand out and stop himself from slamming into the floor. He had been weak even before he had arrived, now he was being pulled apart by the newly awakened jewels. But his torment was nothing compared to what Nellore must have been experiencing.

Her eyes blazed bright with a terrible power she couldn't possibly understand. She was held fast by that tiny connection between one fingertip and the pile. Her hair stood out from her head in a wide arc and steam rose from her jacket. If he didn't do something soon she would be burned up completely.

Errol closed off his mind as if he were sparring with Father Andro back at Emmass Fawr or trying to hide his thoughts from King Ballah in Tynhelyg. It had been part of his novitiate training, and he remembered too the words of Father Castlemilk in his *Introduction to the Order of the High Ffrydd*. There were exercises he knew if he could just concentrate, routines that would lessen the effect of whatever magic the jewels were weaving.

Slowly the tension eased, the sense of having his insides sucked out of him faded away. And as he regained some strength, so Errol saw his aura, tight around him like a second skin. It *was* a second skin, one he could control if he could just concentrate enough. He had used it, extended it and wrapped it tight around that rose cord of Grym that linked Magog's malign essence to Benfro. Perhaps he could do the same with Nellore. If he could just get a little closer.

He had to hurry. Her skin was turning red now and she was shaking so hard her scream sounded more like a gurgle. Ignoring the cuts from the glass strewn all over the floor, Errol dragged himself towards her. He willed his aura to grow, stretching it out from his arms and hands with all the effort he could muster. In Corwen's cave, and later on the journey through the mountains, he had been stronger. There had been plenty of time each evening to ready himself for the task. His time in the Anghofied had weakened him, and now his aura stuck to him like sweat on a sick man, clinging to his skin and refusing to stretch away.

He shuffled closer, moving as fast as he could. Glass cut through his palms and the pain gave him focus. Just a few feet away from Nellore now. Perhaps he could stand, knock her over and break the contact that way. The effort was almost too much, his balance way off so that for a moment Errol thought he was going to topple back, lose the few precious feet he had already gained. And then he was pitching forward, arms outstretched, still trying desperately to extend his aura and give himself the protection he knew he needed.

It all happened in an instant. Tripping over feet too weak to walk, Errol tumbled into Nellore. They both fell away from the pile of ashes, crashing to the floor in a tangle of limbs. She burned as hot as a fire, her clothes smoking, hair wiry and singed, but she was still alive. Errol rolled over on to his back, his head glancing off the base of the writing desk. For a moment he was stunned, staring up into the dark shadows of the roof, the criss-cross wooden beams hung with things he couldn't quite see. Shapes that writhed and twisted in the breeze like tortured souls. Then he heard Nellore groan, roll over and not so quietly throw up.

'Wha—?' she began, her voice croaky like an old woman.

'Who are you? Why are you here? You should not be here. This is not your place.'

The voice hammered through Errol's thoughts like nearby thunder. Something pale and ghostlike moved in the corner of his vision, and then he was looking at an image of a dragon growing rapidly from the pile of jewels that lay on the floor a few paces away. Not an old creature like Myfanwy or Corwen, but a huge, magnificent beast of legend.

'Gog.' The word was barely a whisper, and yet the image of the dragon clearly heard it. He bent low to Errol, peering first at him then at Nellore sprawled side by side like young lovers in the spring. And finally at the pile of jewels now free of ash.

'I am dead.' The ghostly creature rose from the ground, growing ever larger. 'Killed by my brightest pupil. By my own brother.'

Errol rolled on to his side, then levered himself upright. The jewels were no longer trying to leach the Grym out of everything close by, but he still found it hard to tap the lines for warmth. He couldn't help but notice how thin the air was too, each breath a struggle that left him light-headed. The cold nipped at his feet and hands, his whole body slowly shutting down. How had Martha survived here for months, trapped in the cage and cut off from it all?

'There was still so much to do. So much to learn.' The ghostly form of Gog seemed to have forgotten him and Nellore. It floated around the room, never going far from the pile of jewels as if it were tethered to them. Errol remembered the cave behind the waterfall in Corwen's clearing, the nexus of the Grym and the mage's jewels laid to rest there. Corwen had been able to appear in the clearing and looked more corporeal than Gog, but it was clear that the ghost of the dragon could not stray far from the source of his power.

'But how is it that my jewels have been reckoned? Who performed the ceremony? Who conjured the Fflam Gwir? Who fetched cedarwood and Delyn oil? I see no sign of it here.'

'There is one who can breathe the Fflam Gwir. I have seen him do it.'

For a moment Errol thought his words had gone unheeded, the spirit form of Gog ignoring him completely. But then the ghostlike creature turned slowly, moved through the upturned writing desk and peered down at him.

'Breathe the Fflam Gwir?' it asked. 'But no dragon has done that in millennia. Not since before even I was hatched. It is a magic long lost to our kind.'

'Not to Benfro. I have seen him on more than one occasion. He saved me from certain death, burned the man who was attacking me to a crisp.'

Gog's spirit shrank back on to its haunches. 'A burning flame is not the same as the Fflam Gwir. Our wild ancestors could produce a breath of fire, but it is not something cultured dragons do.'

'The fire that killed my attacker left me unharmed. Indeed it gave me strength and healed my wounds. Is that not your Fflam Gwir, then? That can tell friend from foe?'

Gog's spirit scratched at his aethereal head in puzzlement. 'It sounds very much like it. And Benfro was here. Where is he now? I must know more.' He looked about as if his eyes still functioned like a living dragon's. 'I cannot sense him anywhere. But then I can sense very little. Ah, me. This is most distracting.'

'Who you talking to?' Nellore struggled upright, wiping at her mouth with the back of her hand. Her face was a mess of red blotches and flaky dry skin, as if she had spent too long in front of a roaring fire. Her hair still stood on end, dry and thin. She looked at Errol through puffy eyes, then followed his gaze to where the spectral image of Gog sat. 'Oh.'

'Ah. So it was your essence that woke me.' The dragon spirit peered down at her, silent for a moment before speaking again. 'You are Nellore Henriksdotta, from the arid plains of Stondal where the great bondaris trees grow. Your village are a superstitious lot who worship my kind as gods.'

'You ain't gods, and all my village are dead cos of you. Almost killed me too.' She stood up on shaky legs, began to smooth out her coat then stopped when chunks of it fell off.

'This is true. But now I am dead.' Gog turned once, an action that reminded Errol strangely of a dog preparing itself to lie down and sleep. The image of the great dragon mage looked around the room, searching for a while before he finally spied the pile of jewels that marked its last resting place. He leaned over, attempted to pick them up, but his aethereal fingers simply slid through jewels and floor alike. Once, twice, three times he tried, like a child unable to comprehend why the world didn't work the way he expected it to. Then he turned back to Errol and Nellore.

'I cannot remain here. This is no resting place for a mage's jewels. Come. Gather them for me. We shall place them where it all began.'

Errol felt the compulsion behind the words, but it was weak. He shrugged it off easily, closing down his mind as he had been trained to at Emmass Fawr. Too late he remembered that Nellore would have no such resistance, and she had been the one to awaken the jewels, was already linked to them. She stepped quickly across the room, knelt down and scooped up the pile in her fingers. At her touch, the image of Gog faded to nothing, sucked into the jumble of stones in her hands. She turned back towards Errol, a puzzled look spreading across her face, opening her mouth to say something. And then with a faint *pop* she disappeared.

He knew in an instant what had happened. Nellore had no skill at magic, although she had shown some aptitude for seeing the lines. But she had been touched by Gog, joined with his spirit in ways beyond comprehension. Clearly the dead dragon had been unable to move his own jewels and so had pressed the young girl into doing it for him. But where had they gone?

Errol studied the lines around the spot where Gog's reckoned jewels had lain. They were thick there, swirling with the Grym. The whole tower-top room was filled with the stuff. The white gems had clearly disrupted the magic of the place, and now that the dragon's essence had fled it surged about Errol as if looking for another outlet. He could tap it easily, feel the warmth spread through his body, his strength return as his aches and bruises disappeared. It was a heady sensation, all too easy to bask in the power that filled him, lose himself to it. But Nellore had disappeared. Gog had taken her somewhere. If he could just work out where that was, he could follow. Help her.

Even as he thought it, so the path opened up to him. It seemed so easy, too easy, and as he focused on the task, he wondered if this was how Martha had always seen the world. She had been here, he knew. Going after Nellore meant he would not find her soon, no matter how much he longed to be with her. For a moment he hesitated and the Grym began to leach away from him, the path fading from his aethereal sight. There was no time to think; now was the time for action.

Pulling his aura tight around him, Errol stepped into the lines.

16

Of all the palaces of Gwlad, none were so grand as great Claerwen, home to the line of Palisander of the Spreading Span. He who could claim direct descent from Rasalene himself. More vast city than dwelling, the palace stretched for leagues in every direction. Some say you could set out from the South Gate at dawn and fly north for a full day before clearing the far wall. Others question why any would want to, for within that vast circle of stone lay wonders collected from all the corners of the world. Why travel to Eirawen when its finest fruits and greatest artworks could be found at Claerwen? Why cross the Gwastadded Wag to the plains beyond in search of the finest beef when the kitchens of Claerwen could provide for even your most gluttonous desires? Why seek out the knowledge of the ancients when it already lay waiting for you in the greatest library ever collected?

These at least are the claims of ancient myth, for should you seek Claerwen today you will find naught but dust. The palace is gone into memory, the kitchens nothing but a lingering aroma on the breeze, the library burned and scattered to the winds who whisper its secrets to this day.

For Claerwen was the hatching place of Gog and Magog, those brothers of legend who warred over who should love Ammorgwm the Fair. In their battling they broke Gwlad in two, or so it is said. But before then they laid waste to their hatchright, the most magnificent palace of them all.

Sir Frynwy,
Tales of the Ffrydd

It was like being submerged in a warm bath. Iolwen felt no panic, just a strange sensation of breathlessness as the darkness pressed in all around her. Sounds enveloped her, but they were muffled and hard to distinguish. Was it conversation?

Iolwen floated above the ground, caught in a current, mid-step. She didn't walk, couldn't move at all, and yet she was aware of travelling a great distance even though she could not have said how she was aware. It should have been alarming, but the warmth of young Prince Iolo, clasped in her arms and one tiny hand just touching her neck, was all she needed to stay calm. This would be over soon, she understood. That was what the voices were telling her in their strange, muted language.

When she noticed the light it was as if it had always been there, faint in the distance. It didn't so much rush towards her as slowly increase in brightness, sharp and white so that she was forced to squint. She could feel the temperature dropping too. In the cavern beneath the Neuadd the air had been warm, smelly and muggy, breathed by thousands and laden with their mixture of personal odours. Now it was chill and fresh. There was a smell to it that sparked a memory, but before she could place it, her foot hit the ground and she stepped out the other side.

The memory came to her at the same time as the word. Snow. It flurried around her, whipped up by a vicious chill wind. Prince Iolo let out a wail of surprise and Iolwen could hardly blame him. Candlehall had been sunny, enjoying the last heat of autumn, but wherever the tunnel had taken them it was deepest winter and gripped in the tight embrace of a storm.

'Your Majesty. Thank the Shepherd you're safe.'

Iolwen turned in the direction of the shouted voice and saw Usel huddled beside a massive stone wall. Looking up, she couldn't see the top of it, which was lost somewhere in the swirling mass of white. The medic hurried over to her, and as he did, she noticed several others from their party crouched in the lee of the wall. It wasn't providing much shelter, the wind eddying around like a drunkard, flinging snow in their faces whichever way they turned. All of them looked as cold as Iolwen felt.

'Where is everyone else?' she asked as she joined Teryll, Anwen, Captain Venner and Mercor Derridge.

'Some are along the wall a bit, ma'am. Those as came through last. The rest, your guess is as good as mine.' Captain Derridge rubbed his hands together and blew on them for warmth. 'If I'd known we were going to the mountains I'd have worn me coat.'

'Mountains?' Iolwen asked the question, but it made sense. The air was too thin and cold for them to be anywhere else. But the nearest mountains to Candlehall were days on horseback. She had taken only one step in the tunnel.

'Reckon we'd be somewhere in the Rim, up near Emmass Fawr. Winter can come early in the north, and the higher up you are the worse it gets. There's plenty peaks there never lose their snow one year to the next.'

Mention of the monastery that was headquarters to the Order of the High Ffrydd sent a shiver through Iolwen which had nothing to do with the cold. It was her sister's place, and that of the hated Inquisitor Melyn. She might only have been six when her father offered her as a hostage to ongoing peace with Llanwennog, but she'd understood early on that Melyn's voice had been a key decider in her being sent rather than Beulah. For some reason the inquisitor had always favoured the middle of King Diseverin's three girls.

'What about the tunnel? Where's the exit?'

'There is no exit, ma'am. People just appeared out of thin air. Not all in the same place neither. I was a hundred paces over that way. If it weren't for a lull in the wind I'd probably be lost.' Teryll shivered in his thin tunic, hugging his arms around him.

'Well, we can't stay here,' Iolwen said. 'We should follow the wall. There's bound to be a gate or something.'

'My thoughts exactly. We were just waiting for you to arrive.' Of all the party, Usel was the only one who seemed unaffected by the weather. But then as an adept he could easily enough tap the Grym. Iolwen reached out for the nearest lines and did the same, clutching her son close to share some of that warmth.

It wasn't easy going. The snow had clearly been falling for some time, and it had piled up in drifts against the wall that in places were three or four times Iolwen's height. Where it wasn't plastered in thick white, the wall was featureless, built from huge blocks of smooth black granite cut so neatly and set so close together no mortar could be seen. Occasionally Iolwen would glance up at the bruised sky, straining against the wind and the swirling snow. Sometimes she thought she could see the top, when the wind died for a moment, but she could never be quite sure. What she saw was so high, so far away, as to be almost inconceivable. What manner of mason had built this?

Some of the party were flagging badly, stumbling as they went. Iolwen saw the predicant, Trell, fall, try to stop himself with his bad hand and then disappear into a drift. When Captain Derridge hauled him out, the lad looked as pale as the snow that clung to his face and the front of his black robes.

'Do predicants not have training in magic any more, lad?' Usel asked. Trell just stared at him, but it might have been that he was simply too tired, too cold, to understand.

'It's no matter. Here.' The medic placed the palm of his hand flat on Trell's chest and Iolwen felt the surge in the Grym as he pushed warmth into the young man. She shook her head. It was a simple working she could do just as easily. The first magic she had learned was how to tap the Grym for warmth; the second how to pass that warmth on to others less skilled.

'Everyone come close,' she said, casting her eyes over the group to see who looked coldest. Teryll had the waxy complexion of a man about to keel over, so she went to him first.

'Give me your hand,' she said and then tried not to gasp when she took it. The stable lad was almost completely frozen, and yet he hadn't complained at all. Iolwen reached out for the Grym, strong all around her. She took just enough for warmth and passed it through her hand into Teryll. The colour leached slowly back into his cheeks and his eyes lost their glazed expression. After a few minutes he started to cough, his breath coming out in steaming gouts.

'Don't let yourself get so cold next time.' Iolwen patted him on the shoulder. Then she turned to Mercor Derridge, only to find that Captain Venner had already attended to him, while Lady Anwen was giving warmth to the young lad who had seen Dafydd disappear. Beyn, that was his name. He was small and skinny so had probably chilled quicker than anyone.

'Is everyone warm now?' Iolwen checked that they were before releasing the smallest amount of warmth into Prince Iolo. At least he was well wrapped, and carrying him close meant she could keep an eye on him. This wasn't weather for babies to be out in though. They needed to find shelter soon. 'Right. Let's keep moving. And if anyone who knows no magic begins to feel too cold, tell us. The last thing we need is one of you collapsing.'

They set off in the same direction as before, and soon the wind began to die down, the snow falling in straight lines rather than being thrown in their faces. Then it stopped, and they could see the wall more clearly. It stretched away into the gloom in an unbroken arc. For as far as she could see, Iolwen spotted no towers, no gates, not even a buttress. Skywards, it climbed at least two hundred spans, looming over them like a black curse. She said nothing, but the others had eyes too and it was clear that none of them saw much hope in their situation either. What had become of the rest of the people who had escaped from Candlehall was a mystery.

Something flickered in the corner of Iolwen's sight, high up and inside the wall. She stopped walking, straining through a brief flurry of fat snowflakes to try and see what it was. Just the clouds moving in the wind higher up, perhaps? But no, it had moved differently to a cloud. Then something roared overhead with a thunderous sound that shook snow from the stone and sent it crashing down around them. More snow exploded from a drift a few dozen paces ahead of them as noise erupted behind and to the side. Too late Iolwen understood. They had all stopped in their tracks at the first sound, and now they huddled together. No one even breathed as they all tried to force themselves into the unyielding granite at their backs. Desperate to get away, to hide.

Desperate not to be eaten by the three enormous dragons that had them trapped.

The first thing he noticed was the warmth.

Still dressed only in a nightshirt, Errol felt the wind tugging at the loose garment, whistling over his shaven head and brushing the tips of his ears, but it wasn't the ice chill of Gog's tower or the snow on the riverbank where Nellore had found him. This was a summer afternoon, a hot sun high in a sky so cloudless and blue it was almost black.

The second thing he noticed was the stone.

It poked up out of the ground like the point of a spear broken off after a giant's stab at the heart of Gwlad. Deepest black, leaning at a slight angle, it rose in a series of jagged steps. The land around it undulated gently into a hazy distance, covered in low scrubby bushes and little else. Was that trees he could see? Errol couldn't be sure. The heat of the day made the air shimmer so that it was almost impossible to make out anything more than a few tens of paces away.

The third thing he noticed was Nellore.

She knelt at the base of the stone, hunched over so that at first Errol couldn't see her head. He started walking towards her, which was when he realized how hot the ground was beneath his bare feet. The sun had baked the sandy soil hard where the spiky shrubs didn't cover it, and sharp stones poked out of the surface here and there to catch out the unwary. He hopped from foot to foot, moving forward in a series of jumps that brought him finally to Nellore's side and a shallow beach leading down to a wide pool. Sluggish water trickled in one end and out the other, but the surface in the middle was as flat and calm as mirror. The sun reflecting off it dazzled his eyes.

'You all right?' Errol asked as he turned away from the water to where Nellore knelt. She was scooping away at the sand with her bare hands, the pile of Gog's jewels lying just to one side. He didn't think she could have been here for more than a few minutes, and yet in that time she had dug deep. Now water was leaching in from the pool, slowing her down and crumbling away the edges of her hole. So intent was she on the task, she didn't seem to hear him, so he reached out to put a hand on her shoulder.

'Do not touch her!'

The voice filled Errol's head like a thunderclap. At the same time some invisible force shoved him back so that he sprawled in the sand. One hand flung out to break his fall slapped the surface of the water, and the sound disturbed a flock of pigeons roosting among the stones. They clattered away on noisy wings, whirling around in the air for a while before warily coming back to rest. Errol found himself breathing heavily, as if he had just run up the many steps to Inquisitor Melyn's rooms at the top of Emmass Fawr.

The water was cool on his hand, easing away the heat of the day. Gathering himself together after the shock of the voice, he shuffled around and dipped his bare feet in it, startled when a large, fat fish swam idly up to see what they were. He kicked out at it, but it just circled, not scared in the least. Reaching out with one hand, he tickled it under its chin, something that seemed to send it into a stupor. Errol pulled his hand and feet from the water, and looked around the calm spot, the still pool and jagged rock. The faintest of winds rustled the bushes, adding a high note to the quiet trickle of the stream. The only other sound was the noise of Nellore digging.

Standing, Errol looked further away. The ground rose from the pool, blocking the distant view as effectively as the heat haze, but a few paces away from the far bank he could just about make out the sand-covered remains of some ancient building. It was mostly buried, and at first sight looked like a natural mound. Here and there he could see the edges of cut stone. The more he looked, the bigger it became. A magnificent palace had once sat here.

Glancing back at Nellore, Errol hesitated. He wanted to go to her aid, break whatever spell Gog's jewels had woven around her that was compelling her to dig, but he knew he had little chance. Switching his focus, he brought the Grym into view and saw clearly how it swirled around her, directed her and fed her. This place was awash with power, all converging on the jagged rock and the pile of jewels currently resting on the sand at its base. He could do nothing until she had finished the task; he just hoped it didn't take much longer. Already her aura was thinning and turning a pale, sickly colour. It was too much to watch, so he turned away, looked for something to distract himself.

The sand at the water's edge was cooler than the sun-baked earth, so Errol followed the bank around until he reached the stream. Three small stone steps brought him to the other side, and from there it was a short walk to the mound that was the start of the building. He scrambled up it, finding a wide flat area on the top dotted with more of the wiry bushes, but sparser here than on the other side. Nellore still toiled at her digging as Errol traced out the shape formed by the stones. He knelt down and dug away a little of the sand himself, revealing colourful tiles just beneath the surface. Tiny squares, they seemed to make up some kind of picture, although from the small area he cleared he couldn't begin to see what it was. He'd seen something similar though, back at Emmass Fawr in the inner halls of the great library. The floors there were vast mosaics showing scenes of forests and wild animals.

Errol stood up so quickly he felt his head go light. It came to him in that instant exactly what this place was. A magnificent building had stood on this spot, extending for hundreds, thousands, of paces in all directions. Like Emmass Fawr, it had not been men who had built it. Or at least not men for whom it had been built. This was a dragon palace, one so old and abandoned so long ago it had virtually crumbled to dust. But it had been home to beasts of legend once. He knew that now.

'This is it. The place where they were both hatched.' Errol spoke the words even though Nellore was too far away to hear, and too wrapped up in her task. He hurried down off the mound, back to the edge of the pool. The sun reflected off the surface too brightly to see below, but somewhere in the depths surely there lay the final remains of Gog's mad twin, Magog. This was the place Benfro needed to find.

'You are right, Errol Ramsbottom. This is indeed the place of my hatching, though much about it has changed in the millennia since that great moment.'

He should have known better than to look for the source of the voice, and yet still Errol spun round, half-expecting to see the ancient dragon Gog standing behind him. But there was only the low rise, the scrubby bushes and the hot bright sun beginning to lower in the afternoon sky. He turned too swiftly back to the pool, overbalanced and took a step forward to stop himself from falling. Only on this side there was no gentle beach, just a steep bank disappearing into the depths, and with a horrible sense of inevitability he fell headlong into the water.

It was surprisingly cold, shocking the breath out of him, and for an instant Errol panicked, flailing about as if he might drown. He remembered the night Trell had pushed him and Martha into the pool at Jagged Leap, the night he had first encountered a dragon mage's memories. Sir Radnor's jewels had been buried alone at a nexus in the Grym, away from the mingled remains of most of his kind. Clearly Gog had chosen this spot for his own endless solitude. Did he know that his hated brother's remains lay so close by?

Kicking out with his feet, Errol swam away from the bank where he had fallen in, headed for the beach on the other side. The water was cool and refreshing after the heat of the day and it washed away the last vestiges of the terrible stench that had ingrained itself in his skin down in the Anghofied. When he reached the centre of the pool, he trod water for a moment, trying to see the bottom. It was too dark to make out anything except for the pale shapes of the fish that had begun to swim around him, occasionally darting in and nipping at him with toothless mouths. Not painful, but it was disquieting, so he swam as swiftly as he could for the beach, dragging himself back on to dry land as Nellore finally finished her digging.

'Now I can be laid to rest here where I was hatched.' The voice filled Errol's ears as Nellore reached over and gently picked up one jewel, held it up to the sun for a moment and then placed it deep in the hole she had dug. That done she took up another and performed the same ritual. Then a third, and a fourth. One by one she presented the jewels to the sun, then buried them in the ground.

'Arhelion, who is mother to us all, watch over these the last remains of Gog, Son of the Winter Moon. Keep him safe as he watches over your fold.' Nellore spoke the words, but Errol could hear them in Gog's voice echoing deep in his head. This was a ceremony that should have been performed by a great dragon mage, and yet here the greatest of them all was reduced to forcing an innocent young woman to do his bidding.

'I am sorry for that. Truly I am.' Gog's words were only in Errol's head this time. 'My children have lost interest in the subtle arts. Not all of them, but more and more each year, almost as if they are cursed.'

'They are cursed.' Errol recalled the tales Benfro had told him. 'Your brother's parting gift when you split the world, the same as yours was to curse all the dragons who stayed with him and gift the power of magic to men.'

'Such was our folly. My hatred for my brother died centuries ago. Indeed I had all but forgotten him, wrapped up in my own studies. So much to learn and so little time.'

Errol tried to imagine the span of Gog's years, thousand upon thousand. It was impossible; he had not yet seen eighteen summers himself, would do well to see sixty more. What secrets had the dragon mage uncovered in all that time? How could there be more to learn?

'His hatred has burned deeper than I could imagine. Perhaps I am to blame for that, the agent of my own downfall.' Gog's voice was fading now, barely a whisper over the rustling of the dry bushes and the gentle trickle of water in the stream. Looking over to Nellore, Errol saw that the pile of jewels beside the hole had grown very small. With each gem laid in its final resting place, so the spirit of the great dragon mage seemed to fade further.

'I must rest. Think about what has happened. Farewell, Errol Ramsbottom. Farewell, Nellore Henriksdotta. We shall not meet again.'

'Wait. What do you mean not meet . . .?' Errol started to ask the question but a vast pressure gripped him, squeezing him tight. For a moment he thought he was going to pass out. It was as if the world twisted, or he twisted and the world stayed the same. And then as soon as it had come, the sensation was past and everything was changed. He thought he could feel something go out of the air, as if he had been hearing a noise for so long he'd stopped noticing it, but now it was gone. And then Nellore let out a low moan of pain, toppled sideways to the sand, clutching her hands to her chest. Errol shook away the odd, dislocated sensation and rushed to her side.

'What happened? Where am I?' She pushed herself slowly up and he could see the sand caked on her arms, the front of her dress and all over her legs. Her eyes were bloodshot and weary as she looked around, confusion written loud across her face.

'The jewels brought you here. This is where he was hatched – Gog. He made you bury them here.' Errol pointed at where Nellore had dug her hole. It was filled in now, and the next flood would scrub away any sign the ground had been disturbed. Bringing the lines to his sight, he saw a powerful intersection, a nexus in the Grym far greater than the one where Sir Radnor's jewels had been laid to rest. This truly was a place befitting the greatest mage to have lived, even if part of him wanted to dig up the shiny white gems and scatter them to the furthest corners of Gwlad.

'What happened to my hands?' Nellore sat inelegantly on the beach now, staring at her fingers. Errol moved around to face her, taking them in his own. The sand had rubbed away the skin in places, leaving them raw and bloodied.

'Here. Let's wash them clean first.' He helped her up, led her to the water's edge where it was shaded by the towering rock above them. Bare-footed and still damp from his earlier swim, he didn't hesitate to walk in, but Nellore shied away.

'It's all right. The water's not too cold.' Errol crouched down and slowly Nellore did the same, still keeping her feet dry. She winced as he dipped her hands beneath the surface and gently splashed at her arms until the worst of the sand was gone. Then he reached out for the Grym, so abundant in this place as to be almost overwhelming, focused it and channelled it into her.

Errol wasn't entirely sure what he was doing, and yet he somehow knew how to heal Nellore's wounds. He had never used the Grym this way. It felt natural though, to divert some of that power into the young woman's hands and arms, to encourage them to heal more swiftly. He could see the tight weave of her aura, clinging to her like a thin shift, sickly with her weariness. Slowly, as the power of the land seeped into her, the colours began to swirl, first around her damaged fingers and then reaching up her forearms, over her shoulders. At the same time Errol felt the Grym warming him, easing away his own aches and pains. It was a joining both comfortable and profoundly uncomfortable, something much closer than he had ever had with Martha. The thought of her made him step back, dropping Nellore's hands with a twitch of guilt.

'I'm sorry,' he said and then noticed that the sun had sunk low on the horizon, pinprick stars appearing in the sky. The air was chill too, and when he looked down he could see the skin of his bare feet puckering with hours spent in the water. Where had the time gone?

'What just happened?' Nellore held up her hands, turning them this way and that in the failing light. She flexed her fingers a couple of times, then laughed. 'Why are you standing in the water, Errol?'

One of the fish took that moment to nip his ankle. Unlike most, this one had sharp teeth. Errol let out a yelp of pain, kicking up first one foot and then the other as he rushed to get away from it. Nellore backed up swiftly, the look on her face more of glee than concern. The cut on his foot was tiny, but it bled profusely as he hopped up the beach to a dry spot and sat down heavily with his back to one of the bushes. In the chaos Errol trampled over the soft sand where Gog's jewels lay, but the dead mage made no sound.

'Ow. Bloody thing bit me.' Errol rubbed at the cut with his thumb. 'Didn't think they had teeth.'

'This one does. Ugly-looking thing too.' Nellore was down by the water, bending over something, and when she stood up again she had the fish in her arms. Errol couldn't understand how she had managed to catch it, unless in his rush to escape he had somehow brought it with him on to the beach. It was a good size, and the young girl looked very pleased with her trophy. 'Least now we'll have something for supper.'

17

When blizzard hides the summer's sun
And hidden roads reveal'd
Locked doors no longer sealed
Once two, now become one.

The Prophecies of Mad Goronwy

'Keep very still and do not make a sound.'

As advice went, Iolwen felt Usel's words were rather unnecessary. No one was moving so much as a muscle. The three dragons had them effectively penned and were poised for attack. The flurrying snow had the effect of making them seem even larger than the great beast that had eaten Seneschal Padraig, and they stood tall on their hind legs, long necks raised and wings half furled.

'Why are they not attacking?' Captain Venner asked. He had not conjured his puissant blade, Iolwen was pleased to see.

'I don't know, but let's not provoke them, shall we?' She cradled young Prince Iolo closer to her breast, feeling his breath on her skin, and willed him to stay silent. Was it possible that the dragons hadn't seen them? By the way they were standing it was almost as if they were waiting, but for what?

As if frustrated by the lack of action, Prince Iolo took

that moment to let out a wail, timed perfectly with a lull in the wind. His lungs might have been tiny, but the noise was like the loudest crash of thunder, the roar of the mightiest of waterfalls. The nearest of the dragons cocked its head slightly at the sound, lowered itself slowly on to its arms and leaned in close, sniffing. Iolwen was frozen to the spot by something beyond terror as the enormous head of the beast came nearer and nearer. She could see its scales, even the tiny ones that surrounded its eyes in intricate patterns. Its mouth was closed, but fangs pierced those leathery lips upwards and down. Nostrils the size of her head flared as it took in a deep breath, then let it out again. Iolwen tensed, expecting the stench of rotting meat that was the mark of the creatures she had seen in the Neuadd, but instead this dragon's breath was sweet-smelling, almost spiced and intoxicating.

So close now she could feel the heat radiating from its skin, the dragon studied her with something more than sight and smell. Iolwen had tightened her mental shields the moment she had stepped out of the tunnel; now they withered under a pressure unlike anything she had felt before. Not even King Ballah had been able to break through so easily. She felt like a little girl under the disapproving scrutiny of a severe nanny.

Then as quickly as it had begun, it ended. The dragon's mind withdrew so completely it was as if the beast was not there. Astonished, Iolwen took a moment to see what was happening and then let out an involuntary gasp. Unnoticed as all her attention was taken up with the dragon, Prince Iolo had rolled over in her grip. His arms were short, but the creature was close enough, and so he had reached out and touched the delicate tip of its nose. And now the infant let out a little squeal, not of fear but of delight.

The dragon snorted more of that odd-smelling breath, then as slowly as any predator it withdrew. It took two steps back, folded its wings completely and then finally spoke in perfect Saesneg.

'Welcome to Nantgrafanglach, Princess Iolwen. I am Sir Conwil. Please accept my apologies for our wariness, but recent events have shaken our community to the core. Not least the arrival of several thousand of your people. Do not worry for them; they are being tended to. We will never turn away refugees even when there are so many.'

'You . . . you know my name?'

'Your people speak of little else, although I will admit that I was not sure it was you until I sensed your party using the subtle arts. And your kitling, he is strong with the Grym. He would grow to be a powerful mage were he one of our kind.'

Iolwen shivered, both from the cold and the dragon's words. Something about it – him, she corrected herself – struck her as not quite trustworthy. Perhaps it was just a lifetime of considering his kind troublesome when she considered them at all. And the memory of Seneschal Padraig's violent end was never far from her thoughts.

'We have much to discuss, the terrible actions of my fellow dragons among them. But I fear this place is not conducive to such things. Perhaps we would be more comfortable out of this storm.'

Iolwen was about to ask how far it was to shelter, aware that some of the party might not be able to walk much further, but before she could say anything the sky darkened around her. The snow disappeared and a feeling not dissimilar to that of stepping through the tunnel from Candlehall smothered her like a warm blanket. Prince Iolo let out a quiet gurgle, and she hugged him close to her as the darkness faded to light again, revealing somewhere else entirely.

It was a hall, but built on such a scale as she could scarce imagine. Bigger even than the Neuadd, it stretched away into a distance she couldn't clearly see. There must have been a ceiling high overhead somewhere, since the wind had died to nothing, and snow no longer fell. All Iolwen could see was an endless series of bright crystal chandeliers floating above her and spreading into the distance. They cast light over a smooth marble floor that was remarkable both for the warmth radiating from it and for its utter emptiness. She turned slowly on the spot, noticed that they had arrived a hundred paces or more from the nearest wall and door. Counting the members of her small party and finding all present, Iolwen saw that most looked pale, and Teryll was hunched over, trying hard not to be sick.

'What is this place?' she asked. The strange journey from outside had left her with no ill effects, but she could imagine how it might be disorientating for some.

'The Grand Hall of Nantgrafanglach once echoed to the voices of many.' Sir Conwil drew himself upright as he spoke, and Iolwen noticed then that the other two dragons were no longer with them. 'Dragons would meet here to discuss all manner of things, and men have always been welcome. But the years have not been kind to our race. We have dwindled in number and many have abandoned the subtle arts in favour of much baser living. Those . . . creatures, I believe you have already met. But come, you must be hungry. Please, eat.'

The dragon gestured, and when Iolwen followed his hand she was astonished to see a long refectory table laid with cutlery and plates. The stomach-rumbling aroma of roasted meats wafted across the short distance, coming from the large platters that were lined up along the centre of the table and covered with huge silver domes. The table had benches to either side, a tall-backed chair at one end. Iolwen hung back, wary, but most of the party had no hesitation in crossing the floor, sitting at the benches and helping themselves. Soon they were tucking in, chatting together like old friends. The goblets filled with dark red wine from a slender jug probably helped break down the social barriers as much as their shared experience. Most of all though she felt the influence of the dragon, the compulsion that hid behind his words. It was something she was used to resisting, but even without it she couldn't blame her companions; it was very possible none had eaten much all day and the city had been on siege rations before they had all fled.

'This place is filled with strange magics, Your Majesty, but I think we can trust our eyes here.' Usel had not left her side to go and eat with the others; no doubt he had felt Sir Conwil's suggestion too and was equally able to resist it. For himself, the dragon merely waited patiently, his head tilted ever so slightly to one side like an indulgent parent.

'I must feed my son first,' Iolwen said, then noticed

another less pleasant aroma wafting up to her nose. 'And I will need to find somewhere to clean him.'

'Of course. There are facilities just here.' The dragon waved his other arm and Iolwen almost jumped. Where before they had been standing far from the nearest wall, now there was one immediately beside her, a door half open just a few paces away. She stepped over to it, peered in and saw basins, towels. There was a scent of rosewater and soap about the place and a cleanliness that only reminded her of how grubby she was. Turning back to the dragon, Iolwen gave him a nod by way of a curtsy, the best she could do while carrying Prince Iolo.

'Thank you, Sir Conwil. Your hospitality does you credit.'

'The least I can do after the trauma my kind have inflicted on yours.' The dragon returned Iolwen's curtsy with a bow. 'And now I must go, I fear. There is much to do. Please eat, rest. You will find all you need here. I will return as soon as I can.'

Iolwen opened her mouth to speak. There were so many questions she didn't know where to start. But before she could say anything Sir Conwil simply vanished.

It wasn't easy preparing and cooking a fish without any tools, but the Grym was powerful in this magical place and Errol found he could tap it with an ease he had never known before. It took a while to persuade Nellore to collect dry wood and pile it up, her complaining all the while that they had nothing with which to light a fire. Only once they had a decent stack did Errol reach deep into the lines and draw out the power from them, directing it to the nearest branch. He had seen warrior priests and the elder quaisters produce flame with a click of their fingers. It wasn't something he had ever been taught how to do, but somehow it seemed obvious here and now.

Soon the wood was blazing away merrily. They used a broken stick sharpened on a rock to first gut the fish and then spear it through. It sizzled over the hot coals, giving off a smell that rumbled Errol's stomach long before it was ready to eat. And when it was finally done they both fell upon it with hungry fingers. For long minutes the only sounds were the ripping of flesh and the sucking of bones, and over them the soft sigh of the wind.

'He's really not coming back, is he?' Nellore asked as she reluctantly tossed the last few bones and scraps of skin into the flames, wiped fish scales and grease on the hem of her skirt. Errol huddled close to the fire, more for its light than its warmth. The night was chill now, but he reached out with barely a thought, tapped the Grym for warmth, felt the energy of it fill him.

'Gog? I don't think so. It was strange when you covered up the last jewel. It was as if the world stopped for a moment, then started again.' He looked up at the stars spread overhead like grains of sand strewn across a black cloth. There was something about them that was bothering him, but he couldn't say what it was.

'So how're we going to get back then? Seeing as we don't even know where here is.'

Errol shrugged. 'I could try walking the lines. I did that to get here, after all. But I don't really know where I'd go, and that's a good way to get lost. I've never taken anyone with me either. Don't even know how that works, really.'

Nellore moved closer to the flames too. Unable to tap the Grym, she would be feeling the cold now despite being better dressed than him. It would probably be a good idea to keep the fire going all night if they could, which would mean searching in the dark for more wood. If the moon rose then it would be easy enough, but for now there was only starlight to guide him.

'The stars!' He stood swiftly, taking a couple of steps back from the fire as he tilted his head and looked up.

'What about them? Stars is stars, int they?'

'No. Well, yes they are. But I recognize these.' Errol walked around the fire to where Nellore still sat, crouched down behind her and pointed up. 'See there, those five stars close together? They form the shape of a wolf's nose and ears? That's the first of Blaidd Rhedeg. And over there's the Shepherd's Crook. I know these stars.'

'So?' Nellore shivered and turned her gaze back to the fire.

'I didn't know the stars back in your village. I wasn't there long, but it bothered me at the time. Walking north to the mountains too. Some of them seemed to be in the right place, but there were some missing. This is the sky I remember from growing up. These are the stars I learned as a boy. And we were taught about them at Emmass Fawr as well.'

'Still don't know why that's so exciting.'

'It means I'm back in my own world. Or it means there aren't two worlds any more. Maybe that's what I felt when Gog withdrew. Maybe the spell they wove, him and his brother, maybe that's gone now and Gwlad's whole again.'

Nellore stared up from the fire at him, her face worried. 'Sure that fish only bit you on the foot?'

Errol just laughed. He dropped back down on to the sand beside her and held his hands out to the flames for warmth. 'You remember what I told you when we were walking through the forest. About Gog and Magog and how they'd split the world?'

'I thought that was just a story. Like my dad used to tell when I couldn't sleep. Thought you were just trying to take my mind off the walking.'

'But you met Gog. Well, you met his remains. And I know Magog existed too. And this is where the two of them were hatched, where they grew up. There's the ruins of a palace on the other side of the pool. It goes on for ever, far as I can see.'

'So how do we get home then?' Nellore shoved her hands into her armpits and hunched closer to the fire. 'Don't even know where home is any more.'

Errol could think of nothing to say to that. He reached out and touched Nellore's shoulder. When she looked around at him he could see tears in the corners of her eyes, shiny in the light of the flames.

'We should probably try and get some sleep. I'll go see if I can find some more wood for the fire. Keep it going through the night.'

Nellore sniffed, wiped her nose with the back of her hand. 'Ain't you cold? Just wearin' that nightdress?'

'Not really. The Grym is everywhere here. It's almost like I have to work to keep it out, not draw it in. I'll have to find something better to wear, but we can worry about that in the morning.'

He left Nellore trying to find a comfortable position on the sandy beach to sleep, and headed away from the pool around the back of the tall rock. The stars didn't cast much light, and he groped around in the darkness looking for firewood. The Grym was no help, even though the lines were easy to see here, pulsing with life and power. They overwhelmed his other senses, and besides it was dead wood he was after.

Nellore was fast asleep by the time he had collected as much as he could carry and taken it back to the fire. Errol stoked up the flames a bit, put the rest of the wood to one side and set out again for more. By the fourth trip he reckoned he had enough to see them through until the dawn. He settled down by the fire, then lay flat on his back and stared at the familiar sky. He knew he should have been tired, but he was buzzing with energy now, his whole body jittery as if the Grym was pouring into him. He cast around, looking for the source of it, and his gaze fell immediately on the rock.

It speared up towards the Guiding Star almost as if it were the fulcrum around which the heavens turned. Jagged and tilted slightly, it would be easy to climb, and the view from there might give him an idea of the lie of the land. He might be able to see deeper into the pool now that the sun wasn't glaring off the water's surface. Maybe see if Magog's bones really were still lying in the depths.

Before he knew really what he was doing, Errol had stood up, dusted the sand off his legs and walked across to the base of the rock. Without effort, his aethereal vision came to him, layering over the mundane and the bright, swirling mess of lines that was the Grym. Together they showed a clear route to the top, not an easy climb but neither so hard as to present too much of a challenge. In the darkness any lingering fear of heights was lessened too, and soon he found himself near the top. The wind ruffled the hem of his nightshirt and chilled his shaven head, but he pushed on, reaching a flat area strewn with bits of nest and bird droppings. Stepping carefully to the edge, he looked down.

Starlight reflected in perfectly still water, speckling the surface like a sky in reverse, the pool took the shape of an enormous eye, staring up at the heavens in eternal vigilance. Errol stood, transfixed by the sight of it, oblivious to anything else as he gazed deep into that blackness. It felt like the pool was a hole in the world through which the Grym welled up and flowed out across Gwlad, giving life to everything.

'It is magnificent, isn't it.'

Errol startled at the words, quiet but so close they could have been whispered right in his ear. Standing at the edge, he might have fallen had he not grown accustomed to hearing such voices. Instead of spinning round, he turned slowly, stepping back towards the centre of the flat area at the top of the rock. As he expected, there was no one there, but when he focused on the Grym he could see shapes swirling and pulsing up from the patch of sand where Nellore had buried the jewels earlier.

'This was your hatching place,' he said to the air. There was no response, and he couldn't be sure he hadn't imagined the whole thing. Still, it was peaceful up there on top of the rock, so he sat down, warmed by the power rising out of the pool, and stared into the night.

If he slept, Errol couldn't have said, but time passed

and he thought of nothing. Shapes began to form from the darkness, distant monsters lining up to attack. As the dawn pinked the sky, they transformed into trees much closer than he had expected, a familiar range of mountains far distant. Benfro had carried him high into those mountains, and the two of them had walked down the other side into the Llanwennog Northlands.

'Errol? Where'd you go?'

This time the voice was real, and anxious. Looking down at the beach and their fire, Errol saw Nellore stretching, yawning and looking around. The fire had almost gone out, the pile of wood he had worked so hard to collect in the dark still sitting to one side unburned.

'Up here.' He waved as he shouted, waiting until Nellore had seen him. Her face was still red with the after-effects of Gog's possession, her hair awry and her clothing shabby.

'What you doing there?'

'Just looking. I can see the forest and the hills. Reckon I know just about where we are.' He stood up, peered over the edge, looking for the way down. And that was when he realized the mistake he had made. Climbing in the dark had been easy, using his aethereal sight to find hand- and footholds. He had no sense of height, no fear of the drop. Now he could see just how steep the rock was, how tiny the cracks he had used on the way up. Getting down without falling would be tricky. He walked slowly around the edge of the flat top, looking for alternative routes. None presented themselves save one, and it was a somewhat extreme idea. But the more he thought about it, the more sense it made. The pool was deep, that much he knew from his impromptu swim the day before. He wanted to dive as far down into it as he could anyway. If this truly was the hatching place of Gog and Magog, where Benfro had first found the red jewel, then at the bottom of the pool there should be bones. If he could retrieve one, even just a tiny fragment of one, then they were one step closer to freeing Benfro of that malign influence.

Errol recalled all too well the fall from the rock at Jagged Leap. This was higher, but not enough to be dangerous. And he wasn't going to be tumbling half-stunned by a blow to the head this time. No, he would go in feet first and with a lungful of air.

'Build up the fire, Nellore. I'll be down in a moment.' He shouted the words as much to give him the necessary courage as to make himself heard.

And then with a deep breath he stepped forward into nothing.

18

Once the arbiter of justice throughout the whole of Gwlad, the Council of Nantgrafanglach has dwindled in importance over the centuries and millennia since my once-beloved's self-imposed exile at the top of his high tower. Gone are the times when the leaders of nations would bow before it, accept its judgments and depart peacefully after decades of war. Gone are the times when scholars would seek its wisdom on matters of the subtle arts. Gone are the times when the most skilled and powerful of dragonkind would deem a place at its table the greatest of all honours.

Much as our kitlings have left the great palace, abandoned the ways of civilized dragons and returned to our feral roots, so has the Council of Nantgrafanglach become something far less than it was. Now its members convene but rarely, discuss inconsequential things and leave the running of the palace to the men who were once their most humble servants.

And so with heavy hearts I have left my seat empty these past few hundred years. There is no answer to be found in dry discourse that can explain the sickness that has afflicted our kind. I go out into Gwlad to study, to gather information, and yes, to heal those who will accept that gift. I can only remember the glory that once was, and hope that in the future it may once more come to be.

From the journals of Myfanwy the Bold

They wanted for nothing. Doors opening from the great hall led to washrooms, bedrooms and smaller reception rooms. There were clothes for all of them, correctly sized though perhaps not in the latest fashion. Whenever they needed food, it was there. If a towel was left crumpled and wet on the floor, it would be replaced with a clean folded one the next time she went into that room, although Iolwen never once caught sight of a servant. She even found a small nursery with a crib and everything an infant could possibly need, but there was no getting away from the fact that their small band were prisoners.

It was a comfortable jail. Usel found a small library filled with books written in dragon runes that filled him with unreasonable delight as he set about teaching Predicant Trell how to read them. The young man's hand had given him a lot of pain until the medic had found yet another room filled with herbs and poultices. Iolwen could have sworn she had already explored that corridor to its end, and yet no sooner had Usel mentioned how much easier it would have been to treat wounds if he had just a small selection of medicines than a room filled with the tools and ingredients of the healer's trade had appeared. It was as if the great hall could read their moods and provided what it thought they needed.

Lady Anwen seemed content to wait upon Iolwen and

help her look after young Prince Iolo. Mercor Derridge and his grandson Beyn had set off on the first day, intending to explore the great hall, only to return a couple of hours later from the opposite direction having seen nothing at all. After that they had kept to the small rooms they had chosen for themselves, coming out only to eat a couple of times a day.

At least Iolwen assumed it was a couple of times a day. There were no windows in the hall, just the huge crystal chandeliers high overhead. The rooms were lit by smaller lanterns that came on by themselves whenever someone entered a room. There were spaces on the walls where windows should have been, but the shutters would not open, and nor did they let in any light through cracks. Were it not for the predictable regularity of Prince Iolo's demands to be fed, she would have had no way of measuring time at all.

By that unconventional reckoning at least three days had passed and they were all sitting at the table at the edge of the cavernous, empty hall, picking at a breakfast that was the equal of any banquet Iolwen had eaten but which might as well have been dry biscuits.

'Have you found anything to help us out of here in those precious books of yours yet, Usel?' she asked. The medic had brought one with him to the table, something he would never have dared to do in the presence of royalty before they had been thrown together like this.

'Alas, no, Your Highness. There is a lot of ancient history, some treatises on magic, or the subtle arts as dragonfolk call them. But I've yet to find any clues as to the building of this place.'

'Such a book would be beyond your understanding,

Usel of the Ram. And as far as I am aware, no such work has been undertaken as yet.'

All heads turned at the words, even though Iolwen recognized the deep tones and slightly strange pronunciation of the Saesneg language. Sir Conwil stood a few paces from the table, though she could have sworn he had not been there an instant before.

'You are rested?' he asked. 'You have had all you require?'

'Apart from our liberty,' Iolwen said. At her words the dragon dipped his head in something half agreement half apology.

'It was necessary, I am afraid. For all its size, Nantgrafanglach has a small and dwindling population, both dragon and man. Your thousands have swelled our ranks more than tenfold, and you have come at a time when we have suffered a grave loss. The Old One would never have allowed the needy to be turned away, but it takes time to assess them all and decide what to do with them.'

'The Old One?' Iolwen asked.

'The father of us all, really. This is his great city. From here he commanded the whole of Gwlad once, or so it seemed. Events of late have led me to re-evaluate that particular version of history.'

'And my people? What has become of them?'

'They have been found places to stay, work to keep them occupied. It is not easy, since the men of Nantgrafanglach speak only Draigiaith and lack the skill to master your Saesneg quickly.'

'May I see them?' Iolwen asked. 'May I speak to them?'

'Of course.' Sir Conwil inclined his head again. 'Although you may wish to hear what I have to say first.'

Iolwen sat back in her chair, Prince Iolo resting in the crook of her arm. The other members of the party had fallen silent at the dragon's appearance, all eyes on him. She knew that they needed to understand what was happening as much as she did, but she also realized that Sir Conwil wanted some privacy. She let him wait a while longer before relenting. Rising, she handed the prince to Lady Anwen.

'Please attend to him and remain here until I return.' She gestured to Usel. 'Come. I will need your wise counsel.' Finally she went over to where the dragon sat, trying not to be overwhelmed by his size, his musk and the sheer weight of his presence. 'Shall we walk a while?'

'Better yet, I will take you to meet ...' Sir Conwil paused a moment as if considering his words. 'I hesitate to say leader, as that means something entirely different in your tongue. But yes, she is our leader at the moment.'

Iolwen opened her mouth to speak, but before any words could come out she felt that familiar sensation of motion without moving, the darkening of all around her to a black so deep it seemed to suck the life out of her. And then she was somewhere else.

Dafydd would have been the first to admit that he was not his own best company, but after a week on Merrambel he began to get used to the solitude. The first few days were spent half in panic wondering how he would survive, half in pacing the beach close to the spot where the dragon Merriel had left him, praying for her return.

Each evening he would forage for dry wood and light a fire, as much for the cheer of it as any heat. The nights here were warm, the days almost unbearably hot unless he hid in the shade of the great trees that rimmed the shore-line. He had worried about food at first, but the sea teemed with fish quite unused to being hunted, and the bushes lining the path to the great dragon statue were heavy with fruit. Some of it he even recognized, at least from books, and nothing he had eaten had poisoned him.

The first day, and for many days afterwards, he had not wanted to stray too far from the beach lest he miss Merriel's return. Each evening he would settle himself by the fire and try to find the trance state that would let him enter the aethereal. The peace and quiet helped, and soon he could slip in and out of a trance with barely a thought, but he was so far removed from anything he knew it was impossible to do much with the skill. To strike out over the featureless water was to invite dissipation, and whereas when he had practised this magic in his grandfather's palace at Tynhelyg the life force of all the people for miles had been easy to detect, here the utter silence only confirmed for him how truly alone he was.

As the days became first a week and then two, so Dafydd began to grow restless. He made short forays into the woods, struggling through vegetation far more lush than anything that grew in Llanwennog. He visited the valley with the statue of the dragon every day, studying it from a distance. The base of it was hidden from view by thick undergrowth that made approaching it all but impossible, especially in the heavy, damp heat. Each night he would return to the beach and his fire, stoke up the flames and wait for Merriel's return. She did not appear, and the longer he waited, the more he realized that if she was coming, she would find him wherever he went. She had found him at the Neuadd, after all. Surely she would have no trouble locating him halfway up the steep-sided mountain that formed the bulk of this island, what had Usel called it? Mount Merram? Sitting at his fire and staring out across the endless sea, Dafydd decided that the next day he would explore further.

He rose early, breakfasted on fresh fish and then followed the stream that splashed down from the mountain to the beach. Without any means of carrying it, he dared not venture too far from his only source of drinking water. It took him back to the valley of the statue and he spent a while looking at the great work once more. The dragon had been carved in relief, standing tall and with its wings folded closed so that their tips – the joints, he realized – rose above its head. What had Usel said the beast was called? Eirawen? No, that was the land far to the south of here. Earith, that was it. And she was a healer venerated in human form by the Order of the Ram, the travelling monks and medics among whose number Usel counted himself. Of all the men of the Twin Kingdoms, it was Rams who could most be trusted. That much Dafydd knew. His own father had insisted Dafydd be stitched up by a Ram when he'd injured himself out riding many years ago. Prince Geraint had shooed away the palace healers as soon as he had heard one of the order was visiting. Sent for him straight away.

Dafydd smiled at the memory, remembered the scar that his father had been so proud of. That wound should have left him with a permanent limp, but it scarcely bothered him at all now.

He pushed through the undergrowth beside the stream,

wishing he had something to chop away the heavier leaves. Then with a laugh he remembered his training and conjured his puissant blade. It blazed bright even in the sunlight, the power of the Grym potent here. For a moment Dafydd hacked away, clearing himself an easy path, but each frond cut felt like a violation in this untainted place, his destructiveness no better than the ugly mess wrought by the dragons who had demolished most of Candlehall. After just a few minutes he extinguished his blade and pushed on without it.

As if it understood and appreciated his gesture, the forest seemed to clear itself out of his way. Dafydd soon found himself standing at the base of the statue, where the stream emerged from a dark cave between the creature's legs. He approached the cave mouth, peering in. Sunlight filtering through the trees lit only the first few paces, but a cool breeze wafted out of the cave, suggesting there was an exit somewhere, and a well-built stone path led into the darkness alongside the stream. Intrigued, Dafydd stepped into the mountain.

At first he was comfortable with the dark and the gentle burble of the stream as it ran beside the path. And then he saw lights flickering in the distance. Not the magical glow of the Grym, but something more earthly. The fire of flaming torches. His eyes accustomed to the darkness, Dafydd could see the shape of the cave. The path was wider here as the stream narrowed almost to nothing, cutting deep into a cleft in the rock. He could step over it easily and head towards the light. As he took that pace, a small leap that was as easy as climbing a single step, it felt like the whole world twisted around him. He paused, one foot on either side, the invisible stream deep below him, and for an instant he imagined he was cut in half. The sensation passed as quickly as it had come, but it left him with a lingering sense of wrongness that was hard to shake.

Walking swiftly so as to put some distance between himself and the odd feeling, Dafydd soon reached the opening through which he had seen the lights. Warm air caressed his face, bringing with it scents of spice and something else he couldn't identify, but it was the sight that greeted him as he stepped out of the cavern that was so confusing Dafydd could only stand and stare.

It had been morning when he had left on this adventure, and surely not more than an hour had passed since then. Now he gazed down upon a city bathed in the darkness of night. Not a city deep underground; he could clearly see stars speckling a distant sky. Buildings stretched away from him, down a shallow slope towards a calm sea reflecting a sliver of crescent moon. The flickering orange light he had seen was cast by dozens of flaming torches set at regular intervals down a long street, wide enough for a dozen carts to pass. The houses to each side were low, single-storeyed with flat roofs.

Without realizing he was doing it, he walked towards the nearest, and only then understood the scale of the place. The cave had brought him out above the city, and the low buildings were higher than some of the smaller palace wings back home in Tynhelyg. It took Dafydd far longer to reach the first one than he had expected, and when he turned to see where he had come from, there was only forest, dark and impenetrable, behind him.

The breeze carried new aromas to his nose: cooking

meat, spices and more delicate scents. It also brought the babble of conversation, impossible to understand at a distance. He pressed on, and the further he went, the more he heard words that he simply didn't understand. He had studied many languages, was fluent in Saesneg and Llanwennog and could get by in some that very few people spoke any more, and yet the voices he was hearing now were as alien to him as the dragons.

The road opened up into a huge square and he began to see them now, people much like himself though perhaps better dressed and certainly cleaner. At first none seemed to notice him. Too busy about their trading, for this was clearly a market though one far larger than any he had seen before. As he entered the square though, the first stallholder and his customers fell silent. Dafydd did not know what was compelling him, but he ignored their stares and carried on walking. The cacophony of voices fell silent behind him as he came closer and closer to the centre. He felt the heat of a thousand pairs of eyes on his back, and yet he still felt no fear.

A shallow raised pool filled the centre of the square, a fountain leaping up from the middle. Its splashing cooled the warm night air and reflected the light cast by a dozen or more brass torches. Low, wide steps led to the water's edge and Dafydd climbed them with weary legs. He had been walking only for a couple of hours, he was sure, but his stomach rumbled with hunger and the water smelled sweet, so powerful was his thirst. It hit him all of a sudden – exhaustion as if he had been marching for days. His mind told him not long had passed at all, but his body suggested a different story.

There was no sound save the rustling of the breeze in the frond-like leaves that sprouted from the tops of the narrow-trunked trees. The whole square, which had moments earlier been abuzz with the noise and bustle of commerce, now held its breath. Unaware of the tension, Dafydd slumped to his knees at the water's edge, bent low and plunged his hands through the cool surface. He scooped refreshing liquid into his mouth, gulping it down as if he had not drunk in days. Scrubbing at his face he could feel the bristles of a substantial beard on his chin, the grime of a long trip on his cheeks. Running his fingers through his hair he realized it was lank and long. And then the ripples disappeared and he saw his reflection in the surface. A gaunt, thin face, cheeks hollow, stared back at him with his own eyes.

'What happened to me?' He looked at his hands, which were caked in dirt as if he hadn't washed for a month. On the beach just that morning he had cleaned himself thoroughly, as he had every day since arriving there. Yet now he was as filthy as a beggar at the city gates.

'You crossed between the worlds. Such a thing can take its toll on mind and body both.'

Dafydd tensed at the words, his head aching as they formed in his mind. Something large cast a shadow over the whole pool, and he saw in the gently undulating water the reflection of movement. He looked up, twisting his neck round to see, and almost fell in. A dragon loomed over him. At first he thought it would attack him, but he was too weary to put up much of a fight, too confused. Then he noticed that the creature was old, hunched like an arthritic. Its eyes were white with cataracts and half the scales on its face and arms were missing. It was no threat, and neither were the men standing behind it in a wide arc.

'Who are you?' he asked. 'Where am I? How did I get here?'

Some of the men started to speak among themselves in their strange tongue, but the dragon silenced them with a slow sweep of its arm. Its voice rose in Dafydd's head again, and he could hear the feminine tones somehow. Not it, but she.

'You came here by a Heol Anweledig that has not functioned for many thousands of years. That might explain why it took you so long to traverse it, though it must have felt like just an instant to you. And as to who I am, well, I am Earith and this is my home, Pallestre.'

19

The Falem archipelago of islands stretches north through the Southern Sea from Eirawen like rocks strewn across the floor by some giant hand. All are centred around single mountains, some of which smoke from their very tops and occasionally belch fire and brimstone. The islands are all now uninhabited, though many show signs of a civilized society long since departed. Legend tells of the men of Eirawen fleeing some natural disaster, heading north and settling the lands that would become the Twin Kingdoms, and perhaps there is some truth in those tales. Though the land is fertile and the seas abundant with fish, the islands of the archipelago are too small and too unstable to support much of a population. A far better explanation for the deserted towns and derelict temples is that the people who built them were driven onwards by some slow-spreading catastrophic change in Gwlad.

From the travel journals of Usel of the Ram

The fall was exhilarating, but it highlighted one big flaw in his plan. Errol had just enough time to register his nightshirt flapping up about his head and exposing the rest of him to all who could see before he hit the surface. Water exploded around him in a cacophony of bubbles and light, finishing the job the wind had done by ripping the thin fabric completely off. In a way that helped, leaving him unencumbered by clothing as he plunged down into the pool. He had no idea how deep his jump had taken him, but it clearly wasn't to the bottom.

Although he had always been a strong swimmer, Errol couldn't recall ever having dived deeper than when he and Martha had fallen into the pool at Jagged Leap. He pushed himself down ever further, kicking his legs and dragging his arms through water that grew darker with each passing moment. The noise dissipated almost to nothing, just a muffled rushing sound and the heavy thumping of his heart. His eyes all but useless, Errol opened his sight up to the aethereal again, astonished at the clarity it brought him in this dark place. He could see fish circling him nervously. Currents eddied slowly, not strong enough to trap him like old Ben Coulter. Below him something glowed faintly in the gloom. He pushed on deeper and slowly the bottom began to reveal itself.

Long weeds swayed back and forth, glowing gently with the Grym. Small creatures scurried about in the sand and silt. The base of the pool was uneven, rising vertically on the side where Errol had fallen in the day before, at a more shallow angle on the beach side. The middle was almost perfectly flat save for a large mound, and as he kicked towards it, so he could better make out its shape.

At first he thought they were branches off some great tree, poking up out of the silt like grasping fingers. Green algae clung to them, moving in the tiny currents, lit with its own Grym. It wasn't until Errol had reached the nearest of the branches that he understood what it truly was: a rib bone thicker than his thigh.

It was what he had been looking for, but still seeing the last remains of Magog came as a shock. His lungs were beginning to hurt with the effort of holding his breath, his thoughts growing sluggish. Errol reached out for the rib, hoping to pull it free, but it was stuck fast in the mud. He used it to pull himself along in a direction he hoped was the head, searching for a smaller bone, something he could hope to take back to the surface with him. Time was running out though. Soon he would have to push up towards the surface or risk drowning.

The bones were hard to see in the aethereal, dead as they were, but ancient magics clung to them like moss, protecting them from decay. Errol went from rib to rib, pulling at them with greater desperation, each as solid as the next. Magog's skull rose ahead of him, half-buried in the silt, cracked open by the rock that had killed him. Vertebrae oozed up out of the mud, as big as his own head and stuck fast, but a few fragments of bone lay within that massive skull. The place where Benfro had found the jewel.

Errol pulled himself forward, swam into the gaping hole that had once been Magog, Son of the Summer Moon. Plate-sized shards of skull lay strewn around, but as he reached for one, he was suddenly overcome with a terrible fear. What if there were more jewels still in the mud of the pool bottom? What if he accidentally touched one? Would he be able to survive the kind of onslaught that had nearly destroyed Benfro? Errol kicked away from the skull. He wanted nothing more than to get back to the surface, breathe, leave this sacred place.

But he had to get some bone. Without it there was no end to the madness. With the last of his strength he dived back into the open skull, reached out and grasped the first piece he could reach. He didn't have the energy to focus on the aethereal any more, and his vision faded to deepest black as his fingers closed tight. A moment's disorientation as he turned head over heels in the water and then he was struggling upwards.

Bubbles escaped from between his lips as he kicked out with weak legs. Weeds wound around his ankles, dragging him back down. He desperately needed air, but up above was as dark as down below. It felt like he wasn't moving at all, just hanging in the water. Was this how Ben Coulter had died? No, he'd knocked himself senseless on a rock, hadn't he? Or was that Magog, brains bashed in by some giant bird sent by King Balwen? Errol struggled to make sense of anything at all. He was cold, so very cold, and tired. He'd struggled for so long, worked so hard, could he not just have a bit of a rest? Get his strength back. Sleep.

Water poured into his open mouth, choking him so suddenly he almost dropped his precious cargo back into the depths. Errol shocked awake, but it was too late. His lungs were spasming of their own accord, gulping down water, losing all his precious buoyant air. He could feel the depths dragging him down again. He would die here, his bones mingling with those of the great dragon mage.

Something grabbed him under the armpits, heaved him up. A body close to his warmed his back, held him tight. In moments his head broke the surface as Nellore heaved him towards the shore, then dropped him half in, half out of the water. Crashing to the sand drove some of the water out of his lungs, and soon Errol was heaving and spluttering, coughing up great spouts of river as he fought to breathe.

It took a long time, and his throat was raw before he could even think about moving. Around about the same time he realized that Nellore was standing close by, just watching him. He looked up at her and tried to grin but could only manage a weak cough.

'What you thinking, Errol? Jumping in off that big rock and staying down there so long?'

He pushed himself up on to all fours, then slumped sideways into an awkward sitting position, holding up his hand with the prize that had almost cost him his life. The piece of bone was smaller than he remembered it from below, coated in slimy green, pitted and worn around the edges.

'Piece of Magog's skull,' was all he could say before collapsing into a coughing fit again, vomiting up half the pool. He couldn't be sure he'd actually managed to say the words. Nellore came closer, sat down a few feet away from him where the sand was dry. The sun had risen well into the morning sky now, and its warmth was welcome as it dried his skin.

'What you want it for?'

Errol looked across at the girl. Her hair was plastered to her head and she'd stripped off most of her clothes before jumping into the pool to his rescue. What she had left on was stuck to her thin frame, accentuating her thinness and boyish lack of curves. He remembered his own nakedness then, couldn't imagine how he could have forgotten it, and crossed his legs in embarrassment.

'Thank you. For rescuing me.' The words croaked out, threatening another coughing fit. He swallowed hard to suppress it. 'It was stupid. Diving in like that. Didn't realize how deep it was.'

'An' all for a manky old bit of rock. What's so important about it?' Nellore reached out for his prize and Errol reluctantly let her take it.

'It's not rock, it's bone.' He watched as she scraped a bit of the green coating away with a fingernail to reveal white beneath. She carried it to the water's edge, scooped up wet sand and cleaned away at it for a while. Errol watched, still trying to catch his breath, still exhausted from his time in the water. How long had it been? It couldn't have been more than a minute or two or he would certainly have drowned. And yet it felt as if a lifetime had passed.

'Seen boy parts before. You ain't got nothing to be embarrassed about.' Nellore came back with the cleaned fragment of skull and handed it back to Errol. He took it but didn't uncross his legs.

'What happened to my nightclothes?' he asked, looking briefly around and hoping they hadn't been carried off downstream. Or worse, sunk to the bottom of the pool.

'I fished 'em out, hung 'em on a bush to dry.' Nellore slumped back down on to the sand. Closer to him this time, much to Errol's discomfort. 'Now what's so special about this bit of rock or bone or whatever it is?'

Errol weighed the piece in his hand. It was heavier than he expected bone to be, and doubts crept into his head. Had he hallucinated the whole episode? Dived to the bottom and brought back a stone? He shook his head. 'This is a piece from the skull of the dragon Magog. The one whose jewel I've been carrying around.' The jewel that was presumably still sitting in a pouch in a wooden chest in a guest room in Myfanwy's house. At least he hoped so, even if he had no idea how to get back there.

'So why'd you nearly kill yourself fetching it off the bottom? An' how come it's there at all. Dint Magog die like a million years ago or something?'

'I told you about Benfro, right? How he's attached to the jewel by magic? How it makes him do stuff and it's trying to take him over completely?'

Nellore nodded.

'Well with this and the jewel, Benfro can free himself of that link. Free everyone of Magog's influence. All he needs to do is put them together and breathe fire over them.'

The Council of Nantgrafanglach was not at all what Iolwen had been expecting. They sat in chairs similar in design if not size to the Obsidian Throne, arranged in a semicircle around a large table. A dozen dragons, all clearly of great age, stared at her with eyes squinting to focus or clouded white and impossible to read. A couple, sitting side by side, didn't stare at all. Instead they slumped so that their heads almost touched, dozing gently. As she watched, the next dragon along reached a bony finger and prodded his neighbour, causing the beast to wake with a start and clatter its head against its companion. Satisfied that all were awake, the dragon who had done the poking turned its attention to Iolwen.

'They call you Princess Iolwen, is that not so?' The dragon who had asked was ancient, but her voice was clear and unmistakably female for all its deep tones.

'I am Iolwen, yes. Might I ask to whom I am speaking?'

The dragon smiled and turned to Sir Conwil. He was still standing, and there were no spare seats. Not a member of the council then.

'I like her,' she said, still speaking Saesneg, then turned back to Iolwen. 'I am Myfanwy. Some call me Myfanwy the . . .' She paused a moment, then shook her head. 'No, we don't need to bother with any of that nonsense. Myfanwy's just fine.'

'Why have you brought me here?' Iolwen gestured around the room. 'Where is here, for that matter?'

'Have you told them nothing, Sir Conwil?' Myfanwy asked.

The dragon produced that half-nod, half-bow motion he had used with Iolwen before. 'It has been a trying time. Hundreds, no thousands of people to rehouse, the prisoner escaping, this terrible storm. You yourself returning to the palace after years of exile, only to disappear without a word. I did not think a few days' delay would harm anyone. Give us time to take stock.'

Myfanwy's irritation was plain for Iolwen to see, the scolding in her voice unrestrained. 'I told you, Conwil. Times have changed. You cannot treat these people as you have the palace servants and their families. They are not of the Old One's world, but of his brother's. Not Gog's but Magog's.'

At the sound of the last name all the other dragons in the room sat upright and breathed in sharply. Some even gasped. Sir Conwil looked over his shoulder as if some mortal enemy were close by.

'Myfanwy, I—'

'Your great-grandfather is past caring whether or not that name is spoken aloud here. He is dead, and by the centuries-long reach of his brother's hand. We all know the spells he wove to keep himself hidden from his twin. Now both are gone and those magics are falling apart. Can you not see that? Or are you as weak in the subtle arts as our kin who have turned savage and gone to live in caves?'

Sir Conwil said nothing in reply, just lowered his head as if accepting the old dragon's wisdom on the matter. She in turn settled in her seat and brought her attention back to Iolwen.

'Please accept my apologies. As you may have realized, things are changing all too rapidly in Gwlad. Or at least the Gwlad we know. I think you have grown up in a very different place. One where our kind are far fewer in number and far less threatening. That was the Old One's parting gift to his brother's folk. He laid a curse upon them that caused them to dwindle in stature. I remember him boasting of it when he was younger, not that he ever spoke much of his brother. You cannot begin to understand the hatred between the two of them.'

Iolwen thought of the dragons she had seen as she was growing up, on those rare occasions she was allowed to visit the circus at the King's Fair. Compared to the massive beast that had killed Seneschal Padraig, they were as mice to the great carthorses that pulled the grain wagons from the Northlands to the city.

'There is more to the story than that.' Beside her, Usel spoke up for the first time since they had arrived in front of the council.

'Usel of the Ram,' Myfanwy said. 'I have heard of your order. You are healers, it seems. A noble calling.'

'I thank you, Lady Myfanwy. Though you might not think so, were you to realize the nature of our healing. We began as battlefield surgeons, stitching up those unfortunate enough to be wounded while slaughtering your kind. It was only once there were no more dragons to kill that we turned our skills to more peaceful ends.'

'You have killed dragons?' The question came from one of the two who had been asleep on their arrival. Now he was awake and alert, something about his stare suggesting that he might soon even become angry.

'No, sire. I have not. Indeed I have sworn an oath to protect those few who remain in my world, and I have spent a lifetime studying them, trying to learn as much as I can about them and from them.'

The old dragon gave a snort that suggested very human-like derision, but Usel ignored him.

'Which is how I have come to hear many of their stories, the greatest of which is the tale of Gog and Magog. The two brothers who battled for the affection of Ammorgwm the Fair and in so doing split Gwlad in two.'

Another member of the council let out a bark of laughter, but Myfanwy waved him silent. 'Go on, Usel of the Ram.'

'Most dragons' tales, at least where I come from, are part entertainment and part teaching. I had always considered the story of the two brothers to be a morality tale, a warning about the folly of selfishness and the abuse of power. And it is all those things, of course, but it is even more because it is true.'

Silence fell across the hall for a while, then Myfanwy spoke.

'It is indeed true, after a fashion. Gog and Magog were brothers, twins hatched from the one egg. They were powerful mages, perhaps the equal of great Rasalene himself. None but the most skilled could have done what they did, and none but the most depraved would ever have tried. Gwlad herself has been riven in two for millennia. That rift has been weakening for years, but now, with Gog's death, she is being made whole again too quickly. This is not something that will happen easily. This blizzard that has raged around us since the Old One's death is no natural storm.'

It made a horrible kind of sense, Iolwen knew. The dragons in this council were ancient, but they were also huge and shimmered with the power of the Grym. The pieces of the puzzle began to slot into place now.

'The Neuadd,' she said. 'That is Gog's hall, is it not? The Obsidian Throne is his seat. That's why the tunnel brought us here.'

'The Neuadd y Ganhwyllau was built by Palisander, but Gog spoke lovingly of it. If that is the place you mean, then yes, it was his hall once Palisander had passed.'

'And so I ask again, Lady Myfanwy. Where in Gwlad is this place?' Iolwen repeated her question. 'What mountains are these that surround us?'

Myfanwy frowned, as if she couldn't understand the importance of the question. 'These are the Rim mountains, surrounding the endless desert wasteland of the Ffrydd, where Magog once had his great palace Cenobus and before that, Palisander's home, Claerwen. Nantgrafanglach lies towards the eastern edge, not far from the Caenant plain.'

'Not much more than a day's flight from Emmass Fawr then.' Usel spoke the words, even though they were what Iolwen had been thinking.

'The home of Maddau the Wise is far closer than a day's flight. Of Magog's favoured, she was perhaps the one closest still to the Old One. Emmass Fawr lies just a few leagues from here. Had it not vanished when Gwlad was split you would be able to see it from the top of the great tower. Except that you cannot see anything in this foul weather.'

Iolwen shuddered at these words. She turned to face Usel and could see that they had given him cause for concern too. No doubt he was thinking the same things as her, for he spoke in a quiet voice that nevertheless carried across the room.

'Then we must pray this storm continues for a long time.'

'Pray?' It was not Myfanwy who spoke, but one of the larger dragons on the council. He still seemed impossibly old to Iolwen's eyes, but there was an impression of relative youthfulness about him. 'And exactly whom should we pray to?'

There was a long silence as Usel failed to answer. 'It is just a figure of speech,' Iolwen said eventually. 'Perhaps hope would be a better word. Better still would be to ready yourselves for the inevitable attack.'

'Attack? Who would dare attack us? We are all-powerful. And besides, Nantgrafanglach is protected by the most sophisticated workings of the subtle arts ever conceived.' The old dragon who spoke wheezed and coughed as his throat caught on his last word, but the murmuring of agreement that echoed around the chamber didn't fill Iolwen with much joy.

'Workings performed by your Old One, I take it?' she asked. The murmuring stopped as the implications of her words sank in.

'They are still potent, and we are not without our own skills in these matters.' Myfanwy cocked her head to one side as if listening for a far-off sound that Iolwen couldn't hear. 'But there is wisdom in what you say. Nantgrafanglach can no longer rely on the protections it once had. I am still unsure what danger could threaten us though. The feral dragons of our world are easily fooled by the most basic of magics. Are those in your yours any different?'

'It is not dragons you should be afraid of. It's men. In particular Inquisitor Melyn and the warrior priests of the Order of the High Ffrydd. Emmass Fawr is their headquarters now, the dragon you knew as Maddau the Wise long slain. If they discover a city filled with your kind they will descend upon it like wolves on a flock of sheep.'

'We are not sheep, young woman!' The wheezy old dragon pulled himself to his feet, then burst into a fit of coughing so violent he had to sit down again.

'You are not, no. But Melyn and his men are much worse than wolves.' Iolwen considered for a moment how best to get through to these elderly dragons. They were not unlike the council of viziers who had met once a month to discuss matters of state and give advice to King Ballah. She had listened in on a few of those sessions, so dry and formal and ultimately pointless as the king trusted no other counsel but his own. Or at a pinch that of his brother, Tordu. These dragons meant well; they had agreed to see her, after all. But they were so old and set in their ways. They needed something to convince them that times had changed.

It was obvious, in the end, what she had to do, but still it took all her courage. She knew the magic but lacked the practice, and here the Grym was so much more powerful than she was used to. Still, Iolwen steeled herself, tapped into that life force and brought forth a puissant blade. She had meant it to be only small, but it blazed brighter and fiercer than any she had seen. A moment's uncertainty almost let the power of it devour her, and she took a hurried step forward, swinging it down through the nearest table before she recovered enough control to let the Grym dissipate once more. Her ears rang with the noise of it, but even so she could hear the alarm among the council members. Smoke wafted up to her nose, the charred table split in two, the elderly dragon fell from his bench and stared up at her with a wild, frightened look in his eyes that must have mirrored her own.

'I am but a novice in this magic.' Iolwen's voice sounded strained, its pitch higher than normal to her ears. 'The warrior priests can conjure and wield such blades for hours at a time. That is what you must ready yourselves for. They are coming, and they number in the thousands.'

Errol's shivering woke him from troubled slumber. He was cold even though he lay by the fire, too tired and confused to concentrate on using the Grym to warm himself. The day had passed in fitful sleep, his dreams a jumble of images that made no sense. Nellore must have been collecting firewood and keeping the flames going for him. Now she sat close by, running grubby fingers through her tangled hair.

'You awake now?'

Errol groaned and sat up. His whole body ached; even his throat was sore. There was a gentle breeze across the clearing, which cooled the top of his bald head, made goosebumps on the skin of his arms and back. Looking down, he realized he was still naked. His thin nightshirt still hung on a nearby bush, but he could see it was torn along one seam and full of holes. Nellore's clothes weren't much better, scorched by her contact with Gog's jewels to the point where they were falling off in great clumps. He needed to find something better for both of them, but how? He wasn't even sure where he was.

Except that he was in Magog's world. His world. Somewhere out there, up near the foothills of the distant mountains, there was a cave. And in that cave there should be a chest. He had managed to bring it to him once; maybe he could do that again.

'Keep an eye out, will you? I'm going to try and get us some clothes. Like I did with food before.'

Nellore perked up at the mention of food, and Errol's stomach grumbled in sympathy. The fish they had eaten the night before had been large, but it was all gone now.

'Clothes first. Then I'll see if I've the energy to find something to eat.'

He settled himself as best he could by the fire, opened himself up to the Grym and tried to form a picture in his mind of the clearing where Corwen's cave lay. It hadn't been that long since he and Benfro had left. A few months at most, though so much had happened in that time. Still, he could picture the meadow grass and the low stone corral, the river he had bathed and swum in as he tried to build strength in his shattered ankles, and the cave where he had slept with its strange-smelling dry dusty earth floor. His clothes chest was in there, tucked up against the wall opposite the sleeping alcove. Slowly he built up the image, going over it time and again until he was sure he had the details right, the feel of the place. Then he felt out along the lines, guided by that feeling.

It was slow work, but the power flowing up from the pool helped him. The piece of skull clutched in his hands was an anchor too. Something that he could easily return to should he become lost. In his mind Errol saw the cave, dark now that the fire had gone out, but still with that strange smell about it. The alcove was piled high with dried grass and heather draped in a blanket that would do if he could reach nothing else. The ground had been disturbed, the pile of firewood kicked this way and that by Melyn's men as they searched the place. For a moment Errol almost lost his concentration. What if they'd taken the chest? Or just thrown it in the river?

He calmed himself, building up the image of the cave again, picturing the spot where Benfro had placed the chest all those months ago. He remembered all the times he had risen, hobbled on sore, healing ankles across the cave and opened the lid. Inside he could see the piles of clothes, worn a little, perhaps getting a bit on the small side, but his. Errol reached out an imaginary hand and took a hold of the rough cloth tunic his mother had sewn for him not long before her wedding. Beneath it lay a pair of soft leather trews that Godric had given him. There were stiff wool socks, smallclothes and more blankets. And there, washed and dried and tidied away, the jerkin he had been wearing when he and Martha had almost drowned. It was too small for him now, but it reminded him of her. For a moment he thought he could hear her voice, calling him, dragging him away from the cave and the chest and the clothes. He hardened himself against it, focused solely on the chest. He knew all too well the lure of the Grym, the distractions that could tear his soul from his body and dissipate it throughout Gwlad. He needed enough to wear, and something for Nellore since her skirt wasn't going to last much longer if they started walking through deep forest. No more than that. They could search for Martha later.

It was strange, rifling through his clothes in his memory. Errol felt no sensation as he picked up one garment then another, but each one he remembered handling before. Not really sure how he did it, he imagined himself selecting the best of what was on offer, tucking things under an invisible arm until he had all he could manage. He still felt the cold stone of Magog's skull plate in the hand of that arm, and as he focused on that sensation, so the image of the cave, the smell of its soil and the rush of the waterfall out beyond it faded away, morphing into the dry wind through the wiry shrubs, the soft trickle of the sluggish stream and hiss, crack and pop of the fire.

As he came back to himself, Errol felt the weight of the clothing under his arm and a sense of elation that he had succeeded. And then at the last moment he felt something else. A rush of the Grym like a surge of water cascading over him. He clung tight to the clothes, fearful they would slip back to Corwen's clearing, or worse be lost for ever in the lines. He squeezed hard on the piece of bone in his hand, digging his fingernails into it and using the pain to remind himself of his own body. For a moment he thought his head was being squeezed tight by some huge hand, then his ears popped and he was pitched forward.

Errol sprawled on to the sand, the clothes tumbling from under his arm and partially cushioning his fall. The effort of reaching out along the lines had left him even more drained than when Nellore had pulled him out of the pool, but he was dimly aware of a commotion over by the large rock. Then he heard Nellore scream in alarm, a high-pitched wail that reminded him just how young she really was, and how helpless. He didn't know what he could do to protect her, but he had to try.

Mustering all his energy, he pushed himself up off the sand and struggled to his feet. The ground swayed alarmingly as he tried to find his balance, searching all the while for whatever it was that had scared Nellore. His vision was dull and blurred with exhaustion, and he had to shake his head, blink a few times until things came into focus. Only then did he see something he couldn't quite understand.

Two figures stood halfway between the great rock and their fire. One was a young boy who seemed strangely familiar, even though Errol was fairly certain he had never met him before. He looked pale and was wiping at his mouth with the back of his sleeve as if he had just thrown up. The other Errol recognized at once, even though she was thin and bedraggled, her hair awry and her long green cloak in tatters. Martha stared first at him, then at Nellore standing on the other side of the fire. Then her gaze narrowed into a deep frown as it returned to him once more. Looked him up and down and up again.

'Who is this girl, Errol? And why are neither of you wearing any clothes?'

20

First you will feel the heat in the tips of your fingers, as if you have grasped a mug just filled with boiling water. Arms and legs are mere conduits for the Grym, so next your stomach will begin to churn, acid leaching through into your lungs and lights as it bubbles through you. The very air you breathe will seem like flames, searing your throat and swelling your tongue until speech is impossible. It is unlikely at this point you will want to do anything but scream.

As the power floods into you unchecked, so the soles of your feet and the palms of your hands will blister. The fire will engulf your joints, twisting elbows and knees, hips and fingers so that you curl up like an ancient man, withered by time. The fluid in your eyes will boil, turning them white like poached eggs as the heat travels up to your brain.

And the cruellest thing is that you will feel it all. For the Grym is power, true, but it is also life. It will hold you in its grip as it devours your flesh from within. Only when there is nothing left for it to feed upon will your self be dissipated and the agony be over.

Inquisitor Melyn,
Lectures to Novitiates

There had been much to distract her as they began the slow task of reoccupying Candlehall. Appointing a new seneschal had been the least of Beulah's troubles, and for the first time in her life she found herself wishing she had more predicants and clerks of the Candle. Dry and humourless they might have been, but they were efficient and skilled in the minutiae of administration. Clun's background as a merchant's son had proved useful in negotiations with suppliers and builders. His reputation as the man who had bested the leader of the dragons helped as well, but there was still a mountain of work to be done before the Twin Kingdoms could even begin to return to normal. Which was perhaps why she had not yet returned to the Neuadd since taking back her city. That and the fear that her beloved hall was almost certainly damaged, the throne sullied by the presence both of the dragons and her sister.

Beulah had persuaded herself that it wasn't safe to venture through the palace until all the damage had been checked and any people remaining had been vetted to see where their sympathies lay. Those tasks complete, she no longer had any excuse other than her reluctance to return to her throne. Until that was done she could scarcely claim to be queen, so finally she had summoned her husband and bade him accompany her. She took no guards, not wanting anyone to see her reaction to the damage she knew must be.

It was not an easy journey. The stench grew worse, and with it the destruction as they progressed through the palace towards the Neuadd. Dust and bits of fallen stonework lay everywhere, the thick carpets ruined by the careless tramping of many feet. Some corridors were blocked by collapsed ceilings, others impassable because of fallen floors. Wherever Beulah looked there was more damage, but most of all it was the lack of people that she found unnerving. Candlehall had always been thronged with folk, the palace a bustle of busyness as only the administrative centre of a realm could be. There should have been black-robed predicants everywhere, quietly discussing the running of the Twin Kingdoms as they moved from room to room. Ministers should have been on hand to advise her on matters of state. Servants should have been cleaning, repairing and generally making sure the palace ran smoothly. And there should have been guards on every major corridor. Instead the whole place was empty.

'There were warrior priests stationed here before Padraig let my sister and her band of rebels in. I wonder what happened to them?'

'Very few warrior priests remained here, my lady, and they were older men, ready to turn quaister and teach the next generation of novitiates. The most able rode with Inquisitor Melyn into the Northlands, the rest followed us on our grand tour or went to Dinas and Tochers to train the armies. Candlehall was never seen as being under much threat, so we left it to Seneschal Padraig to defend it with his own men.'

'And look how well that turned out.' Beulah let out a humourless laugh as they finally reached the stone steps leading up to the cloisters surrounding the Neuadd. It had taken them far longer than it should have to reach this point, constantly doubling back through empty rooms and using the servants' corridors when the main routes were blocked.

'Not so well for the seneschal, my lady.' Clun lowered his head as if in embarrassment, or perhaps sadness.

'How so? He fled with all the others, did he not? With my darling sister and her savage husband.'

'I think not. That mess on the front steps is all that remains of him. If I understand Sir Sgarnog correctly, Padraig sought to negotiate terms with Sir Chwilog and was eaten for his pains.'

Beulah smiled at the news, but in truth her appetite for vengeance was waning with each new discovery in the palace. It was hard to maintain enmity for her treacherous people when a much more tangible threat hung over them all. Hard to even think of her success over the Llanwennogs when her own capital lay in ruins, its people scattered. A hollow victory indeed.

'Come then. Let us see what chaos these creatures have wrought upon the great hall.' Beulah set a foot on the first step, and as she did so a deep rumble filled the air, shaking the stones and causing plaster dust to spiral down from the ceiling. The noise ended as abruptly as it started, and then a great trumpeting roar blasted down the stairwell. With it came the reek of fresh charnel and an unpleasant heat.

'By the Shepherd, what is that?' Beulah covered her mouth and nose with one hand, summoned the Grym to her and conjured a blade of fire in the other. Beside her Clun did the same. They climbed the stairs together slowly.

'Be careful, my lady. I don't think this is one of Sir Sgarnog's fold. There's something familiar about—'

An explosion of noise cut off whatever Clun was going to say. Beulah saw the stone pillar at the top of the steps shatter into a million pieces, just had time to register that it had been swiped out of the way by a massive scaly hand, and then she was turning, ducking away from the cascade of rocks that bounced and ricocheted down towards them both. Her blade faltered and went out, too much effort to maintain as something else stole the Grym from far around. Her knees buckled and she stumbled down the steps, rolling as she hit the floor at the bottom. Something cracked like a dead branch underfoot, but in the chaos she couldn't tell if it was her own bones or those of her consort. Maybe it was both.

'Clun!' The word escaped from her like the scream of a little girl, but all she could see was billowing dust, shards of stone flying like ballista projectiles and pinging off the far wall. She shuffled backwards, noticing for the first time the pain in her leg. Reaching down, she felt a wetness on her soft leather riding trousers, and when she looked at her hand it was stained with sticky red blood.

Another crash shook the building, sending more stone tumbling down the stairs. It sounded like something was trying to rip the roof off and expose them to the sky. Beulah tried to stand up, but now there was sharp pain in her leg, unbearable the moment she put any weight on it. Something was clearly broken. She pulled herself further away from the pile of rubble at the bottom of the stairs, searching for Clun through the dust. Up above the beast roared again, and there was something in the cadence of the sounds that made her realize it was speech. Angry words, beyond angry. There was a righteous fury to the screeching sounds even though she could not understand their meaning.

The dust began to settle, sunlight spearing through the motes at an angle that suggested at least part of the roof was gone now. Still Beulah could not see Clun anywhere. And then she saw a hand, pale and streaked with blood, poking out from a pile of rocks. Did it twitch as she looked? Could she hear a low moan of pain? Her ears were still ringing from the explosions and the noise of the great dragon's bellowing. It had fallen silent for a moment, but she was sure it was still there, sniffing them out like a terrier after rats. She had put up her mental shields at the same time as she had conjured her blade; years of training had made that automatic. Now she strengthened them against what felt like an alien presence in the Grym, testing and poking the lines to see what it might find. As her hearing returned, she could make out more subtle sounds, the occasional chink of stone upon stone, rough scraping as heavy objects were moved aside, the breathing of a creature so big she could scarce imagine it.

And Clun was lying there wounded, unconscious, helpless.

'Do not try to move, my love,' she whispered. 'I am coming to help.'

Beulah pulled herself along the floor, back the way she had just come. Large stones had jammed together at the top of the steps, but even with her hearing dulled, she could tell that something was digging away at them furiously.

Clun lay on his back, half covered in rocks. Blocking out the pain in her leg, Beulah began shifting the smaller ones as best she could, working quickly but quietly. Every so often she glanced up at the jumble of boulders wedged precariously into the stairwell above her. Should a key stone be removed, the whole lot would come tumbling down and that would be the end.

A weak groan focused Beulah's attention. Clun's eyes were still closed, blood seeping from a gash on his forehead, but he slowly raised one hand and began to push weakly at the rocks still covering his chest. He coughed, then let out a sharp gasp of pain. Beulah could see now that his legs were pinned under a heavy chunk of masonry.

'Stay still. I need to work my way round to the other side of you. Help you shift that.' She started to drag herself around the pile of rubble as Clun hacked and coughed, spitting out dust and blood on to the stone floor.

'Are you hurt, my lady?' he asked after a while. Beulah noticed he didn't look up or try to see where she was.

'Not badly,' she lied. 'We need to get you free before those rocks give way though.'

Clun moved his head from side to side, eyes open and blinking rapidly now. His gaze slid over her. 'I can't see anything.'

'It's just the dust, a bit of blood. Keep calm, my love. I am nearly there.' Beulah dragged herself alongside him as she spoke, reached out a hand and touched him lightly on the shoulder. He flinched, then forced himself to relax as she felt his face, wiped at the mess around his eyes and the cut above them. In the gloom she could see no reason why his sight should have failed him, but she buried the worry, turning her attention to the rock that pinned his legs.

It was a piece of the cloister, she was fairly sure of that. The carving on the side facing her was worn smooth with the passing of ages, and the stone had that dark sooty staining much of the palace exterior wore. It was bigger than her upper body and most likely weighed as much as her filly. What chance Clun's legs were not crushed entirely beneath it? What chance of her shifting it even a tiny amount?

'Can you feel anything?' Beulah slid herself closer to Clun, pressed gently on first one leg then the other. He stiffened and grunted at her touch, clearly in agony but unwilling to show it. Still, it was a good sign.

'I'm going to try and move this rock. Can you pull your legs out?'

'I will try, my lady.'

Clun shifted himself, feeling around with his hands to get the lie of the land. He touched Beulah's leg briefly and she winced, biting back the cry of pain.

'I think we are both hurt more than we are prepared to admit,' he said.

'We are alive. Let us try and stay that way.'

Beulah set her shoulder against the rock and pushed. It gave a little, and Clun tried to pull himself clear. It was not enough though, and after a moment he stopped.

'We need help. Go. Fetch Captain Celtin and his men. I'll be fine until they get here.'

'I can't leave you,' Beulah said.

'You must, my lady. Think of our daughter.' He reached out with a hand, searching the air for her. Beulah sat upright, caught it in her own and guided it to her face.

'I can't because my leg is broken, my love. We either get out of this together or not at all.'

*

287

'Gather the men. I have a mission that will require the skills we have acquired over the course of this campaign.'

Melyn sat in King Ballah's throne deep in the palace of Tynhelyg and wondered why it had taken him so long to act. A week and more had passed since General Otheng and the first clerks of the Candle had arrived, taking on the burden of running this newest province of the Twin Kingdoms, and yet he had not set out in search of Benfro, nor ordered his warrior priests to begin the long march back to Emmass Fawr. Instead he had barely moved from this room and the dead king's personal chambers, all the while struggling to calm the storm of new knowledge, the thousand thousand voices that whispered and shouted in his head. He had not been ready, had still been recovering from his wounds. Or at least that was the excuse that he had given himself. Until now.

'At once, sire.' Captain Osgal snapped to attention, clattering a salute off his chest that had him wincing in ill-disguised pain. The wounds Benfro had inflicted on him showed no sign of healing yet, the sores on his face suppurating, his eyes bloodshot. For all his discomfort he was a constant presence at the inquisitor's side. And yet despite his words, Osgal paused a moment where once he would have rushed straight to his task. 'Might I ask what mission?'

The old Melyn, the one who had ridden out of Emmass Fawr in search of a renegade dragon and a back route into the land of his enemies, would probably have struck the captain for the failure to execute his order immediately and without question. But the old Melyn was dead, consumed by the madness that had descended on him when he had finally met his god. The new Melyn was more accommodating, though perhaps every bit as cruel.

'Come here, Captain,' he commanded. 'Kneel before me.'

Osgal did as he was bid, the fear well hidden behind those red eyes and blistered skin. Melyn placed a hand on the captain's head and let the spirit of Magog flow through him into the kneeling man. It wasn't a pleasant healing, not like the gentle touch of the Shepherd as he washed away the aches and pains of years. Melyn had no time nor inclination for such subtlety. In moments he forced flesh to mend itself that would have taken months of its own accord. Osgal clenched his teeth in pain, his breath snorting out through his nose in ragged gasps, but he did not speak, did not cry out. When it was done though, and Melyn removed his hand, the captain slumped forward before struggling back on to his knees.

'Your Grace, I . . .' he began, then clearly felt the healing that had been worked upon him. Amazed hands wandered up to his face, feeling his cheeks, his forehead, and slowly he looked up to gaze into the inquisitor's eyes. His awe was perfect.

'The Shepherd has returned, Jerrim. He is in me. Now I need you to seek out the lair of the Wolf. It lies somewhere to the north of Emmass Fawr, a city hidden by purloined magics. Take the warrior priests who rode with us through the Northlands. Seek out this city and map its bounds. Station men at its gates who know the hiding spell best, then return to the monastery. I will meet you there.'

'You are not coming with us, sire? Osgal's healed face creased into a worried frown, its youthful flesh at odds with the shock of white hair that covered the crown of his head where Melyn had touched him.

'I have unfinished business I must attend to. You have your orders, Captain. Set to them swiftly.'

Osgal scrambled to his feet, still shaking slightly from the pain of his healing. He clapped a fist to his chest, bowed and then without another word scurried from the room. Melyn turned back to the throne, beside which Frecknock stood, waiting patiently like an obedient dog. She looked up at his words. 'You have the book? *The Llyfr Draconius*?'

'I never let it out of my sight, sire.' She reached for the leather bag slung around her neck, unbuckling it and pulling out the heavy tome.

'Give it to me.'

Melyn took the book, feeling the weight of it in his hand, a tightness in his chest where his wound had healed in a band of golden scales. The wound that Benfro had given him. It was a link to the young dragon, as was the throne, the location where the deed had been done. It was from here that Benfro had leaped into the Grym. Melyn knew how that was done now, could step through the lines as easily as crossing the threshold from one room to another. He just needed to open the door first.

'Come, Frecknock.' He reached out and took the dragon's hand, feeling the warmth of it, the soft leather of her palms and the tiny serrations of the scales that covered her fingers. Much like the ones that covered his own. The book, the dragon and the throne. Together they were his anchor as he reached out along the lines, testing them for the scent he was looking for. So much time had passed since Benfro had escaped. Could he possibly hope to track him this way? And what if he found him? Would he let Magog finish the task he had begun, let the most powerful mage ever to have lived be born again? Or would he do what he had always intended and slay the abomination like he had slain its mother? Put an end once and for all to the madness. Melyn walled off the questions in his mind, hiding them away before they could take hold. There was no need to seek out Benfro anyway; the young dragon would come to him.

And then he felt it, the faintest whisper in the Grym. Frecknock must have felt it too, for her grip upon his hand tightened.

'Your Grace. Master Clun!' Terror clipped the edges of her voice, and as Melyn turned his attention to her he saw why. The aethereal sight was never far from him now, and with little more than a blink he saw Clun's body hanging palely in the air between them. He looked sickly, injured, a dull red glow surrounding him like a protective shield.

'Neuadd . . . Danger . . . The queen . . . Caradoc . . .' Barely a whisper, each word caught in his throat as if he were in great pain. Then he looked straight into Melyn's eyes. 'Help us.'

'Keep calm, my lady. Help is on its way.'

Clun had fallen silent for long moments after Beulah had told him of her injury, and she had begun to wonder if he was unconscious, or worse. Before she could understand his words, let alone ask what kind of help he meant, a spear of light appeared from above, bathing his face in gold. Beulah had quite forgotten the creature above them.

Now she looked up to see pale blue sky. Then the light dimmed, replaced by an enormous eye. A dragon's eye. Beulah froze, hoping that the corridor was dark enough for her to remain unseen, but soon enough the eye withdrew and the sound of rocks being pulled out of the way grew louder. Little runnels of dust spilled from the ceiling, covering her shoulders and matting her hair.

'I'm going to try once more,' she whispered. Beside her, Clun simply nodded, then put his arms out, hands palm down to the floor ready to pull himself free.

Beulah leaned into the stone again, feeling along its edge for the best way to lever it. Ignoring the jabbing pain in her broken ankle as best she could, she braced herself against another rock lying nearby and heaved with all her might. As the stone shifted, further this time, the hole in the ceiling grew larger, lighting up the corridor all around them. Something shifted high above, and then a crashing noise shook the whole palace. Clun was struggling back, grunting in pain as he tried to drag his crushed legs out from under the rock. Beulah felt the air move above her. Instinctively she ducked, and a talon passed through the space where her head had been. It arced past her, catching the edge of the stone and flipping it aside as easily as if it were made of feathers. Freed from its weight, Clun scrabbled back until he hit the far wall.

Beulah fell flat, all her pent-up strength suddenly pushing against air. Her leg twisted and she let out a shriek of pain cut short as she slammed into the flagstones, the breath knocked out of her lungs. Some sixth sense kicked in, and she rolled over as the jumble of stones above finally gave way, crashed down the broken stairwell and spilled out across the corridor. Somehow she managed to avoid being squashed, and ended up alongside Clun, hemmed in against the back wall by a ring of broken masonry.

It took a while for the dust to settle, and then the earth shook again as the dragon began to descend, dipping its massive head low, sniffing the air as it came, and with a shock Beulah recognized the creature.

'Caradoc.'

Clun looked up at her voice, but she could tell he wasn't seeing anything. Now there was enough light, she could see his eyes were glazed with white. She had occasionally seen something similar in the most ancient quaisters at Emmass Fawr, and more worryingly in some of the mindless. Great age could cloud a man's sight, but so could the Grym if not handled properly. Had he lost his concentration when the ceiling had collapsed? Not managed to safely extinguish his blade of fire?

There was no time to speculate. The great dragon shoved itself further into the hole it had created, reaching towards them with its enormous head. Fangs the length of her arm speared down from its upper jaw, those jutting upwards only slightly shorter. Was it possible that the beast was larger than she remembered, from back when it had snapped her beloved horse Pathia in two? The fog then had made it hard to gauge size, but she had no such problem now. It opened a mouth that could easily swallow her whole and spat out a string of sounds that screeched in her ears, breath souring the already stale air with the taint of rotten meat and unclean teeth.

'Ah, I understand now.' Clun spoke quietly, letting his

head drop to his chest. He took a couple of deep breaths, then began to speak in a loud, clear voice. Beulah couldn't understand the words, but recognized the language as the same he had spoken with Sir Chwilog and Angharad the Red. The language of dragons. How could a merchant's son with scarcely twenty summers behind him know such things? It wasn't the first time she had wondered.

'He blames me for the injury to his arm, of course. He wants his naming ring back.' Clun coughed, a horrible bubbly sound that suggested it wasn't just his legs that had suffered in the rockfall. 'And he's not too happy about Inquisitor Melyn using Frecknock to lure him in, let alone the attempts to kill him. He's most angry with us because we killed his mate, though.'

'His mate?'

'Morwenna the Subtle. The dragon who nearly put an end to Duke Glas.'

Beulah remembered then, back on their grand tour. The beast Glas had captured, whose head Clun had cut off when it had broken free of its chains and tried to kill them. She knew little about these creatures, and most of it was demonstrably false, but it surprised her they cared so much for one another.

'So it wants revenge.' She reached out and took Clun's hand. 'I am sorry, my love. I never meant for it to end this way.'

'I am sorry too, my lady. I swore I would protect you, and I don't intend to stop now.'

Beulah felt the air chill around her as Clun tapped the Grym, his blade of fire appearing once more, red and angry. He held it high and shouted something at the dragon, waving the blade this way and that. Perhaps the effect was meant to be frightening, but it merely underlined the fact that he was blind. Still she thought it might be working, as Caradoc withdrew slowly from the hole, screeching in that foul language all the while. Beulah had a moment to almost relax, and then with a speed quite at odds with its size, the dragon struck.

She couldn't see what happened, almost passed out as the Grym was sucked from the room, the lines and deep within her self. Clun's blade blazed, swinging with swiftness and deadly accuracy. Caradoc howled in pain, his head glancing off the remains of the ceiling as he reared back. Something hot spattered across Beulah's face, burning her skin like acid, and then with a wet thud a severed dragon's forearm slapped on to the ground beside her broken leg.

Sunlight flooded the corridor as the dragon withdrew completely. Even if she couldn't understand its language, Beulah could hear the pain and outrage in the noise it was making, and something more, as if it were calling for help.

'You are full of surprises, my love, but I fear we have only bought ourselves a brief respite. Unless we can get deeper into the palace, where even these creatures cannot reach us.'

'Fear not, my lady. Help is here. I merely had to distract the beast a while.' Clun slumped back against the wall and for a moment Beulah thought he was dead such was the pale stillness about him. Up above, she heard the sound of Caradoc screaming again, felt the air chill as something pulled in the Grym from all around. Her ears filled with a buzzing noise like a million angry bees, and then the dragon's voice stopped abruptly. A moment later something massive smashed into the cloisters above her. Cracks crazed across the ceiling, pouring more dust and rock over her and Clun. Something blocked the light, and for confused seconds Beulah thought the rocks jammed at the top of the stairs were tumbling down to crush her. But it was just one rock, rolling and bouncing and spraying something harsh and wet over her face and body. It somehow missed both her and Clun, coming to a halt a few paces off. Not a boulder, but the head of a vast dragon, its eyes staring blindly in death. The head of Caradoc.

Beulah opened her mouth to speak, then shut it again as she could think of nothing to say. Clun stirred beside her, a pained smile sliding slowly on to his face. He opened his eyes once more, staring up the steps towards the cloister even though he could not possibly have seen anything. 'Welcome, Your Grace, Lady Frecknock.'

Beulah followed his blind gaze up the rubble-strewn steps to the hole above where once there had been cloisters. A dragon looked down at them, but not one of the beasts that had sacked the city. This one was smaller, though seemed less timid than the last time they had met. And standing beside her, glowing with Grym and far healthier than Beulah had seen him in years, was Inquisitor Melyn.

21

When healing a fractured bone, it is important both to immobilize the patient and to fit the broken pieces back together as close as possible to how they were before whatever accident led to the break. Common practice is to bind the limb tightly, often with a splint of wood or similar. While in theory this is sound, in practice it is often done far too soon, before the break has been correctly aligned and the patient is sufficiently well sedated. Pain can cause muscles to contract, making a break all but impossible to set, and too tight a bandage will restrict the flow of vital healing humours.

In time, even an ill-set bone will knit back together, but it will be weak and a source of constant pain. Better to break a bone again and set it properly than allow such poor healing to go unchecked.

Archimandrite Boreray,
A Guide to the Healing Arts

Benfro lay on his side in mouldy straw, staring at a tiny square of light high overhead. The torchlight from outside shone through a small iron-barred window in the cell door, painting the distorted shape of the bars on the rough-hewn rock. It was impossible to get comfortable, partly because the cell was so small, but mostly because the wound in his side ached terribly in the cold. He was deep underground, cut off from the Grym, and while that meant he was for the moment safe from Magog's influence, it also meant he could neither keep himself warm nor speed his healing.

His captors had not cared that he was wounded, forcing him down here with kicks and prods. He could only guess that his two guards Borth and Carno were sons of Sir Nanteos, or at least from the same clan. They shared the old grey dragon's disdain for him, as well as his drab colouring. They had forced him into the cell and locked the door firmly behind him. Neither of them had said a word as they left, their footsteps echoing away to nothing and leaving him with only his thoughts for company.

How long he had been down here was difficult to judge. He had slept a little, but mostly he just lay on his side shivering and wincing as the pain lanced ever closer to his heart. He couldn't judge time so far from daylight, and the days spent in the shuttered room where he had crash-landed had played havoc with his sense of day and night anyway. Many hours had passed, of that he was sure, and no one had come to see him since they had locked the door and left. No one had rattled the door or even brought him water. The only companions he had were rats, and they kept mostly to themselves.

Where had it all gone so horribly wrong? Benfro rolled on to his other side, feet kicking against the door, and tried to remember when last he had been happy. Recuperating in Pallestre had been nice after the aches and pains of his near-death experience at the hands of Fflint had begun to recede. Visiting the Mother Tree had brought him hope that soon his ordeal might be over, and finding Gog both alive and apparently willing to help had been a moment of pure joy. And then Melyn's arrival – Magog's arrival really, for Benfro could see how the inquisitor had become the instrument of the dead mage – had ruined it all. Ever since then he had been fleeing, fighting for his life, his goal of finding a way back to the place where Magog's bones lay ever further out of reach.

And even if he managed it, broke through the spell that protected the place, he no longer had Magog's jewel. Without jewel and bone, he would be unable to use the Fflam Gwir to stop the dead dragon mage.

The Fflam Gwir. Of course. Benfro sat up so swiftly he banged his head on the ceiling, starring his vision so that for a moment he thought there really were Llinellau Grym in his dungeon. The stabbing in his side brought things more sharply into focus, reminding him of the wound that had almost healed before his captors had reopened it with their rough handling. He shifted about until he found that awkward position where the pain was bearable, at least until his muscles gave up. Listening carefully now, he searched for any noise. The silence was as oppressive as the low ceiling and carved stone walls, which made it feel like the mountains were pressing in on him. He could hear nothing but the steady rhythm of his hearts and the soft *scritch* of a rat searching through the straw for something to eat. With his blind eye Benfro could see something of the aethereal, although this far from the Grym it was a dark, featureless world. Through the heavy wooden door, the corridor climbed slowly to a large room with a high vaulted ceiling cut with much greater finesse than his cell. In the other direction, it dropped away, until at the end there was just a black maw opening on to nothing. Even the aethereal shunned that place, and it felt like it would suck any Grym down it into oblivion. He would not go that way.

Confident he was not about to be visited, Benfro shuffled around until his head was close to the door. It was made from oak so old it was as hard as stone, hung on heavy iron hinges with a thick bolt on the other side. Had he been uninjured, he might have hammered at it for days without causing it any damage. Instead, he took a long slow breath in, focused his mind on the metal and blew.

The flame was thin and palest yellow. It splayed across the door as he breathed out, and then his lungs were empty. Benfro slumped back, exhausted by the effort. His sight dimmed and he thought he might pass out. Then he saw that the yellow clung to the hinges like an aura. Heat seeped into the cell, welcome at first but then stifling as the ironwork began to glow. The oak charred, giving off acrid smoke that swirled around his head, watered his eyes and made him cough. From darkest red to burned orange, the hinges grew hotter and hotter. Orange turned to white and then the iron began to melt, dripping to the straw-strewn floor in great sizzling blobs. Too late Benfro realized his error as the damp straw dried and then ignited. The flames and the glowing iron lit up the cavern as he kicked out, panicking even though his scales would take far more than a bit of burning straw to crack. One foot hit the door and it buckled outwards, hinges and bolt collapsing into puddles of molten metal.

Benfro scrambled out of the cell as quickly as he could, all too aware that while his bedding might not burn him the molten iron would. By the time he had reached safety, the straw was well ablaze and belching thick black smoke out into the corridor. It billowed down from the ceiling, flowing swiftly towards the large room. Beyond that, stairs would take it up to the lower floors of the palace through which he had been marched earlier. There was no way his escape would go unnoticed.

Benfro heard noises above the crackling of the flames, dragons maybe, or people, shouting through the smoke. They echoed down the corridor like an army baying for his blood. He couldn't hope to escape that way, but to go the other was to risk being trapped, and after he'd escaped once, how much more securely would they lock him up? His stomach was empty; there was no way he could hope to breathe more flame without first eating something.

He had no choice but to follow the corridor downwards, the smoke now so thick it smothered him in choking hot ash and fragments of burning straw. He stumbled at first, until he reached fresher air, grabbed the nearest torch from its sconce on the wall and used it to light his way. The corridor grew narrower, its ceiling scarcely high enough for him to pass without crouching. Benfro counted two dozen cells, the first ones with doors big enough to allow him entry. He pushed open a few, peered inside but saw no way out. When the doors became too small for him, he stopped looking, hurried on towards the end and that blackness.

There must have been something, for he could feel a cool breeze on his face, a hint of a scent that wasn't quite as unpleasant as the choking black smoke but not nice all the same. It reminded him of nothing so much as the privy house around the back of the big hall in the village where he had grown up. Normally it was as clean as a fresh-running stream, but in the early morning after a feast it had that old dragon smell he had always associated with Ynys Môn, Sir Frynwy, Ystrad Fflur and the others. Thinking of them brought a lump to his throat, but with it a determination to survive, to remember their names and to avenge their deaths.

Beulah woke from dreams of pain and suffering, the vivid image of Caradoc's great head tumbling down the steps still in her eyes as she stared up at the cracked ceiling of her royal bedroom. Her ankle throbbed where the palace doctors had set the broken bone and wrapped it tight. The break had been bad if their tutting and head-shaking was anything to go by. It made sleeping difficult and left her constantly drained.

'You're awake. Good.' Melyn emerged from the shadows in the far corner as if he had been there all along. Beulah blinked away the memory of the dead dragon as he crossed the room. There was something about the inquisitor that was different from the old man she remembered. He had always been healthy, hearty even, but now he walked with the vigour of youth. Were it not for his shock of pure white hair she might have mistaken him for someone her own age.

'I hope you're feeling better.' Melyn approached the bed, and as he passed into the light Beulah gasped in surprise. He held his hands clasped together across his front, and she could see the skin on his fingers was gold and shiny. His eyes shone as if there were a fire in his head, and he gave off an aura of power that she had only ever felt before in the presence of the Shepherd.

'What has happened to you? You've changed.' Beulah meant only to think the words, but they spilled out of her in a low whisper. Melyn approached more slowly now, drew up a chair and settled himself down by the bed. He didn't answer at first, just sat there staring at her until Beulah began to feel self-conscious.

'You are right, Your Majesty: I have changed. Something did indeed happen to me. Something both terrible and wondrous. It won't be easy for you to understand, let alone accept. I couldn't, not at first. I went a little mad, as the mindless at Emmass Fawr found to their . . . distress.'

Beulah found herself transfixed by Melyn's eyes again. The pupils were far larger than she remembered, dark and speckled with tiny flecks of red that seemed to flash and spin. They reminded her of something, but she couldn't have said what. Not human eyes, for certain.

'The Shepherd does not exist,' he said. 'He is a sham.'

Beulah stared, aware that her mouth was hanging open and yet unable to close it.

'Perhaps I should rephrase that. The Shepherd is not who you think he is. His power is real.' Melyn lifted up his hands, fingers splayed, and Beulah saw tiny golden scales all over them where skin had been. 'He can perform things we might consider miracles – heal the sick, give strength to the weak and life to the elderly – but he did not create us, did not put us on Gwlad to guard it for his return. And he certainly did not make us in his image. Well, not entirely.'

'I don't understand. You met the Shepherd? He did this to you?'

'I held his heart in my hands. Only it wasn't a heart. It was a jewel, a vast red jewel taken from the brain of a living dragon many thousands of years ago. This is not something the common people need to know. Indeed, the fewer who know the truth the better. Our whole way of life, the Twin Kingdoms, the religious orders, all are predicated on the existence of, reverence for, the Shepherd. He is the glue that binds our society together. To suggest he is nothing but a lie, that King Ballah might have been right all along, will only lead to chaos.'

Beulah could see the sense in that, at least. What she couldn't understand was how Melyn could have succumbed to such a delusion.

'So why tell me?' she asked. 'Would it not be easier to keep the secret if you were the only one in the know?'

Melyn paused a moment before answering, shrugged slightly as if to suggest he had considered it. 'It will come out, in time. Something like this cannot be hidden for ever. And besides, the lie is already unravelling before our eyes. Where do you think all these dragons are coming from?'

'They are creatures of the Wolf, surely. They presage the return of the Shepherd, not his demise.'

Melyn shook his head. 'The Wolf? I suppose after a fashion. Some certainly follow the evil he represents. It is not as simple as that though. Wolf and Shepherd are just two sides of the same coin, and it is a coin minted millennia ago by two dragon brothers.'

'This cannot be. Dragons are . . . Your order's charter is the eradication of their kind. The Aurddraig . . .'

'The Order of the High Ffrydd will be needed now more than ever, my queen. You have seen the kind of damage these creatures can do. We will have to defend ourselves from the coming storm.' Melyn bowed his head in her direction. 'And we will need a strong leader to rally behind. Balwen fought off these beasts in ancient times; it is only fitting his heir lead the fight against them now.'

Beulah shifted in her bed, her leg uncomfortable in its tight bandage. 'As long as they don't come too soon. It will take weeks for my bones to heal.'

'I think not weeks but days. Don't you?' Melyn looked back towards the corner where he had first appeared, and as Beulah's gaze followed his, she saw the impossible. The shadows were not so deep there that she couldn't make out the shapes of the furniture, the play of the light on the wall. And yet all of a sudden the dragon Frecknock stood there. Beulah shuddered both at the sight of her and the suddenness of her appearance. And yet Melyn was clearly at ease in the dragon's presence. True, she was but a fraction of the size of Caradoc and the other beasts that had broken Candlehall; she was still large enough and strong enough to injure her should she wish. And she smelled like a dragon. Not the powerful musk of the feral beasts outside, but something undeniably alien all the same.

'Frecknock has no desire to hurt you, Beulah. Quite the opposite. She has saved your life on more than one occasion, mine too.' Melyn stood, moving his chair away from the bedside so that the dragon might approach, although for now she remained where she had appeared. 'She is an excellent healer and has already administered to His Grace the Duke of Abervenn. How is Clun now?'

'I have stopped the bleeding in his lungs and begun the process of mending his legs. He will walk again, although it will take him a while to recover fully.'

Beulah felt a skip in her heartbeat at the words. Was this some kind of cruel joke? Clun's injuries had been so severe the palace doctors had declared it a miracle he wasn't already dead.

'What of his eyes?' she asked.

'Alas, that is beyond even my skill to repair, Your Majesty. They will clear with time. Hopefully. He is young.' Frecknock's voice was full of trepidation, as if the dragon feared for her life should she fail. Beulah could not quite understand how she was still alive anyway. Melyn had said she would live no longer than she was useful.

'And yet you think I should let you try to heal me?'

'Bones are not a problem, ma'am. If you will allow it, I will make sure they are all aligned correctly before encouraging them to knit back together.'

'Encouraging?'

'It is not an easy thing to explain.'

'Frecknock will not hurt you. I give you my word on that.' Melyn beckoned the dragon over, but she remained in the corner. Beulah could almost taste her fear. She reached out with her mind, skirting over Frecknock's thoughts for any sign of subterfuge, but the creature was as open as a newly welcomed novitiate. She was in awe of Melyn and bound to him by something Beulah couldn't begin to understand. She would die rather than let the inquisitor come to harm, and Frecknock extended that strange fealty to Beulah too.

'Come forward,' Beulah said, and finally the dragon

approached. She was much smaller than the others and had a way of shrinking in on herself that made her smaller still. Even so she towered over the bed, at least until she knelt. After a moment's pause, she held both scaly hands out over the bedspread, palms down and fingers wide. Beulah felt a surge in the Grym quite different to the chill of someone conjuring a blade of fire. The dragon closed her eyes for a moment, muttering something under her breath in that strange language. Then she looked straight at the queen and dipped her head towards the bed.

'May I?'

Beulah nodded, and Frecknock untucked the bedspread with surprising dexterity, revealing the queen's injured leg. The dragon shook her head slightly, making a noise very much like the tutting of an unimpressed teacher.

'Is there a problem?' Beulah asked.

'The leg should not have been bandaged so tightly, and certainly not without aligning the bones correctly first. This will heal, but if left like this you will always limp, and when the weather turns cold or damp your bones will ache at the memory of where they were broken.'

Beulah looked to Melyn for confirmation. The old man merely dipped his head once.

'Do what you must then,' Beulah said. 'Just try not to make me scream. I can't promise my guards won't cut your head off.'

'Frecknock is trying to help, you know.' Melyn pulled his chair up close and settled himself down. The dragon extended a single talon and delicately cut the bandage away, whispering her strange incantations all the while. Beulah felt the release as the tight wrap fell away, but the dull throb turned to a stab of pain that made her breathe in sharply. Before she could say anything, Melyn had placed a hand on her shoulder. His touch was soothing, something flowing from him into her. She looked up at his face, seeing how fresh and young his skin looked, incongruous under that mop of white hair. His eyes were impossibly black, no iris around the pupil at all, and deep within them the flecks of red light sparkled like tiny jewels.

'This will go easier if you sleep,' he said, and Beulah realized how easily she had been fooled. Too late to fight, too late even to raise any mental shields, she was swept up in that gaze and away into blackness.

How long he walked for, Benfro could not have said. In his rush to escape, he just pushed on, hoping for the best. It wasn't until he noticed that the torch he had taken from the wall no longer cast as much light as it had before that he stopped, worried it was going out. Then he realized that the flame no longer reflected off the tunnel walls. He wasn't banging his head and the tips of his wing joints against the ceiling either. He stopped walking, listening for sounds of pursuit, but could hear nothing. Turning slowly, he looked back the way he had come and saw nothing. It was as dark as a cloudy, moonless night in the deep forest, no hint of the torches he had left behind and no scent of burning straw either. Reaching out, Benfro couldn't feel the walls. He walked a few paces in what he thought was the right direction, noticing the surface of the floor through the soles of his feet for the first time. Had there been flagstones before? He thought there might have been, but now it was just rocky ground strewn with small sharp stones and grit. He bent down, holding the torch above his head with one hand as he felt with his other. The larger rocks were deep black and glistened in the light as if they were wet.

Benfro strained to hear anything in the total silence. The torch gave off the faintest of noises, a quiet *shffff* with an occasional *pop*. Apart from that and the sound of his own breathing there was nothing.

'Hello?' He listened for the echo of his voice, surprised when it described a much larger cavern than the narrow tunnel down which he had come.

'Hello? Hello? Hello?' Benfro felt a bit foolish repeating the word over and over, but as he said it and moved his head, so he began to form an idea of where the nearest wall was. Inching carefully and never quite trusting his full weight to just one leg, it took him long minutes to reach it, and when he did, it was made of the same black stone as the floor. He had thought it might reflect the flame from his torch, but instead it seemed to absorb all the light. He could only be sure it was there by touching it, and when he did it was surprisingly warm.

Close by, his questing fingers found an opening. The passage was narrow, but just about big enough for him to walk down without damage. His torch lit up a rough-hewn surface and a floor packed hard by the passage of many feet. Warm air blew into his face, bringing with it a melange of scents. Mostly it was an overpowering stench of ordure, but mixed in with it he could just about make out the individual odours of many people.

Benfro had always prided himself on his sense of smell,

the ability to separate different ingredients from the mass. Some of his earliest memories were of helping his mother prepare medicines and unguents for the old dragons of the village. Identifying all the varied oils, minerals and herbs that went into each preparation by their smell had been a game, although now he could see it had been a part of his mother's subtle training of him. And it had been worthwhile, for he could identify individual scents in the miasma, men all of them. Some had been here ages, others recently arrived. They all smelled unwell, underfed and exhausted. There was death here too, bodies rotting or dried to leathery skin and bone.

He found the first of them in a small cave just off the tunnel. Dark and musty, the fireplace at its centre was cold, embers as dead as the rag-bundled corpses that lay around it. Benfro's missing eye could see nothing here, no Llinellau Grym, no glimpse of the aethereal. The bleakness of the place sucked at him, draining away any hope he might have had, any happiness. He backed out swiftly but not before he had caught an edge of a scent that sparked a memory.

Following it gave him purpose and helped to block the dread that tugged at his every step. Benfro sniffed his way down the tunnel until it opened out on to another large cavern, dark as pitch. Holding up his torch threw strange shapes around the floor nearby, and when he approached the nearest he saw that it was a cart, overturned to reveal metal wheels that would have run along tracks in the floor. Half crushed by it, a man lay on his back, eyes staring into the darkness. Benfro thought at first that his skin was black, but peering close he saw that it was simply covered in such a thick layer of filth the original colour could no longer be seen. He was dead of course, had been for some time.

The overturned cart lay beside a mound of night soil that rose into the darkness. Waving his torch around, Benfro could see no end to the stuff, and the overwhelming stench and the flat quality of the silent air suggested it was a mountain rather than a hill. Where he stood, the surface had dried and cracked, a few darker stains leaching out from underneath. The man had obviously been shovelling from the pile and taking it somewhere in his cart, but for the life of him Benfro couldn't imagine why.

More men lay dead, splayed in a wide circle around the pile as if some giant had swiped at them with a massive hand. And then his missing eye picked up something else. Glittering like spider webs in dawn sunlight, thin strands of silver wrapped around the wrists of most of the dead men, shackling them to their carts with something akin to the Grym. Bending to the nearest and taking it in between finger and thumb, Benfro felt a jolt of restorative energy surge through him as the glow dissipated from the chain. Moving over to the next dead man, he felt the same lift and only then began to realize how exhausted and drained of hope he had been feeling.

One by one he stooped by each dead man, leaching the last remnants of strength from the silver chains until none were left. He was still weary, still worn down by the oppressive nature of the darkness that loomed all around, but he had escaped the dragons hunting him. Now all he needed to do was find a way out.

There was another tunnel, wider than the first and

with its floor scored with parallel tracks along which the carts must have been pushed. Beyond it the air changed once more, the light from the torch swallowed by what felt like an even vaster darkness. There was a burned smell, like hot stones knocked together, the singe of hair and again that faintest trace of a familiar scent. It had been overpowered by the huge mound of ordure in the other cavern, but now Benfro recognized it.

'Errol.'

He turned this way and that, seeking out the faintest trace that might give him a clue. The scent was old, but not so old that it had dissipated entirely. Errol had been here, had spent enough time to imprint some small part of himself on the walls and floor, lingering in the fetid air. Benfro didn't want to know how he might have ended up here, he just had to be certain Errol had escaped.

Out in the passageway again, Benfro sniffed the air, then dropped down on to all fours and sniffed the ground. He might have felt faintly ridiculous, but the scent was clearer here. Still difficult to gauge the direction Errol had taken, he struck out the way he had originally come anyway.

As the smell of the dung heap lessened, so it was easier to follow Errol's trail. Still Benfro was surprised when he came to the first fork in the path. He didn't remember noticing one on his way in; indeed he had come further along the passage than should have been possible. Where was the first open space he had stumbled into after escaping the dungeon? Now he thought of it, he couldn't detect any trace of the smoke from the straw fire, and the stench from the dung was just a faint reminder, clinging to his scales and feet rather than hanging in the air. There was the scent of Errol and a fresher taste to the air that spoke of cold running water and snow.

He stood up again, noticing for the first time that the tunnel had narrowed, its roof now lower than his wing joints. He had to hunch to move forward, holding his wings close in an awkward manner that put pressure on the wound in his side. For a moment Benfro nearly panicked as he realized that he couldn't turn round. If he wanted to retrace his route he would have to crawl backwards, something that would be almost impossible with the torch. But even as he had the thought, he noticed the spreading light up ahead, palest blue and flickering slightly.

The noise came quite abruptly, as if someone had opened a door. One moment he was stooped low and shuffling towards the light in muffled silence, the next his ears were deafened by a roar he found both familiar and comforting. He hurried on, squeezing into the ever-narrower tunnel and cursing the greater bulk his gift from Magog had given him. The dragon who had fled the village so long ago could have walked through standing tall. Instead, the final stretch was a struggle, his wings twisting back behind him in a manner horribly reminiscent of Fflint's attempts to pull them off. Then with a last heave he was through.

Cold seeped up through Benfro's feet, now standing in puddles of icy water. He stared at the inside of a waterfall, cascading down one entire wall of the cave and filtering the daylight from beyond. The Grym flowed into him and the aethereal sight flooded back into his missing eye. It was such a contrast to the pitch-black blindness of the past few hours that he winced, covering up the empty socket with one hand as if that might help. It didn't, and neither did the guttering flame of the torch still clasped in his other hand. He set it down against a damp rock wall, and that was when he noticed something impossible.

Shadowy, ghostlike and imprinted over both his seeing eye and aethereal was the form of a dragon. She floated in the air in a manner she had never been able to do in life, and Benfro felt his hearts try to leap into his mouth as he recognized the form he had never thought to see again.

Morgwm the Green.

His mother.

22

Of all the healers in Gwlad, wise Earith was ever the foremost. Her skill was such that some said she was life itself given dragon form. Hers was the skill to knit bones, make lost limbs regrow, mend even broken hearts. She would turn none away if they needed her help, be they friend or foe, dragon, man or wild beast. But not even Earith could save Ammorgwm the Fair when the violent magics of the warring brothers Gog and Magog struck her down.

Who cast that killing spell, no one will ever know. Such was the madness that possessed those twins it could have been either. Or it could have been both, the combined power of their workings too much even for one such as Ammorgwm to survive. The whole of Gwlad froze in that moment, and it is said that Earith herself, thousands of leagues away in distant Eirawen, fell into a faint and did not wake for many days. And when she did finally awake, such was her sorrow that she cut herself off from the rest of Gwlad, so that her miraculous healing was lost to all.

Sir Frynwy, *Tales of the Ffrydd*

Dafydd woke to the sound of birds trilling. At first he thought he was on the island, that he was hearing the endless call of the gulls that lived around the long stone jetty. Why they stayed there he couldn't understand. Gulls were scavengers, reliant on fishermen and other sailors for their food, but the island was deserted and rarely visited. They had pestered him for days after he had arrived, landing beside him without any show of fear, pecking at his hands until he gave them the food he had prepared for himself.

But these weren't gulls. The sound was too pleasant for one thing. Not the incessant shrieking, the demand for attention worse than any unfed child. This was more like the songbirds that had been a fad among the richer ladies at court a few years back. Poor creatures caught and caged simply so that people could enjoy their song. Most had just thought it pretty, but he had heard the melancholy in their chirping, and Iolwen had too. He remembered well how she had set free the pair gifted to her by one particularly wealthy benefactor anxious to gain favour with the king.

Iolwen. The memory of her jolted him fully awake. Dafydd sat upright too quickly, his sense of balance taking a while to catch up. For a long while he had no idea where he was. The room was vast and airy, a high ceiling of ornate plaster reflecting golden sunlight as it filtered through tall windows. There was no glass, just painted wooden shutters folded back to let in the air.

The bed in which he lay was big enough for ten, and yet he was alone. Dafydd clutched the white sheets to his chest, feeling the coolness of the fabric. They smelled faintly of spring flowers and were softer than the finest down. A gentle breeze wafted past him, bringing scents of the sea and beyond the trilling of the birds, the sound of voices. He couldn't make out what they were saying, and he had no idea where he was. He could remember being whisked to the island by the dragon Merriel, could remember exploring and discovering a cave. After that everything was a blank.

Climbing out of the bed was more difficult than he had anticipated. It was wide, but it was also tall. He felt weak as he shuffled over to the side and let himself down to the floor like an intrepid mountaineer. As he pulled away the sheets, so he understood why. Dafydd had never been as brawny as his father, tending more to the wiry frame of his great-uncle Tordu. He had always been strong though, with the muscles of a man used to outdoor pursuits. He could shoot a couple of hundred arrows without tiring, and hold his own in a sword fight. But now his arms and legs were like sticks, the thinnest covering of flesh clinging to them. Feeling his face, he could trace the hollows in his cheeks with his fingers, the bones hard against skin like a badly mummified corpse.

'We have done the best for you we can. In time you will regain your strength and vigour.'

Dafydd wheeled round at the voice. The words had been spoken in heavily accented Llanwennog at a volume that suggested a large man but in a timbre that was unmistakably feminine. For a moment he was confused, seeing only a wall of dark shiny scales, like the armour in his grandfather's collection that he had been told was worn by the fighting monks of the Southern Isles. It took him a while to realize that he was looking in the wrong place, and to raise his head until he saw the head of the dragon who had spoken.

'You have slept a long time. Many days and nights. The Heolydd Anweledig can have that effect on people. Especially when they have been forgotten.'

'Heolydd . . . what?' Dafydd leaned back against the bed, his legs not quite strong enough to hold him upright. He should have been alarmed, being addressed by such a creature, but that was too much effort.

'The loose translation in your tongue is "invisible roads", I believe. They are an old magic, not something we have much use for any more. Well maintained, they allow those not skilled in the subtle arts to travel along the Llinellau Grym between distant points. When not well maintained, they either fail altogether or draw their power from those using them rather than the Grym itself.'

Dafydd shook his head gently, hoping that might help. It didn't. 'I'm afraid I have no idea what you're talking about. Or, indeed, who you are.'

'My apologies. It is only natural you will have forgotten. I am Earith, and this is my home in the city of Pallestre.' The dragon made a bow, arms spread wide as she bent her head towards the ground. Dafydd felt his ears burn with embarrassment as he understood that the dragon was his hostess. It still made no sense to him, but there were some things that were universal and courtesy was one.

'I am sorry.' He tried to bow but gave up when he realized committing properly to the gesture would see him fall over. 'I am Dafydd, son of Geraint, Prince of the House of Ballah. I am very grateful for your hospitality.'

The dragon clapped her hands once, and two young men appeared from a door Dafydd hadn't even noticed. One held a white robe over his arm and the other pushed a strange contraption that looked like a chair fitted with small cartwheels. They smiled at him, the first offering the robe and the second pointing at the chair as if to indicate he should sit. Both spoke, but the words meant nothing to him, jarring on his ears and filled with odd throaty noises.

'I do not think you are yet ready to walk very far, Dafydd, Prince of the House of Ballah.' The dragon nodded her head slowly in the direction of the chair. 'If you would perhaps robe yourself and allow my servants to wheel you out to the gardens, there is food waiting.'

It was only at that point that Dafydd noticed his nakedness. He had no idea what had become of the clothes he had been wearing on the island, but someone had removed them and washed him. They had shaved his face too, now he came to think about it. How long had he slept? How soundly that these things could be done to him? And yet no one had harmed him; quite the opposite. This was a peaceful place. He was safe here.

'Thank you,' he said as much to the two young men as the dragon. He pulled on the offered robe, feeling that same soft cool material as the sheets on the bed. It was well suited to the damp, muggy warmth that hung in the air. He took a couple of experimental steps, hoping that the chair would be unnecessary, then collapsed into strong waiting arms and allowed himself to be seated. The journey across the bedroom and out into a wide courtyard was short, the young men wheeling him to a low table beside a pool of water in which swam fat golden fish. A fountain at the centre sprayed water into the air, helping to counter the oppressive heat from a blazing sun high overhead.

'Eat, Dafydd. You have a lot of strength to rebuild.'

The dragon Earith sat down on a low bench on the other side of the table, waving a massive hand at the waiting food. Dafydd's stomach gurgled in anticipation, but he couldn't bring himself to begin. There were too many questions unanswered.

'What is this place? How did I get here? How long have I been asleep?'

'You have slept five days, but from the state you were in when you arrived, I would imagine you spent a good deal longer in the Heol Anweledig.'

'I . . .' Dafydd paused, his mind as befuddled as his body was tired. 'How is that possible?'

'Trust me. Of all the many things that could have gone wrong, this is perhaps the least terrible. The magic woven around that road should have disappeared many thousands of years ago.' Earith reached towards the table and picked up what Dafydd had thought was a large jug. With a surprisingly delicate motion, she lifted it to her mouth and took a sip of the liquid within. He caught a whiff of ginger and was instantly taken back to Tallarddeg, the start of the great mad adventure he and Iolwen had embarked upon. Was she safe and well? How could he even begin to start looking for her?

'Tell me. The place you left before arriving here. What was it like?' Earith took another sip of her drink, and Dafydd reached for a similar but smaller cup on his side of the table. He couldn't immediately identify the fruit that had been juiced to fill it, but it tasted wonderfully cool and refreshing. Sitting calmly, observing his every move but never threatening, the dragon left him as much time as he needed to answer her question.

'It was an island at the north end of the Felem archipelago. Merrambel. At least that's what I think Captain Azurea said. We visited it months ago, blown off course on our way to Abervenn. I guess that's why Merriel took me there. It's where we first met her, after all.'

'Merriel?' Earith stood up so swiftly she sloshed liquid out of her cup, but seemed not to notice. 'You saw Merriel? You spoke to her?'

'She saved my life. At Candlehall, when I was separated from the others. Thought I was going to end up being eaten like poor old Seneschal Padraig, but Merriel appeared. She saw off the other dragons and then whisked me away to the island. I've still no idea how she did that.'

'She used the Llinellau Grym, of course. But if she could use them to get to your island, then why not use them to return home?'

'Home?' It was Dafydd's turn to look surprised, but then his tired brain caught up with him. 'Merriel, daughter of Earith. That's what Usel said her name was. So she's your daughter?'

'She is indeed. And she has been missing for over a year.' Earith placed her cup back down on the table, wiping away the dampness on her hand as she spoke. 'I searched for her, called for her, but it was as if she had ceased to exist. And yet I would have known if she had died.'

'The last I saw of her, she was going back to Candlehall to save Iolwen, my wife.'

'Candlehall.' Earith rolled the word around as if it was unfamiliar, then switched to her own tongue. 'Y Neuadd y Ganhwyllau, of course. Gog's favourite place aside from his beloved Nantgrafanglach. But it was Palisander's palace, so it stayed in Magog's world when they cast their wicked spell.' She turned her gaze back on Dafydd, hunger for knowledge in her eyes. 'You live in this Candlehall?'

'No. Quite the reverse. We sought to capture it from Queen Beulah while her attention was focused on the north. We succeeded, but then the dragons turned up and made an alliance with her.'

'These dragons. You mentioned them before. What were they like? Were they like me?'

'Not at all. They are brutish and violent. They killed hundreds of the people in the city. Maybe thousands. One of them ate Seneschal Padraig.' Dafydd paused a moment, recalling the terrible incident. 'But they are your size. Bigger even. The dragons I knew as a boy were little bigger than a horse. And they couldn't fly.'

Earith said nothing for a while, just sat back down and took up her cup again. Dafydd drank some more, then turned his attention to the food that had been prepared for him. Most of it he couldn't identify, but it smelled good and tasted even better. His stomach was tender though, as if he were recovering from a long illness, and he could eat only a little before feeling sick.

'It begins to make sense, as much as anything makes sense any more. I suppose I should have seen it when Benfro arrived, but I thought . . .'

'Benfro?' Dafydd asked. Earith appeared to be talking to herself, but focused on him at his question.

'A young dragon who I think would be more at home in your world than mine. Only I fear there is no longer any difference between the two.'

'I don't understand. My world?'

Earith let out a sigh and put down her cup again. 'Long ago, Gwlad was riven in two by a pair of warring dragon brothers. Gog and Magog were their names. I ended up in Gog's world. He was the less mad of the two, I suppose. But the Hall of Candles stayed with Magog. Even the most powerful of magics must fade in time, especially if the dragon who wove it can no longer maintain it. This is what I suspect has happened with Gog and Magog's great spell. I had thought it would unravel slowly, but something has sped that process up. Old hidden roads are reappearing. Dragons disappear and others appear in their place. Men come from nowhere, speaking a tongue that none can understand. I should have felt it. I should have known.'

'Should have known what?' Dafydd asked.

'That Gog is dead. And now worlds that have been divided for over two thousand years are merging back together again.'

For long moments all he could do was stare. Somewhere in the back of his mind Benfro was aware his mouth was hanging open. He could almost hear Ynys Môn saying, 'That's a good way to catch flies,' as the old dragon had a hundred and more times back on their hunting trips. Slowly he drew it closed, never once taking his eye off the impossible apparition in front of him.

She was motionless, scarcely visible at all. For a moment he wondered if he was hallucinating. It had been a long time since last he had eaten or drunk anything, and he had breathed the Fflam Gwir, which always left him empty. The caverns and tunnels he had stumbled through had been unsettling too, places so devoid of any Grym it was as if they had sucked out his will to live. But he had survived. He had escaped, and even as he thought it, he could feel the life flowing back into him. He glanced briefly up at the point in front of his eyes where the rose cord that linked him to Magog's jewel hung in a loop in the air. It was so pale as to be almost invisible, the dragon mage no doubt concentrating on business elsewhere. Benfro looped his aura around it anyway, tugging the knot as tight as he could without losing sight of the vision in front of him.

'Is it really you?' he asked. The dragon made no reply, did not move at all. Benfro took a step closer and she seemed to recede from him. Another step and she was hanging in the curtain of water. He took two steps back and she followed him, hanging in the air.

'How is this possible?'

Still she didn't answer, and Benfro began to doubt himself again. Tired and hungry, dirty with the grime and filth of the caverns, he was so thirsty he could barely speak above a whisper. Keeping his eye on the vision, he paced in a wide arc until he could reach out and touch the water. He washed away the worst of the muck from his hands before cupping them under the flow and then raising them to his mouth. Nothing had ever tasted quite so sweet and refreshing. Colder than ice, it chilled his throat and made his stomach clench, but he went back for another handful, and another and another. It gave him a little strength, and with it the image of his mother grew steadily more solid. Still she did not move, did not look at him, just hung in the air, her feet a hand's width from the wet stone floor.

Benfro took a step towards her again, and once more she receded. It was infuriating, the worst kind of torture. To be reminded of her was bad enough; he couldn't look at her without seeing that terrible fiery white blade slicing through the air, without hearing that horrible thud as her head hit the ground and the slower sigh as her body crumpled.

'Why are you doing this to me? What do you want?'

The vision gave no answer, and all Benfro could do was sit, stare at her and sob.

It wasn't until much later that he became aware of the Llinellau. They had been there all along, his missing eye showing him the Grym and the aethereal layered on top of the mundane. He had grown so used to them that he scarcely noticed them any more. He had looked for the rose cord, of course. Knotted it tight with his aura even though there was no sense of Magog. He hadn't paid much attention to any of the other lines, the patterns they made about the cave and the way they curved around the vision as if she were a puppet and they were her strings. Corwen would have chided him for his lack of observation, but the old dragon was gone, his jewels taken by Melyn, just as the inquisitor had taken Morgwm's.

Except that he hadn't taken all of her jewels. One had remained, and Benfro had performed the reckoning ceremony. He had not been able to breathe the Fflam Gwir then, or perhaps he had just not known how. But he had used the herbs and the Delyn oil. His mother's body had been consumed by the flames and he had found one perfect white jewel in the ashes. Errol had fetched it from Corwen's keeping when Melyn and his warrior priests had found their hideaway. Benfro remembered the way it had made him feel when he had seen Errol holding the jewel, how he had snatched it away, spurned the boy and almost frozen to death because of his foolishness. But where was it now? Had Errol still had it with him when he had come this way? Was he close by? Was the jewel?

So many questions, and it was only as they dredged up his memories that Benfro remembered why he was here in the first place. He had been following Errol's scent, but it ended here at the water's edge. He struggled to his feet, feeling the numbness in his tail where it had gone cold. Checking first one end of the waterfall then the other revealed no obvious way out, so he must have gone through. Even close up to the cascade, Benfro could make out nothing of what lay beyond. He had no idea whether it was a long drop or a short one, whether there was a deep pool in which to fall or jagged rocks to break his bones upon. He tried looking with his aethereal sight, but the water messed with his vision and his tiredness was making it increasingly hard to concentrate. He could stay here and stare at the vision of his mother until the cold took him and he froze to death, or he could take his chances with the waterfall.

He chose a spot far enough from the hanging vision that she did not disappear from him, and pushed one arm into the flow. The water was cold and fell with enough force to tug him off balance. Benfro snapped back, pulling his arm out before he plunged in unready, but not before he had felt different air on his outstretched hand. The waterfall wasn't so thick, but it must have been falling from a fair height above the cave. Hoping that meant it didn't have too much further to go, he took one last look at the image of his mother, drew in a deep breath and plunged into the deluge.

The drop wasn't as far as it could have been, but it was enough to knock the air out of him as he crashed into the pool at the base of the waterfall. The water mixed with air, bubbles of all sizes boiling around him as if he had been plunged into a vast cauldron over an even larger fire. They robbed him of his buoyancy, slowing him only slightly before his feet hit the gravel and silt of the bottom. Benfro struggled to keep upright, pushed this way and that by the swirling currents. He kept his wings clamped as tightly to his sides as he could, ignoring the pain in his side as the wound tried to rip itself open again. Taking one step, then another, he walked away from the cataract and into thicker water until his body began to rise like a cork. As his head broke the surface, he managed one huge gulp of air before the current dragged him down again, spinning him round.

He kicked out weary legs, stiff with the cold, breaking the surface once more and stealing another breath. It took too long, but slowly, weakly, he struggled away from the waterfall and the treacherous eddies in the pool at its base until finally his feet touched the bottom while his head was still above water. With the last of his strength, Benfro waded out on to a wide beach, feeling sand beneath his feet but seeing only snow all around. He was sheltered from the wind he could hear howling high overhead, but great fat flakes floated down, settling on his head and back, leaching away what little warmth he had left.

He flopped down, casting out for the Grym and sucking it into him like a greedy kitling. He knew it was only borrowed heat, borrowed strength. He needed to eat, to sleep and, most important, to heal, but first he needed to find shelter.

The vision of his mother was still with him, staring back at him, hovering over the water in the middle of the pool as he checked the area for any signs of life. She was pale again, ghostlike. He could see right through her to the far bank, but as he approached the water's edge, she didn't move. He took a step back into the water and still she stayed where she was. His missing eye showed the Llinellau Grym and the aethereal vision of this place as a jumble of contradictory forces. The flowing water disturbed everything, but the trees glowed bright with life even though they were heavy with snow. Creatures moved about in the forest or were hunkered down waiting for the weather to change. And there in the midst of the flow, so bright it broke through the turmoil all around it, a single point of white light shone directly beneath his mother's ghost.

Benfro needed no more prompting. He waded into the water, ignoring the jab of pain in his chest and the ache of muscles close to cramping. The current tugged at him, but it was lazy here, lacking the urgency of the falls upstream. Three paces on firm gravel brought him to the point, the water reaching up to his stomach, not so deep as to make him float. There was not enough light left to see the bottom with his good eye, but the missing one showed him all he needed to know. One deep breath and he plunged down, arm outstretched towards that point of light. It lay among the gravel like any other stone casually tumbled by the flow. Or dropped by a young man struggling for his life. His hand dug deep in the grit, then closed around the light. And as he touched it, so he recognized the feeling of his mother's jewel, felt the joy in it as it reconnected with him.

He burst through the surface like a salmon at the spawning falls. And then Benfro just stood, letting the flow push past him as he basked in the warmth of his mother's embrace. He clutched the jewel tightly to his chest, unheeding of the tears that trickled down his cheek, unaware of the cold that crept into his legs and froze his tail. Nothing mattered now. He had found his mother's jewel.

And then slowly, as if his thoughts had grown sluggish too, he began to notice something. Not the deathly cold but the presence nearby of many men hidden by the subtle arts. Slowly so as not to cause any more noise than the babbling of the water over rocks, Benfro sunk down low into the stream. His feet were deep in the gravel now, and he used that contact, pulled the Grym into him to ward off the chill. At the same time he scanned the woods with his missing eye, searching for the hidden. Then, with a shimmer, some appeared on the beach, popping into sight as if they had just stepped out from behind an invisible wall. He didn't know them individually, but he recognized all too well the clothing they wore.

Warrior priests of the Order of the High Ffrydd.

23

Most workings of magic live only as long as their conjuror. The Grym, which is the source of all life and all magic, is a fluid thing. It shifts and changes constantly, so that only the living can mould it to their will.

There are some materials which are naturally resilient however, both resisting magical influence but, once imprinted with it by one with sufficient skill, retaining it for centuries or even millennia. Crystal jewels are renowned for their ability to trap the Grym, especially those found growing in the brains of dragons. Pure metals such as gold and silver are also potent repositories of magical influence.

It would be heartening to think that this knowledge is used for the betterment of mankind, that the Grym is stored in a benign form to aid those at their weakest and most needy. Such would be the better part of our nature, but is all too uncommon. More often high-value objects such as rings and amulets are cast with curses bound up with such life energy that when the touch of some unwary fellow releases it they are more often than not consumed entirely by the ensuing conflagration.

Father Andro, *Magic and the Mind*

Melyn paced the corridors of the palace like a caged animal, frustration gnawing at him from all sides. He could feel the presence of the Shepherd – of Magog, he corrected himself – all around. These halls were steeped in the dragon mage's power. Everywhere he turned there was a reminder of the great lie that had shaped the Twin Kingdoms. Tapestries brought to life the ancient story of how the Wolf had taunted the Shepherd, how it had tempted his people to turn from his teachings. Like all such stories, Melyn could see the moral in it, the warning not to stray from the true path or risk eternal damnation. But he could also see the parallels with what had actually happened and how the long march of years had twisted the tale into its current form.

'All stories are teachings. It is our way.'

The voice was deep inside his head. Melyn might once have fought against it, when he was young and wilful and swift to anger. Had he known at his initiation into the Order of the High Ffrydd that the god who had chosen him was false, then he would have done anything in his power to drive that voice away. But he hadn't known. He had welcomed the Shepherd into him with open arms, blessed by the attention that none of his fellow novitiates appeared to have received. He had been selected for great things, his innate abilities recognized, his swift rise to the top of the order inevitable. For all the lies, his life had not been a bad one to live. Now he was more powerful than any man in Gwlad. He had the secrets of the Shepherd, the knowledge and skills honed over millennia. And he was the one alive, the one in control.

'We will do great things together, Melyn son of Arall.

But only together. It is true I am dead, but without me you are nothing. Your power is nothing.'

Melyn felt the twinge in his joints and a pressure in his forehead, just the barest hint of discomfort that nevertheless promised much agony should he try to do anything of which Magog disapproved. With a laugh that disturbed Frecknock, standing a few paces behind him, he shook the feeling away. It was true the dragon mage had power over him, but with each passing day he grew more confident in his own abilities. And besides, their aims were very much aligned.

'Is there something troubles you, Your Grace?' Frecknock asked. Melyn turned away from the tapestry to face her. She was his constant companion now. Perhaps the only one he felt he could trust. The warrior priests looked at him with awe and fear, it was true, but he wasn't sure he had their respect any more. Even Beulah was distant, though that might have had something to do with the pain from her broken leg and her worry about Clun. It surprised him just how much she genuinely seemed to love the lad; he had thought her quite incapable of anything so uncalculating.

'There is much that troubles me and much we must do. The whole of Gwlad is in flux. Can you not feel it?'

Frecknock paused a moment before answering. She was always thoughtful, he noticed. She considered her answers before voicing them, unlike all too many of the captains and warrior priests under his command.

'The Llinellau, the lines as you have them, are in turmoil. I have never seen anything like it, except maybe in the forest of the Ffrydd. There great magics were unravelling. It had been a slow process, probably begun when Magog died, but Corwen's jewels held it all in check. When you removed them from their resting place, everything collapsed more swiftly, and . . . well . . . you remember what happened there, Your Grace. At the lake. It is much the same now, only where before it was the forest that was affected, now it is the whole of Gwlad. Things that have been hidden for millennia even from dragons are reappearing. Gog's world is merging with Magog's and it isn't an easy reunion. There is too much difference between the two for them to simply snap back together unnoticed.'

'Like these dragons that have been appearing all over the place. They are exactly the menace the Order of the High Ffrydd was tasked to deal with.' Melyn cast his aethereal sight out through the tall windows that overlooked the parade ground to the front of the palace. A strange collection of dragons lay there, basking in the weak sun, creatures that had arrived with Caradoc but sworn allegiance to the inquisitor the moment he had slain their leader. The beasts that considered Clun their leader had all taken up residence in the courtyard surrounding the Neuadd. The two groups – folds as they would call themselves – were very suspicious of each other. It reminded him of nothing so much as two packs of wolves. As long as there was someone stronger than both of them, they would behave, but he had to be constantly on his guard for any challenge. He didn't like the way they all sneered at Frecknock either.

'You would kill us all?' Her voice was level, but Melyn could hear the anxiety in it, the shock and horror.

'It would be foolish even to try. My warrior priests are too few in number for one thing, and they lack the skills to tackle such powerful beasts, even if they have shunned your subtle arts. Many of these dragons are more skilled than they let on. Sir Gwair, for instance. He wears the Grym around him like a cloak of armour. He has skills he is not willing to show in front of anyone. Oh, the youngsters are all headstrong brawn and no discipline; they would be easy enough to dispatch. But there are too many wily ones, old and skilled. They will flee if I attack, regroup and wait until the time is right to overthrow us. And these are not the ones that worry me. These beasts are predictable. Give them plenty of food, forest to hunt in, and they are happy. I am more concerned with the learned ones. Gog's kin in their mountain palace are too powerful, too arrogant and distant to mix easily with a world where men wield the power we do. They will try to take the Grym away from us, and that is not something I can allow.'

'You think like a dragon, Your Grace.' Frecknock bowed her head as she spoke, then raised it again suddenly. 'I meant no disrespect by that, sire.'

Melyn laughed where once he might well have conjured a blade of fire and cleaved her head from her shoulders. 'Is it any wonder? When I carry deep inside me the essence of the greatest dragon ever to have lived? He took me as a young boy and moulded me into what I am today. I have been thinking like a dragon all my life, just never realized until now.'

Frecknock bowed her head again, but he could see her thoughts clearly enough. Not every dragon, they said.

And she was right. Not all dragons shared Magog's lust for power, but Melyn did. Not all dragons trampled over the feelings and desires of others in their pursuit of that power, but Melyn did. That was the true nature of Magog, a far cry from the loving, caring Shepherd.

'Come, Frecknock. We will pay Master Clun a visit. I need you to stay with him, speed up his recovery.' He strode past the dragon, noting the look of worry on her face as she made to follow him.

'Is it wise to push him so, Your Grace? Time is always the best healer, especially when damage is severe.'

'If I had the time, I would leave him be. The queen is preoccupied with his recovery, and that is as good a diversion for her as any. You will stay with them while I am gone, administer to their needs. Heal them as you healed me.'

'You mean to leave here? To leave me?' Frecknock's panic was almost palpable. Understandable perhaps, given that outside she was at the mercy of dragons twice her size and more, curious and hostile. Inside she ran the risk of offending a warrior priest, and they were all enough on edge to do something rash. But he could not always protect her, and her skills were needed here.

'I must return to Emmass Fawr, and possibly Tynhelyg too. There is much preparation and training needed if the warrior priests are to be an effective force against the dragons of Gog's world. None will harm you while I am gone, and if you heal both queen and consort you will have two more powerful allies. The time of mindless persecution of all dragons is over, Frecknock. Now we fight only to bring peace.'

For the first time in what felt like weeks Dafydd woke feeling refreshed and strong. He rose from the massive bed, his muscles firm as he walked across the room and out into the warm courtyard beyond. It had only been a few days since he had arrived weak and thin, but Earith's magic had worked wonders on him.

'You are looking well, Prince Dafydd.' Earith was waiting for him as she had been every morning since he had first woken here, sitting on her low bench in front of the breakfast table.

'Thank you, Lady Earith. I feel much better now.' Dafydd took up a small earthenware pot that he knew would be full of a strong, dark and bitter liquid that ought to have been disgusting and yet was curiously delicious. Lifting the lid, he took a deep sniff before pouring some into a tiny cup and finally taking a sip.

'So much so that I should really start trying to work out how to get home.' He put the cup back down and surveyed the foods laid out. It was mainly fruit, some grains, nuts and berries, but no meat. For all her imposing fangs and talons surely designed for hunting, Earith appeared to favour a vegetable diet. Dafydd wasn't about to upset her by either commenting on it or asking for something different to the fare he had been offered though. He was all too aware of how dependent on this dragon he was.

Earith took up a slice of something that looked like melon but was green-skinned and had flesh the colour of a new wound. Dafydd had tried it himself, finding it rather tasteless and watery. 'That will be no easy task,' she said after carefully swallowing her mouthful. 'The Hall of

Candles lies many thousands of miles to the north, across the Southern Sea. And that is assuming the Gwlad I knew is still the same now.'

'How can it not be? Surely the land cannot change.'

'On some scales you are right, of course. Eirawen is as it ever was, and the land you call Llanwennog, the Hafod and the Hendry is much as I recall from my youth. The mountains and islands are the same, but the climate is very different. The Ffrydd I have known for two thousand years and more is a blasted desert where nothing grows, yet Benfro knew it as a lush forest full of enchantments.'

'Benfro?' Dafydd asked. The name sounded familiar, but he couldn't say why. 'You mentioned that name before. Who is he?'

'A dragon from your world. From Magog's world, I should say. He stumbled into this Gwlad and fell in with a bad bunch. I patched him up and took him to see the mother tree, but where she sent him I know not.' Earith paused a while as if considering something, another piece of the red and green melon hanging from her loose grip. 'I suppose we could go and look for her again, but she has never shown much interest in the ways of men.' She focused her attention on Dafydd again. 'I mean this as no insult, but your kind do not have the skills to perceive her. At least, you don't have in this world. I very much doubt you would be able to comprehend what you were seeing should you find yourself in the presence of the Mother Tree.'

'I am afraid I don't even know what a Mother Tree is,' Dafydd said.

'No.' Earith shook her head, placed her melon back down on her plate uneaten. 'No, I don't suppose you do. And it's not *a* Mother Tree. There is only one. She is the Grym, in many ways. She is Gwlad and all the living things within it.'

'So how then? How can I get back home? Are there boats I could sail on? A crew willing to make the journey?' Dafydd knew even as he said it how hopeless it was. He had no money to hire a ship, and working his passage would rely on someone else wanting to go that far north. That the idea of working his passage didn't fill him with horror was a surprise. The carefree Prince Dafydd who had ridden out of Tynhelyg so many months before would have baulked at the idea of even getting his hands dirty.

'It's unlikely. And it would take months even if you could find a captain willing to try it. The Southern Sea is not easy to cross. We could try the Heol Anweledig that brought you here, but that will only get you as far as Merrambel, where Merriel left you. After your last journey on the hidden roads you're probably not too keen to try that anyway, I'd guess.'

Dafydd slumped back in his seat, sipping the last of his bitter, dark drink. It matched his mood. 'I have to get back. Iolwen needs me. Iolo needs me. What if something happened to them and I was sitting here in the sunshine, enjoying fine food and your generous hospitality?'

'Do not blame yourself, Dafydd. It isn't your fault. If any are to blame it is Gog and Magog, and their mad mentor Palisander before them. We are all touched by their cruel fate.'

338

'Palisander?' It was a name Dafydd didn't think he had heard before.

'The bards would have it that he was the greatest dragon ever to live. Second only to Rasalene himself, who was father of us all. Arrant nonsense, of course, but bards always love to dress stories up.' Earith poured herself a much larger mug of the dark drink before topping up Dafydd's cup.

'Palisander was a great mage, but he was also reckless. He didn't care what he did to increase his power, his hold over the Grym. It killed him in the end, but not before a lot of my kind went missing. He was old by the time Gog and Magog came along, but he doted on the pair of them as if he was their father. By the moon, maybe he was.' Earith shook her head. 'Nothing would surprise me any more. He died when they were both about two hundred summers old, but not before teaching them much of what he had learned.'

Dafydd sipped, unsure what to say. Earith's stories were meaningless to him, her talk of events many thousands of years ago baffling. How could she have lived that long?

'There is a way of getting you home,' she said after a while.

Dafydd sat up straight, leaning forward in his eagerness to hear more. 'There is?'

'There is, yes. It's the same way you came to the island, if I understand your telling of it right. But it is not an easy thing to do. It worked for you and Merriel because you had both seen that place before, were both linked to it by a shared experience. I have memories of Merrambel, but

339

they are old and faded. And we have only met here before. Nothing else links us.'

'You're talking about moving along the lines. The Llinellau as you call them.' Dafydd recalled the unpleasant sensation of his journey from the Neuadd to the island, the feeling of being torn apart, his essence pulled in every possible direction. He had been desperate then, and the island fresh in his memory from seeing the dragon. Could he maintain his sense of self again? He didn't know, but it was worth it. Better to die in the trying than risk never seeing his wife and child again.

'I . . .' Earith began, then stopped, her head twitching to one side as if she had heard something, although Dafydd could not have said what.

'Merriel!' Earith set down her cup and stood in one motion. She moved swiftly, heading for the wide arch that led from the courtyard out to the gardens beyond. All but forgotten, Dafydd slid off his own seat and followed. He had to trot to keep up, but the bitter drink gave him energy and sharpened his thoughts.

Out in the gardens a group of men and a couple of other dragons stood in the middle of a wide lawn, neatly trimmed and dotted here and there with tiny white flowers. They were fussing over something but moved swiftly aside as Earith reached them. Dafydd had time to see another dragon lying prone on the ground, her wings twisted and slick with blood, and then Earith had gathered up her daughter in a fierce embrace, wrapping her own wings around the still body. For a moment it felt as if the whole world went dark, then he realized that the Grym was being sucked from everything close by, himself included.

He hurried towards them, moving in as close as he dared. Merriel had been injured in some terrible fight. He reached out, placed a hand on her arm, felt the stickiness of her drying blood. He reached out to the Grym, that small part of it that Earith was not already tapping, and added it to the healing flow.

'Use my strength. Take all that you need.'

They flitted in and out of his vision like sprites from one of Sir Frynwy's more fanciful tales. Were it not for his missing eye and the clear view of the aethereal it gave him, Benfro might not have noticed them at all. He had been pulling so much energy from the Grym himself he had not seen them as they crept stealthily through the snow-silent woods. How they had missed him, he couldn't be sure, except that men had poorer vision than dragons and far less sensitive noses. They were concentrating on their concealment spells too, perhaps not expecting to meet anything sinister out here in the wild. It would only take one warrior priest to feel the tug on the Grym for him to be detected though, so slowly, reluctantly, Benfro let it go.

The cold seeped into him immediately. He had scarcely warmed himself up from the tumble through the waterfall, and now the icy water leached that heat away. Every instinct told him to wade out, find a sheltered spot away from the wind and the falling snow, but Benfro suppressed the urge, dropping lower still until the surface came almost to his nostrils. He edged out further into the river, legs stiff and reluctant. At least the distant roar of the falls and the babbling of water on the stones covered any noise he might have made. That and the muffling effect of the increasingly heavy snow. He gripped the tiny white jewel tight in his hand, terrified of dropping it here, where it would surely be lost for ever. It gave him a kind of warmth, lifting his spirits even as his body froze.

The light was fading fast now, though whether from the ending of the day or the heavy purple clouds overhead, Benfro could not tell. In the middle of the river the current was swifter, the water deep enough to give him buoyancy without his feet being lifted off the gravelly bottom. He let himself be swept gently downstream, his good eye always on the bank, missing eye scanning the aethereal for the warrior priests, counting them as if that intelligence might somehow be useful rather than terrifying.

There were far too many.

They spread out through the forest, each one keeping a good distance from the next. At first Benfro could not think why they weren't marching together on a road, or at least keeping close. But then he realized they needed the distance to maintain their concealment. It was much like the simple spell that Ynys Môn had taught him all those years ago, more a trick than any working of the subtle arts. The same trick he had used to hide himself, Martha and Xando when Sir Nanteos and Cerys had almost caught them. It wasn't so much a case of using the Grym as diverting it around you, distancing yourself from it so that your essence sank into the background. The warrior priests were using the technique with a twist, somehow letting the Grym flow through themselves without any disruption to the Llinellau. Benfro had no idea how they were doing it, but it seemed to take up much of their concentration. Otherwise he would surely have been spotted by now.

The river deepened and widened as he floated downstream, but it also slowed. The cold was almost unbearable; he had to clench his jaw tight to stop his teeth chattering, and he feared he would never feel his tail again. Ice began to form on the scales of his nose and the tufts of hair that grew out of his ears. All the while the snow kept falling. As he rounded a bend in the river, the wind picked up and threw it at him. Benfro was glad then to be almost completely submerged. The water might have been cold, but the storm above it was colder still.

And still the warrior priests were making their stealthy way through the woods. Benfro lost count at around five hundred, and those were the ones his missing eye showed him. He did not know how many of the hated order there were, though having seen the size of the monastery at Emmass Fawr, he could only assume they numbered in the many thousands. They appeared to be working their way uphill, and he was moving slowly down. He hoped that he would pass through them shortly, but he was going to have to haul himself out of the water soon or risk not having any strength left at all.

He studied the banks, searching for a good spot for a quiet exit, and that was when he noticed that the current had sped up again. Steep cliffs of rock rose on one side, forming a wide arc as the river took another bend. On the other side the bank was a jumble of massive boulders, trees poking out from between them at strange angles as if they were drunk. The wind dipped and that was when he heard the roar echoing off the stone. Another waterfall, bigger than the last and not far away at all.

There were still warrior priests out there, some close by if his missing eye was to be believed. Should he risk being seen as he hauled himself out and climbed the boulders to the woods above? Or could he survive going over the falls? Without any idea as to their size, the latter option wasn't really worth considering, except that he had no defence against warrior priests if they found him. Not in his weak and wounded state, with a stomach empty and unable to breathe fire.

In the end, cold desperation drove him from the river. Benfro struck out for the shore, muscles complaining. At least the current lessened the closer he came to the bank, and the boulders strewn across the bottom made it easier to find footholds. He tried to move as quietly as he could, but even over the sound of the waterfall and the roaring of the wind in the trees it felt like he was drawing too much attention to himself as he climbed out of the water. It cascaded off him, sloughing from his too-heavy wings and sliding down his numb tail to drip off the tip, each droplet exploding on impact with the surface.

No one heard him. It was all in his exhausted mind. He clung to the first boulder for several minutes, alternately reaching out for the Grym to warm himself, then shrinking back from it lest he be detected. Finally, when his trembling arms and aching fingers threatened to make him drop his precious jewel, Benfro gave in and let the warmth flow into his body. He couldn't exactly remember when he had learned the skill, but it came naturally to him like no other aspect of the subtle arts ever had. Perhaps it was something to do with being reunited with his mother – that tiny stone clenched in his fist was a bright, warm point he could focus on, one that burned away all worry about Magog and his malign influence.

But the rose cord was still there. Benfro could see it with his missing eye, looping away into the darkness as the last of the warrior priests stalked silently through the forest. Somewhere out there the jewel was waiting for him, biding its time. As he had chilled in the river, so his aura had shrunk around him, the knot unravelling and leaving him dangerously vulnerable. He stretched it back out as best he could, struggling at the effort as he reset his defences.

The climb up to the forest should have been easy. Back when he was still a kitling, shimmying up trees and rock faces had been his favourite pastime. Now, with the ache of the wound in his side, his muscles stiff from the cold and his empty belly weighing him down as if it were filled with stone, the slow ascent from boulder to boulder was torture. It didn't help that he could only use one hand properly, the other clasped tightly around his mother's jewel. The boulders themselves were an awkward size too, smooth-faced and covered in slippery green growth. The higher he climbed, the stronger the wind grew and the heavier the snow. Benfro could tap the Grym for warmth and some energy, but not enough to rid himself of the sticky white coat that stuck to his wings and back.

It felt like he had been climbing all night by the time he finally hauled himself up over the last block and slumped down. The tree above him was an old pine, spearing into the storm like a tall tower. Strong and healthy despite its age, he tapped it for more warmth, reaching out to the other trees all around so as not to put too much of a strain on any one. There was an odd feel to the essence flowing from them, and it took Benfro a while to understand that he could feel their stress, longer still to work out what the problem was. These trees were filled with summer's sap, their needles fat and ready to drink from the sun. And yet the weather was something from the deepest winter. This storm was out of kilter with the seasons. Could it be that as the two worlds, Gog's and Magog's, merged back together even the weather was ruptured?

A question for another time. Now he needed to make good his escape. Bad enough that he had been fleeing the dragons who had thrown him in the dungeon, the sudden arrival of warrior priests made things even worse. Benfro pushed himself up on to weary feet, scanning the darkening twilight for any sign of movement. The massive trees stood sentinel, spreading away further than he could see, but their summer needles filtered out the worst of the snow, leaving just a light white carpet on the forest floor. With his missing eye Benfro saw the last of the hidden men working their way slowly up a slope to his right. Clutching the memory of his mother in his frozen fist, he turned left and started to walk.

24

When beast and man walk the forgotten roads
And empty minds are taken from their shells
When winter comes afore the summer's done
The war to end all wars will be begun.

The Prophecies of Mad Goronwy

'I have never seen such fury, such violence. It is almost as if they were being held back from their base natures before, but something has changed.'

Dafydd sat to one side of a massive sleeping platform piled with soft linens, upon which Merriel lay. She looked in much better shape than when she had arrived, cleaned of all the blood that had stained her scales and the worst of her wounds sealed up, but she was still battered and bruised.

'I came across them in the Northlands, while I was searching for Princess Iolwen. She was at the Hall of Candles, where I found you, Dafydd. Only she was hidden from view, deep underground. I tried to reach her, almost made it, and then she disappeared.'

'And the other dragons attacked you?' Dafydd remembered the great beast that had smashed around inside the Neuadd.

'Them? No. They were quite civilized in comparison. This was later. I had a sense of the princess in the north, the mountains that surround the Ffrydd. Only it was no Ffrydd I recognized. There were trees everywhere, ancient and huge. And there were old magics too, unravelling as if they had been held in check until just recently. It was a horrible, confusing place.'

Earith sat on the other side of the platform, tending to her injured daughter with the care only a mother can bring. Dafydd sensed how she was drawing strength from the Grym and feeding it gently into Merriel, building up her strength.

'Who were they?' she asked. 'We know most of the folds that have abandoned the old ways. They've never given us any trouble before.'

'They were a ragtag bunch,' Merriel said. 'But I recognized their leader. Caradoc seems to have left the Twmp fold.'

'Caradoc.' Earith's eyes narrowed as she spoke the name. Dafydd had always considered her gentle and kind, but there was steel in that single word. Venom too.

'You know him?'

'Aye, too well. He is young, scarce five hundred summers old, but he has always been proud. Claims lineage back to Gog himself as if that was something special. All of the dragons hatched after the schism are of Gog's line.'

'He is worse.' Merriel pushed herself upright, the pain showing in her movements. 'It is as if he no longer cares for anything save himself. And those he has drawn about him are no better. They fight constantly among each other, unless there is someone else for them to pick on. They have razed every settlement of men within a day's flying of their camp, and I did not like the feel of that place at all.'

'Gwlad is changing. Your disappearance is evidence enough of that.' Earith stood as Merriel eased herself off the sleeping platform, helping her daughter find her feet. 'And young Prince Dafydd here too. We both know that the lands to the far north are frozen plains of ice and snow, but he speaks of lush ground where barley grows in abundance and gold can be found in the creeks.'

'The Ffrydd is a mighty forest to the west of my grandfather's kingdom,' Dafydd said. 'If that is the place you mean. It is a haunted woodland where few dare to venture. Legend has it that there is a hoard of jewels and gold hidden deep in the middle of it all, but none of the men who have set off in search of it have ever returned.'

'Magog's palace at Cenobus lay in the centre of the Ffrydd. And claerwen is not so far to the east of there. That is where they were both hatched, and where he and Gog fought their last great battle, where Ammorgwm the Fair sought them out, determined to put an end to their endless warring. It is where she died.'

Earith spoke as if these tales were things she had lived and witnessed, and in that moment Dafydd believed that she might well have done. She looked old, worn down and exhausted by the effort of healing first him and then her own daughter. And worn down by a life so long he could not even begin to imagine it.

'I hardly dare ask, but did you find Iolwen?' Dafydd thought Merriel might be angry at the question, or resigned, but instead it seemed to give her life. She ruffled her wings, stretched the muscles in her neck and shoulders, and stood a little taller.

'I sensed her at Candlehall, as you men call it. She was

with the one called Usel who speaks passable Draigiaith, and a group of others. They were underground, deep beneath the hall, and I thought I would just step through the Llinellau to them. But the place where they were repulsed me. It is hard to describe to one who doesn't know the subtle arts well, but it felt like a great wrong had been done to the very essence of the world.'

'Like the collection of countless dragons' jewels?'

Merriel considered for a moment. 'No. This was no hoard. That would have welcomed me in rather than pushed me away. A hoard is a difficult thing to resist, especially for the unwary and unskilled.'

'And Iolwen disappeared.' Dafydd tried to steer the conversation back on track.

'She, Usel and all the others. There was a twist in the Llinellau, and then they were gone. I flew high, tried to track them. That was when I began to see things I recognized, at least after a fashion. The Twmp is unmistakable, but the forest surrounding it was sickly, dying. And then I came across a vast fortress in the mountains, heavy with the Grym and yet teeming with men.'

'Emmass Fawr. The headquarters of the Order of the High Ffrydd. It is as well you did not land there. They have hunted and slaughtered dragons for millennia.'

Earith and Merriel both looked at him aghast as he spoke what was for Dafydd just a matter of fact.

'But why? What could they possibly hope to gain by doing such a thing?' Merriel asked.

'It is the law handed down to them by their god, the Shepherd. And they collect the bright red jewels that grow in your heads. They are a source of great power, I'm told.'

If Dafydd thought the two dragons were disturbed by his first revelation, this new one left an even more terrible silence hanging in the air. Merriel slumped slowly back on to the sleeping platform, and Earith stood so still that she looked like a statue.

'It is terrible, I know,' he said after an awkward pause. 'My own people have not been much better in their treatment of your kind, but at least we haven't hunted and slaughtered them to extinction.'

'You do not understand.' Merriel spoke, her voice soft even though she was clearly in shock. 'A dragon's jewels must be reckoned on death. Our bodies must be consumed by the Fflam Gwir so our memories and experiences can be set. Only then can we join our ancestors and live on through the Grym. Only then can we be added to a hoard.' She shook her head slowly, staring at her hands for a moment before once more looking up at him. 'These jewels in the cavern underneath Candlehall. Are they clear and bright, or red like anger?'

'Near the centre of the chamber, by the pillar that supports the ceiling and the Obsidian Throne above it, they are white. But as the cells go further out, so their contents turn red. They whisper too. A thousand thousand voices that might turn a man mad if he tried to listen to them.'

'Cells?' Earith asked. 'What do you mean by this? The jewels are not piled high, all intermingled?'

It was Dafydd's turn to be confused. 'No. They are in individual piles. I had assumed each was from a single dragon, although some of the piles were much larger than others. And they are arranged in little cells carved out of solid rock pillars, spiralling out from the centre.'

'And some are white, you say? Those nearest the centre?' Earith went back to her bench and slumped down upon it. 'Ah, this is monstrous. Bad enough that men should covet our unreckoned jewels, but I suspect they have only continued something begun by one of our own. No man could produce the true flame, the Fflam Gwir, and yet if what you say is true then dozens, hundreds of dragons have been sacrificed for a purpose I can only begin to guess at. And that guess is too terrible to contemplate. It is a horror. An abomination. No wonder it drove you away, my daughter.'

'You think this is the work of Gog and his mad brother?' Merriel asked.

'Gog was just as mad as Magog. He only showed it in a different way.' Earith stood once more, her shoulders drooping as if she carried the weight of Gwlad upon them. 'And I've no doubt this foul practice has something to do with them, but it must go back earlier still. This is Palisander's work, and it must be destroyed.'

'Destroyed?' Dafydd asked. 'But how?'

'I do not know. A dragon's jewels must be burned with their body in order for the reckoning to succeed. At least that is what I have always understood. If these jewels you have seen are unreckoned, ripped from the skulls of the slaughtered, then their bodies are long since turned to dust and dirt. What hope of setting them right? They must be in such torment, such mad pain.'

Dafydd stood up, his only possible course of action now obvious. 'Take me back there.'

'What?' Merriel and Earith both asked.

'Back to Candlehall. If you cannot enter the chamber,

then I can. I have been there, seen it. At the very least I can free the jewels from their cells. Mix them all up together like they should be.'

The two dragons stared at him for a while, then Earith shook her head. 'To mix the reckoned and the unreckoned would be worse torment than they are currently in. And a hoard of unreckoned jewels on its own? I have no idea what manner of beast that might be. Mad, certainly. And powerful beyond imagining. But the reckoned jewels, the white ones. If they are truly the last memories of dragons who lived in Palisander's time, then they will almost certainly have knowledge lost to me. They may know a way to deal with the others.'

'So I collect together only the white jewels, leave the red ones where they are.'

'It will not be easy. Even dragons can be overwhelmed by the power of a jewel hoard, which is why they are usually left in the care of the most skilled mages. You will need the utmost mental discipline, and you must not physically touch any of the jewels. That would be fatal.' Earith spoke to herself as much as to Dafydd, pacing back and forth as she did so.

'I will take my chances. It's the least I can do to repay the kindness you have shown me.'

Earith stopped her pacing, looked straight at him. 'You truly mean that, Prince Dafydd. It gives me hope that not all of your kind are tainted by Gog's curse. Very well. I shall take you back to the Hall of Candles and we will put an end to this madness once and for all.'

She reached out a hand for him to take, but Merriel stepped between them.

'I shall take him, mother. We have travelled the Llinellau together before, so it will be easier.'

'No, Merriel. You are not strong enough. Your wounds—'

'Are healing. I will be fine. And you need to stay here. Prepare Pallestre for the wounded I am sure will be coming soon. People and dragons both.'

Earith opened her mouth to speak, and Dafydd could almost see the arguments she was mustering. But then she closed it again, drew herself up tall. 'I've known for a long time now there's no point arguing with you, Merriel. So go, take Prince Dafydd to the Hall of Candles. But be careful, be safe. And come home as soon as you can.' She turned and left the room swiftly, but not before Dafydd had seen her tears. He had not known dragons capable of them.

'Are you ready then?'

He turned back to see Merriel with her hand outstretched, exactly the way she had been on the steps in front of the Neuadd.

'As I'll ever be.' He reached out, grasped one massive finger as best he could. And tried not to think about how he was going to get into the chamber without Iolwen or his son to open the door.

A day and a night passed before he was able to relax, convinced that he had evaded all the warrior priests. Benfro trudged through the forest, always heading downhill, using his missing eye and the aethereal view it gave him to keep from going in circles. He would have hunted, or at the very least scavenged for berries and herbs to dull the gnawing emptiness in his stomach, but the snow hid everything, and the cold meant even the hardiest of beasts was tucked away in shelter, keeping its head down and praying to whatever gods small beasts prayed to for an end to this storm.

The morning of the second day saw that prayer answered. Benfro was so weary, stumbling as he half-dozed, half-walked, that he didn't notice when the snow stopped, didn't register the transition to silence as the wind died away to nothing. It wasn't until he tripped on a tree root and went sprawling face first into a mixture of mud and fat brown leaves that he saw the change. Even then it took a while to register, his mind racing in panic that he might have dropped his mother's jewel.

But no, it was still there, clasped in a hand so tight it had seized completely. He needn't have worried about dropping the tiny stone; more difficult would be to put it down intentionally.

Wiping dirt from his snout with the back of his hand, Benfro rolled over and pushed himself up into a sitting position. The wound in his side took that moment to remind him it was still there. His sight dimmed, and he spent a long while breathing hard, fighting back the pain and the terrible sensation he was about to pass out.

When the darkness lifted and his hearts returned to their more normal rhythm, Benfro saw that he was sitting at the top of a steep rise, looking out over a wide valley softened by a canopy of oak and elm trees. The sky was still grey with clouds scudding swiftly in the direction he had walked from, but off in the distance he could see patches of blue, pale as a stolen egg, the occasional ray of sunshine. Distant mountains curved in the haze, only their upper flanks dusted with white. As he stared at them, a flock of birds took off suddenly from the closer treetops, clattering into the air as if startled by something below. They wheeled around two or three times before coming back to rest in another tree nearby.

And that was then he started to recognize the shape of the place.

Benfro couldn't have said how; he'd only ever been here once before, after all, and he was on the other side of the valley this time. But somehow he just knew he was right. Perhaps it was the familiar curve of the distant hills, or maybe it was the smell – a thousand different scents that he could name with ease. As the air began to warm with the growing day, so the animals stirred too. He heard the barking of deer not far off, and then with a busy rustling a nearby bush shook itself open to reveal a sow surrounded by a litter of piglets.

Even though he kept himself perfectly still the sow must have smelled him. She backed up swiftly, squealing at her brood to follow. Benfro's stomach gurgled in anticipation, but he was too far from them to even hope to be able to catch one. He struggled to his feet, leaning on the nearest tree trunk as the world swayed around him. After a moment, when things had begun to settle down, he carefully picked a route down the slope, angling between the trees as he went.

He found herbs as he walked, snapping off flower heads and chewing on them to help with his hunger. A massive honey fungus grew out of the side of one old elm tree and he carefully cut it away. It was better cooked, but thin strips sliced off with one extended talon soon began to fill the hole. By the time he reached the bottom of the valley, Benfro was beginning to feel a lot better. All he needed was a stream to slake his thirst, and he could hear the sound of water not far off.

The trees thinned as he walked towards the water. Coarse grass underfoot had clearly once been a pasture. Saplings had taken it over though, the grazing animals long gone. A few wildflowers bloomed in the spaces between the young trees, but soon the forest would reclaim this place completely.

A shallow stream ran straight and true, its banks quite obviously not shaped by natural forces. Benfro waded in, drinking his fill and eyeing the fish that darted away from him over the gravel riverbed. They would have been a welcome addition to his diet, but he was still too tired to think straight, let alone catch anything. Climbing the bank opposite to where he had entered, he pressed on across the valley.

When he saw the first building, it was with a mixture of surprise and relief. Surprise at quite how more derelict it looked than he was expecting, relieved that it was here at all. He had never actually been here and walked among the ruins, but he had looked down upon them from nearby. Ynys Môn had stood at his side, told him a little of this place called Ystumtuen, of how he had saved the king of men from being gored to death by a tusker boar, and in so doing freed dragons from centuries – millennia – of persecution at their hands. Benfro remembered the story, but now he saw it in the wider context of what he knew.

He walked through the ruins of the hunting lodge, marvelling at the way nature was reclaiming the place as her own. The stone walls of the larger buildings still stood, though some were beginning to crumble at the top. All the roofs had caved in, and trees grew in what must once have been stately rooms. Everything was on a scale for men, which wouldn't have seemed so small when first he had seen it from afar. Now, close in and peering through doorways he would struggle to enter, he could scarce believe the tiny, fragile creatures who had built them could have hunted down and killed his kind.

Past the main collection of buildings, Benfro found an area that must once have been formal gardens. The plants here had grown wild, but they stood in straight lines and were too exotic to have found their way here by chance. A bit beyond them, a low stone wall still stood strong, even though the area enclosed by it was beginning to succumb to the encroaching forest. There were more lines here, but instead of cultivated plants there were stones, ornately carved and shaped. Some had the writing of men on them, and as he stared Benfro understood that they were gravestones. He had heard how men buried their dead in the ground, bodies and all. Did they even have jewels like a dragon? Somehow he didn't think so. The Grym would take them back as it did all base things.

Moving on, he climbed a steep bank that took him into the forest proper, turning every so often to check back, adjusting his course to a memory from a much happier time. When he found the spot where first he had viewed the abandoned buildings, it was almost a disappointment. Had he been expecting a flash of magic and for it all to have never happened? Perhaps in a tiny part of his mind he had. Nothing changed though. He was still battle-scarred and bruised by his experiences. His mother was still dead at the hands of Inquisitor Melyn, her only remaining jewel clutched tight in his regrown hand. Ynys Môn was still dead too, and all the other villagers with him, most of their jewels isolated from each other in Magog's repository at Cenobus. That was a task he would have to attend to, if he ever managed to rid himself of the dead mage. But for now he had a simple mission. He hadn't known it until he had found the old hunting lodge, but seeing it had planted the idea in his mind. He knew the way from here, knew the forests like he knew his own tail.

He was going home.

'Summon the warrior priests, the quaisters and the novitiates. I will address the whole order in Ruthin's Hall in one hour.'

Melyn shook snow from his robes as he strode through the front gates of Emmass Fawr, shouting his command to the captain of the guard. The man stared at him for a moment, slack-jawed. Perhaps that was fair enough; the inquisitor had just stepped out of nowhere to appear before him.

'Your Grace ... how ...?' he began, and then his training caught up with him. Snapping to attention, he slapped a fist across his chest in salute. 'One hour, sire. Do you require an escort?'

Melyn stopped, stared at the man for a moment. 'Do I look like I need an escort?' He shook his head and carried on walking.

Emmass Fawr was huge, built on a scale far greater than human. As a novitiate, warrior priest and finally inquisitor, he had sometimes wondered about the width of the corridors, the height of the ceilings in the most ancient parts of the complex. Even deep in the mountain upon which it had been built, the dungeons were cavernous and went on for miles, carved from the rock and then lined with straight-cut stone blocks as tall as a man. The histories had it that the monastery had taken a thousand years to build. Melyn didn't doubt it, although he knew now that it was not men who had done the building.

He viewed the structure with new eyes, his own memories of the place coloured by Magog's. This had been the home of Maddau the Wise, ancient even when the twin brothers were still hatchlings. With a humourless laugh, Melyn recalled the story of how King Brynceri I had fought the great dragon Maddau, losing his finger and Balwen's ring in the process. Only with the help of Ruthin had he managed to defeat the fearsome beast, cutting open its belly and presenting ring and finger both as a gift to the wandering monk. Ruthin had become the first inquisitor of the Order of the High Ffrydd, the ringed finger passed down the generations as the order's most sacred relic. Emmass Fawr, so the legend went, was built on the spot where Maddau had died. Now he knew better.

'Maddau was ever a thorn in my side. Always favoured my brother over me.' Magog's voice in his head was almost Melyn's own now. 'And yet when we split Gwlad, she chose to remain here.'

'So you gave Brynceri the power to kill her?'

'She deserved no more. She knew of my brother's treachery, how he gave magic to your kind and set them to the destruction of all dragons. And yet rather than help me fight, she withdrew and cast a spell of secrecy over her home. Had she not been such a coward I would surely still live.'

'But if she withdrew, then the tales of her terrorizing the

local population are just that. Tales.' Melyn spoke aloud as he strode the long corridors to the inquisitor's tower, ignoring the strange looks he received from those few people he met. Most were more fearful than anything, scuttling away or backing into the shadows at this approach.

'It is true she took some coaxing out. And first I had to convince that arrogant oaf Balwen that I was a god. It became easier after he died, and your kind live such short lives. His heirs soon learned that respect and honour for the Shepherd was something worth cultivating.'

'But why have her killed? And why take her palace as the centre for our order?'

'Emmass Fawr is a place of great power, but it is also close to my brother's mountain retreat, Nantgrafanglach.' Melyn felt the hatred as the word formed in his mind, pictured the high tower and the endless roofs below it. 'Were it not for this storm, you would see its lights from the northern walls, out across the Faaerem chasm. It always made sense to have my most loyal followers based here, best placed to watch for his return.'

Melyn approached the wide courtyard that would normally have been filled with novitiates practising their swordsmanship. Snow piled against the entrance and dusted the floor of the open passageways, brought in by a wind that howled like no storm he had ever seen in his decades of service to the order. It was the middle of the day, but only twilight made it through the heavy cloud, revealing a narrow path towards the rougher stone-built block that housed his room and the inquisitor's chapel. A small group of young men were shovelling for all they were worth.

'You there. Fetch Father Andro to my quarters.' Melyn's

shout alerted the men to his presence and they all snapped to attention. The one he had commanded saluted swiftly, his shouted 'At once, Your Grace' almost lost to the howling wind. Melyn reached out and drew deep from the Grym, ready to warm himself before setting off across the open courtyard, then let out a curse as the power flowed through him far more swiftly than he had intended. With a flick of the wrist, he dispersed it in a sheet of flame that rolled out over the snow, melting it to slush.

'Begging pardon, Your Grace, but the Grym's acting up proper strange here. None of us dare tap it for warmth more'n a second or so.'

Melyn rounded on the hapless novitiate who had spoken, saw the fear in the young man's eyes. He was beneath contempt, but he was also correct. The lines pulsed and whirled in a manner he had never seen before, and where usually they were the palest white, now they were tinged with red, as if something had bled into them.

'You are one of Clun's year, are you not?' The inquisitor stared at the lad, trying to dredge a name from his memory. There was too much else to remember, his own experiences and the much longer life and life in death that Magog had endured.

'Yes, sire. Quaister Mendrim tasked us with keeping the walkway clear for your return.'

Melyn looked at the path his fire had cleared, already beginning to cover over again as the storm continued to rage.

'Well step to it then. I'll be back shortly and I don't want to be wading my way over.'

He picked away at the Grym in tiny, quick bites as he

fought with the wind all the way across the courtyard. Emmass Fawr was always cold in the winter, but so naturally powerful that even with a full count of many thousands of novitiates, warrior priests and quaisters no one truly suffered. Except perhaps the servants, and they had fires to warm them. It was only autumn now, but the chill had settled deep into the land. With the lines so tangled and unpredictable, a lot of people would be feeling cold. One more reason to give them something to do.

The guard house at the bottom of the building was empty, and for a moment the inquisitor's anger threatened to boil over once more. There should have been a full troop present, ready for his command. But then he remembered how he had come here. Alone, using magic no one else in the entire monastery was aware of. Word had probably only just now reached Father Andro of his arrival, so it was hardly surprising no one had detailed a guard for him. Most of his best warrior priests would be out in the mountains with Captain Osgal, seeking out Gog's palace and mapping its entrances. Soon they would be ready to attack.

The plan was there, already fully formed in his mind, as Melyn climbed the steps to his rooms. With each passing moment the difference between himself and Magog became harder to distinguish. He should have been disgusted, alarmed, horrified perhaps. But instead he was exhilarated. Power and knowledge were things he had striven to achieve all his life.

'We are destined for great things, you and I.' Melyn spoke the words out loud in the empty corridor, and whether they were his or Magog's he neither knew nor cared.

25

Not all dragons are masters of the Grym and the subtle arts. Some have no natural talent, whereas others find the years, decades, centuries of study too tedious to contemplate, preferring the immediate thrill of flight, the hunt and other more carnal pleasures. Men have no ability whatsoever, though some show a degree of sensitivity to the Llinellau. What then if they are needed half a world away?

A mage, or even a skilled adept, can travel with ease along the Llinellau to any place in Gwlad. With but a thought, the distance from Nantgrafanglach to Pallestre need be no more than stepping through an open door. Yet for his retinue, his household servants and followers, a simpler means of travel is necessary.

The Heolydd Anweledig, the invisible roads, are such a means. A permanent link along the Llinellau, they allow for any living thing, dragon, man or beast, to move in an instant from one place to another.

Such magics must not be undertaken lightly though. Fixing a working of the subtle arts to a place rather than a mage runs the risk of that working becoming unstable, with unpredictable results. Travellers along a failing Heol Anweledig might find the journey takes no time, but ages them as if they had walked the distance on foot. Or the exit might move from its intended target to somewhere else entirely, perhaps deep under the ocean or in the heart of a mountain. Worst of all, the subtle arts anchoring the road may simply unravel as it is being used. If this is the case then any traveller on the road will be dissipated into the Grym and vanish as if they had never existed.

Corwen teul Maddau,
On the Application of the Subtle Arts

It was almost as if he had never been away. Dafydd stood on the top step in front of the fallen doors into the Neuadd, staring out across the courtyard at the devastation wrought by the dragons. The only thing that had changed was the weather. He had grown accustomed to the heat of Pallestre, and here the cold wind cut through him like a knife. Overhead, the sky was leaden grey, and flurries of snow swirled around. A light dusting lay on the cold cadavers spread around the courtyard too, and all around was a terrible silence, as if the city had been abandoned.

'How long have I been away?' He released his grip on Merriel's finger as the nausea of the trip began to fade. Instinctively, he reached for the lines, tapping their energy for warmth. Or at least he tried. At first he could find no trace of the Grym, and then it surged into him like a storm. For a moment Dafydd thought it might overwhelm him. His skin prickled with the heat, his scalp itching as his head grew hotter and hotter. Then, as quickly as it had come upon him, the power died away to nothing. He stumbled forward a step, breathing heavily.

'Have a care. The Llinellau are bent and twisted out of shape. It is fortunate we were both here together before. Without that memory I might have been lost. We might both have been lost.'

'What is causing it?' Dafydd brought the lines to his vision and saw something strange and alien. Where all had been order, the Grym gently flowing between the myriad forms of life on Gwlad, now it was pulsing and writhing like a nest of snakes disturbed.

'The death of Gog has undone a working of the subtle arts so immense, so all-encompassing, that it threatens to destroy Gwlad herself. The Llinellau, this weather,' Merriel indicated the snow, thickening now as the temperature dropped, 'these are just the easy signs to see.'

'How can we stop it? How can we put it right?'

Merriel turned so suddenly, Dafydd thought for a moment she was going to hit him. 'We? Put it right? This is magic so far beyond my understanding it can't even be imagined. I doubt even my mother knows what those mad brothers did when they split Gwlad in two, let alone the consequences of that spell unravelling. No, Prince Dafydd, there is nothing you or I can do except stay alive and help others to stay alive too. Gwlad must be given the space to heal herself. And we can start by righting Palisander's wrong. There is an entrance to this cavern that does not require the travelling of the Llinellau, I take it?'

Dafydd looked once more around the deserted, ruined courtyard and wondered where the dragons who had almost killed him and Iolwen had gone. 'There is an entrance built for men. You would fit in the corridor leading to it, but the stairs to the chamber are too narrow and winding. And if the door has been locked then I am not entirely sure how I will enter the chamber myself. It is protected by magics that deny entry to any who do not carry the blood of King Balwen in their veins.'

Merriel fixed her gaze on him, those massive eyes seeing straight through to his thoughts. Dafydd knew he should have told her and Earith the whole story, but there had not been time.

'And who in this city carries that bloodline?' she asked.

'The queen herself is the only one I can think of. I could ask her if she'd let me in, but I think it unlikely. And there's the small matter of the key as well.'

Merriel frowned. 'Only the queen?'

'Well, her daughter, I suppose, but she is just an infant.'

'Then she is unlikely to put up much of a fight.' Merriel looked up at the snow swirling down from the sky. 'But we should step into the hall now, much though the smell of the place sickens me. The dragons are returning.'

'They are?' Dafydd followed her gaze, unable to make out anything in the deepening gloom. He could feel it though, a sense of unease as if something were reaching out to touch his mind. Instinctively he closed down his mental barriers, turned and leaped up the steps, disappearing into the darkness of the hall itself just as the swirling sound of the wind took on a different note. Merriel followed him, wrinkling her nose against the meaty stench. The two of them made as swift a path as they could to the dais and the great throne. Outside something heavy thumped on to the ground and then a voice began bellowing in the tongue of dragons.

'Gwynedd Bach.' Merriel managed to put so much venom into her voice Dafydd was surprised she didn't breathe fire as she spoke.

'The big one? Black as night and, how can I put it, fat?'

'The same. She visited Pallestre once. Stupid and vengeful cow, tried to eat the stallholders in the market place. Mother protected them of course, but there was no persuading Gwynedd that men were not prey. In the end we had to drive her off, wipe her memory of the place. There was no reasoning with her.'

'That's what Seneschal Padraig found, to his cost.' Dafydd recalled the incident all too vividly, shivering at the memory. 'What is she saying?'

'Mostly that she's hungry and that her mate is a useless hunter. It surprises me that any dragon would find her attractive in the least. But then those who abandoned the old ways have become so feral that they have lost all sensibility.'

'What if she comes in here? Sees us?'

'She won't. This is a male dragon's place now. They have marked it as their latrine, and the courtyard outside as their feeding ground. It is disgusting but it is also predictable.'

Dafydd looked around at the mess that had once been the grandest hall in all of Gwlad. The polished marble beneath his feet was scratched by talons and smeared in dung. Shards of glass lay everywhere, and chunks of carved stone from the ceiling littered the ground. He caught a glimpse of a face and thought for a moment it was a man before realizing it was part of a statue. Other figures lay discarded and shattered as if the craftsmanship that had gone into their carving were worth nothing.

'So this is Palisander's great Obsidian Throne then.' Merriel turned from the doorway and the screeching dragon beyond, her head tilting back as she looked up to the top of the vast black structure. Even compared to her it was massive. She climbed the dais, approaching the throne with the same caution Dafydd might have approached a catlion. Reaching out one hand towards the stone, she almost touched it, then withdrew as if it were hotter than fire. She maintained a constant distance as she circled it once, taking in every tiny detail. He had no doubt that the dragon was seeing the throne in the aethereal as well as the mundane, teasing out all its secrets and traps.

'For two thousand years and more the kings and queens of the House of Balwen have ruled from this throne,' he said as Merriel finally dragged her gaze away from it and back to him. 'They use the power of the Grym that flows through it to read the minds of their enemies, to influence the people and make everyone love them. Or they cannot handle the voices and go swiftly mad. The bloodiest wars in these lands have not been between our two nations, but within the Twin Kingdoms itself.'

'It has been adapted so a man can sit upon it, I see.' Merriel pointed one taloned finger at the awkward blocks of stone that had been inserted into what had been the original seat. Steps led up to a platform that was wide for a fat man and must have been uncomfortable to sit on even without the whispering voices. Dafydd could hear them now, chattering away, pecking at his mental barriers. It was hard to concentrate for all the noise they were making, and the confusion in the lines didn't help.

'Hold yourself together, Prince Dafydd. We are close to the source here. You must keep your wits about you.'

'Close, yes.' Dafydd looked down at his feet, imagined the solid rock giving way to the huge chamber deep underneath. 'But there is no way in from here.'

'You are wrong, although it is perhaps unfair of me to say so.'

'Wrong? How?'

'There is a way from this throne to the cavern beneath us. Here, at the back of the seat.' Merriel walked swiftly behind the throne, and Dafydd had to run to catch up. 'Here in the space between the legs, where later masons have tried to blend impure stone into the original design, there is a doorway. Hidden by the subtle arts.'

Dafydd stared at the stonework, remembering it from his brief visit before he, Iolwen and Usel had been chased out by the twins. It looked no different to the rest of the throne to him. Deepest black, polished to a shine that mirrored his features darkly back at him. 'I see no doorway.'

'Then look again.' Merriel's voice had an edge to it, almost a taunt, and her eyes showed a curious twinkle, as if she were enjoying his lack of ability. Dafydd couldn't understand how she could be so calm, here in the heart of enemy territory and with feral dragons just outside. At any moment one of the male dragons might come in and see them. Attack them.

'Relax. Calm your thoughts. See the throne as it truly is. We are as safe here as anywhere in Gwlad.'

Dafydd was not convinced, but he steadied his breathing and willed his heartbeat to slow. He had never been as adept as his grandfather at achieving the trance needed to see the aethereal, but he knew he could do it. He just needed to concentrate, block out all distractions.

It came to him slowly. First the edges of the throne began to sparkle as if it stood outside and a fresh sun had newly risen. Then veins of pure white Grym appeared in the shiny black stone, criss-crossing it in regular patterns and flowing over the carved surface. Seen like this it was easy to tell the difference between original throne and later additions. The men who had added to the stonework might have been skilled masons, but they knew nothing of the Grym, nor of how to weave life into lifeless rock.

'You see it now.'

Dafydd turned his head and almost dropped out of his trance. Merriel was a magnificent creature in the mundane, but in the aethereal she glowed.

'Concentrate on the doorway there.' Her voice echoed in his head, the compulsion in her words impossible to ignore. He studied the joins between the blocks that made up the back of the throne, seeing how they were arranged and how they might be made to move. All he needed to do was reach out and press that point there . . .

Something clicked in his head at the same time as the stone in front of his eyes shifted. Dafydd snapped out of the trance with such force he was flung back, tripping over his feet and tumbling on to his backside. In the corner of his eye he saw Merriel reach out an arm, swift as a striking snake. He half feared she would cut him in two, half expected to feel her strength as she caught him.

Neither happened, and he fell to the floor with a crash that drove the wind out of him and sent a jolt of pain lancing up his spine.

'What the—?'

'Just a little something left behind by the last adept to use this doorway.' Merriel held up her hand, clenched tight into a fist, and then brought it down hard on to the floor a few paces away from where Dafydd lay. He didn't need the aethereal trance, or even the Grym sight, to see the power she had somehow trapped. The marble cracked like ice, shattering into a thousand pieces at her touch. The noise engulfed him, so loud it left his ears ringing and must have been heard far beyond the courtyard. Beyond the city walls even. Dafydd felt the heat blast through him, momentarily expelling the chill that had seeped into his bones.

'Was that a curse?'

'Originally, yes. A working of the subtle arts to prevent anyone from using this entrance who was not supposed to. It is ancient though. Far older than me. Time has warped it, and if what you say of the chamber below is true, that perversion of magic has twisted it too. I almost didn't see it myself.'

Dafydd looked more closely at Merriel as she spoke. He had thought her merely winded by the sudden movement, but now he could see that catching and destroying the curse had cost her dearly. She stooped, her legs trembling beneath her as if they could barely carry her weight. The hand that had smashed into the floor was now bent and twisted like an old woman's, the talons blackened.

'Are you . . . Are you all right?' It seemed such an

insufficient thing to ask, but he really didn't know what else to say.

'I will be.' Merriel glanced up, past the edge of the Obsidian Throne towards the entrance. Noises filtered through Dafydd's hissing ears that suggested the sound had indeed carried far and alerted many to their presence. 'But I cannot stay here. I must return to Pallestre before the turmoil in the Grym becomes too much even for that.'

'Go, then. I will find my own way into the chamber.'

'That much will be easy, Prince Dafydd. Look.' Merriel nodded wearily, indicating the back of the throne. Following her gaze, he saw that the stonework had opened up, revealing an entrance large enough for a man. 'Go swiftly, and I will close the door behind you. In the chamber you must build all the white jewels into a pile, as close to the centre as you can. Be ready though. The dragon memories will be hurt, angry. Some may even be mad, and others simply desperate to reconnect with life. Do not touch any with your bare skin, and leave the unreckoned jewels where they are. At least for now.'

The commotion on the other side of the throne was growing louder, and as Dafydd's hearing began to clear, he could make out individual voices shouting in guttural Draigiaith. He felt a brush of thoughts questing at his own mind, closed himself off as best he could and scrambled back on to his feet.

'I will be fine. Do not worry about me.' Merriel responded to the question before it could reach his lips. Dafydd merely nodded once, then walked through the door. Steps spiralled down, narrow and tight. He took one last look back, seeing the dragon's hand reaching out for the entrance. Then the stones seemed to slide back over the doorway and he was plunged into darkness.

Far fewer people had fled through the tunnel to Nantgrafanglach than Iolwen had thought. Sir Council had spoken of thousands, but in truth their numbers were not that great. Iolwen could only hope that the majority of the people of Candlehall had made good their escape through the other hidden roads and not fallen into her sister's merciless hands. She had no doubt that Beulah would put many of her subjects to death for their collusion in the fall of the city, even though the destruction of Candlehall had been the queen's own doing.

Their initial meeting with the council had not sparked much in the way of action, and Iolwen had found Sir Conwil evasive afterwards, as if he did not like her conjured blade, nor the way Myfanwy had chastised him. She recognized the type, even though he was dragon not man. Set in his ways like Tordu, he didn't take kindly to being told what to do. Instead of arguing the point with his leader though, he simply turned his ire on Iolwen and her party.

They had moved from the great hall to a smaller suite of apartments in a building Iolwen had discoveed was Myfanwy's own home. Usel, Teryll, Anwen and the Llanwennog guards stayed with Iolwen, but Mercor Derridge and his grandson Beyn had soon left to find family. Iolwen was sad to see them go but understood their need; she missed Dafydd after all.

The few hundred men, women and children who had arrived at the great palace were beginning to integrate, helped in no small part by the deep magic of the dragons and their willingness to share it. Most of the Candlehall folk spoke passable Draigiaith now, and were working in teams with the local palace servants to restore rooms that had fallen into disrepair over years, possibly centuries, of neglect. Iolwen couldn't help thinking they would be better off training to fight. The storm might still have raged outside the windows, but she was certain Inquisitor Melyn was out there, planning his attack.

Partly to take her mind off such worries, partly because she could find nothing else to do, Iolwen had taken to exploring the endless corridors and rooms that made up the central building of the palace. A vast tower rose from the centre, its spiral staircase daunting to one as small as her, so she wandered through the smaller wings, although these in themselves were bigger than the entire palace at Tynhelyg. The scale of Nantgrafanglach was beyond imagining.

'You look lost, Princess.'

The voice startled her. Iolwen had paused at the end of a second-floor landing and was staring out of a thick glass window across the snow-covered parkland towards the distant wall. It was hard to make out in the endless whirl of the storm, but the view soothed her, made it easier to think. Now she turned to see the old dragon Myfanwy standing close by.

'Not lost, no,' she said. 'Well, not physically. I'm confident I can find my way back to the others. I hope I'm not intruding.'

'If there were parts of Nantgrafanglach we did not wish you to see, you would not be able to see them.' Myfanwy tilted her head slightly, a mischievous glint to her eyes.

'It is a wondrous place. I have never seen building on such a scale. It makes even the Neuadd seem small.'

'It is still one dragon's folly. There is room here for thousands of our kind, tens of thousands of yours. More. And yet we number in the few hundreds. Your people have more than doubled our ranks but scarcely need one wing to house them all.'

'A hard place to defend from attack then.'

'This man, Melyn. You truly believe he will come for us?' Myfanwy asked.

'I do. He is driven by such hatred of your kind and he is so powerful in the ways of magic. His order have slain almost all the dragons in our world, taken their jewels and collected them all together beneath the Neuadd. That is the power that has kept King Balwen's bloodline - my bloodline - on the Obsidian Throne for two thousand years.'

Myfanwy stared out the window for long moments, as if searching the raging storm for any sign of approaching menace. 'The council will not accept it, but it was a man who killed Gog, and my son Enedoc too. He wielded a blade like the one you conjured in the meeting, only his burned red with anger. If this is your Melyn, then he is more dangerous even than you think, for he is possessed by the dead spirit of Magog and the hatred between those two brothers has almost destroyed Gwlad once before.'

Iolwen was about to ask the old dragon to explain. She had heard the stories from Usel, but there was more to them than the medic knew. Before she could open her mouth, Myfanwy turned to her, a renewed urgency in her stance.

'Tell me, Princess. These jewels beneath the Neuadd, are they reckoned?'

'Reckoned?'

'White and pure, but if I have to ask then that answers my question. They are red, I can see it in your mind. And sorted into individual cells too. Ah, what mad hell is this? No wonder Gwlad writhes and screams. Such abomination. Such injustice.'

Iolwen felt the brush of Myfanwy's thoughts on her own, more delicate than anything her teachers and old King Ballah had ever managed. Unlike them, the old dragon shared her own concerns, and with them her resolve to find a solution to the situation. Still, it was a shaky foundation.

'But how can we hope to fight one so powerful?' she asked. 'And if we cannot fight, then where can we run? There is nowhere in the whole of Gwlad we could hide from him.'

'Magog can be stopped, and with him your Inquisitor Melyn. Cut off the source of his power and he is just a man.' Myfanwy placed a gnarled hand softly on Iolwen's shoulder, her touch light even though the dragon could have crushed her if she chose. Together they stared out at the growing storm. 'There are plans already afoot to break Magog's hold on this world. Let us hope - pray even - they come to fruition before it is too late.'

26

For every working of magic there are consequences. That is hardly surprising, as otherwise there would be no point in seeking to manipulate the Grym to your own ends, but not all consequences are intended. If the working is small, then the potential for mischief is most often equally so, and likewise if it is simple. As workings become more complex, however, so the potential for danger increases. Worse yet is when an ancient working, left behind by some long-forgotten mage, goes unnoticed. The mixing of magics is a delicate art at the best of times, to do it unawares risks disaster.

A powerful mage can maintain a great many workings of the subtle arts, holding them apart or combining them in just such a manner as to prevent them feeding on each other. A wise mage knows to limit the use of his power and to undo such workings as are no longer needed. And when a mage feels the end approaching, for all must die in time and merge with the Grym once more, then he must go about untangling the magics he has made throughout his long life, lest they cause untold damage when he is gone.

Great mages manipulate the Grym with scarcely
a thought, but the greatest of them all leave no trace
of their subtle arts once they are gone.

The Llyfr Draconius

'You are perhaps all wondering why I am here and yet none
of the warrior priests who rode out with me has returned.'

Melyn stood on the raised platform at the top end of
Ruthin's Hall. The largest room in the monastery, he now
knew that it was where Maddau the Wise had held parties
for her friends thousands of years earlier. Like most of the
great complex of buildings that made up Emmass Fawr, it
was vast by the scale of men, merely ostentatious by the
scale of the dragons who had built it. Either way it was big
enough to hold the massed ranks of the order with plenty
of room to spare. Even had not more than half of his warrior priests been out in the field, the hall would still have
held them all.

'Some of you may ask how it is that I arrived here without being noticed. That is a lesson for another day.'

Shifting his gaze to take in both the Grym and the
aethereal, the inquisitor considered for a moment giving
them all a demonstration of his new skill. He could easily
enough step from the dais, disappear and reappear at the
far end of the room. The mad fluctuations in the lines
quickly convinced him otherwise. They mirrored the
storm raging outside and spreading ever further south
across the Twin Kingdoms and beyond. Best to couch
things in language the order had been trained to
understand.

'The blizzard outside and the turmoil in the Grym are a sign. A sign that the Wolf is at our door and the Shepherd himself is returned to Gwlad.'

Melyn did his best to push the words out to the assembled thousands, but it was not easy. The hall itself was so vast it swallowed his voice, and for once the lines were not his ally here. Nevertheless, those close by heard him well enough, and the message soon spread through the crowd like fire.

'I have seen the Wolf, faced him in his lair.' He waited for the news to ripple out before continuing. 'With the Shepherd's aid, I have slain the Wolf.' And this time his words aligned with the shifting of the lines, thundering through the entire hall. The effect was better than he could have hoped, those nearest the front clasping at their ears as the message almost deafened them.

'His death has shaken Gwlad itself. That is why we have blizzards in summertime. That is why even the Grym is twisted and hard to control. These things will pass.

'But his children still live.' Melyn spoke more quietly now. 'They live, and they are close. Given time they will recover from the blow they have been dealt, and they will come seeking mischief and revenge. Not just the Twin Kingdoms, not newly conquered Llanwennog, but the whole of Gwlad is at risk if we do not seize this moment.'

He let the silence grow for a while, the murmur of whispers as neighbour conferred with neighbour, the message morphing as it spread through the entire hall. Behind him the senior quaisters and Father Andro were tense, until now no more wise to his message than anyone else.

'We must take the fight to them. Destroy the Wolf's lair and his children both. I have new magic, the Shepherd's magic, and I will teach it to you. But go now, prepare yourselves well. For tomorrow we march upon the enemy. Tomorrow we put an end to the Wolf and his tricks.'

The journey through the forest took far longer than he had expected. Benfro followed paths he had known as a kitling, only to find they led to places he didn't recognize or looped back on themselves and returned him to his camp of the night before. The forest was different in many ways. Some were subtle, like the strange animals scuttling in the undergrowth, creatures he recognized more from his time with the dragons of the Twmp than his days spent hunting with Ynys Môn. Others were far more obvious. He spent a whole day trekking across a wide sandy clearing where scrub grasses clung to arid soil, and the cracked yellow rocks looked like they had been baked under a hot sun for centuries. The rain spattering off their dusty surfaces was a reminder of how Gwlad was changing all around him, as was the rapidly shifting weather. Only the storm at his back was constant, a dark menace that blotted out his view of the mountains. Gog's tower, the place of his death, was the point around which all the magic was unfurling.

Despite this, Benfro felt happier than he had in as long as he could remember. The wound in his side still gave him pain, but it was healing, and as long as he didn't do anything too stupid it would soon be mended enough for him to try flying. The aches and pains of his fall and the treatment dealt out to him by the dragons of Nantgraf-anglach were fading now, as was the worry about finding Errol, Martha and Xando. He had his mother with him, clutched tight in his hand. Nothing else really mattered.

When he finally stumbled into the village where he had grown up, Benfro almost walked straight through without realizing. The forest here was lush and green, enjoying a warm wet summer even though blizzards raged in the mountains. The front gardens, so lovingly tended by Meirionydd, Sir Frynwy and all the others, had turned to jungle, overrun with brambles and wildflowers. Butterflies flitted between buddleia bushes, resting on petals of deepest mauve and purest white, and it was only his memory of the well-tended shrubs so beloved of Ystrad Fflur that made him stop walking and look at them more closely. That was when he saw the cottage.

It was almost completely overgrown with vines, and what had once been a small apple tree in the front now towered over him, heavy with fruit. Benfro stared with his one eye, picking out more and more detail. The shape of the door was outlined in twining honeysuckle, thorny rose bushes filling the spaces where the windows had once been. He remembered how the path had wound in a gentle S from the gate by the track all the way to the front porch. Now it was tall grass, fat seed heads waving in the gentle wind. His missing eye painted a very different picture.

The Grym flowed through the land here more strongly than anywhere he had seen it, rolling along the lines in great surging waves. All the trees glowed with it fit to burst. There was so much life filling the place it was hard to reconcile it with his memories of that fateful day Inquisitor Melyn had ridden in with his troop of warrior priests. And yet as the aethereal image of Ystrad Fflur's cottage overlaid the mundane, so Benfro was sure of it. This was where he had come so many times as a kitling, listened to the old dragon's tales of travel and adventure. What would he have made of Benfro's own experiences?

Hearts almost in his mouth, Benfro pushed through the long grass where the gate had been, treading a careful path to the front door. There was a peace about the village, a quiet that was both mournful and joyous. At his approach it seemed almost as if the undergrowth slithered away from him, revealing the smooth stone threshold and the solid ancient oak of the door. There was a glamour on this cottage, a protection woven long ago. It would have deterred any who meant ill, but Benfro it recognized, welcoming him in like an old friend. When he reached for the black iron latch, lifted it and pushed, the door opened for him on almost silent hinges.

He stood in the hall for a while, just breathing, remembering. The last time he had been here had been the day of Ystrad Fflur's reckoning. He had been so proud to carry the amphora of Delyn oil for his mother, and yet so ignorant of the honour he was being accorded. What would they make of him now, breathing the Fflam Gwir like some throwback to a bygone age? Some of the villagers would have been appalled, but others, Ystrad Fflur among them, would most likely have been delighted.

The front room where the body had lain was empty now, but oddly dust free. It put Benfro in mind of Magog's repository. That too had been abandoned for countless years and yet had never changed until he had arrived. But of course it wasn't ages since Ystrad Fflur had died, just a few years. His cottage had lain empty until Frecknock had made a start on clearing it out, sure that any day the galant Sir Felyn was going to come and sweep her off her feet. Benfro almost laughed; Melyn had certainly done that.

The furniture was still pushed back to the walls, the old open-backed chair Ystrad Fflur had sat in by the fire still shiny from years, centuries of use. Behind it Benfro found the carved wooden table and the heavy jar the old dragon had kept his crystallized ginger in. He reached out tentatively, took hold of the lid and lifted it off. If he had been expecting a familiar waft of spice, he was disappointed. But of course it had never actually contained crystallized ginger. That had been a ruse. Ystrad Fflur had used the subtle arts to bring his favourite treat to him, taken from some unsuspecting merchant's storeroom in distant Tallarddeg.

Not quite knowing why he did it, Benfro slipped his own hand into the jar. He could feel the Grym all around him, so powerful here it was overwhelming. It linked everything, everywhere, and even though the undoing of the terrible magic that had rent Gwlad apart was putting the Llinellau in turmoil, still he could remember the feel, the smell, the taste of that sweet, sharp root. He had never been to Tallarddeg, had no idea where it was other than far to the east, but he knew another place where ginger was grown. A place he had visited not so long ago. And as he remembered it, remembered his slow healing at the hands of Earith, so the memory formed links within his mind.

There was a knack to the working. Benfro was still unsure exactly what he was doing, but as the idea of ginger formed in his memory, so he felt it through the Grym and in his fingers. For the briefest of moments he was in two places. It would have been the easiest thing to step through the Llinellau, reappear in Pallestre and seek out

Earith's help. Something stopped him though, some sense of self-preservation. The Grym was too powerful and turbulent, his skills too meagre. He would be lost, or worse he would be open to Magog. Clenching his fist against the idea, Benfro pulled his hand from the jar to find it clasped around a half-dozen pieces of sweet-smelling crystallized ginger root.

'His bones are knitting well, Your Majesty, and the wounds inside are all healed. It is only his eyes that still give me concern.'

Beulah didn't think she would ever grow used to having a dragon around, even one as small as Frecknock, but the days made her presence more familiar, and her usefulness was without question. She wasn't as threatening as the great beasts wandering the parade ground and the courtyard outside the Neuadd either. As far as the queen was aware, Frecknock had never stolen cattle from the nearby farms or, indeed, eaten any people. And it couldn't be denied that her skill as a healer surpassed that even of Archimandrite Cassters. The old Ram had taken one look at Beulah's broken ankle after Frecknock had done her work on it and declared that there was no point in him being there any more. As far as she knew, he'd taken himself off to his order's headquarters, the hospital that dominated the western end of the city, there to administer to those unfortunates who had been injured during the siege.

'He still cannot see?' she asked, and Frecknock didn't need to say anything for Beulah to know the answer. It was written in the dragon's face, her shrunken posture and general air of wretchedness. Since Melyn had left, she had kept so close to the royal apartments that Beulah suspected she was sleeping in one of the servant corridors. If she ever slept, that was.

'I will attend to him now. You may leave us.'

The dragon bowed, then backed away before turning so that her tail would not sweep Beulah's feet from under her. Whatever magic Frecknock had performed on the queen's ankle, it had been a miraculous healing. She barely felt anything more than a slight tightness in the muscles, and had been walking limp-free for almost a week.

Clun slept, as he did for much of the time now. Lying in a bed that would have been vast for two, he looked like a small child. The softest of pillows cushioned him, enveloping his head as if it were some strange creature trying to eat him alive. As Beulah approached, she could sense the disturbed thoughts of a man troubled in his sleep. His face twitched and frowned, but when she sat on the chair placed at the bedside, his features smoothed, his breathing settled and after a few moments he opened his eyes.

'My lady. You are looking well this morning.'

Beulah tried to smile at his joke, but it was hard to do. Clun's eyes were milky white, clouded like those of an old man. They did not settle on her face, but stared unmoving at a patch on the ceiling far beyond her shoulder. She reached out and took the hand lying on top of the bedspread, let the warmth of the Grym flow through her and into him.

'You were having a bad dream, my love,' she said, and the frown returned to his face.

'I was not asleep. Well, not technically. I have been refining my aethereal vision, since there is little else I can do until my body has healed itself. At least Frecknock's potions keep away the pain, and her ministrations are speeding up the healing. It's just a shame my injuries were too extensive for her to treat the way she treated yours. Your ankle is as good as new.'

Beulah looked down at her foot. She had taken to wearing court gowns and pale sheepskin slippers simply because trousers and stiff leather boots were difficult to get in and out of when her ankle was swollen and sore. The swelling had gone, and it had been at least a week since last she'd felt any pain, and yet she still wore the clothes of a queen.

'They suit you.' Clun reached up and gently ran his fingers down the arm of her pale yellow jacket. 'Although I think on balance I prefer the tomboy look.'

'How can you . . .?' Beulah was unsure if she was annoyed or scared that he could read her thoughts so and that he knew what she was wearing despite having no sight in either eye.

'I saw you in the aethereal, my lady. Without my eyes, it is so much easier to enter the trance. Sometimes I am almost there and here at the same time. If I could just learn how to do that at will, I would not need these any more.' He lifted a hand vaguely in the direction of his face. 'I would see so much more than the mundane world.'

Clun let his hand drop to the bed, then struggled upright, pushing himself against the headboard until his head was on the same level as Beulah's. It took all his strength and caused him considerable pain, she couldn't help but notice. And yet he bore his misfortunes with the same good nature that had attracted her to him in the first place. How could a young lad from the back country have

387

caught her eye so? How could he have adapted so well to court life and elevation to the nobility? And how could he have mastered the magic of the warrior priests when the rest of his year's intake of novitiates had not even ascended to the priesthood yet? He was an enigma, but he was also her strength.

'Frecknock tells me your injuries are healing well, and if it is true you can see after a fashion then I am heartened by the news, my love. We are facing difficult and dangerous times.'

'The dragons?' Clun asked.

Beulah paused a moment before answering. 'This isn't how I imagined it would be. All my life I have wanted just one thing.'

'Just one?' Clun smiled in an attempt to lighten the mood.

'I'm serious, my love. My sole aim as queen was to put an end to the warring. To unite the Twin Kingdoms and Llanwennog. I should be happy I have achieved that, and yet everything is turned to dust.' She ran a finger along the back of the bedstead, which was thick with white powder. Above her the once-fine corniced ceiling was cracked, great chunks of it missing altogether. The palace of Candlehall, indeed the entire city, had been reduced to near-ruin by just a handful of dragons over the course of a few days. 'This is not the homecoming I had anticipated, not the kingdom I dreamed of ruling.'

'But it is the kingdom you have, and you will rule it well.' Clun placed a hand on her arm, the warmth radiating from him like a summer sun. Beulah took strength from it, even though she knew he could scarce spare any. Just to have him by her side was enough. One constant in a world changing far too much and too quickly for her liking.

'But what of all these dragons appearing everywhere? What are we to do about them? I can see those mad bastards that call themselves the Guardians of the Throne rejoicing that the end times are upon us. You've seen the way they behave, their fanaticism. This is exactly what they've been waiting for, this chaos. How do we put a stop to it? How do we put a stop to them?'

'By sending the dragons away, my lady. They cannot exist alongside us. Not the way they are now. Sir Sgarnog and his fold have shown me that much at least. Caradoc too.'

'Send them away? How?'

'That's the question. I imagine many of them will simply go, maybe to Eirawen, or east across the Gwastadded Wag. There is much more to Gwlad than just the Twin Kingdoms and Llanwennog.' Clun turned to face her, and Beulah shivered. His milk-white eyes looked so old in that boyish face. 'Some will not be so easy to persuade. Sadly the likes of Gwynedd Bach and Caradoc will only respond to violence.'

'Sadly?' Beulah asked. 'She ate Seneschal Padraig, and he nearly killed us both. I would have thought their deaths would be something to rejoice.'

'Indeed they would. Not even the dragons mourn Caradoc and few of them will miss Gwynedd when she's gone. But how many more are there like them? How many must we kill before they leave? And how many of us will they kill in return? We sought to unite the Twin Kingdoms with Llanwennog to put an end to centuries of war and bloodshed. I fear it will be as nothing compared to the carnage yet to come.'

27

The empty plains, the Gwastadded Wag, to the east of the Hendry lands, are renowned for their inhospitable nature. Nothing but league beyond league of emptiness, rough grass and soil so thin it yields but a single cultivated crop before turning to dust. The weather is unpredictable in all aspects but its harshness, decades of drought punctuated by month-long storms of such violence they shake the very core of Gwlad. Few creatures survive out there, and fewer still thrive.

One notable exception is the Gomorran horses, who roam the plains in herds a thousand strong and more. Theirs is the knowledge of this unforgiving land, the location of the few oases in the endless sea of dry grass and sand. A hardy breed, the mares are much prized, bringing hybrid vigour into the horses of the Twin Kingdoms. The men who ride out into the wastelands to hunt and catch them are a rare breed themselves, tough beyond reckoning.

Gomorran mares are difficult to capture and harder to break, but once in a hundred years a lucky rider will trap a Gomorran stallion. None of these magnificent beasts have ever been broken, but breeders prize them beyond anything. One stallion will serve a hundred mares and not think it too many.

His offspring will be strong, smart and loyal to their owner. Traits which will pass down generations.

Gomorran stallions are never kept. Men have tried, but always the great beasts escape. A wise breeder will put the stallion to his mares but once, then let it go. Back to its own kind in the endless, forbidden wastelands it calls home.

Moorit of the Ram,
The Gwastadded Wag, A Geography

The taste of sweet ginger still on his tongue, Benfro left Ystrad Fflur's cottage and returned to the track winding its way through what had once been his village. The forest had taken it back completely, far too much to be entirely natural. He suspected the hand of the mother tree, enveloping this place and protecting it, although from what and for what reason he could not imagine. To see Meirionydd's garden a riot of colour and filled with life was bittersweet. Close to the great hall, her tumbledown cottage had been one of those the warrior priests had put to the torch, and little of it remained save for a jumble of stones. He had such fond memories of visiting here, of the dragon who had been second only to his mother in importance in his life.

Turning away from the pain, his eyes swept over what remained of the central green and the hall. The trees had not invaded the open space here, save for some sturdy saplings that had rooted through the ashes of the dead villagers. They rose in the middle of the green, a tight copse surrounded by fallen stonework and the glint of heat-broken glass. Benfro approached slowly, the chest-high grass tickling his scales as he pushed his way through to where the old oak doors had stood. He had only ever seen them closed twice in his life, on the day of Ystrad Fflur's reckoning and on his fourteenth hatchday, when his mother had acknowledged him as the head of the family and he had finally been freed of the crude spell Frecknock had cast upon him. Now they lay flat on the ground, almost completely hidden by the vegetation, their ancient surfaces charred.

Benfro stepped over them carefully. He had been meaning to enter the hall, the doorway still framed by its heavy stone pillars, but as he approached it seemed to shrink. For a moment he thought it some cruel trick, some ancient spell that denied him the melancholy pleasure of seeing the place where his extended family had died. And then he realized that it was no trick at all. He was too large to fit through the entrance without squeezing now, his wings too bulky to let him pass. The hall he had always thought vast was not so great any more, and the tight-packed trees that speared up from the cracked flagstone floor made it seem smaller still. Perhaps it was for the best. There was little to be gained from standing here, mourning those who were past caring.

Sir Frynwy's house stood on the other side of the green from Meirionydd's. Benfro had visited it often, and though it had been set on fire by the warrior priests, it had mostly survived, protected by the old bard's magics and the solidity of its construction. His missing eye showed him the shape of it more clearly than his mundane sight. Like everywhere else in the village, the forest had overgrown it as if trying to hide it from view. He approached it cautiously, remembering the time he had been brought in front of the old dragon accused of stealing Sir Frynwy's most prized possession.

Pulling aside the twisting clematis that obscured the doorway, Benfro saw that the door itself had been broken down, shards of timber lying in the hall. Too much to hope that the *Llyfr Draconius* would still be inside, and like the great hall behind him this doorway was too narrow now for him to enter comfortably. His missing eye showed him all he needed to know: the traces of ancient spells still gently unravelling, the more recent touch of less skilled or less subtle hands. Melyn had been here, had broken through the protections woven around Sir Frynwy's library. Not just the *Llyfr Draconius*, but all of his books and scrolls had been taken. Was that why Frecknock had stayed with the inquisitor? Because he had her precious, beloved book? Benfro wanted to believe it was that simple, but he had seen her at Tynhelyg, and before that when Melyn had tracked him and Errol down to Corwen's cave. Both times she had warned him to flee, done her best to protect him. He couldn't begin to understand what she was going through, or why. But somehow she had managed to stay alive. Standing alone in the overgrown remains of the place he had once called home, Benfro realized that Frecknock was truly all he had left of that life. Frecknock and his mother's one remaining jewel.

He held up his hand, fingers stiff from clasping the tiny stone, and opened his palm. It caught the sunlight filtering through the leaves, sparkling in his one working eye. The missing one saw a different picture, a shimmering fog of Grym that enveloped his whole arm, creeping up to his shoulder. It was a lovely warm feeling, of being comforted when the night was full of unnamed terrors, of being loved unconditionally, but a part of him could see the danger too. Closing his fist and hardening his aura against the longing, Benfro turned away from the ruined houses and headed out of the village.

As a kitling he had never understood why they lived apart from the rest of the dragons, nor had he ever questioned it. He knew now, of course. The magic that hid the villagers from the sight of men required a focus, and Morgwm the Green had shouldered that task without complaint. Any wanderer straying into this part of the forest would find themselves at the cottage, and so it was that Benfro's tired feet brought him home. The forest had not reclaimed his mother's cottage, nor the clearing in which it sat, but it was messy and untended nevertheless. The vegetable patch he had weeded and dug over so many times before was gone completely to seed, butterflies flitting merrily through a feast of greenery. The house itself looked much the same, albeit smaller than he remembered. A few shingles had fallen from the roof, and the chimney leaked no welcome smoke into the sky.

The clearing was silent save for the twittering of countless birds, the soft rush of the wind in the treetops and the hum of a thousand thousand industrious insects. He wondered idly what would have become of the hives around the back of the house. Their racks filled with honeycomb, would the bees have departed in search of somewhere else to live? How many swarms might have split off now?

He shook his head at the thought. So much had happened, but truly it had not been all that long since he had left here. A year? Two?

And then the wind veered round, as it so often did in the clearing, bringing with it the scent of the cottage itself. Benfro stopped in his tracks, not quite able to believe what his nose told him. He flitted between confusion, fear and then rage, breaking into a run and scarce noticing that he trampled the once-well-tended herb beds underfoot. One leap took him on to the porch where before he had needed to climb each of the three steps in turn. The front door hung crooked, never repaired after the warrior priests had kicked it open and rifled through his mother's belongings. His belongings. He pulled it open so hard it almost came off its hinges completely, then shoved his much greater bulk through a door designed for a dragon half his size.

'How dare you!' His roar was the pent-up frustration of everything that had happened since Inquisitor Melyn had ridden into this clearing at the head of a troop of warrior priests. All the enmity he felt towards men boiled up in him at that point, and Benfro could feel the flame growing ready. His missing eye had already told him there was a man in his mother's front room, and that was an insult too far. What it hadn't told him was who that man was, and as he saw him, recognized him, so the anger melted away.

Father Gideon was asleep in a makeshift bed close by the front window. He looked as old as Gog. Older. And his aura was that of a sick man near to death. Perhaps disturbed by the noise of Benfro's arrival, he stirred, opened gummy eyes and looked around the room in momentary confusion before focusing finally on the dragon. Something like relief passed across his features.

'Sir Benfro,' he said, and his voice was as weak as his aura. 'I have been waiting for you.'

'Your Grace, is this wise? You are not yet fully healed.'

Beulah looked up from the chair in her chambers where she had been nursing Princess Ellyn to see Frecknock fussing over her patient. For several days now the dragon had been using the ancient leather book that Melyn had left in her charge, reciting passages from it that she claimed would focus the Grym and harness it to speeding Clun's recovery.

'Do not try to stop him, dragon. The Duke of Abervenn is his own man.'

Frecknock stood back as if slapped by the queen's words. She bowed in that obsequious manner of hers that made her seem smaller than she truly was. Beulah rose from her chair, handed her child to the waiting maid and crossed the room just in time to catch her husband as his weak legs failed under him.

'I cannot fathom why you persist in tolerating this creature, my love. All she does is mouth words from that insensible book. I don't know why I even tolerate her presence in here.'

Clun smiled, the gaze of his white eyes passing over her face unfocused. Beulah felt the whispering of the Grym flowing around her as he drew strength from the lines, got his legs back underneath him and regained his balance.

'What's so funny?' she asked.

'How we change. How circumstances change us.' Clun took a couple of wobbly steps, then reached out and put a hand on the edge of a nearby table he couldn't possibly have seen. He turned slowly, as if taking in the room for the first time, then once again gazed blindly at Beulah. 'It is true that not so long ago you would have put Frecknock to death. Hacked open her head and taken her jewels to add to the hoard in the cavern beneath the Neuadd. Yet now you do tolerate her presence. And Inquisitor Melyn relies on her despite the most holy charter of our order.'

Beulah scowled, then looked once more at the dragon. She had taken a few steps back, almost disappearing into the shadows in the corner of the room. It was a useful skill, to be able to divert attention from yourself like that, but it was a cowardly thing too.

'You should not speak of such things in front of her, my love.' She slipped an arm under his, felt him lean his weight against her, and then walked him slowly over to the window. Outside, purple-grey clouds scudded over a sky that was more winter than autumn, the air cold and with the fresh smell of promised snow about it. Only a week ago they had been basking in summer sun, hopeful of many long warm days to come. Now it was as if the year had jumped to its end in the blink of an eye.

Clun leaned towards the window, resting his hands on the stone sill as he lifted his head to the light and breathed in deeply.

'Frecknock is not our enemy, my lady.'

'She is a dragon. It is enough.' Beulah stared out the window in the same direction as her husband. The room they were in overlooked the parade ground in front of the palace, and she could see a motley assemblage of dragons lazing around on the hard-packed earth. She had watched them before; they didn't seem to do much except sleep, occasionally fly off presumably in search of food, and every so often fight among themselves. The other dragons, the ones that had sworn fealty to Clun, kept themselves to the top of the hill, in the courtyard surrounding the Neuadd. She hadn't been back there since the incident with Caradoc, but word had reached her of immense damage to the place, and of the hall itself being used as a latrine by the beasts. Yet one more reason not to trust them.

'They understand violence well enough.' She turned to Clun, who shifted his head slightly towards her, the better to hear. Beulah wanted him to stare at her with that wonder and devotion she craved. She wanted to see that handsome face again but knew it would be ever more marred by those milky white eyes. 'But they know you are injured, weakened. How long before one mounts a challenge? And what real chance do we have when they do? With Melyn away and you like this?'

Clun turned then, reached up and gently brushed the side of Beulah's face with his hand. It was soft, and steady as a rock. 'Then I will crush them, my lady.'

He pushed himself away from the window, and for a moment Beulah thought he was going to fall over. It wasn't so much that his legs were weak, she realized, as that his balance was off. It was almost as if he were controlling his body from a point a few paces away, learning how to walk all over again. She suppressed the urge to help him, just watched as he crossed the room, avoiding every possible obstacle in his way. At the door a guard came to attention, saluted. Clun spoke to him for a few moments, words lost to Beulah as the princess began to cry softly in her cot nearby.

'Just a little wind, I think, ma'am.' The maid was at the side of the cot before Beulah had even decided to go and see what the problem was. She lifted up the baby, cradling it expertly against her chest, her shoulder already covered with a fresh white towel. A couple of pats on the back and Princess Ellyn let out a tiny belch, followed by a dribble of semi-digested milk that soured the air with its smell. Moments later a richer aroma made things worse. Beulah looked back to the door, where Clun now stood alone, the guard gone.

'See to her,' she said to the maid before heading away from the source of the odour as quickly as was proper for a queen.

Clun turned at her approach. 'I would like to get some air, I think. We should maybe go down to the parade ground.'

He set off at a far greater speed than Beulah had expected, successfully navigating his way through the palace as she bustled to keep up at a most un-queenlike trot. The further he left behind the sickroom, the more he stood upright and moved like the young man she had first fallen for. When he finally stopped at the bottom of the steps and turned to face her, she was distraught to see his eyes still the same. For a while she had half believed they might have magically healed.

'Why are we here, my love?' Beulah asked. Clun opened

his mouth to answer, but before he could speak a commotion from the far side of the parade ground distracted them all. A group of warrior priests and some of the queen's own guards were wrestling with the great black stallion, Godric. They almost had him under control, but then the horse must have caught a scent on the breeze. With a great snort that could be heard all the way from the palace, he reared up on his hind legs, kicking out until all had backed away. He bucked a couple of times just to make sure no ropes held him down, then burst into a gallop. Godric crossed the parade ground in moments before slowing to a trot, then a walk, tossing his magnificent head this way and that, eyes wide with triumph as finally he came to a halt right in front of Clun, who lifted a hand up for him to sniff, then patted him gently on the nose. The beast lowered his head further, sniffing at the man he considered his master, and Beulah sensed the concern in his simple, proud mind.

'It's all right. I'm fine.' Clun moved around to the horse's side, his hands sweeping over that massive neck and those glossy, black flanks. Not for the first time, Beulah felt a pang of jealousy at just how easily her husband made friends. With this horse she had bought for him, with the dragon Frecknock, even with their daughter.

'He is pleased to see you, my love,' she said, surprised when he looked blindly towards her to see tears in his white eyes.

'And I to see him.' Clun reached up to the great thick mane that tumbled from the stallion's neck, took a great handful and tried to heave himself on to the animal's back. Beulah had seen him do it before, but this time his strength failed him. Godric bent his head round, sniffing his concern, then slowly knelt so that Clun could clamber aboard.

'Is that wise?' Beulah asked. A fall from the stallion's back on to the packed earth of the parade ground could very easily break Clun's neck, and would certainly undo all the forced healing he had been put through since Caradoc's attack.

'Probably not, my lady. But I need to feel the wind on my face again.' Clun climbed on to Godric's back, leaning close to the stallion's neck as he stood.

'But your eyes. How can you see?'

'I see fine. Better now than I could before.' He squeezed Godric's flanks gently, and the horse turned this way and that, dancing like the most highly trained dressage animal. Beulah noticed Sir Gwair watching with astonishment and, looking over at the rest of his fold, she saw that they too were fascinated. Had they never seen a man ride a horse before?

'Frecknock?' She turned to the small dragon, who was still trying hard not to be noticed. 'Stay with him. See he comes to no harm.'

Frecknock bowed her assent, alarm evident in her expression as she walked down the steps and trotted towards Clun and Godric. Beulah had intended asking one of her guards to fetch her own horse, but the men who had brought Godric out now reappeared leading the white filly. She recognized Captain Celtin at their head, couldn't help but notice the fresh bruising around his eye where he had not managed to get out of Godric's way quickly enough.

'Your Majesty.' He thumped a fist to his chest by way of salute. 'His Grace the Duke of Abervenn thought you might like to go for a ride.'

Beulah looked over to where Clun was still sitting astride Godric's back. He was staring back at her with sightless eyes, a grin on his face. 'We've both of us been cooped up inside too long,' he said. 'Fresh air is by far the best healer.'

'Your Grace, it is good to see you again.'

Melyn looked up at the open door to see the face of Father Andro. The senior librarian was frail, closer to his end now than he had ever seemed. The inquisitor could only remember Andro as being old. He had been in his sixth decade, maybe even seventh when Melyn had first arrived at Emmass Fawr. The touch of the Grym some-times extended the life of a man beyond its natural span, but even so Andro was an exception. He must have been approaching a hundred and thirty but it was beginning to show.

'Andro, please. Come in. Have a seat. Perhaps a drink.'

Melyn beckoned from his simple chair in his austere room, a goblet of wine in his other hand. He had lit the fire for perhaps the first time in a generation, the heat tak-ing its time to soak into the old stone walls before it bothered with him. When he had truly believed in the Shepherd, denying himself the pleasures of the flesh had been a way of measuring his devotion. Now he knew the true nature of his god, now that he had become one with him, such austerity struck him as a waste. There were so many things in life to enjoy; denying them was perverse.

And of course the Grym was too wild to tap for warmth, so a flame was ever welcome.

'Are you well, Melyn?' Andro looked from inquistor to fire to goblet as he stepped into the room, approaching with the same caution a cat approaches a sleeping dog.

'Should I not be, old friend?'

'I don't know. So much has changed.' Andro took the only other chair in the room, moving it slightly closer to the fire, which Melyn couldn't help but notice meant also moving it further away from him. Andro didn't sit though, just leaned against its back. 'Did you really kill King Ballah?'

So much had passed since the taking of Tynhelyg that Melyn was thrown by the question, unable to answer for a while.

'He was old and slow.'

The librarian merely nodded his head slightly, as if placing the piece of information into its correct alcove in the great repository of his mind. 'And the Wolf?'

'Him too, although he went by the name of the Old One at the end. Or Gog to those who have studied history.'

'Gog?' Andro's reaction was well played, but Melyn could see the spark of recognition in the old man's eyes. He brushed the librarian's thoughts, skimming them with the lightest of touches. The old man seemed to be thinking of the address in Ruthin's Hall, of the books that Melyn had found in the dragon village and sent to him, most still not yet translated. He was considering how to break to the inquisitor the tragic news of the burning of the almshouses and the death of Tormod. There were a thousand and one things concerning him, but the thoughts circling that name Gog were locked as tight as any forbidden scroll.

'You must know the old tales, of Gog and Magog.' Melyn pushed and probed at Andro's thoughts as he spoke, using the words as levers. 'The brothers of old who fought over the love of Ammorgwm the Fair and cared not what was destroyed in their warring?'

Andro shook ever so slightly, the tremors of age or perhaps the strain of this battle of wills. Melyn had enjoyed sparring with the old librarian in the past, had learned so much from him over a lifetime of service to the order. But he had never managed to see into Andro's thoughts. He had always been too strong, too skilled. And Melyn had never suspected his loyalty, at least not until now.

'Did you know that Errol Ramsbottom escaped yet again?' Melyn asked. As he had hoped, the question threw Andro off balance, random and unexpected as it was.

'Errol?' The boy's youthful face appeared in Andro's thoughts. He was holding a scroll between his hands, the vellum scratched with the stick-like apparently random lines of Draigiaith runes.

'You knew he wasn't the bastard son of a Llanwennog journeyman and a backwoods herbswoman, didn't you.' It wasn't a question. 'You knew he was the true heir to the Obsidian Throne.'

Melyn almost pitied Andro. Time was the old man would have been able to breeze through a test like this, but now he was starting to slow down, and Melyn himself was sharper, stronger than ever.

'I don't—'

But Melyn could already see his mental barriers crumbling. 'Spare me, old man. You knew before he even came here. Princess Lleyn and that Llanwennog dog Balch? You probably knew before the child was even born. Set your Ram friends to keeping an eye on them.'

'Just as well I did. You had Beulah so well trained. What was it, gallweed? That's low, even for you.'

Had he not been touched by Magog, given the power of the Shepherd, Melyn might well have succumbed to Andro's attack. It was swift and brutal. And desperate. The librarian dropped his own shields to strike, and in that moment Melyn saw everything that the old man had been hiding. Not just his preference for Princess Lleyn over Beulah, but a treachery far deeper, going back far longer.

'The Guardians of the Throne?' The inquisitor almost laughed. 'I would have thought better of you, Andro.'

'Which just goes to show how little you truly know, Melyn son of Arall.' Andro did not move a muscle, but the assault on Melyn's mind doubled in strength. For all his age, the librarian's mental control was remarkable. There were freshly consecrated warrior priests who had only half the youthful vigour, and none of the subtlety.

'Oh, I know, Andro. We are both merely pawns in a battle begun millennia before either of us was born.' The inquisitor shrugged off the attack with as much effort as he might use to remove a crumb from his robes. Andro rocked back on his heels as if he had been slapped, hand darting out to the nearby wall to steady himself. He stayed on his feet though, and closed his mind down to Melyn's counter-attack.

'Where did I go wrong with you, Melyn? The young lad I remember was full of wonder at the world, not hatred.'

'Why assume it was ever your failing, old man? Why assume it is a failing at all?' Melyn took a sip from his goblet, the taste sour on his tongue. Nothing like as fine as the dark red wine he had been served in Tynhelyg. Andro watched him all the while, his pale eyes inscrutable. How much had the old librarian kept from him? How many more secrets were there to be ferreted out of that bony skull? All of a sudden Melyn found he no longer cared.

'Your precious Guardians should worship the ground on which I walk. The Shepherd has returned and he is inside me. Together we have slain the Wolf. Once his followers are dealt with I will take my rightful place on the Obsidian Throne. Then all Gwlad will be mine.'

Andro moved with such swiftness, Melyn almost didn't see it coming. He said nothing, simply stepped forward, arm swinging in an arc as he conjured his blade of fire for a killing blow. Had he been a pace closer and not hindered by the chair he had been leaning on, he might even have succeeded. As it was, Melyn felt his flesh burn as the tip of the blade cut a line across his face, instantly blinding one eye. He stumbled backwards, knocking chair and wine over in the process.

'You dare strike me?' Rage flooded through him, swamping the shock that might have paralysed a lesser man. Melyn conjured his own blade, fiery red and ragged. He could feel the Grym rebounding and coiling, pulsing and ebbing to some impossible rhythm, the heartbeat of a world in flux. Riding that chaos, he fed more power into his blade, and more. His hand burned with the heat of it, but his scales were much more resilient than the flesh they had replaced. Pain meant nothing; there was only anger and the old librarian.

'I am not afraid of you, Melyn.' Andro moved with the ease and agility of a much younger man. Melyn wondered how long he had been playing a part. What magic did he know that could hold back the effects of ageing so well?

'You should be.' He advanced on the old man at the same time as he conjured a second blade. It was more difficult to control, with the power surging and falling all around him, but he had Magog's skill and knowledge to guide him. A flicker of a frown ghosted across Andro's face. A less-experienced warrior might have fallen for the bluff, but Melyn had killed far more skilful fighters. Had he not bested King Ballah himself?

Andro took a step back, clearly expecting Melyn to strike at the opening he was offering. Instead the inquisitor crossed his twin blades and then let them extinguish, pushing the Grym out towards the lines that the librarian was struggling to tap for his own weapon. The effect was as dramatic as it was instant. Andro's blade flared bright in the room, the heat washing over everything as all the energy sought somewhere to dissipate. And then it turned in on itself, consuming the old man from the inside. His mental walls shattered, and for a few seconds Melyn was able to dig deep, pulling out secrets like a desperate thief. Faces sprang into view: Father Gideon and Usel the Medic were hardly a surprise, but Seneschal Padraig's collusion was unexpected. There were very few traitors in the Order of the High Frydd, his men were loyal both to him and

Queen Beulah, but the scope of the conspiracy was a revelation.

Melyn became aware of a keening sound and realized that it was Andro's dying scream. Ignoring it, he dug deeper, through layers of memory, searching for anything that was relevant, knowing that he had too little time. Better to have taken the old librarian alive. A few weeks on the rack would have had him spilling all his secrets. But Andro was too wily for that. Melyn could see now that the attack had been quite deliberate. Either he would succeed and Melyn's threat would be neutralized, or he would fail and die swiftly.

'Unless I do this.' The inquisitor reached for the Grym that was burning the old librarian alive and pulled it out of him, sending it hurtling off into the lines. The walls around him glowed with the heat of it, cracks spreading over the stone with a crackling sound. The thick glass in the narrow windows shattered. And Father Andro dropped first to his knees, then slowly toppled to the floor.

28

Of all the great religious orders of the House of Balwen, it is the Order of the Ram that is held in the highest esteem by the common people of the Twin Kingdoms. The clerks of the Candle are responsible for taxation and present the grey, implacable face of the state. The warrior priests of the High Ffrydd bring with them a reputation for ruthlessness that makes grown men quake in their boots. Only the medics of the Ram are welcomed without hesitation, for they bring healing to the sick and teaching to the young.

Unlike their fellow orders, Rams are wanderers. Their headquarters is the great hospital on the western wall of Candlehall, but in the main they serve their ministry travelling and learning. Often spending years on the road away from the central authority of their archimandrite, Rams are an independent lot, open to new ideas and always experimenting with new magics. It is perhaps no coincidence that whenever the bloodline of Balwen weakens and the Guardians of the Throne work their mischief it is the Order of the Ram that has the ear of the king.

Barrod Sheepshead,
The Guardians of the Throne – A Noble Folly

The spiral steps that led down from the Obsidian Throne were uneven, and Dafydd tripped a couple of times as he inched his way cautiously through the total darkness. If it hadn't been for the walls, close enough on either side for him to steady himself, he might have tumbled head over heel. This was not a good place to be injured, buried deep in the heart of Candlehall hill.

When he reached the bottom, it was with a jarring step, his foot hitting the ground before he expected it to. The shock ran up his back and into his neck, making stars in his vision that shifted and twirled. When they didn't fade, he reached out, his fingers brushing warm stone inlaid with strange runes that glowed from the light beyond. At his touch, the wall melted away, and he fell through it into the cavern. Looking back, he saw the stone of the pillar ooze back into shape, hiding the entrance through which he had come. Yet one more mystery to unravel, but not now. There was too much to do, too much at stake.

The cavern hummed with power, the red, unreckoned, jewels clamouring at him for attention. Ignoring them, Dafydd hurried as quickly as his aching knees would let him across to the nearest alcove and its collection of jewels. He almost plunged his bare hands in, eager to free the spirit trapped inside, but at the last moment he remembered Merriel's parting words. He pulled a cotton kerchief out of his pocket, folded it once for extra thickness and used it to cover his hand before reaching inside.

The touch of the jewels, even separated from his skin by the material, was like plunging his head into a clear, cold stream. He had not full appreciated how deafening was the noise of the unreckoned jewels, the pressure of it on his thoughts, until it was gone. Dafydd made a sling from the front of his tunic and swept the jewels into it, carrying them the short distance back to the pillar and the place where he had walked through it. He crouched, tipped the jewels gently onto the ground, then stood and turned to fetch the next set.

Only there was a dragon standing in his way.

'Who are you?'

Dafydd asked the question at the same time as it appeared in his head, booming in a voice so unlike his own thoughts it had to be the great beast standing in front of him. He took a step back, wary of attack, but the dragon just stared at him, unblinking. Then it raised its head, slowly taking in the chamber, the pillar rising to the ceiling, the rows of stone columns with their alcoves. Finally its plate-like eyes settled back on him.

'What manner of place is this?'

'I am Dafydd, Prince of the House of Ballah. This chamber lies beneath the Neuadd. The Hall of Candles I have heard your kind call it. Once it was the palace of a dragon named Palisander?' Dafydd left the question in his voice, unsure what reaction it might get him. The dragon tilted its head slightly to one side, as if considering his words.

'I know Palisander. An upstart of a mage. Too full of himself, and not a care for the harm he causes others with his meddling. This . . .' The dragon sniffed the air, looked around some more. 'This has the whiff of him about it. But how did I come to be here? I cannot remember anything but darkness.'

'I don't know how you got here. This chamber was empty a moment ago, I could have sworn it. Only when I turned my back to place the jewels there . . .' Dafydd let his words fade away. It occurred to him that this dragon, as big as the feral beasts that had taken up residence in the courtyard above them, was nonetheless speaking in easy-to-understand Llanwennog. And now he studied it closely, he could see the shapes of the stone columns through the dragon's body, only partially obscured.

'You're dead.' He said the words quietly, almost to himself. 'Those are your jewels I just moved.'

The dragon frowned, then shimmered almost into invisibility. Dafydd found that he could see it, but only as an aethereal body superimposed upon the mundane world. Then it spread its wings wide, launched itself into the air and disappeared without another word. He couldn't be sure, but he thought he saw the lines pulse with the Grym as it went. They were shifting and twisting so much anyway it was hard to be sure.

The second pile of jewels, trapped in its own tiny stone cell, was smaller than the first. Dafydd scooped them all into one covered hand, then added them to the pile. He half expected to see another dragon appear, but this time there was nothing when he turned back to the shelves. Neither did anything appear for the next twelve piles, and he began to wonder if he hadn't imagined the whole thing. The cavern was uncomfortably warm, and although each set of jewels was not particularly heavy, the repeated walking back and forth soon brought him out in a sweat. He paused a moment to strip off his tunic and mop down his forehead, then carefully eased the next pile out of its confinement. This was a large collection, and each jewel was as big as a hen's egg. For a moment Dafydd considered splitting the load into two journeys, but that seemed somehow disrespectful. He juggled to get the big stones all wrapped up in his tunic, and that was when one rolled on to his bare palm.

He froze in panic, staring at the massive white gem cupped in his outstretched hand. From what Merriel had said, he had expected to be struck down dead maybe, or at the very least rendered insensible. But all he felt was a deep, deep sadness. It was like the day he had been told of his mother's death, and the days and weeks that had followed. Only this anguish was rolled into one perfectly horrible moment. Such bleak hopelessness that his heart almost broke from it. For long moments he could not move at all, but then the muscles in his arm spasmed, the jewel popped out of his hand and tumbled in with the rest of them, nestling in the folds of his damp tunic.

With the touch of the jewel gone, he could move again. Dafydd sprang to his feet, hurried across to the pile, which was growing to a decent size now, and hastily tipped his cargo on to the top of it. This time the pile glowed at the addition, wisps of palest white smoke twisting up from it in tendrils that reached out for him, circled his head and caressed his skin. Then a white shape shot out of the top of the pile, bursting up into the darkness of the cavern before taking on the form of a magnificent dragon, hovering with wings outstretched, their tips reaching almost to the walls on either side.

'By the moon, what foul . . . what horror . . .?' The dragon's voice was in Dafydd's head, in his own language even though he knew that wasn't really what he was hearing. She, and Dafydd could tell it was a female dragon's form that he saw, circled the cavern, swooping past the columns and swiping at the cells with hands and feet as if to try and destroy them. He could do nothing but watch as the creature grew more and more frenzied until finally, with another blast of despair, she settled back down in the space between the pillar and the shelves. Only then did she seem to notice him.

'You freed me from my prison.' It was not a question, and despite his best efforts at keeping her out, Dafydd could feel the force of the dragon's will push through his mental barriers and sift through his mind. It was not painful, but it was a violation nonetheless.

'I should never have been locked away like that. He should never have been able to do it.' The dragon withdrew from Dafydd's mind, fading a little as she looked down at the pile of jewels. He had thought the stack large, but now it seemed inadequate somehow.

'I am sorry,' he said. 'That this was done to you. I am trying to put it right.'

'I too am sorry,' the dragon replied. 'I should not have forced my way into your memories. But it would have taken far too long to learn what I needed to learn otherwise. You are Dafydd, and I thank you for freeing me. I am . . . I was Angharad the Fair. When I died, my body was burned in the Fflam Gwir and my jewels should have been placed with those of my ancestors. And yet he brought me here, to this abomination of a place. He trapped me, alone, unable to commune with my kin or the Grym, and all to feed a mad lust for power.'

'Who did this to you?' Dafydd asked, even though he knew the answer.

'Palisander, who was so great he needed no other naming. That is who.' Angharad raised herself once more, her anger giving her spectral form greater substance. 'Palisander who was my mate.'

Dafydd said nothing for a while. There was nothing he could think of to say. What little he understood of dragon history he had learned in just a few short weeks, and the names confused him. He had never much thought about hoards of dragon jewels until he had first visited this chamber with Iolwen and Usel, and it had seemed perfectly natural that the jewels were organized the way they were. Was not each creature an individual, after all?

'In death we become one, combining our memories and knowledge for the good of all dragonkind. That has ever been our way. This is as close to hell as I can imagine. These poor trapped souls. You must free them, Prince Dafydd. Free them all.'

Dafydd returned to the set of alcoves he had been busy emptying. He had tried not to count as he was going along, but there were at least a hundred stacked with white jewels in this column alone. There were too many columns to count, radiating out from the centre of the vast cavern.

'I will do my best, but there are so many.' He reached for the nearest pile, then remembered his bare hands. He pulled his tunic over his arms again, using it as an awkward pair of gloves.

'You are wary of touching them unprotected,' Angharad said. 'That is wise, but there are better ways than an old shirt to achieve the same result. See.'

Dafydd wasn't quite sure what the dragon meant, but

then his aethereal sight reasserted itself, his aura swirling around him like a second skin.

'Very much like a second skin. Only one over which you have control. Harden it over your hands and arms, protection against the power that lies within the jewels. Then you can touch them without fear.'

He wasn't quite sure what the dragon meant, nor was he entirely convinced he had full control over his abilities, but as he thought it, so his aura darkened over his hands, forming a thick barrier. Hesitantly, he reached into the alcove and touched the first white jewel. He felt nothing but the warmth of it against his fingers, and the rest of them were just as quiet in his mind. Heaping them into both hands, Dafydd carried them across to the pile, carefully adding them to the top before returning once more to the shelves.

'I could think of nowhere else to hide. I am sorry if I startled you.'

Time had caught up with Father Gideon, it seemed. Benfro remembered the man as being old when he had turned up at the cottage years earlier, startling him and his mother both. But now he looked close to death, and not just on account of his obvious injuries.

'What happened to you?' Benfro spoke in Saesneg even though the old man had initially addressed him in poorly accented Draigiaith. The slump in Gideon's shoulders at the change was a sign of relief. He was propped up in his makeshift bed, the blankets pulled up around him, and yet he still shivered despite the warm afternoon.

'For many years I have walked a fine line between

helping people and treason. This time I found myself on the wrong side.'

Benfro said nothing, turning his attention instead to the fireplace. A pile of ash and damp charcoal was covered with a mess of sticks and dead grass, the fallen remains of a bird's nest, if the little chips of broken eggshell were anything to go by. A pile of kindling and dry logs stood to one side, and with a wrench in his hearts he realized that they were the same ones he had himself chopped and stacked the day before Melyn had come. A chore like so many others he had grumbled about but carried out nonetheless. Part of the daily routine that he couldn't have known would be disrupted for ever.

'It has always been the way with our order,' Father Gideon continued as if unaware of the turmoil in Benfro's mind. 'We minister to the sick and needy regardless of their nation or indeed species. We gather knowledge for its own sake, not for some military advantage, and we share it where it will be most useful.'

Benfro picked a few pieces of kindling and placed them carefully on top of the fallen nest. He should probably have fetched the ash bucket and shovel, cleaned the hearth and laid a new fire. His mother would have chided him for his laziness, but in truth he didn't really need a fire at all. It was just something for the old man, a comfort perhaps.

'I learned so much from your mother when I was young. She never cared what manner of creature needed her help; if it was asked for it was given. Perhaps that's why I came here at the last. I knew she was gone, but this place holds such memories.'

Benfro clutched tight the jewel in his hand, feeling the edges of it dig into his palm. It was his constant companion, the feeling that his mother was just in the next room, waiting for him. He wasn't so overwhelmed by it as he had been when first she had died, nor when Errol had rescued the jewel from Corwen's cave before Melyn could find it and add it to the others he had stolen. But it was still an influence on him, possibly the reason he had walked all the way back here in the first place. Now that he was in his old home, he could feel the jewel for what it was. He knew that his mother was not in the other room, knew that she would never be coming back. And strangely the presence of the old man helped him to understand and accept that. He still wasn't ready to relinquish her. Not quite yet. Not completely. Instead, he opened his hand, picked up the jewel between finger and thumb and then placed it carefully in the middle of the table. Then he bent low to the fireplace, breathing a tiny jet of pure white flame on to the kindling. It caught instantly, crackling merrily as he fed a few of the smaller logs on top.

'You are badly injured.' He turned back to the old man, his missing eye seeing past blankets, clothing and flesh to the damage done. Father Gideon had been beaten severely; several of his ribs were cracked and at least one ankle had been broken. Beyond that, arthritis had taken hold of his joints. The man must have been in constant torment, and yet he seemed to bear it stoically. For a moment Benfro wondered how he had managed to get here, to climb the steps and enter the cottage, but then he noticed the sticks leaning against the wall behind him, just within reach. The crude crutches would have helped him get around, but they would have done nothing for Father Gideon's pain.

'It's as well I have a few friends left in Gwlad, or I might not be alive at all,' he said. 'I was travelling with Queen Beulah's army, carrying out my duties as a Ram and helping the sick and injured. Only some of Melyn's more zealous warrior priests took exception to my helping the Llanwennog wounded. They accused me of being a spy, a collaborator, all manner of things.' Father Gideon managed a weary, pained smile. 'If only they knew the truth of it. I escaped with my life, but only just.'

Benfro imagined the scene all too easily, and the effort it must have taken the old man to travel this far so badly injured. 'Have you eaten anything recently?' he asked, although he knew the answer, could see it in the lines on the old man's face and in the hope that sprang into his eyes at the mention of food. 'Wait there. I will see what I can find.'

It was good to have a task, and not a simple one at that. Otherwise Benfro would have had to think; better just to act. Someone needed his help, and that was an easy enough thing to give. He went back out to the overgrown garden, digging around until he found some vegetables and herbs not too far gone to seed. It took a while to gather together enough ingredients and find his mother's old cauldron amid the mess the warrior priests had left of the cottage, but soon enough he had a pot of soup bubbling away.

Father Gideon watched at first, but soon drifted off into a disturbed sleep as the front room grew warmer and filled with the scent of cooking. Benfro let him rest, squeezing his way into the back of the cottage and the storeroom where his mother had kept all her medicines and herbs. There had been a time not long ago when he could have found anything he needed in here blindfolded, but now he was so much larger, the little wooden drawers and stone jars on shelves seemed too small, too close together. It didn't help that Melyn's men had gone through everything. They hadn't stolen much, hadn't broken much either, but they had jumbled it all up. He had to hold things up to the light to read the labels, recognizing his own neat script on the brown-spotted paper. Each new discovery brought with it a memory of the time when he had prepared it, or presented it to his mother, having successfully foraged in the forest for it.

Eventually he found what he needed and took everything back through to the front room. The soup was simple but filling, and he ate a hearty portion before finding a small bowl for Gideon. He crumbled some of the medicine he knew would help with the old man's pain into the broth before taking it to him, waking him as gently as he could manage. When Benfro had first met him they had not been all that different in size. Now Gideon's head would have fitted in his hand.

'How is it that you have grown so large, Sir Benfro?' The old man set about his bowl of soup with the desperation of someone who had not eaten properly in many weeks. The heat of it brought some colour to his pale cheeks, and the herbs eased his pain, but Benfro could see that it was too little, too late. Nevertheless, he fetched another bowl for him, settled down on the floor as best he could and told Father Gideon the tale. It took a long time, but the old man stayed awake throughout the telling.

'I had thought Magog made me a gift of these wings,

and the size that comes with them. But in truth all he did was lift the curse his brother had placed upon our kind.' He struggled to his feet, went back to the fire and put more wood on it. Outside the afternoon was turning to evening now, heavy storm clouds rolling in from the mountains.

'It is a remarkable tale.' Father Gideon coughed, his lungs sounding watery, then eased himself back into the cushions he had made into his bed and drew the enormous blankets around himself again. 'And it confirms something I had suspected but thought never to see in my lifetime.'

'It does?' Benfro asked. For a moment the old man didn't answer, just breathing in short gasps as if he had run a mile and more. Benfro didn't need his missing eye to tell that Gideon was suffering. He could hear the man's heart beating too fast, sense the tension as he struggled to keep conscious. Had the herbs been too potent? Benfro had only intended to take away his pain, not anything else.

'I . . . I do not think I have much longer to live.' Gideon coughed again, dribbling something on to a blanket. It seemed to clear his airways at least a little. 'I don't fear death. In some ways it will be a blessed relief. But there is something I need to tell you before I go.'

Gideon fell silent again, exhausted by speaking. Benfro waited patiently for him to begin again; there was no point in trying to hurry the old man. He looked across the table to where he had placed his mother's last jewel, saw it twinkling in the light from the fire, reached out for it then stopped himself at the last moment.

'You are aware of the three religious orders of the

House of Balwen, I take it?' Father Gideon's question surprised him, and Benfro realized that the jewel had been calling to him, dragging him back to it.

'The warrior priests of the High Ffrydd you have met. My own order, the Ram, are healers and teachers, and then there is the Order of the Candle. These are dry, boring people but important nonetheless. They keep things organized, running smoothly. At least most of the time.' Gideon coughed again, took a while to catch his breath before continuing.

'These orders can trace their origins back to the earliest times of men, when Balwen was not a king so much as the strongest of a number of tribal leaders. A warlord if you will. But what most have long forgotten is that Balwen's three religious orders were not the first. Men had no magic in those days; that was something only dragons knew. And they – you – were powerful indeed in the subtle arts. Some were too powerful, perhaps, as you now know.

'Balwen was favoured by the Shepherd, who taught him the secrets of the Grym. Most of my people think that the Shepherd took the form of a man, but we both know better than that, I think. It is likely he was actually one of the two brothers, Gog or Magog, and that's how men came to have magic, by and large. They were not the only dragons who sought to mould men though. There were others, not as powerful as those two brothers perhaps, but wiser. They knew what might come of such meddling, and they formed another, secret order, containing men and dragons both. They – we, for I am one of the few surviving members – had a simple task, and one reflected in the name we gave ourselves, the Guardians of the Throne. For thousands of years we have kept a watch on Candlehall and the Neuadd. The Obsidian Throne that sits within it was once the seat of one of the greatest dragons ever to live. Not Gog or Magog, but one who came long before even them.'

'Palisander.' Benfro spoke the name he had heard first in the tales of Sir Frynwy. As he did so, Father Gideon looked up in surprise, then fell to coughing again. It took him a long time to stop, and Benfro couldn't help but notice the pink stain to the edge of the blanket where he wiped his mouth.

'Great Palisander, the wisest of all. He built the throne at the point where the strongest rivers of the Grym intersect. It is the very centre of Gwlad. From it, one of sufficient skill can control every living thing. It truly is Gwlad's greatest treasure, and our order was charged with protecting it until the time when he would return.'

Gideon fell silent again, taking in wheezy breaths and swallowing hard to suppress another bout of coughing. Benfro said nothing; his missing eye could see the old man's failing aura, the wetness seeping into his lungs and the strength leaching out of him. There was nothing he could do to save him.

'But my life of service to the Guardians of the Throne has been based on a lie.' For all his weakness, Gideon's voice was now strong with venom. 'We have protected the throne when we should have destroyed it. We were wrong. What lies beneath it is not the work of a benevolent soul.'

'Beneath it? What lies beneath it?'

Gideon seemed not to hear the question. He pulled

himself as upright as he could, holding the blood- and spittle-soaked blanket tight around his chest. 'Palisander's greatest work has been corrupted, and now the whole of Gwlad is in danger. Something is coming, Benfro. I have seen it. Your mother saw it too. It is not dragon, nor man. Not Shepherd nor Wolf. I do not know what it is, but it must not be allowed to take the throne.'

'I don't understand. What lies beneath the—?' Benfro's words were cut off as Father Gideon forced himself to his feet. He staggered across the room, as much falling on to Benfro as reaching out to him. His face had turned blue, his eyes wide and staring as he grasped one finger of Benfro's enormous hand.

'Promise me you will destroy it. Destroy the Obsidian Throne.'

Benfro reached out to catch the old man as his legs went out from underneath him. Gideon's grip on his finger loosened and he slid forward, then crumpled into the dragon's hand. Slowly, delicately, Benfro lowered him to the floor. Using the blanket as a cushion, he gently arranged Father Gideon so that he was lying in what he imagined was a comfortable position. It seemed the right thing to do, even as his missing eye told him that the old man was dead.

How long he worked at the task, Dafydd could not have said. But eventually one column was cleared. Then another, and another. He should have been hungry, he knew. He should have stopped to drink, except that there was no water down here. Deep in his thoughts Dafydd knew that he was being pushed by the jewels, and none of the dead dragons cared whether he lived or died as long as the task was done. As the pile grew ever larger, so the wisps of white smoke swirled, twisting around the pillar, caressing the stone. Occasionally he would see a dragon's form appear, only to dissolve again. Sometimes two would embrace, merge into one and then disappear. And all the while he could feel joy, relief at the end of torments that had lasted many thousands of years. It kept him going, that and the power of the Grym coursing through his body, but he knew that he was putting himself at great risk. And then finally he reached for an alcove and saw nothing but red jewels in front of him.

'Hold, Prince Dafydd.' Something stayed his arm, though whether it was the spirit of the long-dead dragon or just his utter exhaustion, he could not say. He sank first to his knees, then slid sideways until he was lying flat on the warm hard floor. His breath came in ragged gasps and his throat cracked with dryness as he tried to swallow.

'Am I done?' he asked, the words barely audible. For a moment there was no reply, and then the voice filled his head once more.

'All but one, and I sense she is incomplete.' Dafydd looked along the aisle, the carved alcoves glowing red with the jewels of the unreckoned dead. And there, at the end closest to the cavern entrance, was a faint white glow. Had he seen it before, when he and Iolwen had first come down here? He didn't remember, but his task was not yet complete.

It wasn't until he reached into the alcove and touched the jewels that he noticed his aura had faded almost to nothing. With that first touch, the memories overwhelmed him. He saw a small house in a clearing in the woods.

More houses, a village but not of men. These buildings were oddly sized, and the creatures that lived in them were the kind of dragons he knew from his youth and visits to the circus. Small beasts, their wings just vestigial flaps of skin, not something that could ever hope to lift them into the air. They were impossibly old too.

Then the images changed and he saw a young dragon, just a kitling really. He watched it grow, still small but beginning to reach the size of its elders. And then one final memory burned itself into Dafydd's mind. A white-haired man with mad eyes, conjuring a blade of fire and bringing it sweeping down in an arc that would sever his head.

'Melyn!'

Dafydd tumbled back, knocking the wind from his lungs as he fell to the floor. He had recognized the inquisitor even though he had never before set eyes on the man. Now he recognized too the dragon who appeared, ghost-like, in front of him, even though he had never even heard of her before.

'Morgwm the Green.'

She nodded slowly, eyes closed for a moment. Then she opened them and looked straight at him. 'And you are Prince Dafydd, heir to King Ballah's throne.'

Dafydd pushed himself upright, his back against the stone shelf opposite. Clutched in his hand was one white jewel, and his aura was thinner than sweat against his skin, no protection from the contact at all.

'How . . . how do you know this?'

'I can see your thoughts, feel your exhaustion.' Morgwm looked up the aisle between the two shelves to the pillar and the pile of glowing white jewels tumbled around it. 'This is a noble thing that you have done, but I fear if you do not leave this place soon you will die.'

Dafydd could not argue with that. He needed to rest, he needed to eat and drink something. But the compulsion that had swept over him once he had started moving the jewels was still there.

'Ah, we can be cruel and selfish at times.' Morgwm shook her head, leaned close to Dáfydd and touched an insubstantial finger to his forehead. She was smaller than the other dragons, more in keeping with those in her memories. From this version of Gwlad, not the one where they ruled supreme. 'I am not long dead, and so I have not been kept in this prison for long either. The others are confused, frightened, angry. They are coming to terms with what has been done to them and have no thought for anything else. I cannot believe otherwise that they would have put you through the ordeal you have endured. But it is over now. Add my jewels to the pile, and then you can leave. Then you *must* leave.'

'But how? Where will I go? I cannot climb the stairs to the palace. It is too far, and it's the house of my enemy. I will be caught and killed. Or worse, caught and not killed.' Dafydd struggled once more to his feet, staggered across to the alcove and collected up the remaining jewels. As he carried them up the aisle towards the central pillar, he could feel there was something missing. A jewel. He looked back, but could see none that he had dropped.

'You have the sight. It is true, I am incomplete. My remaining jewel is safe enough. My son has it.'

'Your son?' As Dafydd asked the question, the image

427

of the young kitling swam into his vision. Only it wasn't the young kitling any more, but a giant of a dragon with wings covered in the finest of scales that glinted in the sunlight and formed patterns that looked like the full moon. 'Benfro?'

'You know him?' Morgwm asked.

'No. But I see him in your memories. Only he is different. Bigger.'

'Then hold that image in your mind, for it is not my memory but something else. It will guide you to him, and he will help you if he can. He is no friend to your enemies.'

Dafydd knelt down before the pile of jewels like a penitent at prayer. It towered over his head, heaped up against the black stone pillar with its blazing white runes driving away the dull red glow of the rest of the jewels still trapped in the chamber. Had he done all that? Had he moved all those jewels, handful by handful? He could scarcely remember any of it. All he wanted to do was curl up and sleep.

'No. You must leave.' The voice was so loud, he let go of the jewels, then watched helplessly as they fell into the pile. They all looked so similar there was no way he could have picked the right ones out again. Why did he even think he had to try?

'You do not have much time, Prince Dafydd. Stay here any longer and you will wither and die.' The words were Morgwm's, but when he looked up, he saw the great dragon Angharad towering over him.

'I cannot leave. The stairs . . .'

'Take the Heolydd Anweledig. It is ancient and

powerful. It will lead you to safety.' The dragon threw out one hand in the direction of the cavern wall, and as she did so Dafydd felt the weight lift from his shoulders. A surge of borrowed energy filled him, sweeping away his exhaustion, his thirst and a dull, throbbing headache. He stood up, head light, staggered a little as he tried to find his balance, then turned in the direction Angharad had pointed. The last of the hidden tunnels that Iolwen had revealed now stood open, even though no one with the blood of King Balwen in their veins was anywhere near.

'The Heolydd are older far than your King Balwen. Older even than mankind. Go now, prince of men. I can only hold this portal open for a short while. But know that the dragon hoard of Y Neuadd y Ganhwyllau is in your debt.'

Dafydd felt the compulsion behind the words even more strongly than the command to gather the jewels. He stumbled away from the pillar, past empty alcoves, through the red glow of the unreckoned jewels and on towards the open tunnel mouth. Yet even as he broke into a weary run, he fought the impulse. He had travelled this way before and it had almost killed him. How could he trust this road any more than the one that had taken him to Pallestre?

In the end, he had no choice. Such was the strength of the combined dragon jewels in the hoard and his own weakness, he could do nothing but stumble over the ground, churned by many feet, and fall headlong into the tunnel. Darkness enveloped him. Wind rushed past his face and ruffled his hair as if he were falling headlong through space, and with a shout of alarm he hurtled out into a world of white.

29

A mage might travel to a distant place using the Llinellau, or he might cast his aethereal sight along them in order to see and hear without himself being detected. Both skills are essential for any who would study the Grym and the subtle arts, but both also have their shortcomings. In the aethereal it is all too easy to become lost, distracted by the enormity of the whole of Gwlad. Many a master has spent days, sometimes months, gently coaxing his apprentice back from the Llinellau.

Walking the lines is in some ways safer, but a far more difficult art to master. And going physically to a place also makes it harder to observe it without yourself being seen.

Dreamwalking is a compromise between these two. In the dreamwalk the mage leaves his physical self behind but takes with him enough of it that the distractions of the Grym fade away. And in the dreamwalk he remains invisible to all who do not have the aethereal sight, although he can manipulate objects as if he were truly there. A skilled mage can slip from the dreamwalk to the physical with but a thought, returning to his sleeping body or waking it in the place he has been observing.

A student of the subtle arts might ask why not use the dreamwalk at all times? The answer is simple. Where one in a hundred dragons might show enough aptitude to train as a mage, and one in a hundred of their number succeed, fewer than one in a thousand mages will ever master the skill of dreamwalking.

> From the working journals of Gog, Son of the
> Winter Moon

A dark red sun painted the underside of the clouds as Benfro finished filling in the hole. He wasn't sure what rituals men performed over their dead, but he knew they buried them in the ground. It seemed fitting; it wasn't as if Father Gideon had any jewels in his brain that needed the Fflam Gwir to reckon. Better to place him in the earth, let his body become one with the Grym once more. The old man had been kindly enough, and Benfro remembered well his mother's words so long ago. If there was any man that she would have trusted with the secret of his hatching, then it was Gideon. He deserved at least some respect in death.

All the while he had been digging the hole, and as he had wrapped the body in the purloined blanket and laid it in the earth, Benfro had been mulling over Father Gideon's words. He knew of Candlehall, the Neuadd and the Obsidian Throne of course, but he had never seen them. At least not in the mundane world. To travel to such a place would have been suicide; it was the centre of Melyn's power and Queen Beulah's palace. But he had been there in his dreamwalk, and he had fought the inquisitor there too. He didn't remember much of that experience though; it had been too sudden, too traumatic, and so much had happened since.

Something is coming. That was what Father Gideon had said. Well, Benfro wasn't stupid. He could see the connections, knew all too well what that something was. He had watched it cut Gog's head off, fight and kill Enedoc the Black. It wasn't entirely dragon or entirely man. Inquisitor Melyn and Magog somehow merging into one terrifying monster.

At the thought, Benfro instinctively checked the rose cord and the knot in his aura that choked Magog's malign influence. Both were still in place, but the cord itself was pale. He had not felt its pull for days now, and when he slept he had not dreamed of anything, let alone dreamwalked back to Cenobus and the repository. Was Magog too occupied elsewhere to bother with him? Had he abandoned his attempts to take over Benfro's body in favour of his strange merger with Melyn? Relief and horror tinged that idea in equal measure, and besides, Benfro knew he could never be truly free until the rose cord was gone. Until Magog's jewels were reckoned.

The fire was almost out when he returned to the cottage, the darkness heavy with memories. He put a few more logs on, caught himself thinking he would have to go easy on them or he would need to chop more for tomorrow. But he wasn't going to stay here. Not for more than one night.

The remains of the soup took only a few minutes to reheat. Benfro would have liked some meat with his meal, but he wasn't going to complain. It was good to eat something cooked for a change, and as he sat at the table where he had grown up, he stared at his mother's single jewel lying in the middle. It would be so easy to pick it up and feel her reassuring presence. Just for a moment, to help him with the sadness. But he was so tired. Too weary to reach out, too weary even to stop his head from drooping to the scrubbed wooden surface.

Benfro knew he was dreamwalking the instant he found himself flying over the dark forest. He tensed, expecting to arrive any minute at Cenobus, there to renew his task of sorting the pile of dragon jewels for Magog, but he was not flying over the great forest of the Ffrydd. Nor was he powerless to control his own actions. His wings flexed and he drifted downwards. Sweeping them together brought him back up again. A flick of his tail and he was turning, spinning, diving. He let out a whoop of joy at the sheer pleasure of flight. It had been so long since last he had been able to do it without pain.

And that was when it hit him: there was no pain. None of the ache from the wing twisted in his fall from Mount Arnahi; none of the agony from Melyn's blade where it had neatly severed his hand; no aches from the fall through the trees when he had fled to Gog's world. There was no hint of the damage that Fflint had done. Even the wound in his side was gone. And both eyes saw the vista ahead of him.

A fat moon hung low in the sky, reflecting off the tops of the trees as he sped along. The wind ruffled the tufts of his ears, whistled over his scales and the tips of his wings as he locked them straight and glided. He had no idea where he was going, but he was in control. No Magog riding his thoughts this time. A warm sensation ran through his hand, reminding him curiously of Malkin the squirrel's excitement at flying. Bringing it in front of him, he saw that it was clenched tight in a fist, and when he opened it, there was Morgwm's jewel. He could not hear her voice, but he knew she thrilled at his mastery over the air. Snatching his hand closed lest he drop his precious cargo, Benfro flew on.

The hill rose out of the flat plains far in the distance, the river surrounding it like a ribbon of silver. It might have been a purely natural feature were it not for the angular, spiky mass at its top, piercing the night like a broken fang. Benfro's hearts stilled as he flew with impossible speed towards Candlehall and the Neuadd atop it. He could turn, fly away; nothing was compelling him to go there save his curiosity and the inevitability of it all. Father Gideon had begged him to destroy the throne, and here he was in a dream.

The city appeared deserted as he circled above it, but then it had appeared so the first time he had been here too. It was changed though, damaged as if some vast beast had lobbed great chunks of stone at the walls, smashed in roofs and toppled towers. Even the Neuadd was broken, its doors hanging off their hinges, its windows smashed. Benfro circled it once, twice, looking for any sign of a trap, then finally came in to land. He tensed as he touched the cold flagstones immediately in front of the great hall. Then the ground beneath him turned to water and he sank into it.

For a moment Benfro panicked. He splayed his wings, meaning to soar into the air and fly away, but the cold earth swallowed him up like it had Father Gideon. And then he was falling slowly through a cavern underground. From high up he could see stone columns radiating out from a central pillar. They glowed white near the centre, but soon dulled to an angry crimson he knew too well. As he fell, more like drifting down through water than tumbling through the air, so he began to hear wails and moans, the shrieking of a thousand thousand tormented souls. And so he began to understand something of what the old man had meant when he had talked of the horror beneath the Neuadd. Magog's repository had been an abomination, but at least the dragon jewels he had collected had been reckoned. These were red and raw, and all linked to that huge throne up above. It was a nightmare beyond imagining, but there was worse to come.

As his feet touched the hard dirt floor of the cavern, the clamouring of voices grew in intensity. Benfro began to see shadowy figures, red wisps flitting about between the rows of carved shelves. Like Magog's store and the smaller repository beneath King Ballah's throne room in Tynhelyg, the jewels here were separated from each other by lifeless stone. Quite mad, the dragons whose memories these should have been raged against a torture they could not possibly understand. There was no hope for them, no hope in them. These were the slain of two thousand years. The spoils of the House of Balwen and the true power behind the Obsidian Throne. Jewels pillaged from their slaughtered bodies, bones, flesh and scale left to rot down to pale earth, there was no way to reckon them. And should he even try, then what greater cruelty could there be but to lock them in this state for ever?

'There is hope, Benfro.'

The voice was almost lost in the turmoil. Had he not known it from his earliest memories he would surely have ignored it, just one more whisper hidden in the screams. Benfro searched for the source of it and saw to his surprise that the central pillar was piled around with jewels, white and reckoned. He had been so overwhelmed by the horror he had not noticed them before. Now as he approached, white smoke spiralled from the pile, twisting until it formed into a shape he recognized.

'Mother?' He reached a tentative hand towards her, then withdrew it. Then reached out again, only to pull back at the last minute. He knew too well the danger, but longed more than anything else to be reunited with her.

'You have changed, little one. You have grown so big. Much bigger than your father. And your wings.' The smokey dragon remained motionless, Morgwm's voice inside his head.

'How is it that you can speak to me? You didn't before.'

'My jewels are here, in this hoard. Melyn placed me in the stone cells, but I was freed not long ago. We all were, only I cannot join the others fully as I am incomplete.'

Benfro held up his hand, uncurled his fingers. 'I have the last jewel. I can reunite them and you can be whole then.' He held the jewel over the pile, ready to let it go. But something stayed his hand. This was his last memory of his mother; could he really let it go?

'Someone is coming.' Morgwm's ghostly image still did not move, but her voice took on a sudden urgency. 'You must flee before you are seen. You are too vulnerable like this. I can sense your presence, so others still alive will have sensed it too. It cannot be long before they come looking for you.'

As if her words were a cue, Benfro felt the presence of others nearby, questing thoughts like the brush of Magog's mind on his own. An invisible hand seemed to push him away from the pile of reckoned jewels, his mother sending him away as she had done back at the cottage when he had witnessed her death. Reflexively he clenched his fist once more. Behind him the rows of jewels burned an angry red, and he remembered his mother's earlier words.

'You said there was hope, for the unreckoned.'

'There is. For these poor souls, for all of us. If they can be reckoned, then they can be saved. It will take time for them to overcome this nightmare. Some have been trapped here many thousands of years. It can be done, and you can do it, Benfro. But not if you are caught here, and not if you are overcome by Magog's dead spirit.'

'But how can they be reckoned? Their bodies are long gone.'

'There is a way, or so I have read. The *Llyfr Draconius* speaks of it briefly. It is ancient magic, the most subtle of our arts. But you must go, Benfro. Flee before you are found. If you are caught then there truly is no hope.'

Benfro opened his mouth to ask more questions, but a roar from above silenced him. He looked up to see an enormous dragon descend through the cavern ceiling. For a moment he thought it was solid, but then he noticed the outline of the jagged rocks behind it showing through. An aethereal projection, it scanned the room, tasting the air like a snake before drifting slowly over to the central pillar. It reached out, traced hands as big as Benfro's head over the smooth black surface, reading the runes beneath as it sank slowly to the ground. He was hidden from view, shadowed by the stone columns with their carved alcoves, but that was his mundane self thinking. He had no idea what the aethereal dragon could see, and no idea how to escape this place.

'I smell you, young dragon. You are not of our fold. Nor of those mindless brutes who have come to join us. None of them have much time for the subtle arts, but you? You reek of them. Where are you?'

The aethereal creature's voice was unmistakably male. He glided silently around the pillar, momentarily out of sight, and Benfro reached out towards the pile. He wanted to stay here, to be with her, more than anything, but he had to go. Somehow he had to flee.

'Go, Benfro. Seek out Ystrad Fflur and the elder dragons. They will tell you what you need to know. I will wait for you.' The voice was little more than a whisper, an echo in his head, but the shove that accompanied it was like being hit by a gale. Benfro staggered against the nearest column and his hand flew open. He could feel himself waking back in the cottage so many miles away, but as the scene dissolved to blackness he clearly saw the tiny white jewel arcing through the air towards the hoard.

It wasn't the longest of rides, but Beulah enjoyed the privacy all the same. Just her and Clun, who while frail seemed well enough able to sit atop his enormous horse. They ordered the guards to keep their distance and rode through the hunting park to the west of the city, pausing only when one or other of the great lumbering dragons flew overhead. The creatures annoyed her. Beulah had been raised to despise them. One of her first edicts as queen had been to reinstate the Aurddraig, the bounty paid for the head of any dragon. And yet now they were everywhere, arrogant, destructive and smelly.

'It is turning cold, my lady. There's a storm coming.' Clun drew his cloak around him as he stared off into the distance.

Beulah glanced up at the clouds, dark and threatening overhead. 'We should get back to the palace then.' She turned her horse towards the path that led to the city gates, or at least what was left of them.

'Stone walls will not protect us from this storm.' Clun shook his head and squeezed the flanks of his great stallion with his legs. Godric flicked his ears, snorted once, then turned to follow, picking up his huge feet and clattering them down against the hard earth with unnecessary force. Clearly he was unimpressed with their slow pace.

'Patience, my friend.' Clun leaned down across the horse's neck and patted it firmly. When he sat back up again, he was smiling.

The ride back to the palace took them through the army encampment, still occupied and busy despite their victory. The city barracks had been badly damaged by the dragons, and no one seemed keen to stay within the walls for long except those few who were billeted high up the hill at the palace. Beulah could hardly blame them; the devastation was depressing, and the smell of the rotting dead would take a long time to clear even if the bodies themselves had been removed, buried or burned. Perhaps the storm would bring rain to wash the dried blood from the streets.

'Gwlad is in pain. You can see it in the lines. Something momentous has happened and I can't help but think Inquisitor Melyn is behind much of it.' Clun steered his horse on to the parade ground, and coming up behind him Beulah was relieved to see that the dragons had all flown away. The heaps of bones and pieces of rotting flesh strewn about the place didn't help her mood, and neither did the fat flakes of snow that now began to drift down out of the leaden sky.

'And where is he, our good inquisitor? I've heard nothing from him since he took off for Emmass Fawr in such haste. Has he contacted you?'

'No, my lady. I have heard nothing, seen nothing despite my strong connection with the aethereal.' Clun guided his horse to the steps that led up to the palace, positioning him perfectly so that he could slide off. If he hadn't leaned heavily against Godric's flanks once his feet were firmly on the ground, Beulah might have been fooled into thinking there was nothing wrong with him.

'I do not think he is at Emmass Fawr any more,' Clun said after a while. 'I have tried to sense him there, but the halls are almost completely empty of warrior priests, novitiates and quaisters. Only the servants remain.'

'Where have they gone?'

'I do not know, my lady. I could not follow them. The aethereal is . . . disturbed.' Clun let his head droop as if ashamed that his show of skill was somehow inadequate.

'But you were at Emmass Fawr, in the aethereal?'

Beulah dismounted from her own horse, handing the reins to a groom who approached as soon as she touched the ground. The guards who had ridden out with them were still mounted, and she dismissed them with a wave of her hand. There were more guards in the palace, and it wasn't as if she couldn't defend herself. No groom came forward to take Godric back to the stables, although some strong-looking men stood nervously nearby.

'What are you waiting for? His Grace the Duke of Abervenn's horse needs seeing to,' Beulah snapped.

'Not this time.' Clun addressed the grooms, whose shoulders slumped in relief as he slowly reached up and eased off the rope halter that was all the harness Godric had ever worn. The enormous horse lowered his head to allow the rope to be removed, remained stock still even once that was gone.

'You have served me well, Godric. Now it's time you looked after yourself. The coming battle will not be won by strength alone.' He placed one hand on the horse's head, scratching him behind his massive black ear, then leaned in close, pressing his forehead against Godric's cheek. They stood there, motionless, for some moments, and all Beulah could feel was a growing sense of jealousy. Clun had been hers and hers alone, but now he seemed to have more of a bond with his horse, more of a bond with their daughter. Thinking of her reminded Beulah that the infant would need feeding, and she started up the steps towards the entrance. Clun's words stopped her in her tracks.

'Farewell, my friend. May we meet again some day.' He took a step back, gave the horse one last pat on the withers. Godric snorted, took a couple of slow steps across the parade ground. He broke into a trot, then a canter and finally a full gallop as he sped away towards the gates. The guards that Beulah had dismissed scattered in panic as the great black horse ran right through them and was gone.

'You sent him away? Why?'

Clun looked up the steps at Beulah, his white eyes locked on her face for once. 'The time for riding into battle has passed. It would not be fair or right to cage him in a stable.'

'What do you mean, passed?'

'Do you not sense it, my lady? Can you not see it?'

Beulah glanced around the parade ground, searching for clues. Aside from the destruction the dragons had wrought on the buildings and the remains of their most recent meals, she could see little that had changed. But then that wasn't what Clun meant. There was something else that was wrong about Candlehall, even more so than the snow that was beginning to fall heavily now. It took her a while, like realizing a sound she had always heard had suddenly been muted.

'The throne.' Beulah reached a shaking hand up to her neck, suddenly weak and exposed. 'I can't feel it.'

Benfro woke with a start, jerking his head up from the wooden table where it had lain. Dazed, it was a while before he managed to gather his thoughts and calm his racing hearts. Outside it was still dark, and judging by the state of the fire he had been asleep, dreamwalking, for only an hour or so. He sat for a long while, the events of the night going round and round in his head. He could still hear his mother's voice, but it was overlaid with the darker, deeper tones of the aethereal dragon who had come looking for him.

Even in the darkness he could tell his mother's jewel was gone. Benfro felt the weight of it in his fist, but when he unfurled his reluctant fingers, his hand was empty. Part of him mourned his loss as intensely as he had the day she had died, but another part remembered the dream, the pile of jewels now heaped together rather than caged. And there had been his mother's parting words about the unreckoned jewels and the *Llyfr Draconius*. He hardly dared hope, but if there was a way to reckon a jewel without the dead dragon's body, then maybe he could free himself of Magog's influence even though Gog was no longer alive.

Benfro groaned as he stood up, his body stiff from having slept while slumped at the table. He had neither the *Llyfr Draconius* nor Magog's jewel. He didn't even have his mother's company any more. What he would have given for her calm advice, for the wise counsel of any of the old villagers for that matter. But they were all trapped in Magog's repository half a world away. Except for one. Seek out Ystrad Fflur, that was what she had told him. So that was what he would do.

There was a dreadful sense of finality about the way he went from tiny room to tiny room, collecting those few things he thought might be useful. Benfro knew he would never come back here again; the cottage held too many memories. It also held useful medicines though, and only a fool would have set off without at least some of the more difficult-to-replace unguents and potions. He found a large leather bag in the back of his mother's room. There was nothing in it save for a fine white scarf not unlike the one Meirionydd had given him on his fourteenth hatchday. As he was taking it out, something heavy fell to the floor, wrapped in the cloth for safekeeping. Benfro stooped, feeling about on the rough floorboards until his hand fell upon a thick silver bangle. He had never seen his mother wear any kind of adornment, and in the darkness he could make out little about the piece except that it was smooth and surprisingly warm to the touch. It would have fitted easily around his wrist before Inquisitor Melyn had come to the cottage, but now it was all he could manage to slide it on to one finger. He lifted it up to his face to look closer, and his missing eye showed him a twisting spiral of ancient magics woven into it. When he tried to pull it off again, it wouldn't budge, but far from feeling alarmed by this, Benfro was reassured. It felt right that he should wear it.

Dawn was still some hours off when Benfro left his mother's cottage for the last time. The bag over his shoulder was weighty with all the useful things he had found. He had wound the scarf around his neck, and the ring on his finger gave him strength as he looked around the overgrown clearing, eerily coloured by the light of the setting moon. He didn't really need to get his bearings; he knew well enough where he was going. But still it was hard to start walking. Hard to leave knowing he would never be coming back.

The forest chittered and squawked, nocturnal creatures hurrying about their business as he started his silent march through the trees. As a kitling, this journey had taken many hours, most of a day, but now his legs were so much longer, each stride covering three times the distance. He made such good progress that by the time the sun was lighting the clouds he had reached the steps where the river passed over low waterfalls. Benfro paused a while at the pools, eating some breakfast and drinking from the chill, fresh water. He stepped easily out on to the flat rock where Frecknock had performed her calling, such was his great size now. There was nothing particularly special about it apart from the privacy it afforded. The Llinellau that criss-crossed the area were strong, flickering and buzzing in strange patterns that made his head hurt, pulses spearing through them in what he knew was the direction of Gog's palace. The pale rose cord that linked him to Magog's jewel still hung in the air at his head, but it was quiet now, the turbulence in the Grym acting in his favour.

Benfro reached the cave about the middle of the day. He could have gone straight inside, but he'd expected the walk to take longer and wasn't really ready. Instead, he climbed the escarpment above the cave mouth and sat out in the sun for a while. He had some food and there was water from the river nearby. His missing eye and the forest noises both told him there was no danger. It was the most at peace he had been for as long as he could remember.

It would have been easy to have stayed where he was. The woods were far from any people, too thick to be worth exploring. He could have built himself somewhere to live, hunted during the day and slept soundly at night, knowing that he would not be disturbed. It would have been perfect, had it not been for the insistent throb of the wound in his side. And if he stayed anywhere for long enough Melyn would come looking, or Magog, or both.

Reluctantly he hauled himself to his feet and trudged back down into the forest.

The cave was cool when Benfro finally summoned the courage to step inside. He remembered well the last, and only, time he had come here. Back then his mother had been surprised he had found it, but in truth it had called to him. The whispering voices hovered just out of earshot as he felt his way deeper into the darkness. For a moment he worried he might not fit inside any more, but the walls seemed no closer than they had before, when he had been much smaller. Benfro smiled in the darkness, recognizing the touch of ancient magics about the place. That was why it had been chosen, after all, countless generations of dragons ago.

The chamber where the jewels lay was as still as a perfect morning. The jewels themselves were untouched, piled high in pleasant companionship. It was such a stark contrast to the horror of Magog's repository and the chambers beneath both Tynhelyg and Candlehall that Benfro spent a long time just standing there, staring at them. It took him a while to notice that the voices were becoming clearer, longer still to register their curiosity and agitation. Only when a wispy figure formed above the pile did he realize he had been almost asleep, daydreaming.

'By the moon, if it's not young Benfro! But you have grown so large! And what magnificent wings!'

The lump in Benfro's throat stopped him from replying straight away. He had not forgotten Ystrad Fflur, but time and events had blurred his memory of how the old dragon had looked. Even in death he was small, his wings no more than loose flaps of skin, his joints swollen. But he held himself more upright than Benfro remembered, a gleam in his once-milky eyes.

'And what has happened to your face? Your eye. My dear fellow, you've been through the wars.'

'I am fine, Ystrad Fflur. Do not worry about me.' Benfro saw through the image of the old dragon, but where at first there had been just the rock wall of the cave, now other dragons began to appear, faces peering over shoulders, jostling for a better look.

'Well, I can't say it isn't a delight to see you. But what brings you here? I thought Morgwm had sealed the cave so none would come looking.'

'Morgwm is dead. Sir Frynwy, Meirionydd, Ynys Môn and all the others are dead too. Killed by Inquisitor Melyn and his warrior priests.'

'Dead?' Ystrad Fflur's cry was echoed a hundred times and more by the ghostly dragons crowding behind him. 'But how? Why? When? Where are their jewels?'

Benfro slumped his shoulders. The questions were bad enough, but behind them was a terrible sense of shock, of loss and bewilderment that echoed his own state of mind, amplified it.

'They are safe, their jewels reckoned. But they are trapped. I need to rescue them, but before I can do that I must destroy the one who has trapped them. Only then can I bring them all back here, where they are supposed to be.'

The murmuring grew louder, pressing in on Benfro.

'I have a question, Ystrad Fflur. It concerns the *Llyfr Draconius* and the reckoning of jewels.'

'Dear me, Benfro. I'm not sure I am the one to ask about such things. Your mother knew more about the

Fflam Gwir than anyone, and Sir Frynwy was the keeper of the book. Why on earth would you need to know about any of that?'

'I must find a way to reckon Magog's jewels, even though his body has long since gone to dust.'

'Magog?' Ystrad Fflur put so much doubt into that one word, Benfro knew then he would not find the answers he sought here, despite whatever his mother might have hoped. The rest of the voices fell silent, though Benfro could still feel the pressure of their thoughts. A wave of curiosity swept over him, the desperate thirst for experience that Benfro knew would drag him in, keep him here until he wasted away.

'Farewell, old friend,' he said and, hardening his mind to them, he took a step back, then another. It was like moving through a fast-flowing river, his legs heavy and his hearts heavier still. The wound in his side stung at the strain, but oddly that gave him the focus he needed. With a final effort, he turned and without another word strode towards the mouth of the cave.

The scent hit him before he emerged. There were men outside, waiting for him. Terror gripped him for an instant. How had they found him? Could they see the hidden entrance? Would they steal these jewels as they had so many others before? Then the fear turned to anger. How dare they desecrate this place? How dare they steal the essence of beings much wiser than them? And finally his brain caught up with his emotions, the smell sparking memories that filled him not with terror or rage, but with hope. His strides turned into a jog, then a run, and he burst out of the cave into the clearing beyond.

Four people stood there, three of them looking lost and confused as they stared up into the trees. Only one was facing his way, and she smiled as he appeared.

'There he is. Told you he wouldn't be far away,' Martha said, and the other three turned as one. Benfro knew the boy with the broken arm, Xando, but had never seen the young girl before. The third was thin and pale, his hair shorn from his head, but nothing could stop the grin from spreading across his face as Errol recognized his friend.

'Where . . .? Where did you come from?' It was a stupid thing to ask, but Benfro could think of nothing else to say. Martha cocked her head in that annoying manner of hers.

'The place you were looking for. We knew you couldn't risk walking the lines to us. So we came to you.'

30

Fire and Grym
Jewel and Bone
Will ever set
The Summer Moon.

The Prophecies of Mad Goronwy

If only the sun had been shining, it would have been perfect. Benfro sat by the side of the river at the top of the familiar series of escarpments that dropped down towards the Graith Fawr, past the remains of the village where he had grown up and then on to the land of men. He had caught fish in the deep pools higher up, and even now they were cooking on a fire nearby, tended by the boy Xando and the girl whose name he had discovered was Nellore. Martha sat beside him, gazing out across the stream. Her long hair whipped around in the wind; it was cleaner now than it had been in the days they had spent trapped in Gog's palace. She had found new clothes too, and Xando's arm was set in a fresh sling. They had fared much better than him after being discovered.

'What happened to you?' Benfro asked. 'They said you were going to be given over to Mister Clingle. It sounded like an unpleasant punishment.'

Martha picked up a small pebble from the ground by

her feet, turning it over in her hand a few times before flicking it into the water. 'And so it would have been, had it been just young Xando delivered to him. He's a coward and a bully, Mister Clingle. Rules over all the people who live and work in Nantgrafanglach, a position given to him by the Old One himself and one he keeps simply by condemning any who cross him to the Anghofied.'

'Anghofied?'

'A tiny word for a very nasty place. Errol lost at least a month in there, possibly more. Came out stinking so bad they had to shave off his hair. It was beyond washing. Glad we never went there. Not that women ever get sent. Reckon Mister Clingle just gives them to the men to play with.'

Benfro wasn't quite sure what Martha meant, but her tone was clear. 'So how did you escape him then?' he asked.

'Well that was easy. They stuck us in a locked room down by the kitchens. Lines everywhere. It was easy enough to walk along them.'

'Easy? It's the most advanced of our subtle arts. There are dragons who never master the skill.' Benfro remembered Ynys Môn and his love of hunting. The old dragon had not even been able to use the lines to bring things to him without considerable concentration.

Martha merely shrugged. 'Always seemed obvious to me. It's a bit more tricky taking someone with you if they don't know what you're doing, but we managed. Couldn't go all that far though, cos the lines are all jumbled up at the moment. We hid out in the palace for a while; that's a lot easier to do when you ain't got a great lump of a dragon with you.'

'How'd you find Errol? Where was he?'

'Thought he was dead for a while.' Martha stared off into the distance. 'We're close, him and me. I've always been able to sense him. But when he was in the Anghofied it was like he dint exist. Then all of a sudden he was there, bright as day. Course, it took me a while to work out how to get to him. The Grym's all tangled up anyways, but where he was? There's some old, old spells all a-twisting apart there. Would've been easier finding him in the caverns. If I'd known that was where he was all along.'

'The caverns beneath the palace? I've been there.' Benfro remembered his wandering in the dark, how he had followed that scent so faint he couldn't even be sure it existed. And how he had found his mother's jewel in the riverbed. Had Errol escaped the same way? 'How long has it been since we were found?'

'Four weeks, give or take.' Martha picked up another stone, peering at it more closely than the last. Benfro cast his mind back over the days since he had escaped from the dungeons, found his mother's jewel, walked through the forest to the village. Was it that long? He had been in something of a daze, but even so he couldn't remember sleeping more than a dozen nights.

'Time moves differently in the Anghofied. It's a place of old magic, older even than the Grym. That's probably why Gog built his palace there.' Martha put the stone down again, picked up another one. 'It's all a-changing now, anyways. The broken world's mending, but it's going to take a while.'

'The broken world.' Benfro echoed the words. It made sense to call it that, he supposed. 'Is that why there's a storm in the mountains? Why the Grym is all over the place?'

Martha held out the hand with the stone in it, palm up and fingers splayed. Benfro felt a whispering in the Llinellau as she reached out in front of him with her other hand, plucking the stone from nowhere. His missing eye showed him how it was done while his good eye saw only a stone disappear from one place and reappear somewhere else in an instant. It was fascinating to see how effortlessly she manipulated the Grym.

'How did you learn to do that?' he asked.

'Old Sir Radnor taught me most of what I know. And I learned a lot from Gog too. Mostly it just seemed obvious.' Martha shrugged as if the most advanced of the subtle arts should be no more difficult than learning to swim. 'Course it's not so easy now. Nearly lost my way bringing us all here, and I can't go back that way even if I wanted to.'

'You can't? How so?'

'The tower's the centre of it. Where he died.' Martha didn't need to say who. 'Further we get from the centre, the calmer things are. You walked here though, dint you? Came from the river where Errol escaped?'

Benfro nodded, didn't say anything. He was afraid he knew where the conversation was going.

'So you could walk back there then. You know the way.' Martha stated it as obvious, not asked it as a question. Benfro thought of the confusion the journey had thrown in his way, how he had thought he knew where he was going only to find himself back where he had started. But he remembered too the ruined buildings of Ystumtuen and the hunting grounds he and Ynys Môn had roamed in summers past. Once there, he was fairly confident he could find the route back to the river and the waterfall.

'I reckon I could, if I had to. Why?'

'Because we need to go back. To Nantgrafanglach, to Myfanwy's house inside the walls.'

Benfro looked round to see Errol standing on the other side of him. He looked strange with no hair, just the lightest of frizz over his scalp where it was beginning to grow back, matching the tufts starting to sprout on his chin and upper lip. He wore an odd assortment of clothes, as if he had hastily raided a number of different closets. Like Benfro, he had a leather satchel slung over one shoulder.

'But the forest by the palace is thick with warrior priests. Melyn can't be far behind. Surely we should be getting as far away as possible. And I still need to find the place of the standing stone. Though if Gog is dead, then how I can hope to do that is anyone's guess.'

'We need to return there because that's where I left Magog's jewel.' Errol sat down on the riverbank, tugging the leather satchel round until he could reach the clasps. Benfro's hearts sank at his words. He had hoped, assumed even, that the jewel was in the satchel. But then Errol had managed to lose his mother's jewel, so it was hardly a surprise Magog's had gone missing too. The light seemed to fade, and looking up Benfro saw that the clouds had thickened, darkening the sky and threatening rain. Even as he thought it, his missing eye showed him how the turmoil in the Grym and the aethereal was spreading fast.

'What good is the jewel,' Benfro asked, 'if I can't find the place where Magog's bones still lie?'

'You do not need to. Gog took us there already.' Errol opened the satchel and pulled out something flat and white, like a stone that has been tumbled for aeons by a river. He passed it to Benfro, and as the dragon took it in his hands, he felt a jolt of energy, saw again the great skull hidden deep at the bottom of the pool. To his fingers it felt like rock, hard and cold, but his missing eye showed him the rest of the skull, the crashing blow to the head and the massive bird, the Roc sent by Balwen to vanquish his foe, as it rolled the carcass into the water. And at that moment the rose cord lit up in the daylight, crimson with rage. A scream echoed out across the river, so loud and fierce that birds took to the air in a clattering of panicked wings. A surge of pain blossomed in Benfro's head so intense he couldn't breathe, couldn't move. Except for his hands, which spasmed, tipping the fragment of skull away towards the river as he felt the full force of Magog's fury hammer against him.

And then it stopped. With surprising swiftness, Errol sprang forward and caught the piece of skull. Benfro could only watch in astonishment as he slipped it back into his satchel, carefully closing the buckles to make it secure. Then Benfro looked up to where the rose cord speared towards his forehead. Martha stood on tiptoes, leaning close, her hand clenched into a tight fist around the line. It pulsed an angry red but could no longer reach him.

'You should probably pay a bit more 'tention to that now,' she said, a smile on her face and in her voice.

Benfro didn't need telling twice. He pushed out his aura, twisting it into a tight knot around the cord. The thrum of Magog's rage still echoed in his head, but it was something he could cope with. At least for now. 'He will be looking for us. He'll send Melyn and the warrior priests. Others if he can influence them.'

'Then the sooner we get back to Nantgrafanglach and the jewel the better.' Errol scrambled to his feet again, turned back to the fire, where Xando and Nellore were picking at the fish as they sizzled on the embers. 'But first we must eat.'

'It is exactly as you said, Your Grace. The fortress lies the other side of the Faaerem chasm from Emmass Fawr, about ten miles west, where the mountains begin to drop down into the Ffrydd.'

Melyn sat in his apartments high up in the monastery. Outside the wind roared, flinging snow against the thick glass panes of the window. The storm had eased a little, but he could see that it was just a temporary lull.

'What about a way in? Are there gates? How well protected are they?'

Captain Osgal warmed his hands at the fire. He was still dressed in his travelling robes, fresh in from scouting the location of Gog's palace. It wasn't often warrior priests needed a fire, but the fluctuations in the Grym made tapping it for warmth perilous. Two of the novitiates who had been keeping the courtyards clear of snow had self-immolated before Melyn had forbidden the use of magic unless specifically authorized by himself.

'It is vast, sire. Surrounded by a wall so high we could not see the top of it in the storm. As yet we have found only one gate, which opens out on to a road pointing due west. It's wide enough to ride twenty men or more through side by side, but it's barred with heavy oak and iron. I do not think it will be easy to breach. There are other smaller tracks through the woods, from the river to the south and down through the mountains from the north, but they all simply end at the wall.'

'There will be gates at each, hidden by magic.' Melyn leaned back in his chair and let his senses ease out across the distance. He could feel the great palace close by, but it was too difficult to focus, impossible to pin anything down, even for him. The lines were nobody's friend now.

'How can it be? This fortress? On a clear day you could see it from your window, sire. I have led training expeditions through those very woods a hundred times and more, and never has there been any hint of such a place.'

'Did I not tell you that the Shepherd was returned, Captain? Did I not say that the Wolf had returned also? Nantgrafanglach has been here all the time, but it has been hidden by the most powerful of stolen magics. Only now, with the Wolf himself dead, is it showing itself.'

'And this storm? This . . . confusion of the Grym? Is that the Wolf too?'

Melyn considered the captain. Osgal had always been a good soldier, disciplined and with just enough innate magical ability to conjure a good blade of fire, but he lacked the subtlety to become more of an adept than that. In a way, such limited imagination was his protection when wielding the Grym. He was not drawn into it as easily as some. It was surprising to see him putting the pieces of this puzzle together, and perhaps a warning of just how precarious the situation was that he should even dare to bring up the subject.

'It has something to do with him, yes. When—' But Melyn was unable to finish. From nowhere he was seized with an impossible rage. His whole body tensed so hard he sprang up, sending his seat flying into the fire, scattering logs over the hearth and floor. Osgal leaped away in alarm, only the captain's swift reactions saving him as the inquisitor lashed out with twin blades of fire. For some moments Melyn was a spectator in his own mind, his body feeling that it might explode. And then the understanding seeped into him as Magog's thoughts merged with his own. He saw water running through a landscape of boulders and escarpments. Ancient trees towered on the riverbank, full of life. And in his hands, dragon's hands, he held a shard of pure white bone, knew the smash of stone through his skull that had robbed him of life; felt the water filling his lungs as it dragged him down to the dark bed of a deep pool; sensed the crushing weight of passing years, centuries, millennia. He saw through the darkness a face and the body of a scrawny young Benfro, his tiny wings splayed out behind him as he reached closer, closer, and then touched.

Melyn slammed back into himself as if he were bursting through the surface of that pool. Somehow he had fallen to his knees, and now he sank on to all fours, drew in the deep, gasping breaths of a man who has almost drowned. His blades were extinguished, but all around him he could see the damage they had caused. A commotion outside, and several warrior priests burst in, gathering up the burning logs tumbled from the fireplace and stamping out the small fires that were even now threatening to set the room alight. With a wave of his hand, Melyn extinguished the flames. With another he pushed the men back out through the door. His mind was reeling at the information, the realization. But it was Magog's mind, not his own. Or was there any difference any more?

'Sire, are you ill?'

Of all the things Captain Osgal might have asked, this was perhaps the most stupid. And yet, instead of angering him, it made Melyn laugh. He rolled over, still sitting on the floor, hearts racing as he recovered from the shock. Hearts? Only one heart, surely?

'I am a great many things, Captain, but ill is not one of them.' He looked up at the white-faced Osgal, who was standing off to one side and trying hard not to shake. 'I had a vision, you might say. A warning of something that cannot be ignored. The Wolf may be dead, but his followers are not, and they have such evil plans. We must track them down. Destroy them.'

'I . . . I do not understand, sire? Track them down how? Are they not in the fortress across the chasm?'

Melyn paused a moment, squinting at Osgal through eyes that saw the world somehow differently. He went to rub them and noticed that the scales on his fingertips had grown down to cover his entire hands now, his nails turning black and narrowing to sharp points.

'Some of them are, but some are gathering in the south. Take two dozen men. Go as fast as you can to Ystumtuen.'

'Ystumtuen? But it is nothing but ruins.'

'And it is on the direct route from Benfro's village to here. He will pass through there soon, along with Errol and others they have corrupted. Find them, stop them. Kill them.'

Melyn pushed a compulsion behind his words to fire up the captain's enthusiasm for the job, but he needn't have bothered. As soon as he heard the name of the dragon, Osgal's face hardened along with his resolve. He pulled himself up straight, smashed his fist against his chest in salute.

'It will be done, sire,' he said, turned and left. Out in the corridor, the inquisitor heard his shouted commands as Osgal strode swiftly away, a man with a mission and vengeance in his heart.

Melyn looked around the room. His blades had ruined much of the sparse furniture. He went through to his tiny bedchamber and searched through his travel pack until he found a mirror. It was a gift from Beulah, and not something he often had need to use. Now he held it up, surveying his face. The damage caused by Father Andro's blade had healed swiftly, but like all his recent injuries the wound had turned to golden scales, puckering across his cheek. Only his eye had not responded to the Grym and the Shepherd's healing powers. He had covered it with a black leather patch after the attack, and when he lifted it, the eyeball stared back at him white and shrivelled. The socket in which it sat was lined with the finest of scales, already growing over the skin of his eyelids and tugging back the edge of his nose. Soon they would cover the eye socket completely and the ruined eyeball would fall out. It was no matter; he could see fine without it.

'And what am I become?' he asked the darkness falling outside. There came no answer, but in the distance he heard a low, rumbling laugh.

31

Death comes to us all. Savage, swift and unexpected
or drawn-out at the end of a long life well lived.
After but a few short years or at the end of millennia.
We come from the Grym, and to the Grym we
must return. When all else is unpredictable, death is
the only certainty.

But what is death? For the damselfly that lives but
a day or the greatest of dragon mages whose years
pass number, it is the same. An end, but also a
beginning. For the Grym is life and we are all
creatures of the Grym. Death is but a door that leads
from one room to the next. We may step through
naked and ignorant, like the basest of beasts, or we
may take with us all the knowledge and experience
of a long and studious life. In the end it is all the
same, for the Grym cares nothing of learning and
marks all as equal when the time of reckoning comes.

From the journals of Magog, Son of the
Summer Moon

For the first couple of days Benfro couldn't have been
happier. They walked the forests of his childhood, heading ever north and east towards Ystumtuen, and even
though the weather was cold for the season, the clouds

thick and grey overhead, it didn't dampen his mood. Finding Errol was worth so much more than the hope that the young man might lead him to Magog's jewel, or learning that he had a piece of the long-dead mage's cracked skull. The real joy was knowing that Errol was alive and well. Seeing Martha and Xando again, even though their parting had been for a shorter time, also lifted his spirits after the sadness of finding the village once more, of burying Father Gideon and finally relinquishing his mother's jewel. That last was bittersweet, for though he had lost her, she was at least whole and among other dragons. He would have been content just to walk the woods with his companions for ever, never reach Nantgrafanglach at all, but with each passing league he found it ever harder to ignore the wound in his side.

It had always been there, the niggling sense that it wasn't properly healed, that there might be a tiny splinter of wood still in his flesh and burrowing its way towards one of his hearts. Benfro had hoped that it was healing. Cerys had removed the worst of it, after all. But his treatment at the hands of Sir Nanteos and the journey of escape afterwards had taken their toll. He hadn't concentrated on keeping the wound clean, sealing it up tight with his aura, and now the pain jabbed at him with every step.

'You are not well, Benfro,' Martha said as they made camp one evening. Their fire was in exactly the spot were he and Ynys Môn had built theirs not so many years before, the first time he had seen the ruined hunting lodge that lay just a few hours' walk away.

'I will heal. In time.' He stared into the flames, remembering the tale his old friend had told him that night. The story of Gog and Magog and how they had fought over the love of Ammorgwm the Fair. Ynys Môn would have thought it just another tale, and one that Sir Frynwy told much better with his bardic training. But Benfro knew the truth of it now. All dragons' tales were rooted in reality, in things that had really happened.

'Not if you don't let it.' Martha shifted herself closer, turning her head in that odd way of hers. Benfro could sense that she was looking at him in the aethereal as much as the mundane.

'It looks inflamed,' she said. 'There's infection under your scales, see?'

Benfro settled himself, trying to ignore the bickering conversation going on between Nellore and Xando across the fire. He let his missing eye take over, felt himself shift out of his own body and circle it for a better look. From this perspective what Martha said was clear. His wound was not badly infected, but if he did nothing about it that could very swiftly change. He could almost hear his mother's words chiding him for being so foolish.

'I will need to collect some fresh herbs. There is a poultice I can make that will suck out the badness and soothe the pain. I have most of what I need here, but some of the ingredients do not keep well.' He pulled the leather bag he had taken from his mother's cottage over his head, wincing slightly as he stretched the wound and sent a sharp jab of pain through his side. He tried not to let it show, covering up his discomfort by putting the bag down by the fire and going slowly through its contents. Martha watched in silence for a while. Beside her, never far away these days, Errol slept soundly. He seemed to spend a lot of time sleeping.

'That ring. It is full of magic.' Martha interrupted Benfro as he was laying out the ingredients. He stopped, held up his hand and looked at the silver band. He had all but forgotten it, but as he studied it more closely he realized that part of its power was to be overlooked. That might explain why no one had commented on it until now.

'I found it in my mother's cottage, hidden away in this bag. It seemed right to take it.'

Martha peered closer, and Benfro held his hand out for her to get a better look.

'May I touch it?' she asked.

'If you think it's safe. I can't get it off, see.' Benfro grasped the ring between two fingers and twisted it, fully expecting it to remain stuck like it had been back at the cottage. Instead it slid off easily. 'Oh.' He put it in his palm and then held it out for Martha. She peered closer, moved her hands over it as if caressing it only with her aura. A quick peek with his missing eye told Benfro that was exactly what she was doing. Finally she plucked it from his hand, running her fingers around the inside edge. For her it would have been too large even to wear as a bangle. It would have fitted comfortably around her neck.

'There are words inscribed here. Ancient Draigi-aith runes. I can't really see them by the firelight, but perhaps . . .' Martha raised the hand that wasn't holding the ring and conjured a pure white ball of fire. She set it to hover in the air just above her hands as she studied the ring closer still.

'It's a naming ring,' she said after a few minutes. 'It traces your family tree back to . . .' She paused a moment before handing the ring up to Benfro. 'Well, back.'

'Back to whom?' Benfro asked the question even though deep down he already knew the answer.

'Magog's blood runs through your veins, Benfro. That is why he chose you.'

'Chose me? Chose me for what?'

Martha opened her mouth to answer, but something distracted her. Benfro saw it at the same time, and his nose brought him the scent too. Swift as a striking snake, he slid backwards on to his feet, casting his aethereal sight around the trees beyond their camp. His hearts leaped in shock as he made out the shapes, hidden from his senses by twisted magic. Twenty, maybe more, they slid into sight like nightmares, and the greatest nightmare of them all was the man at their head.

Captain Osgal had healed from the Fflam Gwir Benfro had breathed upon him, and now he was more powerful than ever. He stepped into the light from their fire and conjured a blade of light that sputtered and flared with the fluctuating Grym all around them. His voice was all the more horrifying for its calmness, the terror he cast about him overwhelming.

'Kill them,' he hissed. 'Kill them all.'

A shout woke him from a deep dreamless sleep, shocking him into chaos and confusion. Too close to the fire, Errol had to scramble back as Benfro leaped through the flames, snatching up the largest burning log and roaring at something in the darkness. Flaming branches and red-hot coals spilled out, setting fire to the dry grass of their campsite. Risking a glance sideways, he thought he saw Martha standing tall, the angriest expression on her face

465

he had ever seen. Then she disappeared, and two warrior priests filled the space where she had been.

Rage as much as shock spurred him to action. He rose out of his bedroll, searching for the nearest weapon. Errol had never conjured a blade of fire, had no great desire to learn, but in that moment it seemed the simplest of things to let the Grym surge through him and into the two warrior priests. They had barely turned to face him when they were pillars of flame, consumed by the surging turmoil in the lines. He sensed something behind him, ducked as he turned, narrowly missing the arc of a blade as it singed the air above his head. The warrior priest who had swung was young, not much older than Clun, and Errol remembered him from the monastery at Emmass Fawr. There was no recognition in his eyes though, only hatred and a certain measure of madness. This was what the order did to the children it stole from their families.

'You don't have to fight me,' he said, dodging a second swipe of the blade. 'I'm not your enemy. Melyn is the one you should fear.'

For a moment Errol thought he might have got through to the lad. Tanner, that was his name. There was the slightest flicker of doubt across his face, a moment's hesitation. It might well have been that which did for him, although Errol could see how twisted and unpredictable the lines were, how unstable the Grym. It exploded through the young man, burning him up from the inside so swiftly he didn't even have time to scream. He dropped to his knees, then toppled sideways into the fire, the short sword he had been carrying in his other hand falling to the ground. Errol scooped it up even though he had only the vaguest idea of how to use it. He turned just as another warrior priest appeared in front of him, lunging with a knife. His thoughts still sluggish from sleep, Errol barely moved, but the warrior priest's strike seemed to go off course, the point of his blade slashing at the air just to Errol's side.

'Move, Errol!' The shout had him turning, and he saw a brief flash of what might have been Martha, flitting through the darkness. More warrior priests were emerging from the trees now, conjuring blades of fire that sputtered and flared as if they were the work of novitiates, not highly trained soldiers.

A sharp pain lanced through his side. Errol let out a shriek, shying instinctively away. The warrior priest with the knife had finally found his mark, ripping through the fabric of Errol's tunic and cutting the skin over his ribs. The shock gave him focus, forcing the last of the befuddlement from his mind. He leaped to one side, bringing his sword up to parry the next blow even as he noted that Nellore and Xando were surrounded by yet more warrior priests.

'No!' His shout was more panic than intention. Errol had never fought before, never had to defend himself from such overwhelming odds. He lashed out with his sword, catching a lucky edge on his opponent's blade and whipping it from the warrior priest's hand. A step forward brought him in close to the man, and he could see the surprise in his eyes. Errol knew then that he would have to kill him. That was the way fights went. He also knew that he couldn't, not with a blade of steel any more than a blade of fire. He couldn't take this man's essence and add it to the Grym. It sickened him that he had killed two already without truly knowing how he had done it.

'No.' The word was less of a shout this time, and he pushed the warrior priest away as he said it. A moment of confusion, then the man conjured a short blade of fire and advanced again. Errol was forced backwards, tripping over the charred leg of young Tanner, poking out of the fire. He landed heavily and dropped his stolen sword.

'The inquisitor will reward me well for your head, traitor.' The warrior priest raised his blade of fire high. Errol could do nothing but hold up one arm to try and ward off a blow that would strike right through him. Then something barrelled into the warrior priest, knocking him sideways off his feet. The man kept control of his blade, twisting as he fell and grabbing hold of his attacker. Nellore struggled, beating at him with her fists, but she was small and light where he was tall and strong. The warrior priest held her in a firm grip as he whipped his blade of fire swiftly round.

An empty fist swung past her head, the blade disappearing the moment before it would have parted Nellore's head from her shoulders. Errol stared in surprise at his hand clenched loosely around a ball of purest white energy. Nellore wriggled free of the man's grasp, rolling away from him at the same time as Errol began to feel the heat searing his skin. He flicked his hand towards the warrior priest, not really sure of what he intended to happen. The ball of fire leapt from his palm like lightning and struck the man squarely in the chest. He let out a grunt of surprise and dropped down dead. Steam spiralled up from his face and clothes.

'How?' Errol and Nellore spoke at the same time, but before either of them could be answered, a terrible scream echoed through the clearing. Pale blue fire lit up the night, and Errol felt a pull on the Grym as something drew deep on its energy from all around. He rushed to Nellore, helping her up before both of them sprinted for the trees. There were bodies everywhere, all dressed in the robes of warrior priests. Some were clearly dead, their skin blackened, clothes smoking as they had lost control of their conjured weapons. More were unconscious, as if someone had reached into their heads and turned off their thoughts. Only one still stood, and Errol knew him all too well.

'Osgal.'

The captain was dancing this way and that, his blade of fire still steady. The trees gave him the advantage as he fought Benfro. So big was the dragon now he could not easily manoeuvre among the trunks. Judging by the way he moved and the blood slicking his scales he was in trouble.

'Osgal!' Errol shouted the name this time, catching the captain's attention just as he swung around a thin tree, pivoting and sweeping his blade past Benfro's wing as he went. The dragon howled with pain, let rip with another gout of blue flame. It billowed towards the captain but petered out before it could reach him.

'Well, if it isn't young Errol Ramsbottom.' Captain Osgal grinned like a lunatic, then turned his back on Errol and swung his blade once more at Benfro. Trapped by the trees, it was all the dragon could do to avoid being skewered by the fiery blade. Errol tried to focus on the Grym, to reach out like he had before, but Osgal was too contained, his mental barriers too well honed.

'We have to help him.' Nellore went to the nearest unconscious warrior priest and wrested his sword from him. A thick metal blade as long as her leg, she could barely lift the thing, but still she dragged it towards the captain, intent on getting herself killed. Errol ran to her side, grabbed her by the shoulder and took the blade from her.

'You can't hope to fight him.'

'And what about you?'

Errol shook his head and hefted the sword. Osgal and Benfro had moved deeper into the forest now, and he could see that the captain's plan had always been to force the dragon into the trees. Any further and he wouldn't be able to move at all. If he ran out of fire, he'd be completely at the captain's mercy. And Errol knew the captain had none.

'Face me, Osgal.' Errol shouted the words, knowing they were hopeless.

The captain barely slowed in his attack, turning only briefly to address him. 'Patience, Ramsbottom. I'll get to you when I'm done with your friend.'

Errol tried to recapture the feeling when he had taken the blade of fire from the warrior priest. Holding one hand in front of him, he imagined the power of the Grym concentrating there, trapped in a protective envelope of his aura. It was hard to hold on to, the lines were erratic and the Grym itself slippery, but a tiny ball of pure white energy began to form, began to grow.

'I said face me!' He shouted as loud as he could this time, putting all his rage and frustration into the words. As Osgal turned, Errol flung the ball of energy at the captain. It spun lazily through the trees, almost hypnotic, and for a moment Errol thought it would explode in the captain's face, engulf him in flame and consume him utterly. Instead Osgal merely flicked his free hand, and the ball of

Grym veered away from him, smashing into a tree trunk and dissipating to nothing almost instantly.

'Is that the best you can do?' His voice was a sneer that went right back to their first meeting outside the village hall at Pwllpeiran on the day Errol's mother had married Clun's father. Osgal had been there then, pinning him to the ground as Melyn poured thick red wine down his throat the better to force his way into Errol's mind and rewrite his memories.

'It's enough,' Errol said and dropped the sword. Osgal looked momentarily confused, then remembered what he had been doing. He turned back to face Benfro just as the dragon drew himself up to his full height. There was nothing to protect the captain as the pale blue Fflam Gwir engulfed him. He screamed once, the noise cut short as the fire surged in through his open mouth and down into his lungs. His blade of fire sputtered and died, its power surging back into the Grym along with his life force as he slowly sank to his knees and then toppled forward. By the time his head hit the ground it was no more than ash, billowing away into the night.

A kind of silence fell on the woods. Errol could hear only the crackling of flames and the hammering of his heart in his chest. It had all happened so quickly, waking him so swiftly he hadn't been able to think. Now as he caught his breath he began to see the destruction all around. Still mounds by the fire were the dead or unconscious forms of warrior priests. So many of them, he wondered if they hadn't perhaps strayed into Melyn's army. Except that would have meant the inquisitor himself, not Captain Osgal in charge.

Nellore was on her knees by the fire, and at first he

thought she was retching, sick from the carnage. Then Errol noticed the figure lying beside her. He hurried over, all else forgotten as he stooped to see the prone form of the boy, Xando. His face was white, eyes closed as if he were sleeping, but his dark woollen cloak hung around him damply, and when Errol touched it his fingers came away red. He already knew that the boy was dead, run through by a cowardly sword.

'Why'd they do that? He weren't hurting nobody?' Nellore looked up at him with red-rimmed eyes, tears running down her cheeks. Something moved in the darkness behind her, and he sprang to his feet, ready to fight once more, this time to kill. With a whispering of the Grym, Martha stepped out of nowhere, dishevelled, her face dirty, eyes wide. She glanced around the clearing, eyes darting from tree to tree as if each was a hidden warrior priest waiting to leap out and slay them all. Then she looked down, saw the boy and let out a low, keening wail.

'No. No. This is not right.' She pushed past Nellore, knelt and lifted Xando's head into her lap. Errol felt a moment's irrational jealousy before reminding himself that for all the months she had been Gog's captive, trapped in the golden cage or merely held at the top of the great tower, this boy had been Martha's only companion. None of the others knew him well at all.

He reached out, laid a gently shaking hand on Martha's shoulder. She flinched slightly at his touch, then relaxed. 'We will bury him properly,' she said. 'Somewhere he can become one with the Grym.'

Errol was about to agree, but a noise distracted him. How could he have forgotten so swiftly? He whirled to see Benfro still standing where he had breathed fire and put an end once and for all to Osgal, staring at the spot where the captain had died. The last remnants of blue flame flickered and danced in the undergrowth, their light playing across the dragon's scales as he leaned forward, one hand on the trunk of the nearest tree. Slowly he raised his head, turned and faced Errol. Then, with all the grace of a landslide, his legs folded under him and he crashed to the ground.

32

The knowledge and experience of a lifetime are stored in a dragon's jewels, deep within his living brain. A newly hatched kitling will have no memories and so no jewels. A mage of many millennia will not necessarily be possessed of so many as to leave no room in his skull for anything else, but those jewels he has grown will be dark and dense with the learning of his lifetime.

But what if a dragon experiences such horrors he cannot bear to remember them? What if he is driven mad by some terrible calamity? In such situations it is possible to remove one or more of his jewels, and with them the source of his madness.

This is not a procedure that should be undertaken by any but the most skilled of mages, and with the assistance of a healer of unsurpassed ability. Not only must the correct jewel be identified and carefully removed using the Llinellau, but that jewel must be reckoned the instant it is removed. An unreckoned jewel is a dangerous thing. It will latch on to any life it can, leach experience and memory and seek to reassert itself through that contact.

Performed correctly, the procedure can bring much-needed relief to the sufferer, although with one jewel removed the patient will never be quite the same. It is a procedure that can only be recommended when all other possible remedies have been tried, for to fail in it may leave not one dragon mad but two.

From the journals of Myfanwy the Bold

Melyn stood at the tree line and stared out across a narrow strip of clear ground at the imposing wall that towered into the storm-black sky. Snow came in flurries, heavy at times before clearing completely for just long enough to make an observer think it had finished. The cold seeped through his old bones and he longed to tap into the Grym, feel its warmth ease his tired muscles. He could see it all around him, the lines thick and full. But they pulsed erratically, one moment pushing energy into the unwary, the next sucking it out so fast he had seen men simply fall dead. Marching through the forest, they had witnessed trees spontaneously explode into flame, the unlucky recipients of too much power. Others sickened and died, their leaves tumbling on to the snow-covered ground. Only those warrior priests who had mastered the art of Frecknock's hiding spell had any chance of protecting themselves from the unpredictable forces of nature as Gwlad writhed and bucked under the release of Gog and Magog's insane magic. Cut off from the power they had used all their lives, they were cold and miserable.

'Form up the men. We're going in.' Melyn gave his orders in a quiet voice, even though he knew they were not likely to be overheard. The ever-present howl of the wind made it unlikely even a shouted command would carry far. His warrior priests were nervous; a lesser army would have turned and fled by now. Better to keep things calm until there was actual fighting to do.

As the order passed down the line and the men began to form up, Melyn strode out from the trees, crossed the narrow strip of snow-covered ground and approached the wall. At least on this side the ground was scoured by the wind, otherwise the drifts would have made it all but impossible to pass. How quick and easy it would be to traverse the park on the other side was another matter entirely.

Pulling off his glove, the inquisitor reached up and touched the cold stone. The tiny scales that covered his fingers and palm were not affected by the cold, but they could feel magic flowing through the wall, protecting it, sending warnings of their approach to anyone who might be listening. It was unlikely that alarm would be heard, unlikely even the most skilled of dragon mages would be doing anything other than cutting themselves off from the Grym in much the same way as Melyn's warrior priests. It was too wild, too dangerous, especially over distance. Otherwise he might have left these men in Emmass Fawr and walked the lines here all by himself. It wasn't as if the dragons within posed much of a threat to him.

He had studied the wall from the woods, but even so it took Melyn a while to find what he was looking for. This was ancient magic, after all, the subtlest of arts practised by his hated brother. He shook his head to try and rid himself of Magog's influence, but it was becoming increasingly difficult to tell where he ended and the dead dragon began. There was knowledge to be had in that connection, power too, and Melyn had always coveted both.

'Reveal yourself.' He spoke under his breath as the thinnest of cracks became apparent to his aethereal sight. All the subtle arts stemmed from the Grym, so it was no easy task to take that line and ease it open. He had to ride the waves coursing through the lines, anticipate when to let it flow through him and when to withdraw completely. Slowly the crack widened, the spell crumbling around the edges until a stout wooden door wide enough to let a dozen men enter at a time stood in front of him. Set high, an iron handle protruded from the wood, a lever that would lift the latch inside and grant entry were it not for the magical locks that held it firm to all but a dragon's touch. Reaching up as far as he could, Melyn wrapped his scaled hand around the ice-cold iron, felt the rush as a wave of Grym spilled over him. He tapped as much of it for warmth as he dared, letting his senses ride it a short distance so that he could predict when it would become too powerful even for him. Then, with a smooth motion the latch dropped and the door swung slightly inwards.

Without his command, a troop of warrior priests appeared beside Melyn, set their hands to the wood and pushed. It moved slowly at first, and then picked up momentum, revealing a dark tunnel that echoed to the roar of the storm.

'Bring me light.' Melyn waited impatiently until a warrior priest arrived, carrying a flaming torch. How much more complicated life was without the Grym to aid them at every turn. 'Follow me, men. Weapons ready, though I don't expect much of a reception committee.'

He set off down the tunnel, sniffing the air for any suggestion others had been this way. If they had it was many months, maybe many years ago. Nothing lived in here save for the spiders whose webs dangled from the ceiling high overhead.

It took a surprisingly long time to reach the far end of the tunnel and another ancient door that yielded only to Melyn's dragon-scaled touch. This one swung inwards to reveal a bank of snow piled up higher than a man, a thin band of grey light at the top revealing that the storm had returned with a vengeance. Melyn surveyed the lines and the aethereal, riding the waves of Grym which seemed to be a little gentler here than outside the walls. Sensing a lull, he risked drawing the power into himself, then conjured a ball of white-hot flame and sent it into the snow. Steam billowed down the tunnel, engulfing the nearest warrior priests, who cursed at the sudden wetness that added to their already chilled misery. He cared nothing for their hardship; it was not yet cold enough to kill them. His flame billowed out fifty paces and more before fizzling to nothing, leaving a wide trail of damp grass that steamed for a moment before turning crisp with frost. He stepped out into his brother's palace, breathing deep of the freezing air as his army emerged from the tunnel in their hundreds. They fanned out into the snow, heading for the distant pinprick lights that marked the outermost buildings. Warmed by the power that surged through him now, linked to Magog by something stronger even than the Grym, Melyn raised his arms high, gazing at the vast tower that speared up into the clouds, the centre of this storm that threatened to engulf the whole of Gwlad. He would bring it crashing down, put an end to it. To all of it.

'Go, my warrior priests. Seek out the dragons inside

and the traitorous people who serve them. Kill them all. Let no one live. I will wash this place clean with their blood and claim it for my own.'

Screaming woke him from a deep and dreamless sleep. Dafydd sat upright too swiftly, his head taking a while to catch up with the motion. He didn't know where he was, for a moment couldn't even see. Then the light grew brighter as if curtains had been pulled back from a window, letting the day inside.

Had he not spent time in Pallestre, he would have marvelled at the massive scale of the room. It made him feel like a tiny child, so far was the distance between the walls, so high the intricately corniced ceiling overhead. He lay in a bed big enough for an entire family, his feet barely reaching a quarter of the way down the mattress. Dull white light spread over furniture that was at once familiar and odd. Chairs with no backs and far too big for any man to sit in; a wardrobe that would have made a comfortable home for some of Tynhelyg's poorer citizens. The walls were hung with tapestries showing scenes of deep forest, greens and browns shot through with the occasional flash of colour that was a particularly fine bird or some exotic beast. And there, where he had always been expecting them, were the dragons, wheeling above the canopy in a sky of azure blue.

'You're awake. Good. I was beginning to think you were too far gone. The cold is unseasonal, and it is unwise to venture into the mountains without a shirt on, even in the height of summer.'

Dafydd glanced around, trying to locate the source of

the voice. Then an elderly dragon emerged from the shadows by the window. She was small compared to the beasts at Candlehall, but still large enough to make more sense of the room. And she was old, older by far than Merriel and possibly as old as Earith herself. She stooped, her wings hanging from her sides like moth-eaten curtains. Her face was more scarred, leathery skin than scale, and her eyes were white with cataracts though they pierced him with a glare that made him feel naked.

'What's going on?' He struggled with the heavy bedding, pulling himself out from underneath blankets as thick as his fist. The drop to the floor was further than he expected and he landed heavily on weak legs. 'Where's Iolwen?'

'The princess is directing her troops. Well, I say troops, but they're not trained soldiers. Still, there is so much turmoil in the Grym they're almost a match for the men outside. If only I could say the same for my own kind, but we are not skilled in the ways of violence.'

Dafydd limped across the room to the window, only half realizing that he was naked and cold. He began to reach for the lines for warmth, but something stopped him.

'I would suggest not.' The dragon held out her arm towards him. 'This will pass in time, but until it does you are best not using any magic.'

He remembered then the conversation with Merriel at the Neuadd and how the storm that was spreading across the whole of Gwlad was so much more than wind and snow. Through the window he could see plenty of that, swirling across a wide area of parkland that reached out like a white carpet all the way to the distant wall. Dafydd opened his mouth to speak, then his thoughts caught up with him. 'I am sorry. This must be your house, and you have offered me your hospitality. I am Dafydd of the House of Ballah, and I am in your debt.'

The dragon sniffed. 'I know well who you are, Prince Dafydd. I am Myfanwy, and you had best put on some clothes before your wife arrives. I dare say she has seen you naked, but the rest of her retinue might be a bit alarmed.' She nodded towards a large chest that sat at the end of the bed. 'You'll find clothes in there that will serve you better than the thin trews you were wearing when you arrived. If I didn't know better I'd have said you'd been sunning yourself in Eirawen, not trekking through the forest snow.'

Dafydd opened the chest, releasing a brief waft of some unpleasant odour that quickly dissipated as he delved inside. There were clothes aplenty, and soon enough he was dressed more appropriately for the climate. He located the source of the smell too, a small scrap of dirty cloth bunched up in one corner of the chest. He reached in and pulled it out, feeling something heavy wrapped within it.

'Ah yes, that. In all the excitement I had forgotten about that.' Myfanwy was right behind him as Dafydd straightened, and something about her words suggested she was not the kind of dragon who ever forgot about anything. 'May I?' She held out a gnarled hand, palm up, and as Dafydd transferred the cloth to it he felt the hardness inside, something wrapped up. Myfanwy gently teased the corners away with a blunted talon to reveal a small red jewel, ugly and uncut.

'What is it?' Dafydd asked, although he had a suspicion that he knew.

'This is the last remaining true jewel of Magog, Son of the Summer Moon. You may have heard of him.'

'I . . .' Dafydd remembered his talks with Earith and her tales of the warring dragon brothers. 'Yes. But what do you mean by true jewel?'

'You are aware that a dragon's essence is stored in their jewels, I take it?' Myfanwy began to wrap the dull stone back up in its soiled cloth, as carefully as any gold dealer might wrap in fine black silk the tiny nuggets panned from the streams of the Northlands.

'They grow in your brains, I have been told. They are your memories, are they not?'

'Memories?' Myfanwy tilted her head in consideration. 'Perhaps, yes. But they are so much more than that. Red, like this, they absorb the Grym, commune with it, focus and direct it and all who are connected to it. They are the fundamental core of our magic, our subtle arts as we call them. When we die, our bodies are burned in the Fflam Gwir and our jewels become white. The reckoning we call it, and it sets those memories firm. An unreckoned jewel left in the wild, perhaps from a poor dragon who has died alone and unremembered, will slowly dissolve away into the Grym. That dragon is lost for ever, unless someone should stumble upon them. If the finder is weak-willed then the jewel will possess them, and the dead dragon will try to live on. It doesn't ever end well for an unreckoned jewel or the poor soul possessed.'

Dafydd nodded at the cloth, now neatly folded and concealing its dangerous cargo. 'So what is it doing in there? Why hasn't it been reckoned? And why did you call it the last true jewel? Are there others out there that are false?'

'You see to the heart of it, Dafydd. There are more of Magog's jewels out in Gwlad than I can begin to trace. Some have been fashioned into rings, amulets and other items given to your kind. Even though he died over two thousand years ago, his influence is everywhere. But those jewels are ones that Magog tore from himself while he still lived.'

'Is that possible?'

'Clearly, or he would not have been able to do it. But it is a foul perversion of the subtle arts, and quite possibly what drove him mad. Or I should maybe say madder.' Myfanwy closed her fist around the bundle before reaching out, turning her hand over and dropping it. Instinctively, Dafydd caught it.

'Is it dangerous?' he asked.

'Very. It has already sunk its claws into a young dragon who even now battles to save himself from becoming Magog risen anew. Perhaps the only thing stopping that from happening is this storm in the Grym, this cataclysm brought about by the merging of Gog and Magog's long-separated worlds.'

'Can't we just, I don't know, break it? Smash it into pieces?' Dafydd held the cloth in the palm of his hand just like Myfanwy had done earlier. He knew it wasn't hot, and yet it seemed to burn through his skin like acid.

'That wouldn't work. Only the Fflam Gwir can destroy its hold, and only when burned in conjunction with Magog's body. I fear that will have long rotted away to nothing, even if I knew where it was he had died.'

'What should I do with it then?'

'You?' Myfanwy made a noise that was quite possibly a laugh. 'Why nothing, young man. You would be best putting it back where you found it. If we cannot reckon it, then we must strive to stop it from taking control of Benfro when this storm finally blows itself out.'

Dafydd recognized the name, but before he could ask more the door swung open and a group of people hurried in. He recognized only some of them. Usel and Teryll were there as were a number of his palace guard and some of the Candlehall men. But right at the front and running to greet him was Princess Iolwen, their son fast asleep in a sling across her body.

'You woke up. I should have been here.' She wrapped him in the tightest of embraces, and he hugged her to him as if he never wanted to let go. Prince Iolo woke almost at once, stared up at his father, and an infant grin spread across his face that matched the one on Dafydd's own. Both he and Iolwen were shaking with relief that they had found each other after the worry of the weeks that they had been apart. Dafydd was content just to hold his wife and child close to him and breathe in their scent, oblivious to everything else in Gwlad, including the square of torn and stained cloth wrapped around an inert red stone which he had hastily shoved in the pocket of his borrowed jacket.

33

Bronwyn the White was mother to the brothers Gog and Magog, twins hatched of the same egg. Legend has it great Rasalene himself made a prophecy that two dragons so closely linked would lead to the destruction of Gwlad, and so their mother hid them away for many months after their hatching. Gog she named Son of the Winter Moon and his brother, Son of the Summer Moon, claiming to all that they were hatched six months apart. Such swift procreation is unusual for a dragon, but not unheard of. She claimed too that Palisander himself was their father, although he was ancient beyond reckoning by the time they were hatched, and had not so much as looked at another dragon since Angharad had returned to the Grym. Still, he took them under his wing, treating them as his own until the day he died. And yet most of the dragons in the palace of Claerwen knew that he was long since past fathering kitlings. Who their true father was none could ever guess, and Bronwyn never said. There were plenty of lesser families around at the time and any number of virile young bucks who might have performed the task. All could trace their lineage back to the greatest of all dragons, so perhaps the lie was not so hard to swallow.

Whatever their true parentage, the twins grew up believing they were of Palisander's direct line and learned the subtle arts from him. Perhaps if Bronwyn had been more honest and acknowledged the truth, Gog and Magog would have been raised first to hunt and fly. They might not have learned so much of the ways of the Grym, and their warring over the love of Ammorgwm the Fair might have been less damaging to all of Gwlad. But there is no future in might-have-beens, as Palisander himself once said. So the brothers were raised in a lie, and we live with its consequences to this day.

Sir Nanteos teul Palisander,
The Forgotten Halls of Nantgrafanglach

'These are not men but devils. How can we hope to meet such violence?'

Iolwen ducked out of a corridor filled with smoke and the screams of dying men. Dafydd was close behind her, along with half a dozen local men, all dressed in the drab uniform worn by the servants of Nantgrafanglach. All that was save the one who had spoken. The princess had taken an immediate dislike to Mister Clingle and nothing he had said or done since had swayed her mind on that. Older than most of the palace servants, he had a stoutness about him that suggested a man more used to ordering others than doing things himself. The permanent sneer on his face didn't help either, nor his whining tone.

'The warrior priests of the Order of the High Ffrydd are trained soldiers, but they rely too heavily on their magics. The turmoil in the Grym means they cannot maintain their blades of fire for long. We have the advantage both of numbers and a familiarity with these corridors and passages.'

'But we are not fighters, Princess.' Mister Clingle sweated profusely, quite clearly unused to exerting himself.

'Then don't fight. Use the terrain; isn't that the first rule of warfare?'

Mister Clingle didn't answer, merely wrung his hands together as if that would help. Iolwen ignored him, focusing her attention on the young man behind. He at least had managed to arm himself, although the sword he carried looked like it had last seen use when Gwlad had been whole before.

'You, lad. What's your name?'

Startled, the man looked first to Mister Clingle, as if needing permission to speak. 'Meidrim, Your Highness.'

'Well, Meidrim. Here's what you must do. Get the word out to all the servants you can find. Do not engage these warrior priests unless you have no option. You know the palace, so lead them away from the centre. Open doors that will take them to empty halls and corridors. Let them see you only briefly, then disappear down the servant stairwells or through the minor reception rooms. If you have to fight them, then keep back as much as possible. The longer they conjure their blades, the more chance they have of losing control of them.'

Meidrim stared at her for perhaps longer than was necessary. Iolwen's grasp of the language of dragons was not as good as Usel's, but she had been given a swift and painful lesson by Myfanwy and she was fairly sure she had the basics right.

'Go!' She pushed a little compulsion at the young man as she barked the command. He jumped as if stung, made an unsuccessful attempt at a salute and then scurried off, taking the rest of the palace servants with him.

Mister Clingle remained. He had ceased his hand-wringing and now looked at Iolwen with ill-disguised contempt. Not a man used to taking orders from other men, let alone a woman. 'And what will you do while those youngsters risk death? Hide away in the dungeons?' he sneered.

'I rather think that is your place. Prince Dafydd and I will go and speak to the council. If the dragons can be persuaded to act then Inquisitor Melyn's attack will be very short-lived indeed.'

'The council mourn the loss of the Old One. They will not see you.'

'Then I will speak to Myfanwy alone.'

Mister Clingle opened his mouth to respond, and Iolwen knew he was going to say something unhelpful, quite possibly rude. But before he could speak, the door burst open and a wild-faced man charged in. He wore the robes of a warrior priest, but his eyes blazed with a bloodlust quite at odds with the discipline for which his order was renowned. He screamed something unintelligible, conjured a blade more ragged and fearsome than any Iolwen had seen. In an instant he had cleaved Mister Clingle in two, laughing like a madman as his remains slapped wetly to the floor. And then the warrior priest pressed on. Iolwen stepped back, Dafydd at her side. The room they had entered was small by the standards of the palace, but still large enough that they could evade the wild lunges of their attacker's blade. There was only the one door though, and he blocked their route to it.

Iolwen cast out for the lines, trying to conjure her own blade. She could sense Dafydd doing the same, but the warrior priest somehow sucked all the Grym from them, his ragged weapon growing longer and hotter so that it was more like a spear now. As it grew, so she weakened, her mental barriers withering under the onslaught of the man's madness. Then Iolwen felt something behind her and realized that she had been backed into a corner. Nowhere to turn, no escape from that terrible flame. The warrior priest grinned like an idiot, raised his blade high.

And stopped.

The blade disappeared, surging back out along the lines. For a moment confusion replaced madness in the man's eyes. And then he coughed, bright red blood choking past his lips as a huge, leathery, taloned hand appeared in the middle of his chest. Iolwen blinked, and a dragon appeared, standing in the place where the warrior priest had been.

'I would have come sooner,' Merriel said. 'Looks like I got here just in time.'

The smell of burning hair and bubbling skin would take a long time to leave him. Errol had dragged the dead warrior priests to the fire and one by one hefted them on to the flames. It was something to do while Martha attended to Benfro, aided by Nellore. He had thought some of their attackers had survived the fight, but if so then they had fled, for none of the bodies he discovered showed any sign of life. Neither did the pale, limp form of the boy

Xando, who he had moved a distance away and covered with a blanket. They would have to bury him; he was not for the fire or for the forest animals to tear apart.

'How is he?' Errol walked across to where the dragon lay unconscious. Nellore was busy cleaning the blood from his side while Martha held a hand over his forehead and whispered in Draigiaith. Errol could feel the flow of the Grym as it passed through Martha and into Benfro, speeding up his healing and restoring his strength. It was dangerous work, all but impossible to predict if a surge might overpower her, kill both her and Benfro too. Or it might suddenly drain away to nothing, leaching what little life the dragon had out of him.

'He is badly injured.' Martha took her hand away, and Errol breathed out a sigh of relief. 'Without proper help, he will die. We need to get him back to Nantgrafanglach. Myfanwy will know what to do.'

'How? We can't hope to carry him. And I don't know how to get back there.'

'Can walk. Not far.'

At first Errol thought it was Nellore speaking, muttering low under her breath, but Benfro was struggling to get himself off his side and back on to his feet. He used the nearby trees, gripping their trunks tight with his talons and heaving himself upright. He swayed in the pale morning light, gouts of steamy breath jetting out of his nostrils.

'You should rest a while. You need to heal.' Martha reached up and put her hand on Benfro's shoulder, the Grym flowing through her and into him once more. He shuddered a little as if cold, then gently shrugged her away from him.

'There is no time. We have to get to Nantgrafanglach and find Magog's jewel. That's the only way we can put an end to this.' Benfro raised his head to peer through the canopy at the dark grey clouds that blanketed the sky. Soon there would be snow, and that would make their journey even more difficult.

'We must bury Xando first,' Errol said. 'It's the least he deserves.'

Benfro shuffled over to where the boy's body lay. He seemed to gain strength with each step, or at least recover his balance. He knelt slowly, like an old man worried he might not be able to get back up again, then reached out and gently tugged back the blanket to reveal the dead boy's face.

'How did he die?'

'I'm not sure. It all happened so quickly. I think one of the warrior priests must have run him through with a sword. They came out of nowhere.'

'I don't think it's any coincidence they were here. Melyn must know we have the piece of Magog's skull, which means Magog knows too. There can be no other reason he would send Osgal to intercept us. But why try to kill us? I thought Magog was trying to possess me.' Benfro reached up to a point on his forehead directly between his eyes, his hand touching the air and describing the arc of a rope fixed to him. Errol shifted his focus, trying to access his aethereal sight. It wasn't easy; he was too tired for one thing and the shock of the fight had left him unsettled. He finally managed to bring the dragon's aura to light.

The rose cord was still there, pale and lifeless at the moment. Of greater concern was the sickly hue of the colours as they shifted sluggishly around the dragon's body. Greys and greens and dull browns, they were far removed from the vibrant shades that had surrounded Benfro before. And there, at his side, part covered by his damaged wing, a dark black smear cut through him like a scar, reaching deep inside. Errol would have looked closer, but the twisting and pulsing of the lines made it hard to concentrate, his vision fading back to the mundane.

'I didn't know him well, but he did his best to help me when I was in need. This shouldn't have happened.' Benfro stood stiffly, and even without his aethereal sight Errol could see the pain his friend was suffering. The dragon took a step back, indicated that the others should do the same. He took a slow breath in, then exhaled in Xando's direction. The flame that poured from his mouth was almost white, more like steam than fire. It flowed across to the boy's body and settled around it like a shroud. Xando didn't burn, his skin didn't crisp and bubble like the warrior priests on the bonfire. There was no greasy black smoke. Instead, he slowly faded away, drawn back into the Grym, his essence returning to Gwlad and the trees of the forest where he had died.

For a while the lines settled down to their normal stillness, at least in the small clearing where they had made their camp. Errol wasn't sure whether it was indelicate or not, but he stepped closer to his old friend, laid a hand on his scaly neck and let the energy surge through him. Standing on Benfro's other side, Martha did the same, taking the opportunity to bolster the dragon's strength for what they knew would be a hard journey and an even harder fight at the end of it.

The calm lasted until the final wisp of pale flame was gone, no trace of Xando left but the blanket in which he had been wrapped and the clothes he had been wearing. How long they had stood and watched, Errol could not have said. It had been early morning when they started, but the day seemed scarcely any brighter, the sun nowhere to be seen through the lowering clouds. As the last vestige of Xando disappeared, so the lines began to writhe once more, the Grym surging and ebbing with renewed ferocity so that they all had to withdraw from it. Even so, Errol felt refreshed despite his sadness, and Benfro stood more upright, his shoulders less slumped.

'We should go now.' The dragon turned away from the blanket on the ground, looking towards the east. 'There is a long walk ahead of us, and the storm is coming.'

'Earith has conjured a new Heol Anweledig. It leads back to Pallestre from the great hall. It was no easy task creating it, I can tell you. My mother has not set foot in this palace in more than two thousand years.'

Merriel walked so quickly Iolwen and Dafydd had to run to keep up. It was no hardship; they would have run from the carnage even without the dragon to accompany them.

'Why . . . so . . . long . . .?' Iolwen gasped out the question as they reached a pair of wooden doors so huge they made even the dragon seem small.

'That is a question for her, perhaps. I know she does not see eye to eye with her sister for one thing.'

'Sister?'

'Half-sister, perhaps. Myfanwy the Bold always held to

the promises she made to Gog, Son of the Winter Moon, even though the old bastard never kept any of his. Mother couldn't forgive either of them for that.' Merriel pushed at the doors, and with a terrible squealing of hinges they opened.

Beyond lay the great hall where Iolwen and her party had first been taken. Close to Myfanwy's house, it had been pressed into use as a command headquarters; the powerful magics surrounding it made escape easier should the palace be overrun. Usel had a scroll unrolled across the table and was peering at it, running excited fingers over the surface, but it was Anwen whom Iolwen was most pleased to see. Carrying Prince Iolo in a sling around her shoulder, she looked up at their arrival.

'Your Highness. Iolwen. Who is this—?' Anwen began, but Merriel cut her off.

'We do not have much time. The Heol Anweledig cannot stay open for ever. It would be a disaster if these warrior priests were to find it. For those who do not know me, I am Merriel, daughter of Earith. I offer safe passage to Pallestre, escape from this war not of your making.'

Iolwen was only half-listening to Merriel's words, more anxious to tend to her son. She had left him with Anwen that morning, gone out with Dafydd to aid with the defence of Nantgrafanglach, despite her husband's repeated protests. Melyn's men had arrived so suddenly, and spread with such speed and ferocity, she had feared she might never see her Prince Iolo again. Only once she had taken him in her arms and kissed his gurgling, smiling face did she finally understand what the dragon had said.

'Escape?'

'Pallestre is far from here, peaceful. My mother's protection is more than adequate should trouble come looking for us.'

'But what of the people of Candlehall? What of the servants of Nantgrafanglach?'

Merriel's expression was hard to read. Iolwen had spent time with Myfanwy, but she was just one dragon among many, and she was not perhaps the most typical of her kind. Even so, it seemed that Merriel was surprised more than annoyed.

'There is not time.' She waved her hand and an opening appeared in the wall nearby. Warm air tumbled from it, bringing smells of spices, the sea and a deeper, more earthy musk.

'I cannot leave my people. Not when they are being slaughtered like this.'

'I know, Princess.' Merriel nodded towards the opening and as if on cue a line of men began to march from it. 'Pallestre has never needed much of an army, but what it has is at your disposal. I would still suggest you send those less able to defend themselves through the Heol Anweledig. They will be safe.'

Iolwen looked down at her infant son. He had no idea of the horrors unfolding throughout the palace, but that would not stop Melyn from killing him if he was found. She bent low to his tiny face, kissed him gently on the forehead and then reluctantly handed him back to Anwen. Dafydd put out his hand, and for a moment she thought he was going to argue for leaving, but he simply kissed his son as well.

Iolwen nodded. 'Go, Anwen. Take Teryll with you.

Usel, you should go too. You are a man of peace, not war, and Pallestre is full of wonders that should be documented.' She scanned the rest of the group, saw Captain Venner and the last of the Tynhelyg palace guard who had ridden out with her and Dafydd so many months ago. Mercor Derridge was there with his grandson Beyn and a few of the men who had helped them at Candlehall too. What link to her they had that had made Merriel bring them all to this place she couldn't begin to fathom, any more than how the dragon had done it.

'Anyone who is sick of fighting should go with them,' she said as the last of the Pallestre men stepped out of the Heol Anweledig. They formed up in ranks, two hundred and more young men, armed with steel and clothed in oiled leather. Would they be a match for the mad ferocity of the warrior priests'and Inquisitor Melyn? Perhaps they would, for the Grym was not taking sides. And if Iolo was safe, she could hope that they might even win.

If she could only persuade the dragons of Nantgrafanglach to join the fight.

34

Dragons of most ancient legend were said to breathe fire. They were also said to fight each other without provocation and spend all their time either sleeping, killing things to eat, eating them or fornicating. Such is a very narrow view of our primitive ancestors, for while it is certain they breathed fire much like that which burns in the hearth, they could also produce the Fflam Gwir, the true flame, which is something altogether different.

There is no doubt that hundreds of thousands of years ago the wild beasts that would become dragons were less than perfect. A similar development can be seen in the men who serve us today. It is not long at all as measured in our own lifetimes since they were little better than the apes who still live in the distant forests of Eirawen and out beyond the Gwastadded Wag. They dwelt in caves, scavenged for food and caught fish only at the shoreline using sharpened sticks as spears. Now they have raised cities that while small to our eyes are yet marvels of engineering.

As dragons have grown in intellect and sophistication, so we have thrown off some of the more base behaviours of our primitive ancestors. Among these is the ability to breathe fire, and that is to be regretted. For that aspect of our natures was the first of the subtle arts. It was that innate ability that raised us above the common beasts, and to deny it now is to deny our true selves.

Corwen teul Maddau,
On the Application of the Subtle Arts

The battle for Nantgrafanglach was not going well. Prince Daffydd had been here only a short while, had met but few of the dragons who lived here and fewer still of the men. Even so he could tell from their panic that they were not fighters. Those few old soldiers who had fled here from Candlehall were doing their best to whip the men into shape, but they had little skill and fewer weapons. Even the men of Pallestre lacked the expertise of seasoned campaigners. The warrior priests on the other hand were a well oiled machine, each man wielding either a blade of steel or one of fire. Sometimes both. So far most of the casualties among their attackers had been down to the wild and fluctuating nature of the Grym rather than any planned defence.

'We have to fall back, rally everyone around the central tower.' Dafydd paused part way down a corridor, catching his breath as the rest of their party hurried past.

'True. But we also need to persuade the rest of the dragons to help.' Iolwen leaned against the wall, a short steel blade in one hand dripping with someone else's blood. Dafydd knew she had studied fencing and spent hours being tutored by King Ballah in matters of warfare. It was another thing entirely to see her in action. Her face was smeared with sweat and gore, her hair slick with it, and she had not flinched from the fighting.

'The rest of them? There are more?' Dafydd looked back to the main corridor where they had fled an onslaught of warrior priests. He could no longer see much, but the body of one dragon lay where it had fallen, caught up in an explosion when a conjured blade of fire had proven too much for the warrior priest who had wielded it. Others had died before that one, cut down by the ant-like swarm of madmen.

'These dragons are the ones Myfanwy persuaded to come back, to defend their ancestral home. They have no magic, or very little. Just hunters' cunning and brute strength.' Iolwen pushed hair from her eyes, leaving a smear of red across her forehead. 'I had hoped the Council of Nantgrafanglach would join us. They could put an end to this fight.'

'And why won't they?'

'I don't know. Perhaps they are frightened. Perhaps they think that if they hide for a few hundred years we'll all be dead and the problem will go away. Who can fathom these beasts? Not me, for sure.'

'Perhaps I should speak to them.' Dafydd knew as soon as he said the words that they were the wrong ones, simply by the look on Iolwen's face. 'If nothing else, let's try and buy some more time for Myfanwy. She at least seems to have a plan.'

'If not, then at least we can buy enough time for the rest of our people to flee to Pallestre.' Iolwen's glare softened, then changed into a frown. 'Though if Melyn takes Nantgrafanglach then I don't know how long we'll be safe even half way around Gwlad.'

'Your Highness. Ma'am. We need to keep moving, or they'll surely catch up with us. Don't know how much longer we can keep this up.'

Dafydd turned to see Mercor Derridge, flanked by his grandson and a couple of the Pallestre men. They all looked exhausted, covered in grime and gore much like Iolwen.

'Get the message out as far as you can. We need to pull everyone back to the central palace and the tower.'

'We're almost there, sire.' Derridge pointed down the corridor. 'That's if I understand the locals right. Turn there'll take us to the council chambers and the base of the tower. Other way's back through the kitchen block and cut through the city to that big old hall where everyone's trying to escape through one of them tunnels like.'

'The great hall? You can get back there without going through the warrior priests?'

'Aye, reckon so. Lad seemed right keen to head that way and I can't say as I blame 'im.'

A shout split the air from the direction they had come. The corridor was not large enough for dragons, clearly built for the men who served them to pass along unnoticed. That was scant help when it was men who were attacking. Dafydd considered their motley band of soldiers; they really were no match for the warrior priests. Truly the only honourable course was to get as many out of the city as possible.

'Take the men, head to the great hall and on to Pallestre through the Heol Anweledig,' he said.

'Sire? You mean leave? Flee?'

'Exactly so. Iolwen and I will try to spur the council into action, but if that fails then we will join you in Eirawen.'

For a moment Dafydd thought the old soldier was going to argue, but his eyes darted briefly to his grandson before he stood up straight, saluted.

'We'll wait for you at this end as long as we can, sir. Ma'am.' And without another word he was off, gathering the ragtag troop together and urging them on.

'That was very noble,' Iolwen said as she watched them go.

'I can't ask them to fight warrior priests, and we surely can't ask them to die for this place if the dragons who live here won't lift a finger.'

'Some of the dragons. Many have died already. And Myfanwy needs time.'

'Well let's see if we can't persuade the rest to put up more of a fight then. It's their home, after all.'

They followed the troop at a distance, taking the opposite turning when they reached the end of the passage. It led them swiftly to a wide corridor, poorly illuminated by what little light could penetrate the gloomy storm outside and the thick glass set into the tall windows on either side. An opening on one side of the hall revealed a stone staircase climbing up in a gentle spiral. Opposite it and close to their smaller entrance, a pair of massive oak doors stood closed.

'This is it. This is where Sir Conwil brought Usel and me.' Iolwen walked over to the doors as Dafydd scanned the hall for signs of approaching warrior priests. After the screaming and noise of battle further out in the palace, the quiet was unnerving. A *crack* like a tree falling split the air. He whirled round to see the huge doors swing open, revealing another great room beyond. Dwarfed by them, Iolwen stepped inside, and Dafydd hurried to catch up with her as the doors began to close once more. They shut with a dull thud that echoed across the room and reverberated through the soles of his feet.

'Princess Iolwen. I see you have returned. And who is this you have brought before us?'

Dafydd looked up at the faces of perhaps a hundred dragons seated on low benches behind empty tables like so many ancient schoolboys awaiting their master. He looked from elderly face to elderly face, seeing nothing that inspired him with confidence. He had seen more life in the dusty clerics who tended to his grandfather's accounts.

'Good day to you, members of the council. This is my husband, Prince Dafydd. We bring tidings of the battle outside and humbly beg your assistance. Nantgrafanglach is in danger of being overrun.'

A quiet murmur of Draigiaith fluttered around the room as the dragons conferred with each other. One of them, larger than most and with scales of a deep slate grey, finally stood.

'Princess. Your Highness. It is as we said before. The arguments of men mean nothing to us. Your kind measure your lives in tens of years while we have known tens of centuries. We will wait, and in time things will return to the way they were.'

Dafydd sighed, letting his shoulders slump as he looked around the room in the rain hope of seeing Myfanwy. Of all the dragons he had met, she seemed the most attuned to life in the real world. She might have knocked some sense into them, but she was nowhere to be seen. Whatever her plan, she was carrying it out elsewhere.

'It is too late for hiding.' Iolwen spoke. 'Melyn and his men are here already. They have not come for us, but for you. We have done our best to keep them out but we are losing that battle. Many have already died for you. It is time for the dragons of Nantgrafanglach to take up the fight.'

The leader of the council looked up sharply at that last word, as if the very concept pained him. Dafydd knew then that nothing he and Iolwen said would change their minds. Still, he opened his mouth ready to plead once more, but the door behind him boomed as if struck by a giant hand.

'By the moon! Who dares disrupt a full meeting of the council?' The slate-grey dragon moved out from behind his table and strode to the door with surprising swiftness. The other council members began to rise, and Dafydd felt a surge in the Grym as if they were readying themselves to repel an attack. For a fraction of a heartbeat he thought this might have persuaded them of the seriousness of the situation. Then he felt something else building in the air, something that took him back to the earliest days of his training.

Instinct kicked in and he grabbed Iolwen, pulling both of them to the floor as the huge oak doors exploded inwards. Chunks of timber and a million splinters like lethal darts flew across the room in all directions. Had it not been for the bulk of the great grey dragon standing in front of them, they would have been cut into tiny pieces. The dragon didn't fare so well. As the dust and debris began to settle, so he toppled over, slumping to the floor like a dropped sack of flour.

The journey seemed to take for ever and yet no time at all. Benfro had never felt so tired, never known such pain. Even when Fflint had beaten him close to death it had not been the same. Then the agony was sharp, focused on each individual wound, each snapped bone. Now it was as if his body were simply falling apart. Only sustained concentration could keep him together. That and the need to keep walking.

They were a sombre group, all grieving the loss of Xando in their own ways. It seemed so senseless. He had only been with them by accident, had nothing to do with the warrior priests or Melyn and Magog's madness. And yet he had been cut down almost thoughtlessly. Just another tree to be hacked away so that the path could be cleared.

The first night after the attack was miserable. They dared not light a fire, nor seek warmth from the twisting, whipping lines of the Grym. Benfro's missing eye could see enough to warn them should any warrior priests come near, so he sat up most of the night keeping watch. In truth he did not think he would have been able to sleep even if he'd tried. Each breath brought a stab of pain to his side, his hearts thumping out of rhythm so that his head was light and his mundane vision blurred.

In the morning they had left as the first light began to mute the darkness, rising in silence and packing up their meagre camp before resuming their trek through snow-silent forest. Always uphill, always just close enough to the river to be sure they were going the right way.

It was late afternoon when Martha stopped them all with a sharp hiss and raised hand. Benfro had been half asleep, walking without thinking, without seeing anything but the white ground ahead of him. Snapping awake, his missing eye lit up the scene, showing a group of men not far ahead. He concentrated, looking for the signs he didn't want to see and finding them aplenty.

'Warrior priests,' he said in a low whisper. 'Lots of them.'

'The wall is that way. They have the palace cordoned off from this side.' Martha did not appear to have moved, her hand still held up to stop them, but Benfro had seen her aethereal form sweep out through the trees in swift reconnaissance. It was brave, perhaps even foolhardy, given the circumstances and the skills of the men on guard.

'There will be patrols moving around. We can't stay here,' Errol said.

'How are we going to get into the palace? We can't use the lines, and there's no way we could all slip past these guards, even in the snow. Not with Benfro wounded like he is.' Martha turned to face them, and for the first time since he had met the young woman Benfro saw doubt in her eyes.

'There is a way.' Benfro sniffed the cold air, sensing the river not far off. Wind whipped the tall trees overhead, occasionally dislodging chunks of snow down on them, but over the noise he could just about make out the roar of the waterfall.

'The Anghofied?' Errol asked.

'If I can retrace my tracks, we can get back to the palace dungeons. They're right beneath Gog's tower.'

'But what if you can't? What if we get stuck in there and lose days, weeks?' The pitch of Errol's voice rose with his panic. He had not fared in the deep underground as well as Benfro.

'I don't see as we have much choice.' Martha was the voice of unhappy reason. 'We can't walk the lines; there's too much disturbance in the Grym. We can't hope to slip past that many warrior priests either. If there's another way, we must take it. Or give up.'

Benfro knew she had the right of it, even if the thought of that lifeless place filled him with almost as much dread as it clearly filled Errol. He nodded once, then led them down to the riverbank and the waterfall with its hidden cave.

Inside the cavern he retraced his own scent, following it back the way he had come. The journey through the underground world of the Anghofied was every bit as terrible as he imagined it would be, but at least with his three companions close by, Benfro wasn't swamped by the same sense of hopelessness as before.

Errol fared the worst, shivering as if possessed of a terrible fever and muttering constantly to himself. After a while Martha suggested they all hold hands, something that was increasingly necessary given the near-total darkness and utter lack of Grym. The touch of her hand in his was a welcome contact, and from that point on they made better progress. When they reached the dimly lit tunnel mouth that led up to the cells, it was as if a huge weight had been lifted from his shoulders.

Benfro slumped against the stone wall as first Martha, then Errol and finally Nellore scrambled past him. All three hurried further up the passage before stopping, as if the tunnels and caverns they had traversed had been populated with the most terrible horrors imaginable. Perhaps for them they had.

'Are we there? Are we in Gog's palace?' Nellore asked, her eyes so wide Benfro could see the whites all around them. He looked up at the ceiling, then down at the floor of the passage. Both were worked stone, neatly chiselled and smooth. Many feet had come this way over centuries, maybe millennia, each one wearing away at the rock until it shone.

'This is the way I came when I escaped. Uphill will take us past the dungeons. I just hope we don't meet anyone unfriendly on the way.'

He pushed himself upright, wincing as the pain sliced through his side and set his hearts thumpity-thumping out of time. His legs were like stone, heavy to move. His tail dragged behind him like a curse. Every step was a mile, and he couldn't help being reminded of his time in Magog's retreat at the top of Mount Arnahi. Only there it had been the thin air that had weakened him. He had no such excuse this time.

They moved cautiously up the passage, past the burned-out remains of the cell in which he had been locked. Benfro strained his senses, his missing eye showing him a blurry, incomplete aethereal view. Had he the strength he would have pushed further with his magical sight, but it was hard enough just breathing. No sounds reached his ears but the rustle of his companions' clothes and the quiet crackle of the torches that hung from the walls. The passage opened on to the hall where the dungeon guards had been stationed when Benfro had first been led down to his cell. Now it was empty, the fireplace cold. Benfro leaned heavily on the old oak table that filled the centre of the room. The plates of half-eaten food and goblets still brimming with wine suggested somebody's meal had been interrupted. Had they gone off in search of him after his escape and not returned? It seemed unlikely.

'This way leads up to the palace.' He pointed to the wide stairs, his hearts sinking at the thought of climbing them. Even the prospect of walking across the hall filled him with dread. He just wanted to lie down and sleep. 'We must try and find Myfanwy. Or Cerys.'

By the time they reached the top, Benfro's mundane sight had almost completely gone. It was too much effort to keep his eye focused, or indeed open. He walked like a dragon asleep, only his missing eye painting the scene in the aethereal. That was perhaps why he failed to notice anything out of place until he finally stopped.

The main hall was vast. On the far side doors opened on to the parkland that stretched away to the wall. Stairs climbed to a series of landings. Higher still, a great glass dome would have filtered light in from above, were it not darkened by night and the weight of snow pressing down upon it. At this level the hall had contained little furniture, just a few tables in the middle, some heavy chests and sideboards around the walls. That much Benfro remembered from when he was marched through it on his way to the dungeons.

Now it was carnage.

There was a moment's stunned silence, then panic galvanized the remaining dragons into action. Mostly this involved falling backwards over their seats, tipping the tables on end and colliding with each other as they tried to escape. Keeping his head low, Dafydd gripped Iolwen's hand and together they inched back, using the bulk of the dead dragon as cover until they could tuck in behind half of a shattered table.

'Melyn.' Iolwen's voice was a hiss, no question in the word. Dafydd risked a peek, saw a lone human figure standing in the doorway. A crimson blade of fire sprang from one fist and with the other he directed warrior priests into the room.

'We have to find a way out. We can't be captured. He'll kill us both.'

Dafydd scanned what little of the room he could see from where they hid. There were large windows, but the sills stood higher than a man's head, the glass in them thick and heavy. He doubted he could break it with a hammer, and he had no weapon other than his unreliable magic.

'There. The fireplace.' Iolwen tugged at his sleeve, pointing to the back wall opposite the exploded door. The fire was lit, flames leaping up the chimney. Dafydd couldn't think what she could mean, but then he saw it. Like everything else in the palace, the fireplace was built to the scale of dragons, but it was also designed to be cleaned by men. Neat stone steps, presumably to aid with sweeping the chimney, climbed the inside, disappearing past the mantelpiece.

'We'll get cooked in there.'

'Better than the alternative.' Iolwen crouched low, weaving her way across the room until she was at the fireplace. Dafydd took one last look round the edge of the upturned table. The inquisitor was still in the doorway, a seemingly endless line of warrior priests jogging into the hall from behind him, fanning out into the chaos as they conjured blades of fire to attack the trapped dragons of the council. Some didn't even bother with magic, but harried the beasts with steel, raising sparks where they clattered off scales. The noise was horrendous, screaming and wailing that was as much in his head as his ears. It mirrored the chaos of the Grym, surging and fading with no discernible rhythm.

Motion in the corner of his eye, and Dafydd rolled out of the way as a dragon came stumbling towards him. Pursued by a warrior priest brandishing a sputtering blade of fire and oblivious to anything but his quarry, the creature fell over the table. Sticking his leg out, Dafydd tripped the man, reaching for anything that he might use as a weapon. He need not have worried. Momentarily losing his concentration, the warrior priest lit up with fire as the power concentrated in his blade consumed him. Then the flames began to lick at the wooden table, leaping between the splinters of the door that lay all over the floor, heading straight for Dafydd as if they could sense the spark of life within him and wanted to join it.

Dafydd scrambled backwards, knocked into another fleeing dragon and spun round, coming to his feet in a run that brought him to the fireplace just as the Grym from the warrior priest's blade caught the dragon and engulfed it.

'Up.' Iolwen grabbed at his arm as he gazed back at the scene, transfixed. He had never seen anything like it: the power of Gwlad leaping from dragon to dragon, burning them with a ferocity that made the storm outside seem mild in comparison. The warrior priests had mostly extinguished their own blades, content to let their leader do all the work. For that was who was controlling the fire.

Standing in the middle of it all, arms outstretched, Inquisitor Melyn laughed like a mad child.

'Up!' Iolwen shouted over the din, dragging Dafydd back past the real flames crackling over the logs and towards the steps cut in the fireplace. He stumbled, almost fell into the fire and felt the heat of it burn away the hairs on the back of his hand. Iolwen's grip tightened, pulling him back, and he got his feet under him.

The air cooled a little as he followed Iolwen up and away from the flames, but it was still uncomfortably hot. The smoke made it hard to breathe, tears blurring his vision until he could barely see. The steps opened on to a wide ledge that ran around the inside of the chimney, and on the far side of it they found a deeper alcove that took them away from the scalding air and dancing embers. The two of them slumped down with their backs pressed against the rock, faces lit by the glow of the fire below.

'Do you think anyone saw us?' Iolwen asked.

Dafydd had been thinking the same thing. 'If they did, then we're done for.' He reached around and smacked his hand against the stone. 'No way out here.' But when he pulled his hand away, he felt the lightest of cool draughts caress his fingertips. He pressed them against the stone again, running them over the soot until he felt a tiny crack. It rose, dead straight, then formed an arch before coming back down to the floor.

'There's a doorway here. Or something like it.'

Down below the screams of the dragons had fallen almost to silence. The Council of Nantgrafanglach had not lasted long; if he and Iolwen had been spotted the warrior priests would be after them soon enough. Dafydd rubbed away at the wall around the crack, feeling for anything that might be a lever. He tried to get his fingernails in to prise the door open, but it was solid.

'Here. You need to do this.' Iolwen stood up, lifted a hand and placed it firmly on a spot that in the half-light looked no different to any other. With a heavy click, the crack widened and fresh air whistled through the gap. 'Now you can push it.'

Dafydd set his shoulder to the stone and heaved. It moved slowly at first, no doubt stuck from ages of neglect. Then the door swung open, not stone but heavy iron caked with soot. The room beyond was as black as the night, but it was cool and a fresh blew through it. At the very least it was away from the fire, the warrior priests and Inquisitor Melyn. He ducked low through the arch, sliding his foot forward lest there be an unexpected drop. When he was sure the floor was safe, he put out his hand and guided Iolwen through.

No sooner had she stepped into the dark room than the door began to swing back of its own accord. Dafydd tried to stop it, hoping the light from the fireplace would let him see at least enough to find a way out, but it was like trying to stop a tree from falling. The iron slipped from his grasp and with a solid *clunk* the door slammed shut.

The reason Benfro's aethereal vision had shown him nothing awry was clear as soon as he opened his good eye. All the men and dragons lying about the hall were dead. Some had been ripped apart, others cut by blades of such sharpness they could only be the concentrations of the Grym favoured by warrior priests. He scanned the hall once more, searching for any sign of life before venturing out into the devastation. His companions, so keen to forge ahead before, now kept behind him, using his bulk as a shield. He couldn't blame them.

They were halfway across the hall when the massive front doors exploded inwards, snow flurrying in from the darkness outside, wind whipping around them. Benfro froze on the spot, tensed against a rush of attackers. But there was nobody. Then the gale dropped and the doors boomed shut again.

He stepped over fallen men, some dressed in the robes of warrior priests but most wearing the clothes of simple folk. Those few men he had seen in the palace before being taken to the dungeon had dressed in a particular style, and he could identify many of them among the fallen, but there were plenty who wore different clothing.

'Some of these men are from Candlehall.' Martha was the first to speak. She knelt beside a body, rolling it over to reveal a clean-shaven young face. Dead eyes stared into nothing.

'How can you be sure?' Errol asked.

'I spent a summer living there with my aunt, remember?' She reached up and closed the young man's eyes with gentle fingers. 'And I've been here long enough to know what the local people look like too. They have different faces.'

Benfro dragged himself slowly across to the first dead dragon, a great hulk of a beast who lay on his side, wings crumpled around him. He recognized him as Borth, one of the dragons who had escorted him to the dungeons. Not far off, his companion Carno's head was several paces away from his body.

'What happened here?' Nellore asked. 'Who killed them all?'

'Warrior priests.' Benfro pointed to one of the dead men wearing the cloak and dark brown leggings of the Order of the High Ffrydd. He lay on his back, arms splayed. His face was cracked and blistered, one hand missing entirely, the stump of his arm a burned oozing mess. It wasn't hard to work out what had happened to him.

'Why?'

'Because their leader told them to. And he is here, somewhere. I am sure of it.' Benfro headed towards the wide corridor that led to the council room where he had been interrogated. More bodies littered the floor like so much discarded rubbish. Men and dragons were united in death, and he had to suppress the urge to breathe the Fflam Gwir, let everything be consumed by it. There would be time for that soon enough. At least he hoped there would.

He found Sir Nanteos in the chamber off the main passageway where he had undergone his brief interrogation. The old dragon had clearly put up a fight, his chest scored deeply with many burn lines where he had fought off at least the dozen warrior priests who lay dead around him. In the end they had been too many. Benfro stared down at the dead dragon. Sir Nanteos had not treated him well, but he had not deserved this. No one deserved this.

A noise in the far corner of the chamber startled him, and he turned too swiftly to face the danger. The wound in his side was like a shard of ice in his flesh, a cold so deep it burned. Benfro took a sharp breath, felt the fire building within him. The tables behind which his inter-rogators had sat and the low chairs they had used were heaped in a pile, as if someone had stacked them ready to burn. Or maybe used the subtle arts to hurl them there. Now the topmost chair tumbled off the heap, followed by another. And then a hand reached out, dragon-sized and deepest green. The fire died in his stomach as Benfro lurched across the room and began ripping apart the heap as if it were no more than kindling. In his frenzy he quite forgot his pain and weariness. Until he had shifted the last piece and freed Cerys from her prison.

She looked almost as bad as he felt. Her scales were smeared with blood, charred here and there by too-close encounters with the warrior priests and their blades of fire. She was bruised, shocked, frightened and above all else bewildered. Her aura clung to her like sweat, its col-ours muted as if she was trying to draw as little attention to herself as possible. For a long while she simply stared at him with no comprehension in her eyes at all.

'Cerys. What happened here?' Benfro placed a hand on each of her shoulders. At his touch, a spark of Grym ran between them. She stared up at him, her eyes black, no hint of the golden flecks he had seen before.

'Benfro? How can it . . .? You . . .?' Then her gaze slid past his face, focused on the form lying in the doorway. 'Sir Nanteos?'

'Don't.' Benfro reached out to stop her but lacked the strength. Cerys threw off the remains of the furniture that had hidden her from discovery by the warrior priests. She rushed past him, crossed the floor to where the dead dragon lay and knelt down beside him.

'He saved me,' Cerys said without turning to face him. 'Myfanwy sent me to hide. I thought of going up to the room where I first found you, but there were men everywhere, casting the Grym around like it was fire. I was taking a short cut through here when he burst in. Didn't say a word, just pushed me into the corner, threw all these tables and chairs at me. I didn't know what was going on.'

'How long have you been lying there?' Martha had entered the room and was standing a few paces away from Sir Nanteos. Benfro hadn't noticed her come in.

'I don't know. Not long, I don't think. But it all happened so quickly. They were everywhere. So violent. I've never seen such rage. Not even the dragons of the Twmp took such joy in killing.'

Benfro reached out again to place a hand on Cerys' shoulder. She had been tense, but collapsed into him at the touch, burying her face in her own hands.

'How do we get to Go— the Old One's tower from here?' he asked.

Cerys started at the name, looking up at Benfro. 'Why do you want to go there?'

'Because that is where Melyn will have gone. He has to pay for what he has done.'

'But he'll kill you,' Cerys said.

'Not if we can find Magog's jewel first. It was in Myfanwy's house the last time it was seen. Jewel and bone and Fflam Gwir will put an end to his power.'

Confusion creased Cerys' brow. 'But we need herbs and oils to make the Fflam Gwir. A mage to chant the incantations. Where will we find all these things?'

'Think, Cerys. You know what I can do. We do not

need herbs and oils. Dragons never truly needed them.' Benfro took a step closer to the dead dragon. 'Farewell, Sir Nanteos. We may not have met on the best of terms, but I wish you well in the next life.' He took in a shallow breath, then exhaled. Pale blue flame burst from his mouth and nose, spreading out across the fallen dragon as Cerys leaped back. It devoured Sir Nanteos with remarkable speed, fed by the Grym that pulsed through the palace more strongly than anywhere Benfro had ever known. In only a few minutes, the body had been rendered down to the finest white ash, a heavy pile of clear jewels heaped up where Sir Nanteos' head had lain.

'How . . .?' Cerys' voice was almost a whisper.

'I don't know,' Benfro replied, 'but it is not something of which I am ashamed.'

She stared at him with something like fear in her eyes, and then her expression changed. As if she had made up her mind about something, set the past behind her.

'When you killed Fflint with the fire I thought it merely a foul weapon. A cheat of the most base and cowardly kind. But you are right. This is not something to be ashamed of. It is the greatest of gifts. I hope that you will be able to do the same for all the dragons that have fallen this day. Come. I will show you the way to Myfanwy's house. Let us find this jewel you seek. Put an end to this madness.'

35

In the years and centuries before Gog and Magog began their petty bickering over who should win the hearts of Ammorgwm the Fair, the palace of Nantgrafanglach thronged with the great and good of dragon society. Here would ancient Palisander hold his summer court and the young half-sisters Earith and Myfanwy delight and tease their suitors in equal measure. It is said the parties could last for weeks and the palace swelled in size to accommodate all. For such was the hospitality of dragons in those days.

The passing of Palisander brought an end to those carefree times, and soon after the brothers began their squabbling. Appalled by the destruction of Claerwen, Gog cast the first of many spells that would hide Nantgrafanglach away. The parties ended, the dragons dispersed to all four corners of Gwlad, and the massive halls fell into disuse.

Now there are more men living in the vast palace than dragons, scuttling about the darkened corridors like mice. Great Gog, the Old One, keeps to his high tower and is rarely seen. Those few who have not succumbed to his brother's parting curse and abandoned the paths of wisdom and learning eke out their days in quiet contemplation or earnest but dull discussion. Not without reason is the Council of Nantgrafanglach known for its utter lack of mirth.

But the magics that conceal the palace also preserve it. The ballrooms and dining halls stand unchanged since those happier times. And if you should venture into them alone, some say you can hear the music still, echoing down the long centuries from the past.

Sir Nanteos teul Palisander,
The Forgotten Halls of Nantgrafanglach

Errol tried his best not to look at the destruction all around him. Dragons lay dead, their wings twisted, scales black with the soot of a hundred cuts from blades of fire. Their blood stained the marble floors, the going at times so sticky his feet almost popped out of his over-large boots. At other times the floor was so slippery he found himself grabbing for Martha's arm or leaning heavily on Nellore as they hurried down the long, wide corridor.

There were too many dead people too, most dressed in the uniform dark-grey cloth of the Nantgrafanglach servants, but here and there he saw the more gaudy colours he associated with Twin Kingdoms folk. How had they communicated, these people who spoke such different tongues? Had it been enough to unite them that they fought a common enemy, desperation making allies where previously the locals had cast Errol into their foul dungeon?

'Hold!'

Errol froze as Martha put her arm out to stop them. She was at the front, peering round a corner where the corridor intersected with one only marginally less grand.

'Hide!'

They pressed themselves back against the wall, and Errol sank down on to his haunches. He held his breath and drew his aura in around him, cutting himself off from the Grym even more than they had been; the lines still surging and twisting dangerously around them. Martha took hold of Nellore's hand and the two of them slowly faded from view. Glancing back, Errol saw Benfro and the green dragon, Cerys, a few tens of paces away. They did not seem to have heard Martha's warning, nor noticed their companions hiding. Benfro's head drooped, his one remaining eye staring at the floor by his feet. His exhaustion and sickness were evident even without seeing his aura. Cerys was doing her best for him, but Errol could see that it wasn't enough. Benfro needed the attention of a skilled healer or he would surely die. Dropping his hiding spell, he waved desperately at the pair of them, but they weren't watching.

'It's all right. They've gone down a different corridor.' Martha's words came from nowhere, and then she and Nellore melted back into view.

'How many?' he asked.

'Two dozen perhaps. They're headed for the main entrance, I think.' Martha frowned as she looked first one way and then the other. 'Poor Xando. We could have done with his knowledge of the palace now.'

'I worked here for weeks; I can find my way around.' Nellore pointed across the corridor to a smaller opening, more suited to men than dragons. 'That way leads to the laundries. From there we can cut through the kitchens and up to Myfanwy's house.'

'What of Benfro and Cerys? They can't follow us down there.'

'What of us?' The green dragon had caught up with them, Benfro leaning on her shoulder.

'We can't all stick together like this,' Martha said. It's too slow, and too easy for us to be spotted. It'll be quicker if you stay here and hide. Wait for us. We'll bring the jewel to you. Myfanwy too, if we can find her.'

'Myfanwy is not at her house,' Cerys said. 'She has gone to the Old One's tower. She and the elders of the council are trying to stop this storm in the Llinellau.'

'Then you must take Benfro to her. We'll fetch the jewel and meet you there.' Errol looked along the wide corridor towards the stone stairs that must lead up to the top of Gog's tower. This part of the palace was older than the room he had woken up in, less ornate.

'Is that wise? To split up?' Cerys asked.

'Errol is right,' Benfro said, pulling himself upright with an effort of will. 'I need Myfanwy's help. Either hers or Earith's, and I fear Earith is too far away. Without her strength I may not be able to breathe the Fflam Gwir again.'

'Then we must hurry,' Cerys said. 'I will take Benfro to the tower and Myfanwy. You three find this jewel that is so important and meet us there.'

'What about the warrior priests?' Errol asked.

'Pray to the moon that you don't meet any. I will do the same.'

Errol watched as Benfro and Cerys moved off slowly in the opposite direction, then he, Martha and Nellore hurried across the corridor to the small opening on the other side. True to the young woman's words, the passage led to stone stairs that spiralled down into a large room filled with vats of water, strange contraptions to squeeze clothing dry and heaps of dirty laundry. There were no people anywhere to be seen as the three of them hurried through to the far side. Errol wondered whether the warrior priests had come this way, but there was no sign of destruction, no dead bodies, no scorch marks where blades of fire had been used. The place was just deserted, as if everyone had heard the call to arms and run for the main corridors, leaving their tasks unfinished.

It was the same in the kitchens, except that food left unattended halfway through the preparation of the evening meal had attracted the cats of the palace. Dozens of them were up on the tables, sniffing, chewing and licking at anything they could find. A whole ox was roasting in a large fireplace, but left unturned it had charred and blackened, fat dribbled on to the burning wood of the fire. Errol's stomach grumbled at the smell of it cooking, but there was no time to waste.

'This way. It's not far.' Nellore led them down another, wider corridor that ended in the familiar wide low steps favoured by the dragons. They climbed slowly, listening for any sound that there might be warrior priests nearby, but the air was silent. As they reached the main floor of the house, Errol realized what it was that had been bothering him. A large window flooded the hall with light from the parkland outside, and he could see through it to the distant wall. The sky was still heavy with cloud, but it was white rather than the leaden purple-grey of recent times, and the wind had dropped so that inside it could not be heard at all.

'The storm. It's over.'

'The lines are calming too.' Martha held out her hand, palm up, and a tiny ball of light appeared to float in the air just above it. 'Myfanwy must have succeeded.'

'Succeeded? Succeeded in what?' Errol asked.

'In calming the Grym, silly. All the workings old Gog cast around his tower and this palace. The whole of Gwlad for that matter. They've been unravelling since Melyn cut off his head. Why else did you think the lines were all mixed up and that horrible storm was everywhere?'

He had no answer for that, but there were more pressing matters at hand. 'Which way to the room I was staying in?' Errol asked Nellore. The young woman was transfixed by the sight of the tiny glowing orb and didn't seem to hear him.

'Nellore!' Errol shouted this time, earning himself a withering look.

'This way. You were on the first floor. I should know. Spent enough time watching you sleep.' She set off up the stairs at speed, and Errol had to run to catch up. The first-floor landing was lit by another large window overlooking the parkland, the distant mountains showing their white peaks. He paused a moment, transfixed.

Martha stopped beside him, following his gaze. 'The Rim mountains. I recognize this view. We can't be all that far from Emmass Fawr.'

'How would you know the mountains around that awful place?'

Martha raised a surprised eyebrow. 'Really? I spent months looking for you, Errol. When Melyn and that horrible Captain Osgal took you at Hennas and Godric's wedding, I left Pwllpeiran too. Spent a while in the village outside Ruthin's arch, just hoping I might find a way in, but it was impossible. Only the families of those who have served the order are ever allowed in to work in the monastery, and it's protected by such powerful magics I couldn't hope to walk the lines into it without them knowing where to find you.'

'So you went to Llanwennog instead.'

'I hoped I might be able to do something to help. Princess Iolwen was always happy to have the company of people who spoke Saesneg, and I thought there was a chance you might appear there at some time. Melyn could only ever have had you in mind for a spy; if he'd known who you really were he would have had you killed on the spot.'

Who he really was. Errol had barely thought about his true parentage since it had been revealed to him. It hardly seemed important; as far as he was concerned Hennas was his mother, and his father had died before he was even born. He didn't want to contemplate the implications of his real mother being heir to the House of Balwen, his father King Ballah's son. He wanted no claim to any throne, much less two.

'All I ever wanted was to be left alone. To travel Gwlad and learn its secrets. Perhaps help people who were sick or injured.'

'I know. I's all I ever wanted too.' Martha reached out and took his hand in hers. It was warm and the Grym sparked between them as if chiding them for being apart so long. 'But now we need to help Benfro.'

Errol squeezed Martha's hand, reluctant to let it go. Then with a heavy sigh he turned away and followed the wide corridor to the one door that stood ajar. The familiar room lay beyond it, that enormous bed more easy to recognize as a dragon's sleeping platform now. The chest lay at its foot, the lid heaved open. Nellore's backside poked into the air, her feet almost off the ground as she searched inside.

'Have you got it?' Errol asked, approaching swiftly.

Nellore swung back on to her feet, her hair awry, face red from being upside down. She had something in her hand and for a moment Errol felt his heart leap at the thought that they had succeeded. But then he saw what she held. Not the dirty strip of cloth torn from his old travelling cloak, but a neat square of pure white linen, embroidered around the edges in gold thread. She grasped it in frustration rather than triumph, and as Errol hurried over to the chest, peered inside to see everything neat and ordered, so his heart sank.

'It's not here. I've searched, but it's not here.' Nellore held out the handkerchief.

Errol looked at it briefly then handed it to Martha. 'It's gone,' he said.

'I know.' Martha unfolded the cloth to reveal a pattern stitched into the middle. A dragon with his arms spread wide, surrounded by a circle that could only have been the moon. 'But I think I know where we can find it.'

'Where?' Errol and Nellore asked the question at the same time.

'At the top of the tower. With Myfanwy. She must have left this as a sign she had taken it, and as a way to get to her swiftly should we need to.'

'I don't understand,' Nellore said, but Errol did.

'The lines. They are not so confused now. We can use them.' He reached out to Nellore as Martha did the same. 'Here, take our hands and don't let go.' He took Martha's free hand, feeling the crumpled fabric of the handkerchief in it, that spark of the Grym between them. She smiled, the world faded, and then they were somewhere else.

'Leave them. They're all dead.'

Melyn surveyed the room with dispassionate eyes as his warrior priests began to file back out into the corridor. Thirty or more dragons lay dead, and a part of him rejoiced at their passing. This was what the Order of the High Ffrydd had been founded to do, after all: rid Gwlad of the dragon menace. Another, quieter part of him mourned their loss. These had been needless deaths, really. Was there any sense in exterminating all of their kind just because they were descendants of Gog? Were not all the dragons remaining from that bloodline?

'There is still Benfro, still Frecknock. A few others besides. The children of those who remained loyal to me.' The voice of Magog filled his head, his own thoughts not so much lost as dissolved into it. With each passing hour, each act of magic, each dragon slain, so they were becoming more and more inextricably linked.

'Osgal will kill Benfro, and Frecknock is hardly the

grandest specimen of dragonkind.' Melyn spoke the words aloud, attracting a fleeting glance from the nearest warrior priests.

'Osgal has already failed to kill Benfro, and I can do for Frecknock what I did for him. She will be a fine consort, and no dragon queen should have too much unbroken spirit. I shall be rid of my brother's foul taint and free to build our race anew. But first we must put an end to this storm, calm the Llinellau and bring back harmony to Gwlad.'

'And how shall we do that?'

'Go to the top of the tower, where you cut off my brother's head. His body lies there, his jewels. They must be burned in the Fflam Gwir, reckoned and set. Until then they will be constantly at war with me, and Gwlad will never rest.'

Melyn pictured the scene, the huge room he had come to in madness and anger. Benfro had been there, but he had escaped, leaping off the balcony with the green-eyed girl and some young lad. But that was after he had already killed Gog, wasn't it? The memories were fragmented, half his own, half those of the vengeful Magog. He struggled to keep hold of that small part of his mind that was still only him, that part where the Shepherd could not see.

'You. Captain!' Melyn shouted at the nearest officer, action far preferable to the uncomfortable duality of his thoughts.

'Sir.' The warrior priest snapped to attention.

'Do we have the palace secure?'

'As good as, sir. This building is so large it would take months to check everywhere, but this was the most heavily defended part of it, and these look to be the elder dragons. I do not think there are many more left.'

'Good. Leave me a troop. Take the rest of the men and begin sweeping the city.'

The captain saluted again, turned and started giving out orders. They were well trained, battle hardened. It took only moments for them to split into two groups, but as the captain's party marched away towards the palace entrance, Melyn could see how few in number they were compared to the thousands who had begun the attack. The dragons of Nantgrafanglach had not given up their city easily, and the limits of how much magic his men could use had cost them dear. It would take generations to build up their strength again.

'Follow me.' He set off down the corridor in the direction of the great tower, past the sprawled bodies of the dead. He didn't mourn them, but the presence of Candlehall men meant that Princess Iolwen and Prince Dafydd would be somewhere in the palace. Too much to hope that they might have been killed in the fighting. He needed to find them and their child. No one with a claim to the throne could be allowed to survive.

He let out a bark of laughter, startling the nearest warrior priests as they approached the spiral stairs at the base of the tower. What matter the petty arguments of the houses of Balwen and Ballah when Magog would rule over them all? But still, there would need to be a leader of men, someone the simple commoners could accept and understand. Beulah was that person, and he would brook no challenge to her authority.

'Be wary of the Grym here. We are approaching the

centre of the storm.' Melyn knew he didn't need to warn his men, the lines were twisted and fat, crimson where they should have been palest white. Much like in the forest of the Ffrydd when he had taken Corwen's jewels from their resting place, the magics that had built upon each other over thousands of years were unravelling now, loosening that pent-up energy back into the world. He only hoped that Gwlad could cope.

The stairs were wide and low. They were also imbued with magics that should have transported anyone invited there up to the top in just a couple of steps. Melyn recognized the same subtle arts as had constructed the Heol Anweledig. So close to the centre of the vortex, they were unreliable at best, fatal at worst. He guided his troop of warrior priests around them, diverting the unpredictable flows of energy as best he could as they climbed ever higher. Without the helping magics, it was a long, hard journey; by the time they reached the top, breathing heavily in the thin cold air, the line of men trailed back behind Melyn a couple of storeys.

He stepped out into a room at once familiar and unrecognizable. Snow had blown in through the missing windows, covering everything in a thick layer of white. Even now it flurried around, whipped up by the swirling wind. Given the storm raging beyond the broken windows, the whole room should have been scoured clean, but the ancient magics still offered some small protection from the gales. Even so, they were fading like everything else to do with the ancient, dead Gog. Soon they would fail entirely, the full force of the wind given free rein.

'Fetch my brother's head, my faithful servant. That is

all we need.' The voice of Magog urged him on, and Melyn pushed through knee-high snow towards the far side of the room. It was hard to make out details in the gloom, harder still to remember how the place had looked when last he had come here. Something had changed apart from the snow, and glancing around Melyn saw that the body of Enedoc the Black was gone. At the same time that tiny part of his mind that was still his own remembered the pile of ash where Gog's body had been, the fire of palest blue leaping from Benfro's mouth. He knew that flame. It had burned Osgal, left him with wounds that suppurated and would not heal. Melyn had encountered it before that too, when the young dragon had appeared in his aethereal form in the Neuadd. And there had been the ashes of the man killed in the Northlands, the one Frecknock claimed had been consumed by the Fflam Gwir. Benfro was a fire-breather. A throwback to the time when dragons had been no better than feral beasts. Only that made no sense. There were dragons who were no better than feral beasts, Caradoc for one, and yet even they did not stoop so low.

The oddness of the thought gave him pause. Why was fire-breathing such a hated, base ability? That was not him thinking, but Magog. Something of the act filled the dead dragon with shame, disgust, hatred. Or was it jealousy of an ability nature had denied him? Melyn pushed the idea deep into the recesses of his mind where thoughts of rebellion against his false god festered. That Magog had not yet reacted to them gave him some small hope that he might survive, somehow escape that influence yet with the mage's knowledge and skill intact.

Distracted, Melyn almost didn't notice the change in the air as several hidden forms shimmered into view. They sat, huddled in on themselves, arranged in a circle around the room. Seven dragons, unmoving. They had been there long enough for snow to settle on their shoulders and wings, their heads tucked close to their chests against the cold. Only now he saw them could he sense the power that flowed through them as they acted in harmony to soothe the disturbance that had threatened to break Gwlad entirely. He reached out for the Grym, ready to conjure his blade of fire and put an end to these beasts as they slept, but the Grym wasn't there. Casting his sight out, he could see the lines arching up the walls and delineating the edges of the room, but they were twisted away from the centre where he stood, cutting him off from the source of his power.

Cutting him off from Magog's influence.

She had known darkness before, but never something so total as the black that enveloped her now. Iolwen tried to breathe normally, but the total lack of anything made even something as natural as breathing hard. It was as if the absence of light was an absence of everything, even air. She could hear nothing, not even her husband, who should only have been an arm's reach away.

'Dafydd?'

Her voice sounded strange, as flat as if she stood in a open plain on a windless day. No echo greeted her, and neither did her husband.

'Dafydd? Where are you?' Iolwen inched one foot forward, feeling the floor through the sole of her boot.

She held up a hand and waved it slowly from side to side. Nothing.

'Dafydd?' The word stuck in her throat. She turned slowly, feeling for the door through which they had entered, but her hands met only air.

'Iol. Where are you?' The voice was so close, so loud, Iolwen almost fell over. She moved her head from side to side, straining her eyes for any movement.

'I am here, Dafydd. Why did you not answer me?'

A sensation at her side, and then Iolwen felt something brush her arm. Fingers walked down past her elbow to her hand, then gripped it tight. 'I'm sorry, Iol. It was so dark, I thought I would try to see the room in the aethereal. I have never been good at it.'

'And did you succeed?'

Dafydd didn't respond straight away, which answered Iolwen's question for her.

'I'm not sure. It was . . . confusing.'

'Let me try.' Iolwen gripped her husband's hand tight, calmed her breathing and slipped into the trance much as she had in the great chamber beneath the Neuadd. The room was still dark, but it was a darkness born of great size. There were features, walls, a ceiling impossibly high overhead, but they were so far distant it was all but impossible to make them out. At least she could see the floor nearby well enough to know there were no obstacles, but when she turned to see the door they had entered by, there was only a wall just as far away as all the others.

'I think we must have travelled through another of those tunnels like the one that brought me here from Candlehall.' Iolwen slid back into her body, feeling an uncomfortable sensation like submerging herself into a bath of black ink. The darkness was total, the empty silence swallowing her words as she spoke.

'Can we find the way back?'

'I don't know. I couldn't see it, and the lines . . .' Iolwen paused, letting the lines of the Grym swim into her vision. She had been suppressing them before; the twisting, pulsing chaos of them made her feel sick, as it did any with the sight and many who were unaware they had the skill. Now they appeared as she remembered them of old: ordered, mostly calm although every now and then a spasm twisted them out of shape. But it was nothing compared to the way they had been.

'I think Myfanwy must have done something to calm the storm.' She reached out, drew the power in to her and conjured a small ball of fire. The light from it was dazzling at first, her eyes accustomed to the total darkness. Blinking, she looked at Dafydd's face, soot-smeared and sweaty from their time in the chimney. His hair was a mess and his jacket would never clean up, but he looked more beautiful than anything she had ever seen before.

'You look a mess,' he said, embracing her in so fierce a hug that she had to lift her hand high to avoid burning him. As she did, so the light from the tiny flame rolled back the gloom to reveal a huge room. She would have said it was long and narrow, except that its width was still greater than any room at King Ballah's palace in Tynhelyg. Her light was too dim to see how long it was, the darkness swallowing it up before it reached any wall, but for all its vastness, it felt more like a corridor than a hall.

'Which way should we go?' Dafydd asked.

'I don't think it matters. This is not some alcove off the meeting hall. We are somewhere else entirely, if we are even still in Nantgrafanglach.' Iolwen set off towards the wall she judged to be nearest, one hand held aloft for light, the other pulling her husband along behind her. The closer they came to it, the more detail she could see. There were pictures and tapestries hanging at regular intervals, chairs of the kind favoured by dragons for any to sit and rest on their long journey from one end of the corridor to the other. Here and there were huge doors, all closed and with their handles set too high for her reach. Iolwen had noticed how many of the rooms in the palace had entrances more suited to her kind, presumably for the servants to come and go unnoticed. There were no such doors here; indeed the scale of the place was grand even by dragon standards, so that she began to wonder whether she and Dafydd had not shrunk somehow.

'I think we must be underground. In the oldest part of the palace,' she said as they finally reached the wall. Iolwen let go of Dafydd's hand to pat the surface. It felt slightly damp and warm.

'How so?'

'There are no windows and no draughts.' She walked over to the nearest door, bending down to peer through the narrow gap underneath. Only darkness lay beyond. Iolwen sniffed. 'And it smells of mould.'

Dafydd sniffed a couple of times too. 'Well, at least we are away from Melyn and his warrior priests. I only hope that Lady Anwen has made good her escape. I worry for our son.'

'As do I.' Iolwen swallowed hard, feeling the lump in

her throat. It had not been easy to part with Prince Iolo and the rest of their retinue before she and Dafydd had gone to speak to the council. They had never thought Melyn and his warrior priests would penetrate the palace so deeply, so fast. During their escape there had been no time to worry, and she had been avoiding thinking about them ever since, focusing instead on the task at hand. 'Merriel will take good care of them.'

Dafydd reached out, took Iolwen's hand again but said nothing. Together they walked down the seemingly endless corridor, always keeping the wall in sight. They passed huge portraits of ancient dragons, dark tapestries depicting hunting scenes, battles and other less easily recognized stories. Doors every hundred paces or so stood closed, giving off a solid permanence that suggested they had not been opened in many years. This whole place had not been visited in decades, maybe centuries.

It was difficult to gauge the passing of time down in the darkness with nothing but each other and Iolwen's conjured light for company. There was only the endless walking and counting the doors as they slowly came into view then slid into the darkness behind. The floor was shiny, some kind of polished marble that reflected the light and glinted in a thousand sparkles as if it were the still surface of a night-time pool reflecting the pale orb of the moon and the stars. For a while Iolwen was transfixed by the effect, which might have explained how she failed to notice the light coming towards them. Only Dafydd's insistent tug on her arm broke the stupor.

'Iolwen. Look.'

She tensed, expecting to be surrounded by warrior

priests, captured by Melyn and dragged off to the dungeons. Instead the light resolved itself into three people who appeared just as lost as they were. One of them, holding aloft a light almost identical to her own, Iolwen recognized at once. The young woman who had briefly befriended her at Tynhelyg, then disappeared as so many did who grew too close.

'Martha? Martha Tydfil?'

'Princess Iolwen. I had not expected to find you here.'

Iolwen looked at the young woman's companions. A girl of perhaps twelve years who carried herself in the sullen manner of one who cared nothing for rank and privilege. Iolwen's first impression was of someone she could probably like, especially if she was a friend of Martha. Someone who wouldn't stand on ceremony. The other was a young man whose features were strangely familiar. Clearly a Llanwennog, he looked thin, as if he had gone for many weeks without proper food; in the light of the two conjured flames his eyes were deep-set and shadowed. At her name he had looked up, then glanced across to Dafydd. Something in that movement triggered a memory.

'Errol? But how is this possible?'

'I could ask the same thing, Your Highness.' He sketched a bow so slight that some might have taken it as rudeness, but Iolwen could see that it was more exhaustion that stopped him from being polite. Then she remembered the truth of his parentage that Usel had told her.

'I do not think you need to bow to me, nephew.' She smiled. 'But what are you doing here? All of you? And where exactly is here anyway?'

'Not where we thought we were going,' Martha said.

'We were at Myfanwy's house, looking for something. It wasn't there, but this was.' She held up a crumpled white handkerchief trimmed in gold. 'I thought it would lead us to Myfanwy, but instead it has led us to you.'

'Myfanwy's house?' Iolwen's heart thumped in her chest. 'Did you see anyone there?'

'No. It was deserted.' Martha lowered her hand, the light glowing on her face picking out her fine features, her long black hair and piercing green eyes. 'And before you ask, we saw no bodies either. I do not think Melyn's men have been there.'

'Who are these people, Iol?' Dafydd eyed them suspiciously, and Iolwen could see him tensing, tugging at the lines as if readying himself to conjure his blade and strike.

'Friends, Dafydd. This is Martha, who came to me in Tynhelyg, and you must remember Errol?' She nodded at the young girl. 'You I do not know.'

'Nellore speaks only Draigiaith. She is of Gog's world,' Martha said in the language of dragons. Iolwen readied herself to speak the same, but the young woman interrupted her.

'I knowing some Errol's words. Yours not same.'

'What were you looking for at Myfanwy's?' Dafydd asked in his native tongue.

'A small red jewel, wrapped in a piece of stinking cloth,' Errol said. 'It was entrusted to me to look after, but I left it there not realizing I wouldn't be coming back.'

'A jewel?' Iolwen asked. Beside her Dafydd was patting down his coat, checking his pockets, a frown upon his face. 'Why would you need such a thing?'

'Because it is the only thing that can put an end to all

this madness. That much Myfanwy told me, though I don't begin to understand any of it. This is what you're looking for, I think.'

All eyes turned to Dafydd as he pulled his hand from his pocket and opened it. Resting in his palm was a scrap of dark brown cloth that gave off a faint odour of the privy. With delicate fingers, he unwrapped it to reveal a dull red rock no bigger than Iolwen's thumb. She reached out for it, but in a flash Martha's hand was around her wrist.

'It would be best you didn't touch it. No good will come from that.' She let go, and Iolwen pulled back her arm as if she had been burned.

'Bone and jewel. I never thought we'd have them both.' Errol pulled the bag he had been carrying over his head, opened it and reached inside. After a moment he came out with what looked like a flat piece of thick ceramic tile, the sort of thing Iolwen had seen laid on the floor of the bathing rooms in her apartments back at the palace in Tynhelyg. As he held it up, the jewel in Dafydd's palm began to glow the dull red of an iron taken from the blacksmith's forge too soon. 'Now all we need is the flame. All we need is Benfro.'

'So you are Inquisitor Melyn, harrower of dragons and Magog's favoured whipping boy. I must say I preferred the young lad Gog took under his wing. His potential was for greater good.'

Melyn turned at the voice, stepping sideways into the clear patch in the centre of the room. One of the motionless dragons had spoken, and now it raised its head slowly to stare at him. Not it, her. A part of him recognized her, unchanged in sixty years where he had aged a whole life.

'Myfanwy.'

'Oh, so you remember me. I should be flattered.' Slowly the dragon unfurled her straggly wings and stood up on arthritic legs. She had been old when Melyn was a boy, but whatever magics she and her companions had woven to calm the storm in the Grym, it had taken a toll. He could see it in her aura, sickly and pale as it stuck tight to her chipped scales and dry, leathery skin. He could kill her easily. All he needed to do was walk across the room to where the Grym twisted away, up and overhead.

Overhead.

Melyn looked up and saw the cage of gold hanging from its chains, its open end pointed straight at him. He felt something invisible grip him tight. A *click* and the cage was falling towards him, mouth wide like a whale engulfing a fish.

'You cannot catch me that easily.' He fought back against the force that held him, throwing himself to one side as the cage smashed into the floor, toppled over, its door bent out of shape. His tumble brought him close enough to the twisted lines to reach out and tap them for power. It rushed into him on a wave of Magog's fury. That these feeble creatures could hope to entrap him, even in a cage of gold. That they sought to remove him from the Grym when he was not its servant like the rest of them but its master.

The gloom turned crimson as his twin blades of fire burst into life. Melyn leaped to his feet with the agility of a man a third his age, arms swinging so swiftly that the lines of flaming energy blurred into sheets. He cut all the obstacles out of his way on his path towards Myfanwy. The consort of his hated brother.

'I will cut you all down and add your jewels to my collection.' He sprang forward the last few paces. For an instant he felt his wings snap open and catch the air, saw his talons extended ready to rip open that ancient, blind face.

'You are not Magog, little man.'

Melyn slammed into something unseen with such force it knocked the wind out of him and he fell to the floor. His blades sputtered and disappeared, the Grym sucked up by two more of the dragons surrounding him. Something forced its way into his thoughts as if he were no more skilled than a newly chosen novitiate. For a moment he understood what it must have been like for Errol when he had rifled through the boy's memories, discarding those of no use to him, changing those that would mould him into the perfect spy. Then his training kicked in and he closed down his mental barriers, pushed back against the dragon who had entered his mind so easily. Myfanwy rocked on her heels, her eyes widening in surprise, then narrowing just as swiftly.

'So you have some spirit, I see.' She stood up, ruffling her wings like a recently woken bird. 'It will do you no good. This is Gog's place. There is nowhere here for his brother.'

Melyn turned slowly on the spot, seeing the dragons for what they were. Ancient and powerful, true, but also blinkered. They had spent almost their entire lives within the confines of the walls that surrounded the palace buildings. Reading histories, learning the ways of the

Grym, having endless meaningless discourses on matters of no importance whatsoever to the rest of Gwlad beyond their tiny demesne. Over the uncounted centuries those of an adventurous or rebellious nature had left, gone to join the folds of dragons in the wild, slowly losing touch with their magic but gaining an enviable freedom in the process. Only these dusty old beasts remained, too fearful of life to live properly. Did they really pose any threat to him? To Magog? Of course they did. Their very existence was an affront.

'You are right, Lady Myfanwy.' As Melyn spoke, so he saw that the storm outside had abated, the wind died down until it whistled rather than howled. The lines were slowly shrinking back to their normal size as the turmoil in them eased away. These crusty old dragons had done the job he had come here to do, and if Gog's body was nowhere to be seen what did that matter now? 'I do not belong here, am not welcome here. So I shall take my leave of you.'

He turned his back on the aged dragon and walked towards the doorway and the top of the long spiral stairs. As he did so, he reached out to the Grym once more, pulling in the power easily. At the top step, his troop of warrior priests hammered blindly at nothing, as if there were a solid door between him and them. It was easy enough to see the magic that confounded them, cast by one of the dragons in the circle. He reached out and snapped the spell in two at the same time as he barked his command.

'Use your blades of fire. Kill them all.' And turning, he released all his accumulated rage in a ball of flame as hot as the sun, flung straight and true at the dragon Myfanwy.

36

The Fflam Gwir is most commonly associated with the sacred ceremony of reckoning. Properly conjured, the flame will consume all flesh, scale and bone, leaving only a fine white ash while it renders the jewels of the recently deceased clear white and set. Such indeed is the most important task for which the Fflam Gwir is used, but it has many other properties.

Applied to an infected wound, a small Fflam Gwir will sear away only that which is rotten, leaving fresh, clean flesh to heal. As it does this, so too will it aid the patient in their recovery. As a weapon, the Fflam Gwir will burn those who mean harm to one who has conjured it forth, leaving them with wounds that will not heal without the application of the subtle arts. It can melt iron even though it casts no heat beyond that metal, or it can strike down a foe while leaving friend untouched. More, it can give strength or take it, depending on the whim of the one who has conjured it. It can even be used to heal the body of the mage who has created it.

The Fflam Gwir is thus both a weapon and a medicine. The purest distillation of the power of Gwlad. The essence of the Grym.

The *Llyfr Draconius*

Chaos filled the room as a dozen and more warrior priests burst in through the doorway, fanning out into the open space to do their leader's bidding. Some stumbled on the steps, landing face down in the snow. Others conjured swift blades of fire, cutting paths through the debris of Melyn's first attack as they headed for the motionless dragons. The inquisitor leaped towards Myfanwy as the pent-up energy of his conjured fireball exploded in her face. He meant to press his advantage while the light and heat dazzled her, but she swept the fire aside as if it were nothing.

'You will not find me so easy to best, Melyn son of Arall.' She stepped forward, flowing into the Grym and reappearing behind him with a swiftness quite at odds with her age. Two warrior priests crumpled and fell dead as she twisted a hand in the air, pulling all the Grym out of them and their blades before she hurled it at Melyn. He ducked below the blast, feeling the heat scorch the air above him, singeing his hair. Glancing up, he was just in time to see the dragon disappear once more, but this time he was ready for her, tracking her along the lines, anticipating where she would reappear. His ball of fire exploded right in front of her, knocking her off her feet so that she crashed into the overturned writing desk.

'Not so clever now, Myfanwy Bach.' Where the name came from, Melyn wasn't sure. It was something Magog had called her, perhaps, or a taunt. It was not him speaking now, not him in control of his actions. He knew the feeling of the Shepherd's touch well, but this was something more intimate even than that. It felt better, more complete, as if this was how he was meant to be.

Risking a look towards the huge open windows, he saw his warrior priests harrying one of the other dragons. A great hulk of a beast, it was slow and old but its scales were thick, impervious to their blades of fire. Across the other side of the room, two younger dragons were fending off a concerted attack from half a dozen of his men. Melyn's blind eye painted a confusing pattern of aethereal and Grym over the mundane view, but there was something wrong with what he was seeing.

'Give yourself over completely, Melyn son of Arall. There is no need to fight any more.'

Magog's voice expanded through him, filling him with warmth and strength. Melyn had not known he was resisting, but as he relaxed, so his vision expanded, the confusion of the view melting away until it all made perfect sense.

There was only one living dragon here at the top of the tower. All the others were projections, the solid yet ghostly forms of long-dead long-reckoned jewels. A part of him knew that they lay in a hoard somewhere close by, lending their support to Myfanwy. Finish her, and they would dissolve away to nothing.

'Ignore the others. Concentrate on this one.' He barked the order, turning back to Myfanwy. She had recovered from her fall and was backing away towards the fireplace, cold and empty. The warrior priests formed a semicircle, trapping her, their blades of fire humming with power, ready for the kill. Her milk-white eyes flitted from side to side and she threw the occasional ball of fire, but she was clearly tiring. No longer able to just reach into a man and pluck the life out of him. No longer a threat.

A commotion behind him distracted Melyn's attention. Whirling, he saw movement at the top of the steps, the entrance through which the warrior priests had so recently swarmed. A small dragon, female, young, her scales deep green, stumbled across the threshold. Her appearance was quite striking, something Melyn had not really considered in a dragon before now. Her eyes widened in alarm and surprise as she saw him and his warrior priests, and she turned to hurry back through the doorway. Something blocked her way, another dragon who tripped as if exhausted beyond the ability to stand, tripping into the tower-top room.

Had a part of his mind not been expecting him, Melyn would not have recognized the battered and beaten beast. His wings hung from a thin frame, scales discoloured and scratched, missing in far too many places. Someone had taken a chunk off the end off his tail at some point, and the inquisitor couldn't help but find it amusing they had both lost an eye.

'Well, well. If it isn't Sir Benfro.' Melyn smiled, the scales on his face crinkling at the unfamiliar expression. He turned back to his warrior priests, still holding Myfanwy at bay, meaning to order them in for the kill, but the old dragon just stared past him, nodded once.

'They're here. It is time,' she said, and disappeared.

Long before he had recovered himself, before he had even been able to struggle up from the floor, Benfro knew that there was something very wrong. His missing eye showed him the room with dreadful clarity: at least a dozen warrior priests encircled Myfanwy, who had backed into the unlit fireplace. The aethereal forms of several ancient dragons hovered around the edge of the room, but they were dead things, jewel projections like Corwen. For all their magnificence, they were powerless against the trained minds of the warrior priests. And worse still, standing in the middle of the room beside the remains of the golden cage, was a thing that was half Inquisitor Melyn, half Magog.

Then he heard Myfanwy's voice in his head, so quiet as to be almost a whisper. 'It is nearly done, Benfro. Stay strong until I return.'

He looked up at her, saw her nod just once, then she flowed away into the Grym and was gone.

'Always a coward, that one.' Melyn-Magog spun on his heel to face Benfro once more. 'I will get to her in due course. But now what are we going to do with you?'

Benfro struggled to his feet, ignoring the pain that lanced through his side. He could feel the fire growing inside him, fuelled by hatred and anger. He took a step forward, then froze as the creature that had once been the inquisitor raised one hand. With his missing eye Benfro could see the cord as it looped from his forehead into the Grym. Where before it had been palest red, now it pulsed with a dark crimson hue, each surge timed to the beat of his hearts. Melyn's own aura, twisted into a crude dragon shape and shot through with ugly slashes of colour, gripped the cord tight.

'You are mine, dragon. You have been since before you were hatched. Everything you have done in your sorry life has been by my design. Do not think that you can change that now.'

Benfro pushed back against what felt like a fist

crushing him. He concentrated on his own aura, pale and weak, stretching it out to the knot tied around the rose cord. But it was already there, already choking off that foul influence as best he could manage. Still Magog-Melyn's mind pushed into his own thoughts, digging out an image here, an emotion there, as if he were a thief going through someone else's belongings, throwing aside any that didn't interest or excite him. Benfro tried to push the inquisitor away, but he was so tired.

'You will not have him!' Relief came so suddenly, Benfro surged forward, almost falling over again. Beside him Cerys stood tall and defiant, her own aura spread wide as a shield between the two of them and the inquisitor. Benfro thought he might have had a chance to gather his remaining strength for an attack, but Melyn-Magog simply shrugged his shoulders. There was a fluttering sensation in the Grym, as if a bat had flown past him in the night, then Cerys let out a little squeak of surprise and crumpled to the floor.

'What . . . what have you done to her?' Benfro knelt beside the collapsed form, reached out for her, realizing too late that he had turned his back on his attacker.

'Don't worry. She's just sleeping. A prize like her's too good to waste. And besides, I will need a consort when I am reborn.'

Benfro felt the touch like a knife into his flesh. He twisted to see Melyn-Magog standing beside him. He was so small, so frail, Benfro could have swiped a taloned claw and cut off his head, yet he was unable to move.

'Don't fight it, Sir Benfro. This is what you were always supposed to be.'

The voice Benfro heard was Melyn's, that harsh, nasal

tone that he remembered all too well from that fateful day outside the cottage, when Morgwm the Green had met her end. The voice in his head was Magog's, proud and arrogant, the great dragon who had taken him under his wing, promised to teach him all of the subtle arts. They overlapped each other perfectly, fitted together so well they might have been the same being.

'Now you begin to understand how long I have been working towards this end.' The inquisitor held up both hands, weaving them around an invisible ball hanging in the air at head height. The Grym surged and spun, and then a dark red jewel, the size of a hen's egg, appeared in the middle of it. A moment later it was joined by another, and another. Something fell through the air, smacking to the floor with a wet slap. Benfro stared incredulous at the massive fish as it flopped around blindly, gasping in the air. More soon joined it, brought through the Llinellau from wherever they had swum to when he had freed them from Magog's retreat at the top of Mount Arnahi.

Sharp clinks on the stone floor were rings, amulets and other trinkets, their jewels joining the growing mass of red that swirled between the inquisitor's hands. Benfro could do nothing but watch, mesmerized by the light flickering from the tumbling stones, the heat of the twisted Grym that radiated from them. The collected jewels of Magog, son of the Summer Moon, the greatest dragon mage ever to have lived. Or at least the most depraved.

'Depraved, Sir Benfro?' Melyn-Magog put heavy emphasis on the title, sneering at Benfro's powerlessness. 'I rather think inspired. What greater magic can there be?

Had I not preserved myself in my retreat, spread myself throughout Gwlad, then I would truly have died all those millennia ago. My jewels would have lain unfound, unreckoned, reclaimed by the Grym. My knowledge would have been lost for all time.'

'I think that would have been for the best,' Benfro said through gritted teeth. Melyn-Magog held the slowly revolving ball of jewels in his aura, suspended just above one hand now, and with the other he reached out towards Benfro's head.

It was like an explosion behind his eyes. Benfro couldn't breathe, could scarcely see as memories of his earliest kitlinghood burst across his vision and then disappeared. He thought he was going to pass out, heard a distant scream, felt it pouring from his own mouth as if the two were entirely separate things. Then with a horrible popping sound, the pain ended.

Light-headed as if he had drunk deeply of the wine from that endless goblet at Magog's table, Benfro looked up to see a single fat red jewel hovering above Melyn-Magog's empty hand. His own jewel, plucked from his head. His essence stolen.

'Do you see how this goes now?' The thing that had once been the inquisitor sneered and reached out towards Benfro's head again. He moved away as best he could, as if mere distance could stop the desecration of his mind.

'You could have had it a lot easier, if only you'd not fought the inevitable. I would have merged with you through that connection forged when you rescued my one remaining true jewel. But you fought, struggled against me, ran to my brother's hated realm. Now the link is tainted; I cannot use it. It's no matter. Better to purge you entirely, then I will take your mindless body and make it mine.'

The pain cut through Benfro's head again as Melyn-Magog searched for another jewel deep within his brain. He struggled against it, unsure how to protect himself, unsure if it was even possible. He cast out with his missing eye, searching the room for anything that might help, but the power was all his enemy's now, the Grym his to command entirely. The warrior priests watched on impassively; Cerys lay motionless on the floor; even the spirits of the long-dead dragons who had helped Myfanwy to calm the storm that had begun at Gog's death were fading away now, their horrified expressions only making Benfro's helplessness more acute.

And then something glimmered in the Grym behind Melyn-Magog. Benfro's hearts leaped as he saw a handful of figures shimmering into existence. Myfanwy towered over Errol, Martha and Nellore. Two others stood beside them, people he didn't recognize, but that was no matter. It was what Errol held that was important. Magog-Melyn might have summoned all his removed jewels to him, but one jewel, one true jewel, remained. Now it sat in Errol's hand atop a piece of bone so old it was almost rock, and Benfro knew it for what it truly was. Hope fluttered in his hearts as Benfro felt Cerys grasp his hand, heard Myfanwy's voice over the arrogant sneer of his foe.

'Now, Benfro.'

He took in a deep breath as Melyn-Magog turned, realizing at that moment that something was wrong.

'How—?' But Benfro didn't let him finish. With all the

force he could muster, he breathed out the pale blue Fflam Gwir, on and on until there was nothing left in his lungs and he slumped unconscious to the floor.

Errol froze as the fire leaped over them all like it was alive. Melyn twisted as the fire enveloped him completely, choking off his voice. Living flesh and scale it left untouched, warming weary muscles, soothing away aches and pains, but the slowly rotating ball began to fade from dark blood to rose, to palest pink and finally to white. The air boiled, writhing and roiling into angry shapes that distorted the view, forming what looked almost like a dragon in the throes of agony.

Out of nowhere, a wind blew up so violent it carried the broken furniture across the room, whipping it out of the vast open windows and into the void. Screams cut short were the last words of warrior priests caught unawares by the gale and blasted into oblivion. But, enveloped by the flame, Errol felt nothing of it. Pressure built in his head, squeezing his brain until he thought his eyeballs must surely pop out. He tried to move, but the flame held him tight even as it protected him from the raging storm around him.

As the last of the fire drifted away to nothing, the twisting ball that had been floating at Melyn-Magog's head lost its shape, breaking apart into dozens of fat, clear jewels that clattered to the stone floor like hail. With the last of them, the pressure popped away, the wind died to nothing. The being that had been Melyn slumped slowly to his knees, arms hanging loose as he swayed gently from side to side. A thin dribble of drool leaked from the corner of his open mouth, and his one remaining eye stared unseeing at nothing, as if a light had gone off inside his head.

Errol let out a long slow breath, only then realizing that he had been holding it in. The bone fragment that had been in his hand was gone, replaced by a fine dusting of ash on his fingers that drifted off in the breeze. Outside, the clouds had parted, pale blue sky shimmering with the distant rising sun. All around he could hear the sounds of people and dragons coming to their collective senses.

Then the air hummed behind him, and Errol felt the pull on the Grym as a half-dozen warrior priests conjured blades of fire. He wheeled to see them spreading out as they emerged from the fireplace where they had sheltered from the storm that had cleared their comrades and everything else from the room. He was sluggish after the reckoning, and the first attacker was upon him so quickly he had no time to defend himself. With a sickening sense of inevitability, he knew he was going to die.

But the moment never came. The warrior priest stopped mid-swing, his blade sputtering out to nothing as a leathery, taloned hand wrapped around his neck.

'Your battle is lost, little man. It is time to stop now.' Myfanwy squeezed harder, then let the man go. He slumped to the floor, knees striking the flagstones. Errol saw his comrades falter, their blades disappear. They looked to Melyn for leadership, but he merely knelt in the middle of the cluster of fallen jewels, mindless as the empty husks in the almshouses at Emmass Fawr. One by one they dropped to their knees, bowed their heads in surrender. Would that the hundreds still sacking the city below were so easily turned.

'What happened to him?' Errol asked as Myfanwy approached, peering cautiously at the kneeling white-haired old man. She reached out a finger and gently lifted his chin. Melyn's head tilted up, but his one remaining eye was staring at nothing. When she took her finger away, his head stayed at the angle she had left it.

'He gave himself to Magog. To his precious Shepherd.' She passed a hand through the air around Melyn's head, back and forth as if examining him without actually touching his flesh. 'He has begun to turn into a dragon, it seems. When Benfro reckoned Magog's jewels, there was one forming deep inside his brain. I've never seen anything like it before, but it is clear now, not living. The man you knew is dead.'

Errol's sigh of relief was short-lived. Beyond what had been the inquisitor, Benfro lay unmoving, his head flat against the floor, neck outstretched where he had collapsed. Beside him the young female dragon was stirring now, shaking herself awake and drawing in so much energy from the Grym that Errol felt a chill in the air.

'Careful now, Cerys. The Llinellau are much more powerful here than at the Twmp.'

'It is not for me, Myfanwy. Benfro needs our help.' She laid a hand on the unconscious dragon's shoulder, murmuring soft words in Draigiaith under her breath. After a moment's pause, Myfanwy went and stood beside her, adding her own magic to the healing. Then Martha nudged past Errol without a word. In moments she too was by Benfro's side. The three of them joined hands,

Martha looking very small beside the other two, and together their rhythmic chanting filled the room. No one moved, no one dared move as the most potent of magics surged around them. It went on for a long time, the shadows retreating down the walls as the sun rose higher in the morning sky, and slowly, inch by inch, they brought Benfro back from the brink of death.

The inquisitor was still kneeling motionless when Benfro finally let out a choking gasp, then spasmed. Everyone jumped at the noise, even the warrior priests flinched though they had said nothing all the while, but Melyn simply carried on gazing into nothing, his head still at that awkward angle.

'He'll live, but for how long I cannot say. There is a splinter lodged dangerously close to his left heart. I am not sure even I can remove it without killing him.' Myfanwy turned away from Benfro as she spoke, surveyed the room and the kneeling warrior priests. 'You men. Leave. Go back to your stolen monastery and never darken my door again.' Her words were backed with such a powerful compulsion that Errol had to fight to stop himself from obeying them too. The warrior priests stood as one, then filed out of the room, heads bowed. Only Melyn remained, motionless and mindless.

37

Nothing is more important to a dragon in death than that their body be burned in the Fflam Gwir, the true flame. Without this ritual, the jewels that are the core of their being will remain unreckoned and they will not become one with the Grym. But to reckon a dragon's jewels requires both Fflam Gwir and mortal remains, so what of those poor unfortunates who fall prey to accident far from home? What of the jewels collected by men, unreckoned and raw, the bodies that carried them left to rot to dirt?

Theirs is the most terrible of fates, for without bone or scale the Fflam Gwir cannot work its magic. A dragon's jewels left undisturbed in some distant corner of Gwlad will slowly leach away into the Grym until all trace of their existence is gone, and this is the preferred fate. For if the jewels are disturbed, then they will latch themselves on to whatever living thing is close by, be it dragon or man or beast, and seek to live again through whatever host they can.

In the masterworks of the greatest mages there are hints and suggestions of a way an unreckoned jewel might be set pure with Fflam Gwir alone, but none admit to knowledge of the method. Even the

Llyfr Draconius, that ultimate distillation of all
dragon knowledge, is silent on the matter. It can be
done, the mages say. But none will tell us how.

Corwen teul Maddau,
On the Application of the Subtle Arts

The first thing Benfro noticed was the warmth. Sunlight
played across his scales, soothing his battered wings and
warming his aching muscles. He could have just lain
there, fallen asleep and slept for a thousand years, but
something buzzed away at the edge of his hearing,
demanding his attention. With a weary sigh, he focused
on the noise, recognizing who was speaking.

'Dragon fall from nowhere. Benfro not well?'

Something landed on his head, and when he opened
his eye it was to the view of an upside-down red furry
face, big white teeth and long quivering whiskers. A frown
of concern wrinkled the squirrel's face.

'Malkin?' Benfro struggled to remember where he had
been moments before. How he could be here, now. It
didn't really matter in the end. The squirrel's presence
could only mean one thing. He pushed himself wearily
upright, not quite trusting himself to stand, and looked
around to see where he was. Ancient trees formed the
edge of a dark forest not far off, but he sat in the soft grass
and wild flowers of a peaceful meadow that was somehow
familiar. This was where he had woken after his first
encounter with the mother tree, a patch of grassland in
the midst of the great forest of the Ffrydd. Not far off
there would be a river full of fat stupid salmon ripe for the

catching. The thought of them made his stomach rumble; it was too long since he had eaten, and he had breathed so much fire.

The memories clattered into place, each one a weight on his shoulders driving him back down on to the ground. How had he come to be here? Why?

'I brought you here, Benfro. To thank you for breaking the spell that cut me in two.'

Benfro turned slowly at the voice. He knew who spoke and was expecting to see a strange, pale creature. Or perhaps Ammorgwm the Fair. In this incarnation the mother tree was neither, and both. Her form shifted constantly, shimmering in the sunshine like a heat haze. Aware he was staring, Benfro dropped his gaze, but he couldn't help himself from thinking that she looked unwell.

'I am healing.' The mother tree settled into the form of a dragon not unlike Benfro's mother, then knelt beside him. 'It hasn't been easy though. For a while I thought the strain might break me. It was a risk worth taking though.'

Benfro looked up into dragon eyes. 'Risk?'

'Gog and Magog caused so much damage with their warring, and then they caused even more with their infernal magics. The Grym was stretched and twisted to their ends for so long, there was a chance it might never recover. Fortunately for all of us there are still great mages in Gwlad who understand the balance needed. Earith and Myfanwy, Merriel and the girl Martha too. Others have played their part, and now I can hope that the Grym will once more flow unimpeded.'

The mother tree fell silent as a gentle breeze toyed with the grass, swayed the red poppy flowers and blue speedwell. Benfro would have been content just to sit there with her for all eternity, but he knew there was a reason she had brought him here.

'It's not over though, is it?' he said.

The mother tree shook her head. 'I am sorry, Benfro. You have given so much already. But there is still a disturbance in the Grym. Gog and Magog are gone, their jewels finally reckoned. They cannot hurt me any more. But the one who taught them still lurks out in the darkness. His malign influence still spreads through the Llinellau like poison.'

'But I got the bone and the jewel. I breathed the Fflam Gwir. I reckoned his jewels.'

'Magog's jewels, yes. But there are others still unreckoned, and hiding within them is the one who began this all.'

Benfro saw them then, thousands upon thousands, locked away in cells like the jewels in Magog's repository at Cenobus. Only those had been clear and pure; these were red and dangerous. Still reaching out to any who would hear them, still threatening to twist the Grym so that they might live again.

'But what can I do? Their bodies are long since gone to dust. Surely the true flame will have no effect on them.'

The mother tree sighed, and the air in the meadow grew colder as clouds slid across the face of the sun. She looked at him with sad eyes, and Benfro understood then as he always had, really.

'There is a way.'

'Who holds the key to the chamber? Where is it now?'

Beulah burst into the chamberlain's office, startling the

handful of black-cloaked clerks of the Candle who were working away at their ledgers. Newly appointed Seneschal Ioan appeared from the far doorway, which led through to a more secluded office.

'Your Majesty. This is most unexpected. How may I be of service?'

'The key to the chamber beneath the Neuadd. Who has it?'

Ioan frowned, then bowed his head. 'I do not know, ma'am. Your sister did not entrust it to my keeping when she left, and neither was it in the door. I merely closed it. I do not know if it is locked. Surely the magics of the House of Balwen will protect it, locked or no.'

'We shall see. Come with me.' Beulah turned and left the room, meeting Clun coming the other way. He walked slowly, still weak as he recovered from his injuries, and she had outpaced him in her impatience to find the seneschal. Now she was beginning to regret having elevated Clerk of the Candle Ioan to the position. The man was as dry as the parchments he was so clearly in love with, and slow to react to her order. She left them both behind in her haste to get to the chamber, but stopped before she descended the narrow spiral stairs, uncertain whether she dared go in alone. Far from being protected by ancient magics, she could see the door stood ajar as if the treasures within were now so sullied that no one would even dream of stealing them.

'Your Majesty, please. You must not rush off like that. The palace is no longer the safe place it once was. There could be allies of your sister anywhere.' Seneschal Ioan was clearly too self-important to run, but he had developed a method of walking that covered the ground almost as quickly while preserving his dignity, at least in his eyes. He bowed again as he reached the queen, Clun not far behind and followed by Captain Celtin and a dozen warrior priests.

'And I suppose you are all going to want to go down there with me. For my own safety.'

'The door is open, my lady.' Clun took a moment to catch his breath. 'Who knows who, or what, may have entered?'

'Very well then. Follow but touch nothing.'

Beulah led the way down the narrow stairs and into the chamber beneath. It was changed from her last visit, although at first she couldn't tell how. The carved stone columns were still draped with the coverings her sister had used to prevent the people of Candlehall from seeing their greatest treasure. As she stepped into the space between the columns and the cavern wall, she could see the shape of the rock as it arched overhead towards the centre, where the huge pillar supported the mass of the Neuadd and the Obsidian Throne above. And that was when she realized what was different.

'My lady, the jewels have been moved.' Clun stepped forward to the nearest shelf, pulling at the curtain that had been draped over it. Nearby the alcoves still held their collections of blood-red jewels, but towards the centre they were all empty.

'Only the white ones. Are they stolen?' Beulah started forward, but Clun caught her by the arm and stopped her.

'Not stolen, no.' He turned back to Celtin. 'Captain, fetch the dragon Frecknock. And place a guard on the entrance upstairs.'

Beulah shrugged off her husband's hold, annoyed that he had the nerve to touch her in front of the common people. Something called to her from the centre of the room at the base of the pillar. The light there was different, brighter and pale where she was used to a hellish red tint whenever she visited this chamber.

'What do you mean by bringing the dragon down here?'

'My lady, something has changed. Not just here but throughout Gwlad. It involves dragons, and Frecknock knows more about her kind than any save perhaps the inquisitor himself. We should be cautious. The lure of the jewels is far more intoxicating now than it was before.'

Once he had said it, Beulah could sense exactly what Clun meant. Before, the jewels had been a source of power, but undirected. She had been able to tap them, use them to augment her own magical skills. Now it was as if someone else was in the chamber with them. Someone or something. And it was lonely, needy, desperate even. It called to her in a voice she couldn't understand, but which was insistent all the same. Like the incessant wailing of an infant. Unguarded, she had been completely open to its influence. Now she closed down her mind as tightly as she knew how.

'We should check the hidden tunnels.' Clun set off around the edge of the cavern, one arm held aloft just inches from the rock surface. Drawn by the pale glow at the centre, Beulah had to force herself to follow him, Seneschal Ioan just behind her like an obedient dog. At the point where the first tunnel entrance should have appeared, nothing happened. It was the same for the second and third, but the fourth hazed into existence as she touched the wall. Beulah stared into the dark tunnel beyond, sniffing the air. She could smell nothing but damp earth and chill.

'This is not as it should be.'

She looked over to where Clun stood by the fifth and final entrance. It lay open, and by the way his blond hair drifted about his head a good breeze was passing through from the other side.

'How is it still open? Surely only the touch of royal blood can reveal these portals.' Seneschal Ioan stared open-mouthed at the tunnel entrance as Beulah joined her husband.

'Something more powerful than the blood of kings is at work here,' Clun said.

'It is the hoard, sire. Can you not hear them?'

Beulah turned swiftly to see Frecknock emerge from the doorway at the bottom of the spiral steps. She looked around the cavern like a mouse scanning the sky for predators, timid and careful. Beulah hated her more than anything, but she couldn't deny the dragon had more knowledge than any of them. If only Melyn would return, but then Melyn was changed.

'The hoard?' Clun looked towards Frecknock with his cloudy eyes, head tilted questioningly. Then he turned towards the centre of the chamber and the thick pillar rising to the ceiling. 'Yes. Of course.'

'What is it, my love?' Beulah followed his gaze. There were no drapes over the stone columns on this side of the chamber, and she could see down the nearest aisle to the base of the pillar at the centre. Except that where she would have expected black polished stone to merge seamlessly with the cavern floor, now there was a heap of glittering white jewels piled high around the column.

'How can this be?' She started towards the pile, but once more Clun stopped her.

'Do not go too close, my lady. Such a concentration of jewels is not something to be approached lightly. There is good reason why they were all kept apart.'

'Good reason for men, perhaps, but it was an abomination for dragons. A hell. This is how they should be.' Frecknock fell silent, and Beulah fancied she could hear whispered conversations in Draigiaith fluttering through the air like nighttime moths.

'It was a man called Dafydd. A prince, by all accounts.' Frecknock paused again. 'He came through here not more than a couple of days ago. They opened the portal so that he could be with his wife at Nantgrafanglach.'

'They?' Beulah asked, although she had a feeling she knew to whom the dragon was referring. Frecknock opened her mouth to answer, but before she could speak, Clun let out a sharp cry of pain. Whirling, Beulah watched as he pulled out the amulet from inside his robes, its chain still hanging around his neck. An artfully wrought silver disc etched with the markings of the full moon, it was set in the centre with a single amethyst and imbued with deep magics accessible only to those of royal lineage. As he held it up with trembling fingers it shimmered in the light from the jewels, but then disappeared. Clun held up his hands, an expression of horror spreading across his face. The ruby set into his wedding ring, King Balwen's ring, flared brightest red, and Beulah felt the heat of it wash over her face. She closed her eyes for a moment, and when she opened them it too was gone.

Clun let out a low grunt of pain, ever stoical though the burns must have been agony. 'I don't . . .' he started to say, then stiffened as if someone had slid a blade into his heart.

'My love? What is the matter? What ails you?' Beulah rushed to his side, catching him as he slumped to the ground. 'Dragon. Help me!' she shouted over her shoulder, then turned when Frecknock did not immediately come to her aid. The dragon was a good distance off now, walking towards the pile of jewels as if in a trance. No help when it was most needed.

Clun began to tremble, the convulsions growing ever more violent as Beulah struggled to keep a grip on him. 'Hold his legs before he breaks them again,' she snapped at Seneschal Ioan, who was standing like the useless idiot he was, wringing his hands. Soon he would start flapping them about and running round in circles like a headless chicken.

'Pull yourself together, man.' Beulah sent a compulsion with her words, meaning to calm the seneschal enough for him to function, but the Grym surged as she tapped it, feeding far more power into the hapless man than he could possibly control. With a stifled yelp, he too slumped to the floor. With no one to catch him, his head bounced off the stone with an ugly crack. It didn't matter; he was dead before he hit the ground.

Beulah held Clun close to her breast, squeezing him tight as she tried to quell the fits passing through him in waves. Glancing across the chamber, she saw Captain

Celtin emerge from the doorway, backed by a couple of warrior priests. They hurried towards her, and it occurred to Beulah that they should have been with the dragon, Frecknock. What had kept them? Or had she travelled to the chamber along the lines, the way Melyn had told her was possible?

'About time, Captain. Take his legs, hold him down lest he do himself more damage.'

Unlike the useless, dead seneschal, Celtin was a trained warrior priest, battle-hardened and competent. He set about his task swiftly, but even so, Clun thrashed and convulsed with far greater strength than he had shown earlier. Beulah tried to hold his head still, looking about for something to wedge between his teeth lest he bit off his own tongue. She couldn't bear the thought of never hearing him speak again. As her fingers brushed his cheek, a spark of Grym shot between them. She had a momentary glimpse of something in his mind. Fire and pain and utter terror, the dying moments of a god. And then he fell limp.

'Is he . . .?'

'Breathing still, ma'am.' Captain Celtin, bent low, sliding his hands underneath the prone form and lifting Clun up with considerable difficulty. 'We must take him to Archimandrite Cassters. Get him away from here, for starters.' He looked around the chamber nervously.

Beulah nodded, was about to speak when a low, sobbing groan interrupted her train of thought. Turning, she saw Frecknock on her knees, head in her hands. The dragon looked like she had been gut-punched and was retching on the warm stone floor. Then she slumped sideways, tucking her tail around her as she looked straight at the queen with eyes of deepest purple.

'He is gone. The blood oath is broken.'

Beulah felt a chill in her heart. 'He? You mean Melyn? What do you mean gone?'

'I do not know, Your Majesty. He was there, like he is always there, in my mind. And then he was gone. The blood oath I swore connects us, but now that bond is severed. I cannot sense him at all.'

'Is he dead?'

'I . . . I do not know.' Frecknock bowed her head, surrendering herself to her fate.

'Then you are no longer of use.' Beulah reached out into the Grym, feeling the power that surged through the chamber into the central pillar. With a simple thought she conjured a blade of fire, clean and white. It drove the shadows from the empty stone alcoves and turned the remaining red jewels black as she advanced on the supine dragon. Frecknock did not move, seeming to accept that her time had come. Rage consumed Beulah. The thought that Melyn might have died before she could confront him about his affair with Queen Ellyn, that both her beloved Clun and this hated creature had felt his passing where she had sensed nothing at all, fuelled her anger far more than Frecknock's pathetic nature. The dragon had always been weak, despicable. All her kind were alike, two-faced and thieving. Had they not stolen magic from men? She would hunt them down, kill them all.

Her strike was true. It should have taken Frecknock's head off at the shoulders, added her meagre jewels to the collection, but at the last possible moment the dragon twisted her head to one side, raised a swift hand and caught hold of Beulah's fiery blade.

'We did not steal your magic. It was given to you by one of our kind. That was a mistake, I see that clearly now.'

Frecknock's eyes were huge circles of dark purple pricked with tiny flecks that twinkled as they reflected the light of Beulah's blade. She showed no distress at the fiery touch, indeed seemed to be absorbing the Grym and sending it somewhere. Beulah brought the lines to her vision, saw how they pulsed with the power of Gwlad. Always down here they had been ordered, converging on the central pillar before surging up to the Obsidian Throne high above. Now they snaked around the chamber, hugging the stone close as they spread like a net over all the individual alcoves, all the red, unreckoned jewels. The power that Beulah was tapping for her blade came from them, but Frecknock was channelling it away from the pillar and instead into the pile of white, reckoned jewels. Misty tendrils rose from it like smoke, twirling in the heavy air until they began to take on identifiable shapes.

They spun and flew, formed patterns that mesmerized the queen, even as they grew ever larger, came ever closer. And then they enveloped her completely, the spirits of a thousand long-dead dragons. Beulah scarcely noticed her blade of fire sputtering out. She was entranced by the beauty of the shimmering shapes, enthralled by the voices that called her, beckoned her to join them. They had such stories to tell, such knowledge they would happily share.

Her anger and hatred evaporated as quickly as it had flared. She had been so wrong, Beulah could see that now.

For the briefest of moments she hesitated. There were things to be done. Clun needed help, and Princess Ellyn would need feeding soon too. But she could always come back to them; this was more important.

A ghostly hand formed in front of her, as small as her own but with long, thin fingers that tapered into sharp talons. It felt perfectly natural to reach out, take it in her own. Beulah shifted easily into her aethereal form and, leaving her body behind, stepped into the dragon hoard.

He knew the moment he closed his eyes he was dream-walking. Benfro had never truly understood what it was that he did, how he travelled the aethereal in his sleep as if it were no more difficult than climbing a tree, but right now that didn't matter. Here, in this plane, he could fly with ease. Here there was no pain, no tiny splinter of wood working its way towards his heart. Here he was master of the air, master of everything.

That it was night was no more surprising than anything else. It had been dawn when he had breathed the Fflam Gwir over Melyn, but he had lost weeks to the mother tree before. He soared through the black sky, scanning the ground far below in search of something familiar. Twisting, he took in the stars peeking out through occasional gaps in the cloud. One or two looked familiar, but there were too few for him to get his bearings.

The clouds parted and a fat full moon cast its silver light across the land. The familiar shapes of Candlehall and the Neuadd rose in the darkness. He hardened his aura against the onslaught he knew was coming, then dived towards the massive hall. In seconds he was upon it and then sliding through the stone walls into the empty space beyond.

Almost empty. The Obsidian Throne rose from its dais right in the centre. It glowed with the Grym, a strange light that illuminated nothing but itself. And the minuscule figure that sat upon its seat.

'So, dragon. You are here, finally. I was beginning to think you might have died.'

For all her tiny size, Queen Beulah's voice carried like a tempest, battering at Benfro as he hovered in the air before the throne. The Neuadd itself had been damaged almost as badly as the rest of the city. Its windows were gone, the massive doors fallen from their hinges. Cracks split the great pillars that supported the roof, and much of its ornately carved decoration lay shattered on the marble floor. It was the stench that almost knocked him out of the dreamwalk though. Benfro had never noticed any smells before, but now he could scarce breathe for the noxious fumes wafting up from the piles of ordure around the throne. He had smelled something similar in the Anghofied, but this was far worse.

'Don't want to get your precious feet dirty?' the queen taunted him from her throne. 'Perhaps you'd better come here then.' Benfro felt the pull of her magic as if she had wrapped an invisible hand around him. He was dragged forward with such force that his wings twisted back behind his head and he tumbled from the air. He cracked his head on the cold stone of the dais upon which the throne sat, but at least up here he was away from the worst of the mess. He pulled himself to his feet, hardening his aura against Beulah. She waved one hand and he felt the tug of it again, but this time he was able to resist. He stood tall and slowly folded his wings across his back.

'Melyn is dead. The warrior priests are defeated.'

The queen shrugged. 'And what, you expect me to surrender? I don't think so.' A wave of pure aggression rolled from the throne, engulfing Benfro with such swiftness it took his breath away. He recoiled, one foot slipping off the first step of the dais, his tail nudging something vile that stirred up yet more stench. Clenching his fists, he pushed back at the terror, sweeping it aside as he felt the power surge up in his stomach. He took in a deep breath even as he realized his aethereal form had no real need to do so. The magical flame exploded from him, taking on the form of an attacking dragon, wings wide, talons extended. For a moment Queen Beulah looked worried, but then she raised a hand, fingers outstretched, palm towards the fiery beast, which burst apart on the invisible bubble surrounding her and the throne, dissipating into the darkness. And as it went so she began to cackle.

'It will take more than your precious Fflam Gwir to defeat me, Benfro of the Borrowed Wings. Yes, I know all about you and your base magics. I understand more than even Melyn knew about your precious subtle arts.' Beulah shifted in her seat, seeming to grow in size until she filled it completely. The Llinellau glowed bright as the sun as she pulled in the power from all around her. So much Grym should have burned her away to nothing, but instead she absorbed it all, growing larger and larger until the great throne could no longer contain her essence.

The fear swept over him again, stronger still. It held Benfro in an impossible grip as the massive figure of the queen lurched to its feet. She towered over him, head reaching into the vaulted ceiling of the Neuadd as she stretched an impossibly vast hand towards him. Benfro could only watch, frozen by the sight, his thoughts overwhelmed by the sudden shift in circumstances, the dread stench and the corruption of the Grym.

'Do you understand now, little dragon? This hall was built on the jewels of the greatest mages ever to have flown the skies of Gwlad. It is not bound by the Llinellau; it binds *them* to *me*. Melyn was a fool, Magog too. They had such small dreams. But I . . . I will not *rule* Gwlad. I will *be* Gwlad.'

Queen Beulah's form was shifting now, morphing and bulging. Her face began to elongate; massive feet thrust forth great talons that gouged the stone floor. Spectral wings sprouted from her back, a thick, scaly tail from her rear. Her shoulders hunched and with a great crash that knocked masonry from the roof, she slammed down on to all fours. Still the queen, she was also a dragon so vast Benfro was barely as big as her head, and as she opened her mouth he could see nothing but darkness, a void more terrible even than the Anghofied beneath Nantgrafanglach.

'She is not real, Benfro. This is not real.'

The words were little more than a whisper deep inside his head, but Benfro recognized the voice as his mother's. It brought a flicker of hope, damped down his terror just enough for him to spring back and into the air as Beulah's giant fist crashed through the space where he had been standing.

'Still fighting, little dragon? You have spirit, but it will do you no good. You are mine. You were always mine.'

And now the voice was less Queen Beulah, more

something ancient and sinister. It spoke Draigiaith with cadences that reminded Benfro of the old tales Sir Frynwy would recount after all the villagers had feasted well. The first tongue, from the time of fair Arhelion and great Rasalene. This was the language of bards, of Palisander.

'I will never stop fighting. Not until this great wrong you have done is put right.' Benfro swooped to one side as the dragon queen swiped at him with a hand the size of a house. He felt the pull on his aethereal form, knew then that only his dreamwalking protected him from the full force of this attack. His body was far away, sleeping, watched over by Malkin and the mother tree. He was safe as long as they were safe. But to end this fight would require something more substantial.

Bringing his wings together with all the force his aethereal self could muster, Benfro climbed high into the darkness that was the ceiling of the Neuadd. The vast spectral creature that was part Beulah, part something much more ancient and malign, reared up, swinging round in an attempt to swat him like a fly. He dodged this way and that, some sixth sense helping him to predict where the next blow would be aimed. No, not some sixth sense; it was something far more focused than that. He felt the massed memories of a thousand dragons and more come to his aid. He knew what they were, and the sacrifice they made so that he might succeed. He swept up into the highest point of the Neuadd, far above the great black throne, then folded his wings and dived. At the same time he reached out across Gwlad, searching for his true body, and with a snap that almost broke him in two merged with it. Not back in the Mother Tree's clearing, but there in the great hall.

With his body came the pain, the splinter working its way towards his heart, the aches and bruises and a hundred unhealed wounds. Far from overwhelming him, they gave him focus as he plummeted towards the throne. And now he had to take a deep breath, build the fire in his belly. The dragon that had been Beulah had no presence in the mundane. Benfro still saw its vastness with his missing eye, but the physical presence was a twisted wreck of a woman, seated upon a dragon's throne. Benfro was too close, falling too fast. There was nothing he could do to stop himself, and neither did he want to.

'How is it—' The creature's words echoed in his mind as he opened his mouth and let loose the flame once more.

This time there was no stopping it. Benfro watched as the Fflam Gwir spread over the empty throne and the dais upon which it stood, dissolving the man-made blocks to reveal the true obsidian beneath. He let out another great roar, and more fire attacked the ancient stone, cracking and weakening it, reducing it to so much black chalk. And still Benfro fell, gaining speed as he hurtled towards the ground.

He tensed for the impact, expecting hard stone to smash his battered body into pieces. Instinctively, he hardened his aura the instant before impact, and as he hit it, the throne burst apart, chunks flying in all directions. The marble cracked beneath him like an earthquake, and Benfro crashed on through. It was as if his body were rock and the world around it mere flesh and bone. The ground split away from him like water in a pool. Like diving from the top of a high rock into a deep river and swimming down, down, down to dead remains far below.

38

False god on his throne of black
Puppet master in the shadows
Weaver of spells, weaver of fates
Would kill the world so he might live

The Prophecies of Mad Goronwy

Benfro burst through the cavern roof in a hailstorm of rock, shattering the pillar that had supported the massive throne above. It exploded into tiny fragments, shooting out in all directions and clattering off the walls. All the air was driven from his lungs and the wound in his side tore open as he tried to spread his wings to slow his fall. For a moment everything went dark, such was the agony. Then the pain eased as if it had never been there, replaced by a feeling of warmth like his mother's embrace.

Wings wide, Benfro circled the area directly beneath the demolished pillar, searching for a spot to land before his strength left him. He had expected the chamber to be empty save for the collected jewels of generations of dragons, but there were people down here, spilling out of an open tunnel mouth at the edge of the cavern. He snapped his wings together, narrowly missing the nearby stone columns, and saw the hellish red glow from the countless alcoves cut in the stone. Some had been dislodged from their cells by the collapsing roof, scattered over the floor like discarded toys. To land on any of them was to invite disaster. He had been a slave to the rose cord that had linked him to Magog for too long. That was something Benfro did not want to have to go through again.

He turned as sharply as ever he had done at the circus. It wasn't enough. He was still falling too fast, and there was only one place he could aim for. If he hit the stone floor, he would surely be killed, so Benfro crashed into the clear white jewels piled up against the stump of the pillar. They broke his fall, even as the touch of so many memories swamped him. They clamoured for his attention, demanded his experiences while thrusting their own upon him. Winded by the impact, he struggled to keep control of his thoughts as he rolled away from the hoard, scattering jewels hither and yon, white mingling with red in uncomfortable intimacy.

Bursting from the pile, at once gasping for breath and oddly light-headed, the first thing Benfro saw was the queen. She stood motionless just a few paces away from him, and at first he thought she was preparing for an attack. But that couldn't be right. She had been above, in the Neuadd, on the Obsidian Throne. He had breathed fire and destroyed her utterly.

Then he understood. That had been the aethereal, and the figure who stood before him was entirely mundane. Without a thought, his missing eye painted the view for him, the Llinellau pulsing red into the carved alcoves, white into the hoard, bleeding into pink where they mixed. All around him ancient magics were unravelling, twisting the aethereal and making the very air hum with energy. But the queen was a blank slate. She had no discernible aura, her aethereal self departed and destroyed. Like Melyn, she was mindless.

It was hard to walk, so heavy were his legs, and Benfro approached the queen with caution. He waved a hand in front of her face, then extended one sharp talon and prodded her forehead. A single bead of dark red blood welled from the cut, but Beulah did not move.

'She is not there.'

Benfro whirled round too swiftly, his legs giving way beneath him so that he slumped on to his tail. A dark figure emerged from the shadows between two fat stone pillars, and as his head cleared, so Benfro recognized her.

'Frecknock?'

She was smaller than he remembered. Or was it that he had spent so much time in the company of large dragons and had grown so big himself that she seemed a mere kitling in comparison? Her scales were dull grey, and she looked thin. Only her eyes were the same, darkest black with flecks of purple glittering within. She wore a leather bag slung over one shoulder, and Benfro's missing eye could see the power it held.

'I always said you would be trouble, squirt.' She walked up to him slowly, brushing past the unmoving form of the queen, then embraced him in a hug that was as awkward as it was surprising. 'But you killed Melyn, and Queen Beulah is lost to the Grym. We are safe, Benfro. We are free.'

She stepped back again, looking him up and down with that same critical eye he remembered so well. Benfro wanted to hate her; it was her fault that Melyn had come to the village in the first place. But try as he might, he couldn't blame her. She was as much a victim of Magog's scheming as any of them, and she had been through just as many trials as he had to end up at this point.

He realized then why she carried the bag with her, why it glowed in the aethereal. 'The *Llyfr Draconius*. You have it, don't you?'

'It is the greatest treasure of our kind.' Frecknock's hand went to the strap over her shoulder and pulled the bag close to her. Benfro opened his mouth to speak, but a commotion from the side of the chamber distracted them both. Two dragons had appeared at the tunnel entrance now, accompanied by a group of people some of whom Benfro recognized. Errol broke away from them and hurried over towards him, but Cerys swiftly overtook him.

'How is it you're here already?' She looked him up and down, then noticed Frecknock. 'And who is this kitling?'

'I am no kitling.' Frecknock raised herself up to her full height but was still half the size of the other dragon. 'I am Frecknock the Grey, last of the line of Albarn the Bard.'

'Never heard of him,' Cerys said, turning back to Benfro. 'Your wound. It has opened up again. If you don't stop crashing into things you'll die.'

Benfro looked down at his side for the first time since he had landed in the pile of jewels. His scales were slick with blood, and drops spattered the dusty floor at his feet. The warmth that he had felt as the pain lessened now seemed more like a numbness, spreading slowly through him. He tried to stand up but found that his legs no longer wanted to work.

'Let me rest a while. I'll be fine.'

'Oh, but you won't be fine, Benfro Bach. Far from it, indeed.'

Benfro's head snapped up at the voice. Cerys and Frecknock turned as one, all eyes on Queen Beulah. She still stood, but there was a change in her stance now, her shoulders squared and hands clenched into tight fists. The cut in her forehead had dribbled blood down the side of her nose, pooling on her upper lip like a ruby bead, but it was the crimson glow in her eyes that held them all.

'Did you think me lost when you broke my throne, little dragon?' Beulah stepped forward, raising one arm and thrusting Frecknock aside as if she was no more than air. She stumbled on a piece of fallen rock and fell heavily. Cerys put herself between the queen and Benfro, but with another contemptuous wave she was tossed aside. Benfro could only watch helplessly as she smashed into a stone pillar and slumped unconscious to the floor. He was too tired, too weak to fight.

'Oh, I am not Beulah. I am just using this vessel for now. I am not even Magog. This place was my greatest working long before those meddlesome brothers came along, and the people of Gwlad were little better than savages when I ruled its skies.'

'Who are you? What are you?' Benfro struggled to stand but his legs were too weak, the numbness spreading through him more swiftly now. Frecknock lay close by, shaking her head as she fought to regain her senses. Her leather bag lay beside her in the rubble, its strap snapped.

'Who am I? Has it been so long that you have all

forgotten me? I am the greatest mage ever to have lived. I built this chamber and the Neuadd above it to contain my workings of the subtle art so that even in death my knowledge would live on. I am Palisander. So great I need no other name.'

'You're the mad remnant of a long-dead fool. Begone!'

Benfro ducked as a ball of Grym flew over his head and exploded in the air above the queen. The spectral dragon flinched, Beulah's legs mimicking its actions, as Myfanwy surged past him, hand already conjuring another attack. Her speed and ferocity had clearly taken Palisander by surprise, but he rallied quickly enough. Catching the second ball of Grym, he flung it back at the old dragon. For a moment she was engulfed in it, and Benfro thought she was dead, but his aethereal sight showed how she flitted along the Llinellau at the last minute. He searched for the source of the dead dragon's power, but it was everywhere, as if every unreckoned jewel contained a part of him.

The numbness was spreading fast now. Benfro could no longer feel his legs or tail, and his arms were as heavy as his head was light. The blood leached from the wound in his side even as the splinter inched its way closer and closer to his heart. He cast out with his thoughts, trying to communicate with Frecknock where she lay. Myfanwy's fight was a useful distraction, but he knew that she couldn't hope to win, not against a foe spread so far into the Grym. There was only one way to stop Palisander, to stop everything. About that much the Mother Tree had been right.

Summoning the last of his failing strength, Benfro

reached out his hand for Frecknock's bag. As he stretched, so he could feel the traitorous splinter working its way into the edge of his heart. Every movement was agony, only hastening the end.

'Frecknock. The book. Give it to me.' Benfro whispered the words, but the grey dragon didn't respond. Then a human hand grabbed the bag, passing it to him. Errol was by his side, using his bulk to hide from the queen.

'You look like you need this,' he said, despite everything, a grin on his face.

'This and a jewel.' Benfro pulled out the book and unwrapped it from the cloth wound around it. 'Any jewel, as long as it's red.'

Errol nodded, ducked away and returned a moment later with a dull crimson stone in his unprotected hand. Benfro opened the book at a random page, and Errol dropped the gem on to it.

'Now go, Errol. Quickly.'

'But what are you going to do?'

'What needs to be done. There is no other way. Now go.'

Errol looked like he was going to argue the point, but then stopped himself. He nodded once, laid a hand gently on Benfro's shoulder. A spark of the Grym flowed between them, dulling the pain and lending Benfro some much-needed strength.

'Be careful, my friend,' he said and backed away.

Benfro took one last look around the chamber, saw Frecknock slowly coming round, Cerys still unconscious but not badly injured. Myfanwy still battled the aethereal Palisander, but he could see that she was tiring, too old and worn down by the events at Nantgrafanglach. Bringing so many through the Llinellau to the mouth of the Heol Anweledig must have taken a great deal of effort too. As he watched, she stumbled, fell to the ground and didn't get back up.

'Just you and me then, Benfro Bach.' The tiny figure of the queen turned back to face him, surrounded by the aura of a vast dragon. It leaned in close, head as big as Benfro's entire body. Mouth wide and fangs dripping, it made to swallow him whole, to possess him and be reborn. Magog had tried that and failed. Benfro wasn't going to let anyone else have a chance.

'Just you and me.' He felt the splinter pierce his heart, but the pain was no more than a prick from a rose's thorn. With the last of his strength he lifted up the *Llyfr Draconius*, focused on the single red gem in the middle of the open pages and breathed out the last of his Fflam Gwir.

Errol stumbled away through the debris of the fallen ceiling as pale blue flame erupted from Benfro's mouth and nose. It flowed like storm water, engulfing the book and the dark red jewel sitting in it. Over Benfro's arms, his shoulders, flowing down his body like a cloak, it finally covered his head. Then it washed over the floor, leaping up Queen Beulah's legs and over her body. It spread over the cavern with such speed he could not hope to outrun it.

'Do not panic, Errol Ramsbottom. This is the Fflam Gwir, the true flame. It will not harm you.' Errol knew the voice, although he could not have said from where. It reminded him of his earliest dreams, reassuring and peaceful. He stopped running and let the pale flame engulf him.

He was wrapped in a warm embrace, soothing away his aches and pains, restoring his strength so that he could concentrate on the events unfolding across the cavern. With his aethereal sight, he saw the great spectral dragon anchored to Queen Beulah's mindless body and the endless collections of red jewels. But they were not red any more, the colour leaching out of them as the flame grew, leaping along the lines and bursting into each stone alcove. The queen was fading too, not burning like Osgal, but dissolving into the Grym as if her physical essence was feeding the magic as it unfolded.

Then he saw that Benfro too was turning pale. The flame danced over him with unchecked joy, devouring scales, wasting away bruised flesh and cracked bone. And as his battered and broken mundane form began to fall apart, so his aethereal self rose strong and clear.

'Isn't he magnificent? To reckon all these jewels when their bodies are so long gone. Every unreckoned jewel, all across Gwlad. He's saving them all.' Errol felt a hand take his and looked round to see Martha standing beside him. Her mundane form was more beautiful than anything he had ever known, but her aethereal form, bathed in the Fflam Gwir, took his breath away. A human shape clad in the aura of a great dragon. Looking down at his own aura, Errol could see that it matched.

'How is this possible?'

'The Fflam Gwir reveals your true nature, Errol. Do you not think it strange that we are both so skilled at the subtle arts?' Martha smiled and spread the wings of her aura wide.

'But what of Benfro? The flame is killing him.'

'No. It is saving him. His injuries were too severe. He was dying, and now he is one with the Grym. And his parting gift will put an end to the madness that has plagued Gwlad all these thousands of years. See?' Martha raised her free hand in the direction of the huge aethereal dragon that was Palisander. It fought against the flames that stripped it of its essence, flailed about the great chamber and smashed into the columns with their alcoves. One by one they shattered, spilling the jewels on to the floor. And where before they had been crimson, now they were purest white.

Shrinking, the aethereal dragon stumbled on, smashing his greatest and most terrible creation. Errol feared for the ceiling. Already the central pillar was gone and the Obsidian Throne with it. Would they all be crushed if the last of the columns gave way?

'We have to leave. Before the whole place collapses.' Errol shouted over the screeching of the aethereal dragon. He squeezed Martha's hand tight, pulling her towards the tunnel entrance. As he did, another column exploded, fragments flying through the air in all directions. He ducked instinctively, but the stone faded to nothing before it could reach them.

'We have to help Myfanwy,' Martha said. Errol looked over to where the old dragon lay against the cavern wall, then back to where Benfro grew ever larger in his aethereal form. Frecknock lay close by, and Cerys was not far from them. All were bathed in the Fflam Gwir, but unlike Benfro they grew ever more substantial. They were stirring too, as they regained consciousness.

'What can we do? I can't drag something that size.'

Even as he said it, Errol headed towards the centre of the chamber. He ducked as the aethereal Palisander swooped past him, feeling the scrape of ghostly talons against his aura. A nearby column exploded and an ugly crack appeared in the ceiling, spearing upwards towards the hole through to the Neuadd. Was it his imagination, or could he see stars high up above?

He reached Myfanwy first, crouching beside her as she shook her head and struggled to her feet. When she looked at him it was with eyes clear as a spring stream, and her face was fuller too, the many scars gone, missing scales regrown.

'You have to get out of here. The chamber's going to fall in and crush us all!'

Myfanwy's eyes widened as she stared up. Palisander threw himself against wall and ceiling like a caged beast in fear of its life. Errol could sense his desperation and terror. He closed his mind to it as Myfanwy hauled herself to her feet.

'I will take care of the dragons, Errol. Go now. We shall meet again.' She was in front of him, and then with a blink she was standing beside Cerys, helping her up. Another blink and the two of them were hauling Frecknock to her feet, but as they did so Errol could see she was not the tiny dragon he had seen before. Now she stood as tall as Cerys, and her wings drooped low to the ground around her. He had one last glimpse of the three of them, huddled together, and then they were gone.

A last screech from the aethereal form of Palisander turned into a despairing wail. There weren't many pillars left now, the ground scattered with clear white jewels freed from their imprisonment. The air grew thick with dragons bursting into the aether like smoke from dead leaves thrown on an autumn fire. They danced and flew and embraced, their joy in stark contrast to the beast who still careened around the chamber, cracking walls, ceiling and pillars as it smashed into them.

And there, at the centre of it all, Benfro knelt in the midst of his own flame. He was almost transparent now, scarcely any form left to him at all, but he towered over his mundane remains. He stared straight at Errol, smiled and nodded.

'Farewell, my friend,' he said as the last of the pale blue flame flickered to nothing. And as it went, so Benfro disappeared.

The aethereal dragon reared up over the spot where Benfro had been and where now a pile of white jewels lay all on their own. The creature swelled to fill the whole cavern, stretching itself until it was almost invisible. Then with a bang that Errol would hear for the rest of his days, it exploded. The ground shook, cracks spearing through the rock as the remains of the Obsidian Throne and the rest of the Neuadd began to topple into the cavern. Errol couldn't move, stuck between the urge to escape and the need to rescue Benfro's jewels. He could hardly even accept that they were Benfro's jewels. His friend was dead, burned up in his own fire. He had sacrificed himself to save everyone else. How could that be fair?

Errol was too stunned to react, even as the ancient palace fell about him. Then a hand slipped once more into his, warm and familiar.

'It's time we left,' Martha said. And they did.

Epilogue – Rebirth

The Mother Tree's bargain is a simple thing. You give her a story, and she gives you a choice. For generations of dragons of Gwlad, that choice has been to hide away unnoticed by men or to take the long road in search of another world. We who chose to hide grew smaller, more timid, lost the ability to fly. Those who took the long road ran the risk of death at the hands of men, their unreckoned jewels collected and stored in vast underground chambers.

These were not always the only choices, and neither was the mother tree ever obliged to fulfil her bargain. And yet she has ever been a friend to dragons, however capricious or foolhardy they might be. Hers is the power to grant wishes, even if you do not know what it is you are wishing for. For she is Gwlad and she is everything.

Sir Frynwy,
Tales of the Ffrydd

Iolwen stood at the top of the Street of Kings, where once the inner gates had opened on to the parade ground. Now she looked at a deep pit already beginning to fill with muddy water. There was nothing left of the Neuadd, and hardly anything of the old palace. All the buildings at the top of the hill had disappeared into the hole made by the collapse of the chamber beneath.

'We will have to rebuild the city, but the palace and the Neuadd are gone. This place is not for our kind any more. If ever it truly was.'

'A dragon hoard lies deep beneath this hill now. A true hoard, not the abomination begun by Palisander and continued by Magog. You are wise to leave it well alone. Perhaps in time it will become a place of learning, but for now we should leave the departed to themselves.'

Beside Iolwen the dragon Myfanwy shifted her weight and stared across the pit. They had seen a lot of her, and of Cerys and Frecknock, in the month that had passed since Queen Beulah's end. Theirs was an uneasy truce that Iolwen hoped would grow into a lasting peace as the armies once loyal to the queen were dispersed. She had thought Lord Beylin might have been a problem, that he might have made a play for power, but he had proved to be more pragmatic. There was money to be made in the rebuilding of the Twin Kingdoms – the Three Kingdoms as people were now calling them – and Beylin loved nothing so much as money.

'How fares Nantgrafanglach?' Iolwen asked.

Myfanwy turned away from the pit, and the two of them headed back down the road towards the city gates. All around them the sounds of building echoed in the morning, hammers and saws and the shouts of busy men. 'We mourn our dead and repair the damage done. I have sent young Cerys south to Pallestre with my sis— Lady Earith. We will need her help and wise counsel in the coming months and years, I suspect.'

They walked in silence for a while. Iolwen was not comfortable with the authority thrust upon her, for all she had agreed to accompany Dafydd on his mad quest to have their child born on Twin Kingdoms soil. So much had changed since then, it was hard to believe she was the same person sometimes. Dafydd too was different. The loss of his entire family had left him deeply depressed, and while she had no doubt he would recover in time, she sometimes found herself annoyed at his selfishness. They had been her family too, after all.

'There is the matter of Emmass Fawr and the warrior priests.' Myfanwy brought the subject up out of nowhere, and Iolwen could tell that this was the real reason for her visit. The old dragon came often, working the magics that would eventually create a new Heol Anweledig between their two cities.

'Sad to say, but we need the Order of the High Ffrydd more than ever. Most of your kind are content to leave us alone, but there are some who cleave to the old ways. Too many dragons out there look upon this newly rejoined Gwlad as one great hunting ground. I need warriors skilled in the subtle arts, if not to kill them then at least to persuade them to limit where they hunt. I have chosen a new inquisitor. It won't be easy, but I think he can begin to change their ways.'

'Fair,' Myfanwy conceded with a nod of her huge head. 'But who is this person who can earn the trust of Melyn's men?'

'You should meet him. He'll be your near neighbour up in the mountains, after all.' Iolwen and Myfanwy had reached the entrance to the large merchant's house that had been commandeered as a makeshift palace. Two guards, one Llanwennog, the other a Candlehall man, snapped to attention and then pulled open the doors. One of the main reasons Iolwen had chosen this house over the many others lying empty was that it was big enough to accommodate a dragon of Myfanwy's size. The larger beasts still hanging around the ruins of Candlehall had to content themselves with what remained of the parade ground and the churned plain where Beulah's seige army had camped.

'Your Majesty, I received your summons.'

The man who had been waiting for her return sprang to attention as Iolwen stepped into the reception hall. He bowed to both her and Myfanwy, clearly not concerned by the dragon. He was young but carried himself like a much older man, and though he seemed to see without difficulty, his eyes were clouded white. He wore the plain brown robes of a warrior priest, and hung around his shoulders was a sling of soft white cotton in which an infant slept, snuggled contentedly against his breast. It was at once incongruous and the most natural of things.

'Inquisitor Clun, may I introduce Myfanwy the Bold, Mistress of Nantgrafanglach.' Iolwen watched as the young man bowed once more, supporting the child with one hand. Then he addressed the dragon in perfect Draigiaith.

'My lady, I am honoured. I would like to apologize for the actions of my predecessor. I hope that our two houses can coexist harmoniously.'

'Would I be right in thinking Inquisitor Clun was your sister's consort?' Myfanwy asked Iolwen.

'Beulah was the mother of my child, Ellyn.' Clun struggled to lift the sling over his head without waking the sleeping infant. Cradling her in his arms, he offered her to Myfanwy to see.

'Just Ellyn? Not Princess Ellyn?'

Clun shook his head. 'She has no need of titles, no claim on any throne. And besides, my lady Beulah was not of Balwen's direct line, for all that matters any more.'

'How do you mean, not of Balwen's line? Was she not Iolwen's sister?' Myfanwy peered at the child, which was not much bigger than her hand.

'Half-sister,' Iolwen said. 'We shared a mother, but her father was Melyn, not King Diseverin'

Myfanwy seemed to consider this for a while, her focus distant as Clun hung the sling and his child back around his neck. 'And do you not thirst for revenge for your dead wife?' she asked eventually.

'I mourn her, Lady Myfanwy. I miss her. I loved her and always will. But I am not so blind that I cannot see how she was at fault. Nor the way she was manipulated from such an early age. Gwlad is changed. She is whole again, and we share her with dragons once more. There is far more important work to do, building peace where we can, defending ourselves where we cannot. I do not think I have the stomach for revenge. Or the time.' Clun bowed again to both Iolwen and Myfanwy. 'And now if you will permit me, I must return to Emmass Fawr. There is much work to do.'

He nodded once, then walked away, head bowed slightly as he muttered soft words to his daughter. Only when he was out of sight and earshot did Myfanwy finally speak.

'He has a dragon's temperament, to mourn his soul-mate so deeply and yet not let it destroy him.'

'We all bear our losses as best we can, Myfanwy. So much death and destruction, all for nothing.'

A comfortable silence spread between the two of them for a moment, Iolwen's thoughts vague as she watched Clun leave. Princess Ellyn had something of her grandmother about her, but she was also undeniably Beulah's daughter.

'You miss her, don't you? Your sister.'

Iolwen looked round into the old face of the dragon. 'Is it that obvious?'

'When you have lived as long as I have lived, you notice things like that.'

'I just wish it could have been different. Sister or half-sister, it doesn't really matter. I do not miss the Beulah who plotted and schemed, who stole the throne and slaughtered all of Prince Dafydd's family, but I miss the girl I remember when I was six. Perhaps if I'd been able to—'

'Talk to her? Do you really think she would have listened?' Myfanwy shook her head slowly. 'She was too much her father's creation, I fear. If you must, then mourn the loss of your childhood friend, not the woman she became. Be a friend to her daughter as you are to Inquisitor Clun.'

Iolwen considered the old dragon's words. There was much wisdom in them, hard though it was to accept.

'And where is Frecknock?' Myfanwy made a show of looking around the room as if expecting the dragon to be hiding in the corner. 'I had hoped to see her. We have much to discuss, she and I.'

'I cannot fathom her ways. She has grown, did you

know? She's almost your size now. I caught her stretching her wings in the courtyard the other day, thought she might even try to fly.'

'It is her birthright, and now the curse on her line is lifted it's only natural her true form should begin to emerge. I would have thought she would come to Nantgrafanglach, or go down to Pallestre to be with her own kind though. And yet she seems to prefer to stay here.'

'She tends to Melyn even though he is a mindless imbecile now. And physically he is half dragon, growing more so by the day. He is tiny though, in comparison to most of you.'

Myfanwy chuckled. 'The great Magog lives on. That was ever his aim. I suspect if he were aware he would not be so pleased at how it all turned out.' She paused a moment in thought, then added, 'And is there news of Errol and Martha?'

Iolwen sighed. It was something that weighed heavy on her heart that of all who had escaped the collapsing chamber, those two had not been in the palace or made it through the Heol Anweledig to Nantgrafanglach. Yet she could not bring herself to believe they had perished.

'They are gone. I know not where, but I don't believe they are dead. I don't think Errol wanted anything to do with his birthright, so I hope they are somewhere far away, together and happy.'

Myfanwy closed her eyes briefly, let her head droop as if falling asleep. 'Together and happy. Aye, they deserve that.'

Hot sun beat down from a midday sky, baking the rocks and radiating heat from the ground so that the air shimmered with the force of it. Errol paused in his climb, wiping the sweat from his eyes, and looked up at the distant ruin.

'We could walk the lines, you know?' Just ahead of him, Martha clambered over rocks that looked suspiciously like they might once have been a huge column. All around the ground was strewn with blocks, all the same sand-coloured stone. Some were chipped and scored, others almost undamaged and quite clearly carved.

'I've never been to Cenobus. Have you?' Errol took a drink from the water bottle he had filled at a stream that morning. It was already more than half empty; he'd need to ration himself.

'Don't need to have been there to get there.' Martha stuck her tongue out at him, disappeared into the lines and reappeared a hundred paces higher up the hill. Errol sighed and trudged on.

It was well into the afternoon before they reached the massive arched entrance. The wooden gates were long gone, and the courtyard beyond had been scoured by the wind, its flagstones worn so thin they cracked underfoot as he walked across them. Even so, Errol sensed the power in the place, the aftertaste of magics that had preserved it, hidden it then trapped any who might have broken through those enchantments. Like much of the old workings, they were gone now, their potency spent. Soon men would arrive here, driven by legends of gold and treasure. This ancient palace would be looted and the knowledge trapped within its walls lost. Unless he did something about that.

'This way, I think. Looks like Benfro came here.'

Martha, always two steps ahead, stood at the top of a stone staircase that disappeared into the ground. The ruins of the palace sat on a high escarpment, jutting out of the great forest of the Ffrydd like a snapped bone poking through skin. Errol approached with caution, even though he knew the place was safe now. Cenobus might once have been the home of Magog, Son of the Summer Moon, but now it was just a jumble of rocks.

The chill was welcome as they descended into the depths, though Errol shivered as his body adjusted to the temperature. Martha didn't seem to notice. With each passing day, she became more like the impetuous young girl who had dropped out of the tree and into his life all those years ago at Pwllpeiran. He wished he could just shrug everything off so easily, but his experiences weighed heavy on his heart.

'You still miss him, don't you?' Martha conjured a tiny ball of fire to light their way as they reached the bottom of the steps and set off down a wide tunnel.

'He gave his life to save . . . well, everything.'

'He's still here though.' Martha touched her chest with her free hand, then moved it to her head. 'And here.'

Errol dipped his head in understanding. He knew she was right, but Benfro's death still saddened him. That final 'Farewell, my friend.'

'Reckon this is what we're looking for.' Martha held her light up high, revealing a heavy wooden door set with iron studs. Bones lay on the ground before it, men who had come this far only to find they could go no further nor turn back. Shivering at more than the cold, Errol looked up the tunnel with his aethereal sight, relieved to see that it was as he expected. When he looked back, Martha had already opened the door.

'Magog's great repository.' She sniffed, stepped inside. 'Smells a bit.'

Errol followed her into a room that seemed to stretch on for ever. Squat pillars held up the roof, carved with shelves that held books, parchments, treasures, and row upon row of pale white jewels. A heavy writing desk hauntingly similar to the one in the room at the top of Gog's tower in Nantgrafanglach had been pushed against a wall, and the space where it had sat was filled with yet more jewels in a pile. Beside it smaller piles lay ready for sorting, exactly how Benfro had described his dreams when Magog had taken control of them.

'It's just how I remember it,' Errol said.

'Why wouldn't it be?' Martha gave him that quizzical smile he loved so much. With his aethereal sight he saw her harden her aura around her hands, then bend low to the first small pile of jewels and swiftly add it to the larger hoard. 'Come on, Errol. Time's a wastin'.'

He paused a moment to concentrate on his own aura, still not used to the shape it formed around his hands, the talons rather than fingernails. With a thought it turned from swirling colours to solid black, and he plunged his hands into the first carved alcove in the nearest stone column. Scooping up the jewels within, he carried them over to the pile and let them drop. As they clattered against those already there, he thought he heard a distant voice, its tone like that of someone greeting a long-lost friend, but he couldn't make out any words.

Shaking his head, Errol turned back to the stone

columns and the collected jewels of Magog's repository. There were a lot of them to move.

He had been expecting nothing, just an endless peaceful darkness away from the pain and the weariness, the constant fear and battling just to survive. Instead, Benfro gazed up at a sky of perfect blue marred only by the occasional bright white cloud. His wound was gone, not just the constant sensation of it, but he knew that the splinter was no longer there, the muscle and flesh knitted back together, the damage undone. His heart, both his hearts, beat strongly, their rhythm reassuring.

A large bird flew across his view, and that was when he realized that his eye too was healed. Regrown would perhaps have been a better description, since Fflint had gouged it out and flung it aside like offal. Slowly, expecting his joints to creak and complain, Benfro lifted his hands in front of his face, twisted them this way and that as he inspected them. There was no sign of the scars, the chipped talons and scratched scales that he remembered before. Nor could he see the signs of regrowth where Myfanwy had begun her healing magic and Earith had finished the task. His arms felt strong, his whole body rested. And he couldn't remember how he had come to be here.

Rolling over, Benfro got to his feet and glanced about. He was in a clearing surrounded by mature trees. Rolling hills climbed into a distance made hazy by the heat of the sun, but they were covered in green forest and strangely familiar. He looked behind him and saw a narrow river running close by, a track through the grass crossing it at a ford.

In this peaceful place it was hard to remember the pain and the struggle. He knew he had battled first Magog and then Palisander, knew he had breathed fire to reckon all the stolen jewels of Gwlad. As he remembered that, so he remembered too that he had burned the *Llyfr Draconius*, and he felt a moment's panic that Sir Frynwy would be beyond angry with him for that.

But there had been no choice. And if the knowledge contained within that book was the same knowledge Gog and Magog had used to split Gwlad in two, then it was better off burned.

Benfro stood for a long while, the sun warming him as he considered the track. He couldn't shake the feeling he had been here before, but neither could he remember ever having seen it. From where he stood he could turn right and cross the ford, or left and drop quickly into the trees. Both options had their merits, but he couldn't decide which way to go.

The heat of the sun decided for him. The ford would cool his feet for a while, but the trees would give him the best shelter. No sooner had he stepped into the cool of the forest than he began to recognize individual trees, the shape of the land, the little streams that tumbled between the trunks. In no time at all he was walking down the wide track that led through the middle of the village, only where he had expected dilapidated and burned-out cottages, now it was all as he remembered from before when Melyn had come through. The gardens were well tended, the cottages welcoming.

'Benfro. You're looking well.'

He stopped in his tracks, not quite believing he saw

Ystrad Fflur at the door to his house. The old dragon looked different somehow, and it took Benfro a while to realize that he was standing upright, not bent over with arthritis. His eyes were clear too, and the joints of his wings rose high above his head.

'Going to the feast early, eh?' Ystrad Fflur nodded his head conspiratorially. 'Very wise.' And then he turned away, stepped back into his cottage.

Bemused, Benfro carried on through the village. Other dragons greeted him and all were healthier than he remembered, younger, larger. There was Ynys Môn, whittling away at a stick as he sat outside his tumbledown house. There was Meirionydd dead-heading the roses in her garden. Sir Frynwy snoozed in the afternoon heat, slumped in a chair outside his front door. They were all here, all as he remembered them. Better.

The hope grew ever stronger, overwhelming him as he headed towards the centre of the village and the track that would take him home. He paused a while, staring up at the stone hall where he had eaten many a feast and heard many an epic tale. It wasn't as grand as the Neuadd, but it was magnificent all the same. Strong stone and slate roof, glass windows and that stout oak door. It stood open now, and as Benfro looked a dragon stepped out into the sunlight. His hearts almost stopped as he saw her, and he rushed towards her.

'You came back.' Morgwm the Green swept him into a strong embrace, and if Benfro was bigger than his mother now he scarcely noticed. 'I knew you would.'

Acknowledgements

It's been more than fifteen years since I began the fool's quest that would eventually become this epic tale. Back then, at the start of the noughties, I had recently relocated to the heart of Wales, up in the Cambrian Mountains inland of Aberystwyth. Learning about that wonderful country, its language, culture and mythology was a fascinating and magical experience, and although I have now returned to Scotland I still feel a certain hiraeth for the place.

The germ of the idea for the series was born out of taking evening classes in Welsh, and I have to thank my tutor, Ioan Guile, for introducing me to the delights of that wonderful language. Sir Benfro himself would not have existed had not my long-suffering partner, Barbara, pointed out that the Welsh name for Pembrokeshire was also clearly that of a dragon, and a slightly bungling and inept one at that. All my friends from Cwmystwyth and the Pwllpeiran Research Farm deserve a mention too, for the friendly welcome, the work, and the introduction to such interesting sheep breeds as Beulah Speckle Face, Llanwennog, Torwen, Tordu and Clun Forest. Not to mention Divitie and Diseverin the CAMP rams.

Many others deserve a hearty thanks. Stuart MacBride, who persuaded me that sheep don't make such good villains in an epic fantasy; the late, great Dot Lumley who tried so hard to sell my unique vision of epic fantasy to the world; and the effervescent Juliet Mushens who finally succeeded. I must thank the team at Penguin, too. Although it's hard to name everyone who has passed an eye over this tale, you have all left a mark on it and for that I am ever grateful. If I name any, then they must be Alex Clarke, Jillian Taylor, Sophie Elletson and Hugh Davies. I'm hugely indebted to Roy McMillan and Wayne Forrester for the amazing audiobooks too. I can't read these stories out loud without slipping into a soft Welsh accent now. I must thank Andrew Farmer too, for taking my rough scribbled drawings – done for my own reference – and turning them into the rather splendid map of Northern Gwlad that adorns this book.

And last, but by no means least, I would like to thank all you readers who have stuck it out to the bitter end. Special thanks to those dedicated few who picked up Dreamwalker in its original self-published ebook guise and liked it enough to stay the course. You all know who you are, and I love you all equally. Without you I'd probably keep on writing these strange stories, but it wouldn't be half as much fun.